# PRINCES
# AMONG THEIR
# PEOPLE

# Princes Among Their People

## Janet Ball

S I M O N  &  S C H U S T E R

LONDON·SYDNEY·NEW YORK·TOKYO·SINGAPORE·TORONTO

First published in Great Britain by
Simon & Schuster Ltd in 1990
A Paramount Communications Company

Copyright © Janet Ball, 1990

**Simon & Schuster Ltd**
**West Garden Place**
**Kendal Street**
**London W2 2AQ**

Simon & Schuster of Australia Pty Ltd
Sydney

A CIP catalogue record for this book is
available from the British Library
ISBN 0–671–71720–0


Typeset in Garamond 3 11/12.5 by Selectmove
Printed and bound in Great Britain by
Richard Clay Ltd, Bungay, Suffolk

*To the memory of Lore Burgess*

*Fierce in the fair green land,*
 *Hatred and suspicion.*
*Peasant and lordling's band,*
 *Bitter is their division.*

*Close in the city walls,*
 *Jew and Christian merchant.*
*Each man lives in thrall*
 *To the Church and the King's taxation.*

*King and priest and crusader,*
 *While swearing themselves to Christ,*
*Greedy for land and plunder,*
 *Hold all men in their vice.*

# Part I

# *1184–1190*

# 1

The wind was so strong on that day that it blew the family along the road, as if hastening them towards the city for some purpose of its own. It sought out every hole and thin place in their meagre clothing, stung their eyes and tugged at their hair.

The boy's thoughts were of the wind and where it came from. What made it rush about so? Why was it not always still, as it was on those days when the smoke rose straight into the air and not even a leaf stirred? Today nothing was still and Benedict longed for some rest, away from the buffeting and the mad scurries which sent them running and left them again just as suddenly, so that they staggered to keep their balance. Why was this mad gale so fiercely intent on rushing to some other place? Even the sound of it made him weary.

Deep in contemplation of the wind, he stumbled over a sharp stone which scraped his toes, so that he clutched at his mother's skirt to save himself. She, weak and irritable from lack of food, fended him off with a push which almost overbalanced him and he concentrated then on the road, examining every inch with eyes downcast, seeking to ease his painful feet in the soft places where sand had drifted between the ruts. Before him was the sled and the blunt figure of his father, his body thick as a tree-trunk, his arms and legs like ill-attached branches, and somewhere behind lagged the two younger children, who whined intermittently.

Anyone watching the group might have wondered that a child as beautiful as Benedict should belong to such a family, though the keen observer might have detected traces of youthful prettiness in the draggle-haired woman. Perhaps the boy's delicate face bore some resemblance to what she once had been, but it differed markedly from those of his small brothers, coarse already and pinched, like the faces of old men.

Lifting his eyes briefly from the track, Benedict saw in the distance a cluster of rooftops peeping over the top of a long bank, and set into the bank was a square white building which must be one of the gates of York. The sight of the gatehouse should have brought relief, but instead the boy was filled with apprehension, and he glanced again at the purse which dangled and flapped emptily from his father's belt. The boy was sure that because there was nothing left, nothing at all, his father would try again the trick which had failed so disastrously in Stamford. There they had all been sent running down the hill, over the bridge and out of the town in a hail of stones. Now at every fair he was afraid that they would have to flee from a jeering mob, and what would they do today, he wondered, when the collectors came; how were they to pay their dues?

His thoughts returned to the time when he had been exhibited only in the herb-scented rooms of monasteries. The monks were interested in his talent and he would willingly have stayed when the Abbot of Meaux offered to keep him, but the Abbot was not prepared to pay and his father wanted money. So it was that they had begun to tour the fairs, where he hated the crowd and feared the troublemakers who pushed past his father refusing to pay.

The family had been ten days on the road from Lincoln, on a journey which should have taken no more than six. All along the route his father had been tempted into alehouses and whilst he had drunk inside in comfort, his family had huddled away from the wind in the lee of the building. The child wondered if they would ever again have a settled home, for they were perpetually on the move and he had to make an effort to remember that there had once been a house, a hearth, and a meal each day. During this last journey he had watched with dread as his father spent their remaining money and, now that Alyce was gone, how could he alone earn enough to keep them all? He longed to know, but dared not ask a second time, what had happened to Alyce.

As they came to the gatehouse, a brilliant shaft of light pierced the purple clouds and illuminated the new white stonework and the freshly sawn timbers of its palisade. Along the bank the grass was tossed roughly, this way and that, dark green at one moment and flashing silver the next.

One of the guards, leaning over the rail and shouting against the wind, demanded to know their business. Benedict tensed himself, fearful that they were going to be turned away, and his father muttered that he had come to buy provisions. Benedict wished his father would speak louder, for the guards might ask again what he had said, and nothing must be done which would attract undue attention. Wishing only for anonymity, the child wrapped his arms about him in an unconscious gesture of defence and held his breath, but the guard merely laughed and turned to speak to his companion. The guards had clearly heard what his father had said, and the second made a jeering remark about their shabby clothes and enquired if they had enough money to buy two cabbages. That set both men laughing and, to Benedict's relief, no questions were asked about the sled. They were allowed through the arch into streets already crowded with booths and

4

stalls. Now, whatever the outcome of the day, they were inside and might be able to beg or steal some food before they were driven out again.

For an hour they struggled through the crowded streets without finding any vacant plot on which they could pitch their stand. At one place, where the street was wide, a group of musicians was playing and some of the people were dancing and capering, clasping hands and spinning round. Benedict caught a brief glimpse between the press of bodies of a woman's plump, flushed face encircled by her white wimple, the end of which had come loose and was flying horizontally like a banner in the wind. Then someone in the crowd, backing away from the swirling dancer, trod on his mother's foot. She began a loud argument with the people round her and Benedict pressed on through the crowd. There was no time for watching; his father, raging against the weather, drove them on from place to place. He, who had wasted so much time on the journey, was anxious now in case they earned nothing before the inevitable downpour drove the crowd indoors.

The space which they eventually found was amidst the rubble of a demolished house, so that theirs was set back from the other booths where it would easily be overlooked. This new manifestation of ill luck set his father cursing again but Benedict was glad, for though they were half hidden from possible customers they might be missed by the keen-eyed collectors.

'I need some drink,' his father shouted above the wind, 'and if we get no more than ten customers today we shall go hungry again this night.'

Benedict's stomach contracted at the very thought; he knew they must have food soon, and from somewhere near came the delicious smell of roasted pig's feet. On days when he had been less tired and better fed, he often crept away to watch the jugglers and tumblers, but now he stared listlessly at the activity around him, until his father, who was lashing the cross-piece to the two uprights, angrily recalled his attention. The mother joined her voice to his and looking over her shoulder shouted irritably into the teeth of the wind, 'Give me a hand, you idle young wretch. Take the weight of this cloth; don't expect me to do everything.'

The boy gathered up the blanket in his arms and as he held the weight of it off the ground he found some consoling warmth in its grimy folds. He laid his cheek against the bundle of cloth and watched as his mother, with arms raised above her head, tied the strings at intervals around the horizontal pole. Soon both blankets were suspended, leaving between them a space through which people with money to spare could pass to see the boy perform. Benedict let the blanket fall and crept behind it to shelter from the wind. He watched his two small brothers with envy, and while he watched he stood briefly on alternate feet, warming the sole of the free foot against the opposite calf, and clasping his body tightly with his arms all the while. The smaller boys were too young to be of any help, and played no part in the performance, so that they were free to amuse themselves by scraping together little heaps of gravel with their grubby hands.

At last his father took up his stand before the screen and began calling to the crowd. The sled had been dragged behind the curtain to form a platform, and his mother had sat down on the end of it for a few moments' rest. Now she rose, and Benedict stepped wearily up on to it and turned to face the back of the screen.

'My lords and gentlemen, come see the boy who can reckon figures faster than a Jewish moneylender! This boy is a marvel at reckoning. Come, only a groat to see the boy who has been shown before the King at Westminster, at Lincoln, Ely and before the Abbot of St Edmundsbury . . .'

Two loafers, already the worse for drink, conferred together, paid, and pushed their way in, where they stood, shifting from foot to foot, their mouths hanging open vacantly. As nothing happened and his father continued to harangue the crowd, the two customers began to complain, but still his mother waited, and Benedict kept a wary eye on the two men for signs of trouble. Not until four customers stood in the space before the platform did she begin to recite what he had taught her. If it rained soon, he thought as he began, there would be sufficient money for only one to eat, and he knew who that one would be.

His answers were almost as automatic as her recitation of the questions. On days when he had not been so weary, he had managed to present himself with a set of parallel questions, the better to occupy his mind, but no matter how tediously simple the task, he was careful to answer correctly. No one in the crowd would know whether he were right or wrong, but he was proud of his skill.

The performance was brought to a sudden halt by a bellowing voice and, glancing up, Benedict saw the fierce face of a man who was seated upon a huge war horse, and was looking down at him over the blanket screen. The audience, excited by this new attraction, pushed their way out. The Knight glared at Benedict as though he had done him some personal injury.

'Bring the brat out here! I'll give you a groat if he's as good as you say; if not, you'll feel the flat of my sword.'

The bystanders shuffled backwards, treading on each other's toes, warily giving the man a wide berth and taking note as they moved of his sword and the whip which his mounted retainer held, carelessly coiled in the hand which rested on his thigh. Benedict stepped down from the sled, his knees trembling, and as he emerged from behind the screen he saw that there were three horsemen. The third was perhaps twenty years of age and close by in the crush a woman nodded in his direction and said admiringly, 'Is that His Lordship's son? Upon my soul, he is handsome!'

The great man was now the centre of attention and people hurried over to see what was happening. Benedict stood as far as was possible from this awesome figure and his father took up the liturgy of questions. The horseman's patience lasted for less than a minute, before he interrupted once again. 'Stop! The boy knows the answers by heart; let me question him,' and with a grin which held no humour, he began. 'Now lad, if I had one hundred soldiers and forty-five were killed in a battle . . .' He saw the boy's lips move as he made to answer, and stopped him with a severe: 'Wait now! . . . But we then recruited another thirty-three . . .' He hesitated, 'And fourteen of those fell sick . . .' He paused, before finishing briskly: 'But I impressed twenty-seven millers, five blacksmiths, and – what shall we say? -- seventeen little boys like you? How many would I be able to take into battle on the next day?'

The man was obviously pleased at his own cleverness, and had Benedict been crafty in the ways of the world, he would have delayed his answer to make the problem seem harder than it was. Instead he replied immediately, 'One hundred and twenty-three, sir, or one hundred and thirty-seven if the fourteen sick men recovered.'

'Impudent young scoundrel! How could they recover overnight?'

Benedict's eyes flickered nervously in the direction of the sword, but suddenly the man was laughing. Tossing some small coins on the ground, he turned to his companions, and with some jocular comment which was carried away on the wind, rode off without a backward glance, leaving Benedict trembling.

By the time his father had gathered up the coins, their audience was drifting away and no amount of calling would bring them back. Only one man had remained and was watching them from a short distance. He was well dressed, a merchant perhaps, with a fur lining to his brown cloak, and he eyed Benedict speculatively. The family, in their turn, regarded the man with suspicion. Did he wish for another performance, or was he an official of some kind? Now the man was approaching, and stepping up close to Benedict's father he said grudgingly, 'The boy can reckon.' Then, after glancing again at Benedict, he asked, 'How old is he?'

'He will be ten at Michaelmas, your honour.'

Oh, why did his father always say he was younger than he was? Benedict looked quickly at the merchant to see if he had detected the lie, and as he did so, he had a sudden vision of the roaring man on the horse and although he had been frightened by the shouting and the sword, Benedict knew that this quietly spoken one was more to be feared. There was something sinister in the way the man was staring at him so intently, and to Benedict's amazement he now asked, 'How much do you want for him?'

This must be a jest. Benedict knew it was unlawful to sell people; but then he remembered Alyce. Suddenly, his vague suspicion about her disappearance clarified itself into certainty, and into fear for himself.

'It is a groat to see him perform, sir,' his father replied, pretending to misunderstand.

'I saw the boy perform for the Constable of Chester, and you will soon replace him; perhaps these smaller brats will grow to be calculators or,' and a faint and humourless smile flickered across his face, 'is this one the get of some cleric in holy orders?'

The child turned, wild-eyed, to his father, and found that he was scarcely listening, but was staring fixedly at the ground while he counted on his fingers. Benedict realised with horror that his father was assessing how much he dared ask. Then the man uttered the words which they had all been dreading. 'Make up your mind. I could have you driven from the fair. By the look of you, you haven't paid your dues.'

That decided the matter. Taking courage, his father shouted suddenly, 'A silver mark, your honour. The boy is famous throughout the land. A mark if you please.'

Benedict had never seen a mark; they had never had so much as a mark! The man laughed – that was the price of a fur-lined cloak like the one he was wearing – but it was his turn now to glance round apprehensively as, pulling open his purse, and without taking his eyes from the ashen face of the boy, he extricated some coins and tossed them in the dirt. When Benedict's father saw the money which was scattered at his feet, he began to whine an objection. 'This won't feed us for more than the week!' Yet at the same time he was eagerly scraping the coins out of the rubble. Benedict stood transfixed, staring in disbelief. If that was all the man had paid, then his father would give the money back, surely he would? The merchant paid no attention to the complaint but commanded, 'Come, boy!' before moving a few yards off and waiting.

Benedict couldn't move. He felt barely able to breath, and there was a pressure on his ears which blotted out the sounds around him, leaving him briefly in an unearthly silence. His first thought when his wits returned was to appeal to his mother but he hesitated, for if she had done nothing for Alyce, she would do nothing for him. One quick glance at her averted face was confirmation that he was right, but he knew that if he was parted from his family, he could never return to the hamlet on the river Hull, and a wave of homesickness overcame him. He turned again to his parents. He caught the sound of his mother's voice, whining some indistinct words to his father, but he was already dismantling the stand, while the two little boys still played among the small stones, incurious and uncaring.

'Come, boy!' the merchant repeated, and Benedict stumbled reluctantly after him. Fifteen yards off he stopped to look back, but his parents were already tying their things to the sled. Only a few minutes more and they would be gone. He wondered wildly whether he should run back to them but at that moment he felt the man's hand grasp the cloth on his shoulder and, with a sinking heart, he allowed himself to be led away.

They entered a busy, narrow street, filled with people who were going about their business, buying and selling, carrying merchandise and gossiping together. Benedict looked into their faces, but he found no comfort, for none of them either knew or cared that something dreadful and momentous had just happened to him. They were at home here; they knew the streets, the markets, the churches, whilst he knew no one, and cities alarmed him. He had stayed in a city only once before, and that was the night on which Alyce had vanished.

He recalled their trudge along the road towards Lincoln, and the day on which his father had stopped suddenly, and bent to pick up a coin which glinted in the road. Benedict recalled the coin with bitterness. It had paid for a bed and a meal when they reached the town and he knew now that they had been better sleeping in a barn, or under an elder bush. The alehouse where they stayed had been hot and rowdy, and an unpleasant man had taken a close interest in the drowsy Alyce. The man had said things which Benedict had not understood, but which had made him feel uncomfortable. Next morning when he awoke, there had been no sign of his sister, and his enquiry about her met only with a kick and a blow. He had felt then that the coins which his father carried away from Lincoln had some connection with her disappearance, but he shied away from the ideas which began to form. And how quickly that money had gone!

Now the man who had bought him stopped before the stone front of a building and said, 'Here we are. Inside with you!' In silence they passed through a shop, though Benedict, struggling against the tightness in his chest which he felt would suffocate him, was scarcely aware of it, and traversed a dark passage from which he stumbled, blinking, into a cobbled yard. Two young women were folding newly washed sheets which they grasped tightly in the billowing wind. He saw their strong forearms straining, and their cold, red hands clasping the corners of the sheets, before the sun struck from behind the storm clouds and shone painfully on the snowy linen, making him turn his head away.

'See that this boy gets a wash, and find him some old clothes of Master John's,' the man ordered, and without giving him another glance, turned and entered the house by a back door.

'He's a dirty ragamuffin,' said one of the young women, making her way to the well and beginning to let down the bucket.

'Save your strength, Betsy,' replied the other. 'We can use the last of the rinsing water for the boy – and make haste, I want to get to the fair before it rains!'

'Come into the wash-house, little beggar boy,' said the first, and moved towards the door of a low shed. Benedict followed her into the dark interior. 'Take off your clothes, and we'll use them for rubbing cloths, then get into this tub. Here is some soap . . . What! Have you never seen soap before? Rub it all over you, then rinse it off and Joan will bring you something to wear.'

She left, and he stood still, until his eyes became accustomed to the gloom. There was a thatched roof over his head and thin strips of light came in through the walls of interlaced wattles. Then, fearful lest somebody should look in and see that he had not obeyed, he quickly took off his jerkin and footless hose, and taking up the piece of soap from the stone floor, he stepped into the tub.

He had never felt warm water before and the pleasant sensation was such a surprise that he crouched there, motionless, until a sound from the yard outside reminded him of the soap, and he began to rub the ungainly, greasy lump across his chest. Twice he lost it in the water, but by the time he heard footsteps approaching he had succeeded in passing it over most of his body.

The light from the doorway was blotted out, but it was neither of the washing women. Instead, he was surprised to hear a gruff male voice.

'Get out, lad! Here's a towel; make yourself dry and put these clothes on.' As the figure shuffled forwards, Benedict saw by the light from the doorway an old man, who stooped to drape some clothes over a line which was stretched across the back corner of the wash-house. Then the man turned and, handing Benedict the towel, he spoke again in a dull monotone. 'Rub yourself dry before you get cold.'

The boy did as he was told and the man exchanged the towel for a pair of hose. 'And where did he find you?' he asked, as he handed him a jerkin.

The boy replied listlessly, 'At the fair.'

'Are you a beggar?'

Benedict was shocked. 'No!' he shouted, 'I am a calculator.'

'And whatever's that?' asked the old man, his voice betraying the first sign of interest.

'I can reckon faster than anyone in England,' Benedict replied angrily.

'Oh, can you now,' the old one replied. 'Then why are you so ragged?'

Benedict fell silent.

'You're wanted in the house,' said the man, and ushered him across the windy yard and in at the door through which his new master had entered.

At that moment the long-expected rain slashed down behind them, striking the yard with such force that the spray danced a foot above the paving, whilst out in the town it beat the dust, which had been a torment to the eyes, into a thin mud which now beset feet and legs. Traders struggled to cover their goods. The juggler, rushing for shelter, collided with the palmer, who let fall his bag of little pieces of the True Cross which he had whittled from a willow down by the Ouse the previous week. The performing bear stood patiently on its hind legs for the duration of the downpour, obligingly covering its owner's head with its paws whilst he snuggled into its belly fur.

The fair continued, but without Benedict. Whilst he crept into the goldsmith's house in Coppergate, out in the rain-lashed market place the two washerwomen dashed, screaming in mock alarm, into an alehouse already crowded to the door. Their arrival roused the company to laughter and ribaldry. Somehow room was made for them among the packed bodies of the men, and there they stayed until long after the rain had finished.

Benedict and the old servant, meanwhile, climbed the stone stairs of the silent house. He had seen the merchant enter, but the house was so quiet that the boy assumed it to be otherwise empty, and was surprised to find, when the door of the upper chamber opened, that his master's family was gathered there.

Apart from his interview at the Abbey of Meaux, never before had Benedict entered such a fine room. Here was a wall fireplace, a thing of which he had heard but never seen, and beside the fire in a high-backed chair, sat his new master. Opposite on a bench was a woman, and beside her sat a boy of about his own age who stared at him arrogantly. On the plank floor before the hearth, two small girls played with their dolls and conversed in whispers.

'Your father said you were almost ten,' the merchant began without preamble.

'No, sir, I am twelve,' Benedict replied.

'You are very small! My son John here is a great lad compared with you, and he is not yet twelve.' Benedict noted the look of satisfaction on John's face, and not caring for what he saw, he turned again to the man, who continued, 'You can make yourself useful in the shop, the boy we had has just died, and you can teach my son to calculate.'

Benedict was painfully aware that he was wearing the other boy's old clothes, and glancing again at John, he decided that he was not a promising pupil. Some people didn't seem able to understand numbers and it occurred to him that he should warn his new master.

'I tried to teach my brothers, sir, but they couldn't learn.'

'If John doesn't learn you will be beaten, so see to it that he does. Now Will,' the man went on, addressing the old servant who had stayed by the door, 'take the boy to the shop and show him something of the business. You can give him some bread and then he can sleep there under the counter.'

Benedict was ushered out, and as he followed the old man down the stairs he realised that he did not know his master's name and that nobody had asked his.

'What is he called?' he enquired.

'That is Master Peter, the goldsmith. He is rich, and very important in York.'

'It is a fine house,' Benedict agreed, his voice very small.

'This house, my master got from a Jew,' Will continued, pleased to have an audience and warming to his subject. 'They like stone houses, but my master is so rich that he bought this house from the Jew Aaron who went back to France.'

'Is that where the Jews come from?' asked Benedict.

'No!' Will said scornfully. 'They come from the Holy Land, where the crusaders go; have you not heard of that when you've been to church? The Jews it was who crucified Christ!'

'We haven't been to church since we left home,' the boy replied. Then, lest the man should think his family had left home for no good reason, he added, 'My father said the Church had stolen our croft, and that was why we were travelling.' He hoped that the statement gave him some standing. Then he thought to ask, 'What did the other boy die of?'

'He fell down stairs,' was the brief reply.

They had reached the shop, where Will continued with his description of the goldsmith's grandeur, making no attempt to explain the presence of a supercilious-looking youth, who was leaning against the counter.

'So, you were turned out by the monks, were you?' Will said sharply. 'There have been many hamlets destroyed to make way for the abbey sheep. Where did you come from?'

At last, thought Benedict, somebody in this house showed an interest in him.

'From Aike, on the river Hull, near Beverley,' and he found comfort in the repetition of the familiar place names.

'What kin do you have?' asked Will.

'My father and mother and two brothers.' Then he realised guiltily that he had omitted to mention his sister, but to include her now would lead to further revelations about the state to which his family had sunk.

'I'll go and fetch you some bread,' said Will, and left him alone with the languid youth, who now turned from the counter to say, 'I heard that my master bought you in the market place.'

'Did he buy you as well?' asked Benedict, ingenuously.

'Buy me!' the youth exclaimed, making a half-hearted attempt to strike him a blow on the ear. Benedict was usually quick, but tired as he was, he only just avoided the blow. The youth leaned back, set his elbow on the counter, crossed one leg over the other and, assuming an air of superiority, said, 'I am Master Peter's apprentice! My father is a goldsmith of Lancaster; do you know where that is, boy?' As Benedict shook his head, the youth added, 'My father paid a great deal of money for my apprenticeship. Sold indeed!' With that he turned away, and with great deliberation placed both elbows on the counter and began to play idly with a little pair of brass scales.

Soon the old man returned, bringing a chunk of bread which he passed to Benedict; then, glancing at the youth and seeing that they were not observed, he pointed to the bread in Benedict's hand, winked, and pressing a finger to his lips, signalled that he should keep silent, saying, 'And how did your father earn his bread?'

So, Benedict thought, he might speak, but not about the bread. 'My sister Alyce used to dance. We had a performing dog, too, but it died. Then we left Alyce behind at Lincoln . . .' and at that, he began to weep.

'They left her behind . . .' the old man said thoughtfully, 'and sold you . . .' He put a hand on the boy's shoulder. 'Never mind, lad, you'll eat here and you need never be cold again. See the fine clothes they've given you. Eat up now.'

Benedict swallowed hard, and turned his attention to the bread in his hand. He was surprised to find that there was a hunk of cheese hidden inside it. The master had said nothing about cheese. As he chewed, he looked up at Will, who was watching him closely, and attempted a wan smile of thanks.

That night he tossed and turned under the counter, and dreamed that he saw his sister dancing, but as he moved towards her a heavy curtain came between them and he struggled helplessly in its folds. When he got free of the smothering cloth, he was dismayed to find that Alyce had gone, but in the distance he could see his parents trudging along with the sled, his small brothers trailing behind. He set off at a run, trying to call out to them, but his voice wouldn't leave his throat and his feet seemed to be made of lead. As he fought on, vainly trying to reach them, they slowly disappeared into the distance.

# 2

All that year Benedict worked for the goldsmith and tried to teach the idle and unwilling John to recognise the relationship between weight of metal and its value in money. He invented little games which he hoped would help the dull boy to add and subtract, and taught him to use the small abacus with its wires of beads. At first John enjoyed this new skill, but as soon as Benedict praised him, he threw the thing away and would not look at it again.

At meals the goldsmith's wife saved the daintiest morsels for John, who grew both fatter and clumsier. For the girls she cared little; to Benedict, in all the time he lived in the house, she addressed never a word. At night, he still dreamed of his family at Aike and imagined they were happily seated together around the fire, and that Alyce was telling stories as she used to do. His happiness would be shattered when he woke, and he wept to find himself alone in the goldsmith's house. He tried to find excuses for his parents' behaviour, and if anyone asked him about them he would be adamant that they would soon return to collect him.

The goldsmith never chastised his son, but Benedict thought that he did not love him, for he could often be observed staring morosely at John, his chin sunk on his chest, his hand clasped around the stem of his silver cup. While John grew fat, Benedict grew tall, but too thin. 'Outgrowing his strength', Will called it. As he was kept indoors most of the time, he got little exercise and all he saw of the city was on the rare occasions on which his master took him to visit customers. For this purpose, Benedict was dressed in finer clothes and walked behind the goldsmith, carrying a little chest of valuables. Then he had looked about him, memorising as much as he could so that he could describe it to Will in the evening. He longed to see more and began to wonder if, when he was older, the goldsmith would allow him to go about by himself. Surely, he thought, when he was a man he would be free? But were some people slaves? Was he to be a slave to the goldsmith all his life? The idea alarmed him, until it crossed his mind that perhaps he was not allowed to wander the streets in case his family returned to claim him; yet, whilst half hoping that they would, he dreaded a chance meeting. Suppose they turned from him, what would he do? He had a bleak vision of himself, following them down the street, begging to be taken back. He was still haunted by the picture of his parents dismantling the stand for the last time, and knew that if he were rejected again, no amount of dreaming would console him.

He still found pleasure in his calculations, and the diversion was necessary in that unhappy house. There were days when Master Peter flew into unpredictable rages, and on those days even the journeymen avoided him. His master was drunk now more often than he was sober; the little girls fought, pinched, and pulled each other's hair, and their mother paid them little attention, but sat for hours, nervously watching her husband and biting her fingers. One morning at breakfast she had a great bruise on the side of her face and the little girls were unusually silent. Benedict caught the glance which was exchanged between the two journeymen, and inferred from it that the workmen would have something caustic to say later about their master in the privacy of the workroom.

On a day when the master was away, the apprentice cracked the silver bowl which he was raising with his hammer. He ran to the journeymen and pleaded with them for help, but they were adamant that there was no time to anneal the metal before their master returned, and their faces betrayed that they were secretly pleased to see the youth in trouble. Benedict almost felt sorry for the arrogant apprentice, despite the fact that he had never had a word of kindness or sympathy from him, but he held his tongue when the tearful youth ran back with his broken bowl into the shop. Whatever he said, he knew it would be met with sarcasm.

When the master returned, the damage was discovered, and the apprentice received a beating. Although the spoiled cup was none of his doing, Benedict was beaten too. These beatings became more frequent as time wore on. Whenever his master felt aggrieved, or following some particular display of stupidity by his disappointing son John, the goldsmith would vent his wrath on Benedict.

Of all the household, Will was the only one who took any notice of Benedict, marvelling at his ability with numbers, and taking him to Mass in the church at the foot of Coppergate on Sundays. If Will did not go about the town on Sunday evenings, he would sit and talk with Benedict, who related to him his history and described the years of wandering and the places he had seen. He had, he thought, been seven years of age when he had left home, and when he described the little croft, the hens, the vegetable patch and the copse where he had played, Will would sigh and begin to reminisce about a similar hearth and houseplace on a croft long ago at Sherburn in the Forest of Elmet.

'Who taught you the calculating?' Will had asked one evening, as they sat on a narrow bench against the wall of the wash-house, out of sight of the windows and of their master.

'Brother Aidan,' said Benedict. 'He lived in a hut on the common, but on very cold nights he used to come into our house and sleep there.'

'What was he doing, living on the Common?'

'He had some quarrel with the Abbey and they threw him out,' Benedict replied. 'It was always cheerful in our cottage when Aidan came. He told stories from the Bible, and my mother was always in a better temper when he was there.' Then, remembering more, he described how Aidan had brought sand in a bag and had spread it on the floor near the hearth where it was illuminated by the firelight. He had marked out the squares of the abacus and used pebbles as counters. Benedict laughed when he recalled how the rest of the family had looked on with wonder as he quickly learned the system and, later, how to calculate the dates of Easter for future years.

Benedict spent most of the day in the shop, receiving customers or their servants and going to fetch his master when it was necessary. In this way he came to know the richest citizens of York, the most interesting of whom was Josce, one of the leading Jews, a dealer in grain and wool, and a famous moneylender. He, also, took a delight in calculation, and Benedict soon came to look forward to his visits. Whenever he found the boy alone, Josce would set him some problem to solve so that the two of them began to enjoy a measure of intimacy.

At first Benedict found it difficult to understand Josce's speech, and asked Will if this was the language of the Jews, but Will laughed and said that Josce had a French accent.

'Do they speak French in the Holy Land?' Benedict asked, but Will replied with confidence that whilst the English – and he said it with pride – naturally spoke English, foreigners spoke French. That no other languages were mentioned puzzled the boy, for he knew there were people other than the French and the English, but he didn't pursue the matter for he had begun to think that sometimes Will didn't get things quite right, and the old man could be touchy.

Then there came the day which was to change Benedict's life. Josce brought into the shop a casket which had been sent to him from a far-off place he called Constantinople. The casket was opened in the presence of the goldsmith and from it was taken a succession of carved ivory figures which, Benedict understood them to say, were part of a game. He stood on tiptoe at a safe distance from his master, but could see very little, until the goldsmith turned and told him to bring the taper stand closer. Then Benedict saw that around the heads of two of the figures were thin circlets of gold, one of which had been damaged, and it was this which Josce desired to have repaired. During the following week Benedict would creep into the workshop, for the journeymen tolerated his presence so long as their master was absent, and he watched as the crown was repaired.

When Josce came to see if the piece was ready, he insisted that Benedict put the casket on the counter and, refusing the boy's offer to fetch his master, lifted out the repaired piece and held it to the light, considering it for a moment. Then he took from the box a chequered board.

'Is it for calculating?' Benedict asked, thinking the chequered board was an abacus.

'No, this is not just a counting board.' And, placing some of the carved pieces upon the squares at Benedict's side of the board, Josce continued, 'This is to be a surprise for my son, Aaron. Can you play at this game?'

'No,' the boy replied, casting an anxious glance over his shoulder towards the workroom. 'I should fetch my master. Please allow me to get him, Master Josce.'

'Surely that is not necessary,' Josce replied, moving some more of the pieces on to the board as he spoke. 'He leaves you to mind the shop and, in any case, this game is my own property. Now, see here, this is how the board is set out and this is how you begin to play.' He moved one of his pieces, the light from the window glinting on his garnet ring, and when Master Peter entered the shop a little later, he saw the golden curls of the boy and the dark curls of the man close together over the chequer board, both players engrossed in the game.

'Now, Master Josce!' he said loudly, 'Good day to you. Have you called to collect your chequer-men?' He had advanced to the counter and, without seeming to look at Benedict, came very close, kicking the boy's ankle and pushing him roughly aside. The goldsmith's jovial tone did not deceive Benedict, who was in no doubt that what he had just seen had aroused his anger, and while the two men discussed the set, Benedict, in the dark shadows at the back of the shop, rubbed at his arm and ankle, and dreaded the time when Josce would leave.

'Very well,' Josce said at last, pulling up his purse on its long strings, 'What is the cost of the repair?' And, as he brought out the required sum, he continued, 'Now, lend me the boy to carry it home.'

'No, Master Josce, my son John can carry it for you,' and the goldsmith turned towards the passage door.

'Thank you, Master Peter,' Josce replied, smiling, and putting the pieces into the casket as he spoke, 'this boy will do, it is but a simple task and I would not wish you to go to the trouble of sending your own son to my humble house.'

Benedict was at once alert. Was the Jew trying to protect him? His humble house! Why, everyone knew that Josce of Coney Street and his own namesake, Benedict of Spen Lane, lived in houses like palaces, the finest and richest in York. Again, Master Peter tried to persuade Josce to accept a more worthy errand boy, but still Josce was adamant that he would have Benedict.

So it was that they left together, and Benedict was startled as they stepped out through the doorway, for two giants appeared as if from nowhere. His first thought was that they were robbers, but as they took their places at either side of him Josce spoke to them and one stepped aside, motioning Benedict forward, so that the four strode together down the centre of the paved street. It was late afternoon, nearly the end of March, cold now, and the light fading. Benedict trotted along, skipping every now and then in order to keep pace; proud to be walking with them, and not following in servitude, as he had always done with the goldsmith.

The last of the traders were packing up their goods ready for home, and in the flickering light blackbirds shouted hysterically from the housetops. The men talked as they strode along, Josce addressing one as Thurstan and the other as Sirich, so that Benedict, who had taken the giants for foreigners, was surprised to find that they were both English.

In spite of his delight at being out in the street, he remembered his master's anger, and knew that Josce's victory would only make matters worse; a beating awaited him on his return, yet he longed to see the wonders of the great house in Coney Street. The longer he was away, the more angry his master might be, yet the greater the distance from his master's door, the more his excitement overcame his fear.

The famous house glimmered palely in what remained of the evening light. Josce raised the bronze knocker and thundered on the door. Immediately a shutter was drawn aside, an enquiring face looked out, and the door was opened by an old man who took Josce's cloak. Then Benedict and the giants followed Josce up a stone staircase which led them into what seemed to be a grand hall, but as it was almost dark Benedict could only guess at its size. They walked its length, stepped up on to the dais, and passed through a door into a smaller room of dazzling splendour. Benedict hesitated on the threshold, but Josce turned and indicated that he was to follow.

The day on which he had been sold was the only one on which Benedict had been allowed to enter the solar of the goldsmith's house; he remembered how he had been impressed by the painted hangings, but he realised now how crude those had been. The walls of this solar were hung with cloth of such magnificence that Benedict gasped at the sight. The glowing colours were woven into a pattern of lions which looked backwards at their tails, and each lion stood in a circle of silver threads which glinted in the firelight. Benedict stepped closer, amazed at the fine detail, and seeing his interest, Josce said, 'They were woven in

Constantinople, and carried to England in the same Venetian ship which brought the game of chequers.'

Benedict turned then and saw a wall fireplace and a splendidly carved high-backed chair for Master Josce, and then he dragged his eyes from the magnificent furnishings to look at the people.

A tall, slender woman, in a rose-coloured gown came towards them smiling. 'You hammer at the door so, Josce, you almost deafen us!'

A tiny girl, barely able yet to walk, toddled eagerly but unsurely towards Josce, and almost falling as she reached him, grasped the skirts of his gown with both hands. Stooping, he lifted her up.

'I like the whole house to know I have arrived home, Hannah,' he replied smiling. Then, turning to the child who was now seated in the crook of his arm, her face close to his and her arm about his neck, he asked teasingly, 'Have you been eating sweetmeats, little Miriam? I can feel your sticky fingers. You will make marks on the collar of my gown.' She nodded solemnly, and licked her palms in an effort to clean them. Josce turned, meanwhile, to pat the dark, wavy hair of a boy of about ten, who had risen from a stool near the fire and now stood with his arm around his father's waist. Benedict was surprised to see their easy familiarity.

'Who is this?' the woman asked.

'This is Master Benedict. He has the makings of a scholar, and he brought my chequer set from the goldsmith's shop,' said Josce.

'Where is it?' cried the boy, and Benedict, who was still holding the casket, looked enquiringly at Josce.

'Yes, set it down there,' Josce indicated a table which was covered to the floor with a rich cloth. 'Now,' the father said to his son, 'we shall enjoy our game much more.' The boy approached the table and, unfolding the cloth, opened the box and gasped with surprise.

'Does anyone in England have such a set as this?'

'I doubt it!' said Josce, laughing.

'Father, it is wonderful. When can we play?'

'When I have had a drink and changed my boots!' Josce exclaimed.

One of the huge servants brought him a drink from a cupboard on trestles, draped with white linen and set out with splendid plates and bowls and cups of silver. Then Josce sat in his chair whilst the other servant removed his boots.

Benedict's eyes could not rest. The firelight danced on the silver and glinted on the tapestry. Everywhere there seemed to be colour and light. He had never seen such riches or known there could be so much comfort. Never before had he been called 'Master' Benedict, and he felt a glow of satisfaction at the title. Most of all he was surprised by the happiness in the house and the love of this family, one to another. But then he remembered with a start that he must return to the shop.

'Master Josce,' he said anxiously, 'I must go now.'

Josce turned to him frowning, 'Yes, indeed, you must, Benedict,' and, thoughtfully, he crossed to a standing cupboard, and when he turned again, he held in his hand a little carved wooden box. 'Take this to your master as a present,' he said, 'and, as it is dark, I will send one of my servants with you.'

Benedict was reluctant to leave, yet it was a comfort to know that he would arrive at his master's house in the company of one of Josce's impressive servants, seemingly even taller now as he was wrapped in a long cloak. They travelled the streets in silence, for Benedict did not dare speak to the man, and when they arrived, the servant hammered on the door, just as Josce had at his own. This boldness, and the loud noise, made Benedict cold with fear. There was no hope now of slipping in quietly. Will unbarred the door, and as he opened it he said in a voice which betrayed his own fear,

'Benedict, the master wants you!'

Benedict had the impression that Will had been waiting anxiously behind the door.

'My master has sent a present with the boy,' Josce's servant replied in a stern voice, 'and he told me to wait and see it handed over.'

The three of them climbed the stairs together. There was no sound in the house and Will opened the door on the silent room. Benedict advanced to the centre of the floor and, rigid with fear, he held the box out at arm's length towards his master saying, 'Master Josce sent this as a present, sir.'

The goldsmith was slumped in his great chair, his legs spread before him, his heels on the dusty planks, his cup in his hand. As on the day on which Benedict had arrived, the goldsmith's wife sat opposite, rigid and silent, with John beside her. The only change from that first day was that the little girls no longer played, but also sat beside her on the bench, watching, wide eyed. And why, Benedict wondered, should John look like the cat which has stolen the cream; why was he so particularly pleased with himself this evening? The goldsmith's wife rose and crept from the room, leading the girls by the hand, and her going increased Benedict's fear.

'Oh, Master Josce has sent me a present,' said the goldsmith mockingly, but he turned his head as he spoke and took in the presence of the huge servant. There was silence, whilst Benedict stood, still with arms outstretched, offering the box.

'Shall I put it on the table, sir?' he asked, anxious for some resolution. The silence continued for what seemed an age, then Master Peter cast another glance in the direction of Josce's servant and nodded. Benedict moved to the table, and as he placed the carved box on the oak the shaking of his hands made it clatter. He remembered the sumptuous cloth which covered Josce's table and the gaiety and sparkle of that other room.

'You can go now,' said Master Peter to Josce's servant.

Benedict, his back to the room, mistook the command for one addressed to himself, and with a great sense of relief stepped towards the door. His master's voice reached him very quietly, 'Not you, Benedict.'

The hair on the back of his neck stood on end, his stomach felt as if it were full of ice. Josce's servant hesitated, and then, whilst Benedict watched with a feeling of despair, left the room followed by Will. He could still hear their feet slowly descending the stairs, and he turned to face his master. As he did so, he saw the look of pure glee on the fat, red face of John, shining in the firelight.

The blow was unexpected. While he was still puzzling about John's expression, something crashed against his head and he reeled back towards the table. He righted himself by clutching at its edge but he had not been able to turn in time and so did not see the second blow descending. This caught him on the shoulder, breaking his collar bone. The pain made him stagger down the length of the table, bent double with the pain, and clutching at the edge of the plank. John, with unusual alacrity, put out a foot to trip him as he reached its end. On his knees now, he tried to crawl beneath the table for shelter but his master, exerting great strength in his fury, half lifted the other end of it and turned it over on to its side with a crash. The table's trestle caught Benedict as it fell, knocking him flat to the floor. He opened his eyes in time to see the little carved box fly into the ashes on the hearth.

Now his master reached down and, gathering up a handful of the back of Benedict's jerkin, he dragged the boy to the middle of the room where he dropped him again on the boards. The blood was running into Benedict's left eye, but he saw with the other his master's boot, aimed at his ribs. He tried to roll over, but the kick landed on his right side simultaneously with one from fat John on his left. He began retching painfully and was sick on the floor. This drove his master to a frenzy and he and his son aimed kick after kick at the boy's curled body.

It was at this point that Will hurried into the room crying out 'Master, master!' Suddenly the kicking stopped. Benedict was now barely conscious, yet before he fainted he was puzzled to hear Will saying something about 'the other boy'.

# 3

Benedict was pleasantly aware that he was lying on a comfortable mattress, and yet he had at the same time the strange sensation that he was floating above it. It seemed to be evening, and somewhere near music was playing. The idea floated across his mind that it was perhaps the time of the Lenten fair again for it must be a year since he had come to York.

The next time he woke, he could see in the dim light that he lay under a white sheet, and remembered . . . when was it? . . . white sheets which flapped in the wind, reflecting the glare of the sun on a cold day.

He fell into a light sleep one afternoon and dreamed. He turned in his sleep, and half opened his eyes. Through his lashes he could see that a girl was sitting on the stool beside his bed. She had a cloud of shining red-gold hair. She seemed to be part of his dream, and he closed his eyes and slept again.

The third time he woke, it was with a shout of pain. His eyes opened wide and he took in at a glance the whole room. The planks of the floor were swept very clean, and on a stool beside his mattress, someone had left a wooden bowl and a horn beaker. The floors were not usually swept as clean as this. Simultaneously he heard the sound of retreating footsteps; someone was making a careful descent of a ladder and then the same feet crossed a wooden floor. Who, he wondered, had been sitting beside him and watching him whilst he slept?

He looked up at the chink of blue sky showing through the double slits of a high window in the white stone wall, and over his head were rafters and the undersides of roofing stones. It was strange, he thought, that there could have been a room under the eaves without his knowing about it, but although he tried to concentrate on the problem his thoughts would not obey him.

Again he heard the music, sweeter than any he had heard at a fair, and, stranger still, it seemed to be somewhere within the house. He tried to rise, but fell back, sweating with pain, and then the face of his master's son swam before him, red in the firelight and shining with a grin

of delight. With that, the whole of the previous night's events returned
to him. He had tried to shelter under the table and he remembered the
blows and kicks. These he now related to the various pains he could feel
and, drawing one hand from beneath the sheet, he gingerly touched his
head. He found that he was wearing something soft over his hair and
a gentle exploration confirmed that he had remembered the first blow
correctly. They must have brought him up here, and they were obviously
concerned about his welfare, for they had put him on this soft mattress.
Who had carried him up here, he wondered, for he felt sure he had not
climbed the ladder himself?

He remembered Will's voice somewhere in the confusion of the
previous night's violence, shouting something about the other boy, but
surely that other boy had fallen down the stairs?

It was then that he heard feet ascending the ladder, and he lay,
rigid with apprehension, his eyes fixed on the door. A man in a black
robe entered, turning as he did so to hold the door for someone who
followed, and Benedict was amazed to see the wife of Josce appear in the
doorway, where she paused, smoothing her long, heavy skirt with her
hands. Benedict was to remember the graceful gesture long after, when
he could no longer remember her face.

'Ah, little Benedict, you are awake!' and, turning to the man in the
black robe, she continued in a faintly teasing voice, 'Can you always
make your patients sleep for four days? If so, I shall call for you when I
am tired of the English winter, and you shall make me sleep until spring.'

'The sleep will do more good than anything else I can do for him,
Hannah,' the man replied, and they came then and stood over him. The
man's face was solemn.

'Did my master let you in?' Benedict asked, but Hannah, instead of
answering, posed a question,

'Where do you suppose yourself to be, little Benedict?'

'At the top of the house,' the boy replied in a whisper. It seemed to
him to be quite obvious where he was.

'But at the top of whose house?' she asked, raising her eyebrows and
seeming to smile a little. Then the realisation dawned upon Benedict that
a miracle had happened.

'Am I in Coney Street? Am I in your house?'

Hannah turned to the doctor with amusement in her voice. 'You
see, Abraham, my husband was correct, the boy is intelligent and it was
worth the risk he took in order to save him.'

Benedict wondered what the risk had been which Josce had taken
and what 'intelligent' meant; was it the same thing as useful? The
goldsmith had bought him because he could be useful, so perhaps Josce
had bought him from the goldsmith for the same reason.

'Everyone is worth saving,' said the doctor gravely, and there was something in his voice which made Benedict feel sad. He reflected that the man had the same French accent as Josce and Hannah, so he must be Jewish as well. Benedict looked closely at the man's face, and decided that he was someone who could be trusted. Then the doctor addressed him again. 'Now, Benedict, do you feel much pain?'

'Only when I move. If I keep still it is not bad.'

'A cheerful patient!' said the doctor, with satisfaction. 'You must keep still for another day, but I want you to drink some milk, and then on the following day, even if it hurts, I wish you to rise and walk about a little.'

During that week Benedict began to recover from his cracked ribs and broken collar bone. He was fed on fine food, such as he had never eaten before. A tall, strong woman called Isabelle brought him soups made from fish and from chicken meat, flavoured with herbs. Then, when he was stronger, she brought dainty portions of fowls, a jelly made from apples, and some small cakes which, in answer to his question, she told him were flavoured with almond nuts. Benedict had never heard of almonds before. He had gathered hazel nuts in the autumn, and he had once found a walnut from the tree in the manor garden of Sir Robert of Meaux, which a squirrel had taken and had hidden among his father's vegetable rows.

Three children came up the ladder from time to time to look at him. Aaron, the dark-haired boy who had welcomed home the chequer set, announced himself proudly as the son of the house. Later, Francisca, a tall girl of about his own age, came to see him holding the hand of her small sister Miriam, she of the sticky fingers, who was eating something which she held tightly in her other hand. Whenever this small child appeared, she seemed to be eating something. The tall girl had a cloud of brilliant red-gold hair, which was caught in the shaft of sunlight which streamed in through the narrow slit above. Benedict thought he had seen such hair before. The tall girl made him feel shy, and he felt at a great disadvantage, lying there, whilst she looked down at him from what seemed a great height. He was pleased that she had the young child with her, for he was able to tease the little one and avoid conversation with the older girl.

He woke next morning to hear a commotion at the foot of the ladder. All but one of the voices were speaking in French but he listened anxiously, and it seemed that little Miriam had tried to climb up the ladder to see him.

The English voice belonged to Isabelle, the children's nurse who, when she brought his food each day, examined his injuries. She was about forty years old, he guessed, with fair hair showing streaks of pure silver. As he had grown stronger, she had sat and talked to him, telling him that she had been in the household since Francisca was a baby, when Josce and his wife had first come to the newly built house in York. Benedict was surprised to find that the family had an English nurse and to learn for how long they had lived there, for he had supposed that these exotic creatures had just arrived from the Holy Land, speaking in their strange French way. Surely that was what Will had told him, and since that time Benedict had explored this Holy Land in his imagination, confusing it with Heaven. Brother Aidan had told him about the Holy Land, 'A land flowing with milk and honey,' he had said, and had not Benedict been fed on milk and honey over the last weeks?

For the first time in his life Benedict thought about the language he spoke. In all his wanderings he had never spoken with foreigners, and although he knew that the monks used Latin and French, he had not considered how it was possible for ordinary people to know more than one language. Already he was learning new words from the other children; words which at first he had thought must be French but which, having tried them out on Isabelle, he found were indeed English.

It surprised him that these children spoke such good English but then they had been born in England. Perhaps one's language depended upon where one was born. What then of Josce and his wife? Isabelle said they had been born in France; did the English come to them when they set foot in England? What if he went to France on a ship, would he find himself speaking French when he landed at the other side? If that should be so, how would he be able to understand what it was that he was saying?

He could plainly hear the children playing beneath him, for his room was tucked up on a little floor over the solar and their voices came to him quite clearly. Sometimes they spoke in English, but often in French, and he pondered further on this ability to jump from one language to the other. The matter was very puzzling.

At last the doctor ascended the ladder and, after a brief examination and some questions, pronounced him well enough to return to normal life. Isabelle helped him down to the solar, for Benedict was shaky from lying so long, and nervous as they descended. He could hear the voices of the adults and wondered, with a sinking sensation in the pit of his stomach, whether Josce would now send him back to the goldsmith's shop.

It was Friday evening. There was a blazing fire, and, with what seemed to the boy unnecessary extravagance, there were also candles in a branching stand of bronze set on the table. He and Isabelle sat on a bench by the wall. Josce was talking and, to the boy's relief, nobody took any notice of him. The room seemed full of people and when he could look around he saw that most of the company was already known to him. Josce and the doctor sat on stools at either side of an older man, who must be important for he sat in Josce's high-backed chair, and seated on a bench beside Hannah was a woman who must be the older man's wife, though she looked younger than her husband.

Aaron and Francisca sat at the table. To Benedict's surprise, the girl was reading a book, and a long strand of her hair had escaped from the white linen cap which was tied under her chin. She turned and caught him staring at her, and he dropped his eyes, waiting for a while before looking up again. She was no longer looking at him but had returned to her book. Aaron was concentrating hard on an arrow shaft which he held upright in the palm of his left hand, whilst the left forefinger and thumb held an arrow head very tightly to the tip of the shaft. With the fingers of his right hand, he was binding the arrow fast to the shaft, his whole concentration directed to the task and his jaw rigid with the effort.

Josce was saying, 'The Abbot is interested in redeeming Sir Walter's debt, and thus obtaining part of his Lincolnshire estate.'

'Sir Walter is in too deep, and the Abbot surely knows it,' the old man answered. 'These monasteries, the great landowners and the King will, between them, eat up these small landowners. Too much power in too few hands is never a good thing for a country's well-being. I thought, when I came to England, that this country would breed a different type from France. They say that the men of the north-east are descended from the Danes, an independent people, and the Normans seem to have some respect for the Saxon laws. If the lesser nobles would only curb their ambition or attend to the care of their estates, they could surely gain increasing independence, and would have little need to borrow money.'

'And what would become of us?' asked Josce. 'We would make no profit if these wild men became suddenly careful of their inheritance; then our protector the King would have no further use for us, and . . .' He snapped his fingers in the air, 'We should be snuffed out like a candle.' Then he smiled and added, 'But we are safe enough; between the King's taxation and this craze for crusades, we shall be busy for many years.'

Just then the doctor leaned towards Benedict as though to ask how he felt now, but before he had time to speak, the old man seemed to notice Benedict for the first time. 'Is this the boy you brought from the goldsmith's?' he asked. 'Are you going to rescue every boy who is beaten by his master?'

Benedict was gripped by a sickening fear. Would Josce be persuaded to send him back to Master Peter? He looked quickly towards the doctor who, he felt, might protect him, but Josce said, 'It would be foolish to attempt any such thing, the population of York would be about our ears, but this is a special boy, and it is well known that Master Peter killed the last boy he had. I had only to hint about that business and this one was handed over to me very promptly.'

'Even so, the Christians will suspect that you have brought him here for evil purposes. After that business at Norwich, you should be more cautious, Josce. You have now made an enemy of the goldsmith.'

'Benedict!' Josce exclaimed, and the boy started upright. 'We already have so many enemies that one more will make no difference,' and smiling, he added, 'in any case, the boy is your namesake; how could I leave him to die?'

Then Benedict realised that the older man was Benedict of Spen Lane, whose house was said to rival even this one. The rest of the conversation was understood by him only in part, but Josce's words had reassured him, and he breathed freely, looking about at the wonders of the room until he was eventually led away, sleepy and contented, to bed.

# 4

_____

From the very first day, Benedict loved the life of the house in Coney Street. It had in it everything he had been missing, yet had not known that he had missed. He was not a boy given to brooding, so that even at the goldsmith's he had soon become resigned to his fate, reasoning that at least he had food every day and a roof over his head at night. As to the violence, he had been accustomed to it during his family's wanderings, and he acknowledged as a matter of fact that men drank, and that when drunk they were violent.

But Coney Street was like another world, with a different order of things. Men were never drunk there, and no man ever lifted his hand against woman or child. At first Benedict had waited for the violence to begin, but after a while he saw that in this house such behaviour was impossible. Not only were both family and servants kindly and courteous in Josce's house, but there was another aspect in which life in Coney Street differed from that at the goldsmith's. There the journeymen and the apprentice took every opportunity to escape their work and to avoid their master, whilst here everyone worked with a will.

With what delight, also, had he discovered books in the house. Benedict had heard of books in monasteries, and he had seen the Bible in church, but he had not thought that there could be books in a house. This house not only had a shelf of books a yard long, but the conversation in the house was quite different from any he had heard before. When the rabbis came to visit the talk ranged over many topics and Benedict would listen eagerly, trying to make sense of what he heard. They discussed the laws of the Jews and talked of some men called philosophers or Greeks who, it seemed, were men who lived in the time of Our Lord or perhaps even before that, he could not be sure, and who had been filled with learning.

Benedict was amazed to find how much learning there was in the world. He had supposed himself to be the cleverest boy in all England, but he could neither read nor write. When he discovered that Josce's elder children could read and write in more than one language, he conceived a desire to learn everything they knew, yet he hesitated to ask if he could be taught. Josce had been so good to him already that he did not like to ask for yet another favour.

One evening he stood near to Francisca as she sat on a bench by the window, and leaned forward to look over her shoulder at the book she was reading, curious to see if reading were a difficult thing to do. As soon as she noticed him, she exclaimed crossly, 'Benedict! Go and read your own book, this one is mine!'

'Benedict does not have a book,' said Josce severely. 'He may come and stand by me'.

Benedict was scarlet with embarrassment and, determined not to approach Francisca ever again, he went hesitantly to the chair in which Josce sat and whispered to him, 'I can't read, Master Josce.'

'I know you can't,' Josce replied kindly, 'and it is high time you began to learn. Tomorrow you must sit with Miriam, and Hannah will begin to teach you your letters; but now you may look at the pictures in this book whilst I read the words to you. They are written in French, but I will read them to you in English.'

Benedict was happy, but he still felt uncertain of his position in the house. He was given tasks to perform, bringing in the logs, helping Aldred in the stables, sweeping a floor, or stirring a pot for Isabelle. So he was a servant in the house, and with that he was content. He would gladly have served Josce all his life, but was he intended to stay here? He had supposed that Josce had bought him, as the goldsmith had, but one day Isabelle told him the story of his rescue.

She was elder sister to the two huge servants who accompanied Josce when he went about the city. The men, it transpired, were twins, and it was certainly difficult to tell them apart. Benedict knew now that it had been Thurstan who had returned with him to the goldsmith's on that fateful night, and Isabelle described how her brother had stood with Will at the foot of the stairs and how they had heard the table crash to the floor. Then, when Will had groaned and said 'This is how the last boy died', Thurstan had hurried back to Coney Street.

Josce had been very distressed to hear what was happening. 'Go quickly, man,' he had said to Thurstan. 'Bring the the child away and offer money if all else fails,' and he had crammed a purse into Thurstan's hand as he turned to leave. Meanwhile, Isabelle, full of anxiety, had prepared a bed for the unknown child. 'Oh, how I prayed, and I didn't know what you would look like, poor little soul. I didn't know if you were a little bairn of five or so, or a bigger lad about Aaron's age. I put some warmed stones in the bed and I had a hot drink ready, but you were in no state to drink anything, in fact I thought you were already dead when my brother brought you in.' Isabelle was out of breath by the time she had finished her story. She could usually work and talk at the same time, but she had stopped her work and had been wringing her hands as she relived the anxiety of that night. 'I prayed to Our Lady,' she said, 'and she answered my prayer. Give thanks to the Blessed Virgin, child, every time you go to church.'

Benedict knew by now that Isabelle had an affection which seemed to encompass the whole world, and that she held a very special place in the household, being as much housekeeper as nursemaid. Hannah was glad to leave the management of the house in such capable hands, for Isabelle understood the special way in which the food must be stored and cooked; she kept the house in a state of great cleanliness, and chivied the maid about the place. The maid was a strange little person, the daughter of the Jewish baker who had married again since the death of the girl's mother. She had one arm much shorter than the other and a limp which made Benedict think she had one leg much shorter than the other as well, so that although she was of marriageable age, he thought that perhaps her father could find no husband for her. Despite her difficulties, however, the girl had a sense of humour and could relate the small adventures of the day in a way which made everyone laugh. If Isabelle sent her out into the garden during a fine afternoon to gather the eggs, she, who had never played and skipped, would stop to watch the children, smiling as she did so, as though the sight of their playing gave her pleasure.

Hannah was tall, beautiful, and quite different from any woman Benedict had encountered before. Her chief interest was in books, which was unusual even among the Jews, where there was a high degree of literacy. Each day, after giving Miriam her lesson, she would sit reading by the window, or in her flowering mede in the sunny garden.

Benedict would often remember in later years how, in that first warm spring at Coney Street, she would sit on the grassy bank, which had been specially made so that it was like a long seat with another bank behind on which to rest one's back. The grass had been kept very short, and Benedict learned that each autumn Thurstan borrowed a sheep which he kept on a tether while it cropped the grass. Then, when they grew in the sheep-nibbled grass, the daisies and the clumps of violets, the primroses and cowslips were clearly visible.

When Hannah sat there, her gown – fitting close to the body in the new fashion and flaring out into wide skirts – would be spread over the grassy bank. The slender hands, holding her book, emerged from wide fur-lined sleeves, and he could picture how she kept her finger on the place where she was reading if anyone interrupted. Although she would always stop and answer questions, it was Isabelle who came hurrying if Miriam should fall, or cry, or need attention.

Isabelle was devoted to children, and Benedict considered this, remembering many kindnesses he had had from a childless neighbour-woman when he had lived at Aike. His own mother, always cross and harassed, had said that those who had no children were overly fond of fussing them and that if they had children of their own to plague them they would not love them half so well. Benedict thought that perhaps this was the case with Isabelle.

Isabelle and her brothers were the children of a free peasant of Langthorpe near Ripon. Their older brother worked the land, but Thurstan, Sirich and Isabelle had sought work in the town. Isabelle told how Sirich, despite his shyness, had been the first to venture into York, where the street idlers had taken him for a country fool. He asked for directions, and those who stood loafing at the street corner sought to make a greater fool of him by sending him to the door of Josce, then newly arrived in York. Sirich often declared that no one had ever done him a greater service, for Josce and he had taken a liking to each other and, needing trustworthy servants, Josce had been glad to employ the brother and sister as well. Josce relied on the brothers for news of what was going on in the streets of the town, for although he had an amazing knowledge of the doings of the landowners, great and small, it was the servants who knew the undercurrents of city life.

Benedict was proud of the great house, and whenever he approached it along the gentle curve of the street he would take care to walk on the opposite side, so that he could get the longest and best possible view of it as the handsome facade came into sight. He would pause before he entered, and look up to admire the decorated stone of the rounded arch, before he knocked at the heavily studded door. High in the wall were the windows, each a pair of narrow arches set into a wider arch and divided by a slender pillar spiralled with carving. The windows were shuttered from the inside, but while other shutters in York were made to fit their spaces exactly, these were rectangular, and the space at the top of each arch was filled with little circles of glass set in strips of lead; glass so clear that you could almost see through it.Inside, even with the shutters closed and without fire or candle, there was always light. Benedict was delighted at any sign of ingenuity in workmanship and in the windows he took particular delight. Oh, the joy of living in such a house!

In those early days Josce was concerned about Benedict's health, exclaiming over his height and slenderness. 'You are like a plant which has grown in the dark, Benedict. Did you not go out to play after your work at the goldsmith's?' So Benedict related how he had sat sometimes in the goldsmith's yard on warm evenings talking with Will and how, after the evening meal, if he was not required to teach the goldsmith's son he would retire to his bed under the counter. The shop would be in darkness, with the shutters already in place, and there he would lie under the counter, making calculations in his head. He had been quite content with this arrangement and was surprised when Josce replied, 'That wasn't much of a life for a boy. No time for play, and teaching the goldsmith's dull-witted son indeed! You must go out into the garden with the other children for a while each afternoon. They have a ball to play with, and Aaron practices with his bow. Perhaps he will allow you to shoot with it, but don't do what Isaac, the son of Benjamin did!' Benedict looked up, alarmed. At first he thought that Josce frowned, but then he had the feeling that he was suppressing a smile, as he continued, 'The boy aimed so badly that he shot one of Isabelle's hens.' Then Josce did indeed smile, and Benedict was surprised to hear him say, 'Yes, you must learn to play like other boys, and when I ride out on Belazzar, you shall accompany me with the other men of the household.'

From that time on Benedict went to the garden each afternoon for an hour or so. The land contained by the high walls behind the house held a number of most interesting enclosures. First there was a paved yard with a wash-house, like the one at the goldsmith's, but here there was also a stable with room for a horse and a cow.

He had not previously ventured beyond the yard and buildings but he had seen, over a wicket gate, that there was an area bisected by a gravelled path bordered with lavender plants. On the left of the path he had caught a glimpse of a vegetable garden and on the right, when he stood on tiptoe, he saw some rose bushes, a young mulberry tree, and a flowery mede.

Now that he had permission he walked for the first time to the end of the gravelled path and passed beyond the second wicket, and there he found the place where the children played. It was an area of grass, the width of the house, about forty feet in length, and set about with fruit trees. Over by the western wall stood a walnut tree, its silvery bark almost invisible against the limestone, and spread out against the wall was a cherry tree which had been so trained that its branches sprang out to either side of the trunk, exposing its fruit to all the rays of the afternoon sun. In the middle of the grassy space were apple and pear trees, under which was a wicker hen-coop and two beehives of woven straw. One far corner was given over to bushes of lavender, rosemary and sweet woodruff, and he saw that this must be Isabelle's store of strong herbs for strewing on the floors after sweeping.

Benedict soon became accustomed to the children's games, and they showed him all their favourite places. The stable was their chief stopping place on their way to the orchard. Like the wash-house, it was a lean-to building of wicker with a thatched roof. It had a middle passage where a man could stand, and over a strong partition of timber to the left was the place where Josce's beautiful horse Belazzar was kept. In the season of apples, the children would bring back some windfalls after their play and, careful not to let any adults see their wasteful extravagance, would feed the gentle animal over the stable door. On the right was a lower partition behind which the house cow stood when she was not at pasture in the water meadows. Sirich milked this cow night and morning, and was devoted to the animal, though the children found her dull company. A solid door in the eastern wall, close to the stable and well bolted against intruders, allowed the animals to be taken directly into the passage way and so to the street.

The pleasance garden beyond the yard was not intended for children's play though, when unattended, they sometimes stole in there to snatch a handful of green hairy gooseberries. It was Thurstan's domain, and there he planted onions and garlic, poppies, peonies and fennel for their seeds, tall white lilies, rosemary, thyme, and sage. Benedict remembered that his father had grown the more usual leeks, peas, beans and kale, but Isabelle bought such common vegetables in the market.

Josce and Hannah would walk among the scented herbs on warm evenings, and on fine spring days, family and guests would sit in the flowery mede. Here, in the carpet of sweet bright wild flowers, were specimens of fine roses, the white alba, the red gallica, pink centifolia and a moss rose, so dark that the red seemed to shade to black in the depth of its petals. Between the mede and the orchard was a long box hedge, where the briars of sweet eglantine were allowed to spread.

It was the rough orchard grass beyond which rang with children's voices, and it was there that Benedict learned to shoot with the bow and arrows. He was never so expert a shot as Aaron, but the skill he attained gave him great satisfaction. Sometimes, whilst he was waiting his turn to shoot, he would throw the ball gently for Miriam to catch. She could not be persuaded to keep her eyes open as the ball came towards her, but if he tossed it carefully it sometimes fell into her outstretched hands and then she would run off with it among the apple trees, turning to laugh at him as he pursued her, until, turning once too often, she would trip in the long grass and, still laughing, would fall headlong.

With Francisca, the boys would play at throwing and catching the ball, but when her friend Bella visited Francisca did not like to play. Then, conscious of their audience, Aaron and Benedict would throw the ball to each other, harder and swifter than the girls could manage, while Francisca and Bella would watch them, giggling and whispering together as girls do, but looking hurriedly away if either of the boys spoke to them, as though their interest lay elsewhere.

Benedict felt awkward enough with Francisca, who seemed so elegant and knowledgeable about the world, but in the presence of both girls his embarrassment was intolerable. He had not realised that Aaron was aware of his discomfort until one day, tired of their sports, they were lying in the grass when Aaron said 'You should not mind Bella and my sister. I never take any notice of what they say or do; we are men, after all.' The fact that Aaron had noticed his blushes made matters worse, and he tried in vain to adopt the lofty indifference of the younger boy. His nerve failed him, however, and his only defence when Bella came to visit was to find some excuse to keep out of their way.

Benedict became very fond of the two menservants and, though at first they had seemed indistinguishable, after a week or so he found it easy to tell them apart. Sirich was perhaps a trifle broader and rounder in the face, but they differed more in character. Thurstan was full of tales of the past and was eager to talk with anyone, but Sirich preferred to remain silent. Curiously, his interest was in far-away places, and he overcame his reluctance to speak most readily when among travellers, for they could describe to him the roads by which they had come and the towns through which they had passed. He asked them little, but once he had started them on their story, he would sit, intently absorbing the information. By this means he had memorised the geography of much of northern England and, though he had never been further north than Fountains Abbey or further south than Selby, he knew by heart the ways by which the drovers brought cattle down each year from Scotland. He could recite the names of the villages through which travellers would have to pass for thirty miles or so along any road which led out of York, but what fired Benedict's imagination was the description of a great wall, built long ago, and which stretched across the whole of England.

Citizens, when contemplating a journey, would come to the house to consult Sirich and, even if they had a guide, would feel more confident if he had approved the route and described to them the places – which he had never seen – through which they would have to pass. On their return they would visit again, to recount their experiences, to discuss the merits of inns on the way, or to inform him about any broken bridge, or any new one now being built which would make the journey easier.

The brothers took the place in Benedict's life which had previously been occupied by Will. He asked them for news of his old friend, but all he learned was that Will had gone away. So, to them he retold the story of his family's misfortune and wanderings, and in return, Thurstan delighted him with tales of his own childhood on the rich farm near Ripon, of Christmas and harvest celebrations, of dancing to a fiddler in the church at certain times, and of the maids and young men coming home burdened with May branches in the spring. He told him of the Devil's arrows which stood in the fields not far from their home, but he would not say what these arrows looked like, no matter how often Benedict asked, and the arrows remained a mystery. Benedict wished that he could travel north, for it seemed that it was a country of wonder and mystery.

Josce was careful during the first year to see that Benedict should come to no harm from the goldsmith. There were reports that his behaviour was becoming very strange. It was the common gossip of the streets that he declared every man's hand was turned against him and that demons came at night to torment him. So, in that first year, Benedict was allowed out only in the company of Sirich or Thurstan and, eager to explore the city, he sought them out frequently to see if they had errands to be done. They, in their turn, were pleased to take him along, for they were proud of this, the northern capital, and it amused them to see the boy's wonder at each new discovery. Benedict went to the fair with Thurstan and Sirich and looked at the people who entertained with an understanding which his companions did not share. When he found himself face to face with two of the men who collected fees, he darted quickly behind his companions. 'What's the matter with the boy?' asked Sirich.

'It's the collectors!' he whispered, from his hiding place.

Sirich turned to take the boy by the hand. 'They don't want anything from you, child, come out. Whatever is wrong with the boy?'

'He remembers the days when he lived this life,' Thurstan replied, then he pointed out the badges which the men wore on their sleeves so that Benedict learned to identify the collectors of each of the authorities which held a charter to hold a fair.

The city bustled with activity and the river was busy all day long with a multitude of ships passing up and down, loading and unloading, for, deep inland though York was, it was one of the most important ports in the north. The children would stand at the upper windows on the south side of the house to spy the ships beyond the high garden wall, while Benedict and Aaron, though his father would not have approved, would sometimes steal away to the river.

Benedict would persuade the servants to begin and end each expedition with a walk along the riverside, to which there was easy access from Coney Street. On either side of Josce's house an alley led down to the water, and along the banks at intervals were landing places, built high of reed bundles which were held in place by stakes driven deep into the mud. It was pleasant to walk there, the reed embankment clean and springy under foot, and to watch the boats and hear the strange languages of the crewmen.

When the water ran low in dry weather it was difficult for the boats to come near, and Benedict would watch as the fractious boatmen beat up and down the deep channel, shouting and complaining to those on the river bank as they sought a place where they could unload. When the river was high after rain, the work went more swiftly, and the men were in better humour. Benedict delighted to see how, with three strong poles set up in a tripod, a block and tackle and some ropes, huge quantities of timber and great blocks of stone from Tadcaster could be snatched from the bottom of a ship and lifted easily, up, out, and on to the river bank. Sometimes the brothers took him to the King's mill, and while they sat with Henry, the miller, he would sail sticks and pieces of grass on the mill leat to his heart's content.

In the time since Benedict had come to York there had been an increasing demand for the fine white limestone of Tadcaster. The wealthier merchants had been building new houses for themselves, and the new minster was almost finished, its thick walls and rounded arches so solid that it seemed it would last for ever. All over town there was the sound of hammering and sawing. He delighted to linger beside a sawpit until the great log had been successfully sawn from end to end, and to see the underdog climb out, coughing and spitting, shaking his head and beating at his arms to get rid of the sawdust.

He was glad to see, in the rubble where his father had pitched their stand, that a new house was growing. It was a relief to him that the dismal patch of land where he had been sold was soon to be blotted out. He need no longer avert his eyes when he passed, but could look with interest as the house walls grew. The abundance of creamy stone seemed to make the city lighter and the sun shone twice as brightly when it glittered on the white buildings. York, the second city in the land, was growing fast inside its encircling embankment and to Benedict it was a continuing source of excitement.

Foreigners were common in the streets of York. There were Irishmen from Dublin and Wexford, Danes and Norwegians, French, Flemings, and men from so far away that they could converse only with the help of other foreigners who explained to the English what was being said and helped in the process of buying or selling between the two parties. Benedict knew now that Will had been wrong to describe men as speaking only two languages, and he experienced a kind of tender pity for the old man.

One day a stranger came up to the house from the river and spoke with Josce in French. At first Benedict couldn't tell what was being said, for the man's accent was strange. But the family's astonishment made him concentrate harder and he found he could follow the conversation with a fair degree of understanding.

The man was a Jew and he described his journey by boat from a place called Danzig, but his journey had begun much further off, far away to the east, in the kingdom of Muscovy where he lived and traded with the wild people for precious furs. He ordered his men to bring the furs to the house, and they caused great excitement, for such quality had never been seen before. Then his men brought from the ship a neat chest containing walrus ivory, amber, and a dark green stone which, he said, polished well when cut and which he called malachite.

His name was Isaiah and he stayed for some weeks, regaling them with stories of the cold lands in the north where the sun never showed itself in the winter and shone all day and all night in the summer. Benedict thought that anything could be possible in such a world. Isaiah told of endless forests, the haunt of huge packs of wolves, more dangerous than any which could be imagined in England, and of the customs of the people. Other Jewish families came in to sit and hear the tales he told, for it was rare for them to meet a Jew from such a heathen place. The rabbis questioned him about his religious observance, but he assured them that his and the two other families living there kept all the feasts most faithfully. He agreed that, although it was a strange place in which to live, they were safe there from the depredations of Christians, who were too busy fighting each other to pay much attention to the Jews. All they lacked, he said, was the conversation of civilized people, and when he left he took with him a cargo of raw wool, and for himself a quantity of precious books.

Aaron was clever, but not as devoted to scholarship as his father would have wished him to be. He preferred shooting with his bow, or riding on his bay pony. Whenever his father rode out on the beautiful horse Belazzar, Aaron would beg to be allowed to ride it for a while. Sometimes he was allowed to ride the horse all the way home and would appear in the street outside the house looking very proud to be astride such a splendid animal. Aaron often said that when he was older his ambition was to own a black palfrey, as fine an animal as his father's Belazzar.

Benedict longed to learn to ride, but he dared not ask to be allowed to try for fear of being refused. Francisca sometimes rode on a pony which Aaron no longer liked. Her father would keep her close beside him, and Thurstan would walk beside its head ready to grasp the bridle, for the pony had been known to run away with Aaron. Benedict thought it very brave of a girl to ride, but it gave him another reason for hesitating about riding himself. For he feared that if he were offered a ride on this wicked little pony, Thurstan might not walk beside him to make sure the pony didn't bolt. Suppose the pony ran away with him across the water meadows and Aaron and Francisca laughed at him? So, for the time being at least, he decided it was safer to walk.

Josce encouraged Aaron to take a greater interest in matters of business, and Aaron tried to oblige his father, but it was apparent

37

to everyone in the household that his heart was elsewhere. Benedict thought that if Aaron had been a Christian he would have made a splendid knight and, although Aaron was younger by two years, Benedict felt the admiration for him which youth usually reserves for its elders.

Coming into the great hall one day, Benedict saw Josce standing by the long oak table with his hand lying on the metal cover of a book. The light was catching the ornaments and picking out the colours, so that Benedict, always interested in books, hastened forward. 'What is it?' he asked as he approached, and Josce moved his hand, revealing more of the heavy ornamentation. The casket was so heavily decorated that the underlying silver showed only at the edges. The surface was divided by gold wires into a trellis of diamond shapes, and each of the spaces was treated with a different enamel, blue, red, green or white. In each section was set a jewel of some kind and, largest of all, in the centre of the cover was an oval of rock crystal, the size of a pigeon's egg. Elsewhere were white pearls, black pearls, garnets, amethyst and rose quartz, and, as Benedict gazed at it in awe, a beam of light shone in at the window and struck corresponding gleams from the stones.

Aaron strode into the room just then and stood at his father's other hand. 'What is this, Father?' he asked briskly.

'It is a Bible, which belongs to the Abbey of Byland and was made somewhere in Ireland before William the Norman's time. It has been left with me as surety for a debt,' and Josce's voice betrayed his amazement that the Abbot of Byland should have parted with such a treasure. As he spoke, he was carefully releasing the two clasps but, impatient to see what lay inside, Aaron grasped the edge of the cover and began to lift it, then let it slip, so that it flew back and clattered heavily on the table.

'Careful, careful!' said Josce, lifting the cover again, and looking anxiously to see if any damage had been done. Sighing with relief, he gently laid the cover on the table and began to turn the pages, which were brilliant with pictures of saints and strange beasts and gilded borders of bewildering complexity.

'What is it worth?' asked Aaron.

'All the world or nothing,' Josce replied, looking into his son's eyes.

'But what is it worth?' Aaron repeated, as though his father had not understood him.

'To some men it is worth more than life itself; to others, only what they can raise upon it in cash.'

'But it is only the work of ignorant men,' said Aaron, 'Even the monks have seen fit to pawn it.'

'Do not judge,' said Josce. 'Respect other men's beliefs. They may be wrong, but have respect always for others and for the craftsman's work; whatever the worth of the book, a man made this, and he made it well.'

Aaron glanced down once at the book, before striding away to the corner under the stair to pick up his bow.

Aaron had gone with his father to visit a family at Selby, so Benedict had no companion that afternoon and had climbed an apple tree where he intended to read for a while. He had hardly begun when he caught the sound of voices, and realised to his dismay that Francisca and her friend Bella were approaching. He dare not climb down without first securing the book and he struggled to push it into the front of his jerkin, but before he had finished the two girls had sat themselves down upon the stone bench under the high garden wall.

It had seemed to Benedict that, in the few weeks since Bella's betrothal, the two girls were not so close as they had been and that Bella now had about her an aura of adulthood.

'My family will soon choose a husband for me,' said Francisca.

'You will be so happy,' Bella replied.

'They will consult me, I know, and I know I should be happy, but somehow I wish it could be put off for a year or two,' said Francisca.

'But you must wish to marry; everyone does,' said Bella.

'It is not that. It is just that I cannot feel love for any of the young men who visit us here. I cannot imagine lying in bed beside any of them,' and Benedict saw that Francisca blushed as she spoke.

'My mother says that love comes afterwards. That once you know a young man, you are bound to fall in love. You should reject these fancies, and settle your mind to married life and children.'

'Yes, I love children. Even my little sister. Oh Bella, she is so naughty! Do you know what she did last Sabbath when we were all at table? Well, no, I cannot repeat it.'

'You have begun, so you had best go on,' said Bella, and she sounded as though she were addressing someone much younger than herself. Benedict felt a little resentful that she should presume so.

'Look!' said Francisca suddenly, and Benedict froze, high in the branches, afraid that he had been spotted. Then he saw Francisca running away towards the box hedge and the eglantine. 'Look Bella,' and Bella rose to join her. 'Look at this butterfly.'

Just a butterfly. Benedict had had enough of their girlish exchange and he slipped quickly down the tree and took refuge behind the sage bushes in the farthest corner of the garden.

The girls returned to their seat.

'It is better not to touch them. The dust comes off their wings and they cannot fly,' said Bella. 'Now, what were you going to tell me about Miriam?'

'Oh, it was too embarassing. She is so precocious and I am sure my father encourages her for his own amusement. I wish my family were like yours. Your parents are always dignified and your brothers and sisters are very sensible.'

'Your brother Aaron is sensible,' Bella replied.

'Sensible! When all he does is try new ways of binding arrows to shafts and stringing bows!' said Francisca. 'No, Miriam is very sweet but she does say such dreadful things, and her manners at table are not good enough for a child of her age. She stands there, and I know she can't see into the bottom of her bowl, but she fishes around in it with her elbow stuck up in the air, and she crams what she finds into her mouth and then tries to talk.'

'They are all like that at her age,' said Bella.

'But they don't say rude things,' Francisca objected. 'Just when I thought the meal was safely over, she suddenly said "I saw something today", and instead of letting well alone and ignoring her, my father asked what she had seen. She always says something shocking, I feel sure she does it on purpose. Well, she said "I saw Mistress Catherine the draper's wife with her little dog, and the dog lifted its leg by the wall and water came forth from its leg."'

Bella held her handkerchief to her mouth and shook with laughter.

'Oh, don't you laugh as well!' said Francisca. 'She said it in front of Benedict, and before anyone could say something to cover it up, she said "How did it do that?" Then Aaron snorted, because he was trying not to laugh.'

At this, Bella laughed aloud.

'My family is bad enough, don't you laugh too. In any case I haven't finished. My father frowned at him, because he will never let anybody laugh at Miriam. I saw her look very crossly at Aaron, who had his head down over his plate and his hand clapped to his mouth, but Benedict kept a very straight face. Then, as though she hadn't done enough, she said "I thought it was very clever of that little dog. Have you ever seen a dog do that?"'

'And what did your handsome brother do then?' asked Bella.

'He almost burst, and my father said "Go and find Isabelle and get a napkin on which to blow your nose." Miriam asked what was the matter with Aaron; I thought it would never end. Even my father was struggling not to laugh and he said "Aaron is sneezing," but we could all hear Aaron laughing in the next room. I wish my family wouldn't show me up in front of Benedict.'

'You seem to care a great deal what Benedict thinks,' said Bella. 'You are not becoming too fond of him, are you? He is a Christian after all.'

Francisca blushed deeply, and replied vigorously that she was not interested in him.

'Then why have you gone so red? Please be careful not to let your parents see that you like this boy. They would be very upset, Francisca. You really should become betrothed quite soon.'

As time went on, Benedict learned a great deal about Josce's business and how it was conducted. The buying and selling of grain and wool was simple to learn, but the moneylending was a matter of great complexity. Professional chirographers were employed to write out the first section of every loan agreement, but the two copies, written below on the same length of parchment, were often done in Josce's household. When Benedict had proved himself a careful copyist he was allowed to help, and on a sunny July afternoon, two years after he had come to Coney Street, he and Josce were engaged on this task at a table in the cool of the great hall. They worked in a pool of sunlight, while the cheerful sounds of the street drifted in through the open window.

Benedict found the work satisfying. He could now easily read both Latin and French and, although he couldn't understand documents written in Hebrew, he faithfully copied the letters, leaving, as Josce had shown him, a space between each section of about three inches in depth, across which a few well-spaced words were then written. When all was finished, and in the presence of the parties to the agreement, Josce would divide the three sections with a zig-zag cut. The top section was kept by the debtor, the second by Josce, and the third was sent to a place of safety. The Jews called these bonds by a name of their own, shetar, but this was commonly now, by Jews and Christians alike, called starr. In the case of the starrs made by the Jews of York, the third copy was kept by the Benedictines in an iron-bound chest at the minster and often the last part of the transaction was made in the precincts of the minster itself, with the clergy as witnesses.

After a couple of hours of this copying, Josce rose and stretched.

'Come Benedict, let us take a rest,' he said, and led the way to the benches by the empty fireplace. 'You are learning fast, Benedict,' he said. 'How strange it is that your father sold you; if you were my son I would be proud of you, and I am glad that I followed my instinct on that night, although, as everyone was anxious to point out to me, it was dangerous to bring a Christian child into a Jewish household.'

While he had been living in Coney Street, Benedict had learned the story of the murdered child, William, whose body had been found in Norwich. He had heard that even the child's mother was sure the

Jews had had nothing to do with her son's death, but the Church had declared that the Jews had stolen the child away, had fattened him up and sacrificed him. A citizen of York had gone all the way to Norwich on his crutches, and had returned cured, so that there was great enthusiasm in York for Saint William of Norwich. There were other child saints, he knew, in other English cities, also said to have been murdered by Jews, and Benedict knew that each of the cathedrals which held the remains of these children became very rich from the gifts left by pilgrims who visited the shrines.

Josce had remained silent for some time and Benedict thought that the conversation was over, but Josce said suddenly, 'You have heard, I think, of little Saint William of Norwich?' Benedict blushed; it was as though Josce had been reading his thoughts. 'That cost us dearly, as did a similar accusation in London. The Jews dread to hear of a child found murdered anywhere, for it is an excuse for further persecution of our people.'

Benedict had indeed come to realise the magnitude of the risk which Josce had taken in bringing him to Coney Street, particularly as he might have died of his injuries, and now he saw an opportunity to thank Josce for saving his life.

'I am grateful to you, Master Josce, for if you had left me there, the goldsmith would surely have killed me, and you have taught me more than I ever dreamed it possible to learn.'

Benedict had become tense as he spoke; and now he sat clasping and unclasping his fingers, and staring all the while into the empty hearth, for there was something about which he needed advice. After a few minutes of this, he plucked up the courage he needed, and keeping his eyes on the cold hearth he asked, 'How do I know, Master Josce, if I really belonged to my family?'

Josce leaned back in his seat and regarded the youth with interest. 'What makes you think you might not have belonged?'

Benedict hesitated, fearing he had begun on a subject which was going to lead to difficulties, but having gone so far he decided that he must continue. 'I didn't look like the others and I was the only one who could calculate. Then, the goldsmith, when he bought me, said that I might be the get of some cleric. I have often wondered if I was a bastard and that was why my father sold me.' His voice trailed off dismally.

'But he sold your sister as well. Was she like you or like the others?'

'I don't remember anyone saying whether we were alike or not.'

'Do you still feel the loss of your family?' Josce asked.

'I dream of them at night, though not as often as I used to. I often wonder if they are still alive and what happened to Alyce . . . it is worse for a girl to be alone.'

'It is natural that you should dream of them. Do you know the story of Joseph and his brothers? It is a story of my people, but it is told among the Christians. Joseph was sold into slavery by his brothers but God was watching over him and, after he had suffered for some years, God saved him. Joseph became a great man, rich and respected in a strange land.' He thought then for a while before continuing. 'We always think of those we have lost, whether we were deserted, as you and your sister were, or whether we were torn from them by others.' There was a long pause before he spoke again, and to Benedict's surprise he went on, 'My parents and elder brother were murdered in France, many years ago.' Benedict gasped, and the sound made Josce pause for a second, before he continued, 'We are fortunate indeed to live here in York, for in France, since the year which the Christians number 1171, there has developed among them a fondness for murdering Jews. This violence always coincides with the Christian festival called Lent; though why they should celebrate their religious festivals by murdering their neighbours I do not understand. Did you know that Rabbi Yomtob came here with some others of our community after one of these massacres?'

Benedict was amazed at the story, and stuttered, 'I knew only that he came here from J. . .Joigny, but I did not know the reason.' He was alarmed and sat silently for a while, shivering with tension, his hands clasped tightly round his knees. The house seemed so strong, the riches so permanent and he had always thought Josce a powerful man, but now fear sent a shudder through his slim body and Josce, again as though reading his thoughts, continued, 'Riches do no bring safety, Benedict, particularly not for Jews. Your family was very poor but no less vulnerable than we are, in fact our riches make men envious and our religion makes them afraid. No, we are as helpless as the poor.'

'This is England,' said Benedict, trying to bring some comfort to his master, and to revive his own confidence. 'England is better than France. Those things couldn't happen here!'

Josce smiled. 'It is true, Benedict,' he said ruefully, 'that we are under the protection of the King, but so we were in France, and under the same King for that matter.' He was silent for a while and brooded a little before he spoke again. 'Let us hope the madness does not spread. We are rich, as you say, Benedict. We have an enviable life, which in itself is a danger, but with or without violence our lives are precarious. The King, Benedict, the King, as in the game of chequers, takes all. Whenever he wishes to, he can demand money of us, as if all we own belongs to him. Now you might reply that everything the Christians own is his also, and in theory this is the truth, but gradually the Christians are getting greater control of the land. When the Normans first came here, all land was held of the King and if you were to ask the King he would say that it was still so. Yet you have seen for yourself how men now buy and sell manors. One day the English Christians will, I think, own their land without dispute, yet the King can demand money whenever he needs it and while the collectors often come to an arrangement with a Christian landowner, we Jews have to pay in full. Indeed, sometimes the fines are levied only on the Jews.'

Benedict did not know how to reply but Josce suddenly straightened his back, rose, and said more cheerfully,

'Come Benedict, back to work! Let us make some more money in case the King wishes to go on crusade, or marry off his sister, for it is we who shall have to pay.'

By evening they had finished writing out the starrs, and while they waited for the meal to be ready they talked again by the fire which had been kindled.

'Shall I always work for you and live here?' Benedict asked.

'It is a day for asking questions, is it not?' Josce answered smilingly. 'Yes, you are a good worker and you shall stay in my household if you wish.'

'Good,' said Benedict, heaving a great sigh of relief.

'Was that another question on which you had been pondering?'

'Yes, when I was first brought here I thought you had bought me and I asked Isabelle if I would be a free man when I grew up. She said that I would be free, but then I wondered who I would be.'

'And what do you suppose it is which determines who we are?' asked Josce.

'Well, I have no family, so that I live with yours, and you are Josce of York, and rich and . . .'

'But we have settled the matter of the riches,' Josce replied. 'And the fact that you have no family does not diminish you in any way, so what is this difference between us which concerns you?'

Benedict pondered for a while and said, 'You are a real Jew and I am not a real Christian.'

'That is a surprising statement, Benedict; explain to me what you mean.'

'When Isabelle has taken me to church . . .' but before the boy could go on Josce interrupted him.

'You say you are taken, not that you go, now that is interesting in itself.'

'Yes, I go because I must,' the boy replied, and without explaining further he continued solemnly, 'While the service is in progress I admire the windows and the paintings, then if I tire of these things, I count the number of people – without turning round too much, that is why I like to stand at the back so that I can count them more easily – and I multiply the people by the number of pillars, or by the divisions of the window, or some other number of things which I can see.' Josce was smiling now, but the youth had not looked up and his face remained solemn as he continued, 'I think that when you go to the synagogue you do not spend your time counting, Master Josce.' He was startled when Josce laughed aloud.

'There have been moments, Benedict, when I have been tempted – I will admit only to having been tempted – to do some counting of a more serious nature.'

It was a moment before Benedict realised that he was being teased, and then he smiled as well.

'So you do not worship God when you are in church. Do you mean that you do not believe in God at all, or that you would prefer to come to the synagogue?'

'No, the matter which concerns me is that I do not know what the priest means when he talks about God my father.' Benedict hesitated before adding, 'My father, before he sold me, said that the Church was the enemy of the poor. It was the Church which drove us from the land, and I have seen that even the nobles fear the power of the Church. What does all that power have to do with God or with our Lord Jesus, who abandoned wealth?'

He looked at Josce and saw that he looked doubtful. 'You have been good to me, Master Josce. You have behaved to me as Christ said his followers should behave to strangers and to beggars. Yesterday, a priest stopped me in the street, they often do, and asked if I went to Mass every day. I said that I went only on Sunday and on saints' days. Then he said I would go to Hell because I live with you and because I go to hear mass only on Sunday. If God loves me, why will he make me go to Hell? Why does he need me to go to church every day? You rescued me and saved my life, but you ask nothing of me in return. How can it be that God is my father and loves me?' In the ensuing silence, Josce didn't reply, and Benedict went on, 'I don't think that I would like to attend the synagogue . . .' Then he added hurriedly, lest he had given offence, 'Yours is a good religion, your people are charitable, but it is particularly your religion and I do not feel that it could be mine. I hope you are not offended, Master Josce.'

'No, I am in no way offended, Benedict, but I think you should have a religion. It is important to have regulation in your life; to obey the laws of God. What would men be if they had no fear of God? They would be savages.'

'But those Christians in France believe in God, the ones who kill Jews,' Benedict replied.

'I wonder,' said Josce.

# 5

It was September of 1188, and during one of their evening conversations Thurstan proposed that Benedict should go home with him to Langthorpe, to meet his brothers and to see the farm. Benedict was delighted at the idea and disappointed when Josce at first objected.

'I shall have no servants left! It is a good thing that Isabelle and Sirich don't ask to go running off like this or we would never manage the place at all, and now you want to take the boy as well.'

Benedict was less surprised at this unusual show of annoyance than he would have been a few weeks before, and reflected that Josce had been uneasy of late. After a little persuasion, however, he agreed to their going, provided they spent only one night away. So at sunrise the next morning they left the house with many messages from Isabelle for the family, and carrying hunks of bread which she had provided for them to eat on the journey.

They arrived soon after midday and Thurstan's elder brother, Askil, dropped the adze with which he had been working and advanced towards them with arms open wide. He was another giant, whose fair hair had been bleached almost white by the sun, and whose arms were tanned as brown as his leather jerkin.

Thurstan had described the farm so well that Benedict knew it as though he had lived there himself. There, across the yard, was the house, just as he had known it would be, its great cruck beams overshadowed by the thatch. House and barn were one building, divided through the middle. He stepped with Thurstan through the great open doors, crossing the threshold into the cool of the cross passage and, as Thurstan had said, it was wide enough to admit a wagon with its load. It was dark there, in contrast with the bright sunlight outside, but at the far end a chink of light showed through a crack in the timber of the winnowing door. Benedict glanced over the half door on his right, and saw the heads of young calves looking over a pen at the far end of the barn which was otherwise filled with fresh, sweet-smelling hay.

As they stood on the threshing floor, Askil's jolly wife, Maud, entered through the open door on the opposite side of the passage with a ladle still in her hand, and the smell of cooking followed her. The mixture of good smells was almost intoxicating.

They followed Maud into the houseplace, where the sun streamed in, for the shutters were wide open at both sides of the house. On the floor, in a patch of strong sunlight, lavender was spread out to dry. In a cauldron hanging over the fire bubbled a stew, the smell of which made Benedict's mouth water. He looked about the room and was surprised to see a long table of the kind he had previously seen only in manor houses when he journeyed with his master. The place was very orderly; clean and polished tools hung upon the walls or were lodged on shelves beside the door. Benedict could see great hams hanging to smoke under the plastered wattle hood which was suspended over the open fire. When Askil came in they sat down to eat, the four of them and two of the farm men, on long benches at the table, not around the fire as Benedict's family had done at Aike. Benedict had never been inside a rich farmer's house before, and he saw now in what poverty he had been raised.

Askil's wife complained, as she ladled stew into their bowls, that Outhan was late and that the food would be cold by the time he came in, but just then the light from the window was obscured as the youngest brother leaned inside to tell of a cow which had wandered and how he had had to retrieve it. This Outhan was scarcely older than Benedict and stared at him all through the meal. He seemed somewhat in awe of the elegant city youth. Benedict found this embarrassing, and took pains to tell him about the croft on which he had been born, so that they were soon on friendly terms. When the meal was over the two strolled out into the yard where they leaned their full stomachs against the wall of a sty and, to grunts of appreciation, Outhan scratched the sow's back with a stick.

A farmyard was no novelty to Benedict. The comfortable sounds and familiar smells were very pleasing to him. He sauntered then with Outhan to the stack yard, where hens scratched and crooned among the straw and a cock crew lazily, as though reluctantly obliged to proclaim his dominance of the sleepy yard. Outhan pointed out with pride that he had himself thatched the stacks and, when Benedict had admired the handiwork, they strolled to the fields where women and children from the village were gleaning among the stubble, and the team of oxen was beginning on the first furrows of the autumn ploughing. The late sun came in low and golden across the field, picking out the reddish brown of the women's skirts as they bent to their work, gilding the stubble, and making the ploughshare gleam silver against the velvety brown of the earth.

Outhan asked about life in York, and it seemed that he had scarcely believed all his elder brothers had told him of the house in Coney Street. Did they really eat such exotic food? Did they really have splendid hangings on the walls? Could they all read books? . . . and was it true what people said about the Jews?

Benedict assured him that Jews were like other people, and that they did not eat Christian children. Their food was as good as Thurstan had said, and it was correct that even the little children read books. At last Outhan seemed satisfied and they returned to the farmhouse as the sun began to set.

It was the end of harvest and after dark the neighbours came into the house and ate and drank of Askil's hospitality. A piper played for the people to dance and Benedict watched their shining faces glowing in the firelight, his foot tapping to the measure of the tune. Though he loved the excitement of life in York, he thought that he could be happy to live once more in the country.

The next day when it was time to leave, Askil reminded Thurstan to take Benedict home by the road which passed the Devil's arrows but, again, nobody in the house would explain to him what they were, laughing and telling him to wait and see. Outhan accompanied them for some of the way, and as they walked Benedict taxed the brothers with guesses, but nothing would induce them to reveal the secret. Suddenly, before him, there appeared three huge rocks, as high as houses, pointed and slender as tree trunks, and set about at random in the fields.

'The Devil threw them down there in his fury,' declared Thurstan. Benedict didn't argue, but he had begun to doubt all the acts which were attributed to the Devil. He had heard Sirich tell of the great wall which stretched across England from side to side, and he wondered whether a race of giants had lived here long ago, ancestors, perhaps, of Thurstan and Sirich.

Benedict had always been pleased to see with what respect the most prominent citizens treated his master. For some weeks Josce had been planning a banquet to which some of the leading merchants had been invited and which they were eager to attend. But despite this, Benedict knew that the humour of the city was changing. Ever since he had lived with Josce, Benedict had been used to children following him in the street, crying after him 'The Jews will fatten you and eat you', but of late, they were becoming more impudent.

On the morning of the banquet, Benedict walked with Josce and Thurstan to Spen Lane and, turning out of Coney Street, Benedict glanced round in time to see a ragamuffin about to throw a handful of refuse after them. Benedict made as if to chase him whereupon the child fled down the nearest alley. Then, as they turned into Coppergate, they saw in the distance the figure of a white-robed canon who was preaching from the steps of All Saints. As they approached they paid no thought to the preaching but, coming closer, they were able to distinguish his words, and it was clear that he was praising the new crusade and inciting the people against the Jews. A glance of concern passed between Josce and his servants but they walked on determinedly, and now they heard the canon clearly as he flung out his arm in their direction, saying, 'There goes one infidel now. You have seen them in their pride. Their houses are built like citadels, yes, like royal palaces, and there they keep court, like princes among their people . . .' and Josce, Thurstan and Benedict kept their heads high because they could see, without turning their eyes towards the church, that the crowd turned sour faces towards them as they passed.

When they had rounded the corner, Josce said in a level tone, 'That canon is one of the Premonstratensians and a creature of Richard de Cuckney, I have seen them often together. Sir Richard's family founded Welbeck Abbey on their estate in Nottinghamshire for the Order. When we first came here there was a better spirit than this. We were not abused so.'

The incident had left the party feeling uneasy. They returned home a different way and it was with a sense of relief that they came to Coney Street, but as they neared the great house they heard a commotion. To their surprise they saw that gathered before their door was a small herd of swine in the charge of two swineherds, and running about the heels of the swine was a pair of small dogs of the kind used by herdsmen. Instead of directing the dogs to move the animals on, the men were undoubtedly urging them to keep the pigs close and were themselves using their staves to make sure that the animals couldn't stray from the house front. There was such a din of barking and squealing that a crowd had gathered and was laughing at the scene. Isabelle's head appeared out of one of the windows and she harangued the swineherds, but they did not move until Thurstan ran forward and threatened them with his stave.

The swineherds took their time and slowly moved the herd away down the street. Merchants and shopkeepers came out to shout at the men and warn them away from their doors. As the herd disappeared round the bend of the street, the two swineherds looked back and made rude gestures with their thumbs on their noses.

When the pigs had gone there was still a strong smell and the paving before the house, usually swept clean, was littered with filth. Josce had remained at some distance, and Benedict glanced anxiously up at his face, but he was showing no outward concern. As the crowd began to disperse, some of the people made a great pantomime of holding their noses and laughing. Benedict flushed with anger, seeing this as a further insult to his master, and found himself trembling with suppressed rage.

Isabelle rushed from the house, wearing high pattens on her feet to protect her shoes, and the old man who kept the door followed her with a bundle of brooms and heather besoms. Thurstan ordered him to bring water and the servants began a vigorous cleaning of the street, sweeping the dirt away down the side passage towards the river.

'I wonder,' said Josce, 'who it was who gave instructions for those unclean beasts to be herded at my door, and on the day of the banquet?'

Sirich appeared from the direction of Ousegate, and, like Josce, he showed no surprise at the activity only saying, 'I see you have had pigs at the door.'

'You smell them, brother, you are too late to see them,' Thurstan replied irritably, as he applied the broom with greater energy.

'What I did see,' Sirich answered, in a serious tone of voice, 'was two swineherds in conversation with the goldsmith, Master Peter, and he gave them money.'

'Master Peter . . .' mused Josce.

'I'll make more enquiries, master,' Sirich replied, and strode off again in the direction of Coppergate to ask questions among his cronies.

That evening, after the banquet was over and the happy guests had left, satiated with good food and wine, Benedict was helping the other servants to clear away, when he hesitated at the solar door, unobserved. Josce, Hannah and the children were seated around the cheerful hearth, encompassed in the amber glow of the fire, and Benedict experienced a sudden thrill of fear. He felt an impulse to rush forward and fold them in his arms, but he made no move to enter. It was as though, even watching them, he was guarding them, but from what? And how could he, a waif whom Josce had rescued, protect this, the richest family in York? He felt a deep unease, for whilst here in the house all was light and colour and warmth, out there the streets held something sinister.

'Why do they borrow the money?' Benedict asked Josce one day as they worked, 'they only have to pay it back again.'

'They borrow when they have to pay the King's taxes. Wars and crusades demand a steady stream of money. It is as though the country were bleeding to death. The landholders are reluctant to part with property. Land is the only safe place for a man's wealth, Benedict, far safer than keeping it in a chest, and so the laws are all designed to protect land. You see how the monasteries, which have a large income from wool, buy land whenever it becomes available. It is said that even before Duke William came from Normandy, the Church owned one third of all the land in England. Thus the rich men, if any money comes into their hands, immediately put it into landed property. If you should ever find yourself rich, Benedict, put your money into land.'

They laughed together, and Josce went on, 'Then there are dissatisfied landowners, most of whom could manage to live well without borrowing, but they envy their neighbours and, with a show of pomp, must be always competing with them. There are certainly unfortunate men who fall on bad times, but the chief borrowers wish to buy more than the year's income will allow.'

'How do the dissatisfied ones spend what they borrow?'

'Some wish to endow a convent for the sake of their souls, others to buy more land or provide a larger marriage portion, so that a daughter can marry someone rich and powerful. Some have daughters for whom they can find no husbands, so they give both daughter and endowment to a convent.'

'But how do they expect to repay you?'

'Some expect an inheritance, while others hope for a good grain harvest or a heavy wool clipping . . .'

'But the harvest can fail and the sheep can fall to the murrain,' the boy interrupted anxiously.

'You are wise, Benedict,' said Josce. 'If any of these things should occur, or the kinsman should not oblige his heir by dying in time, the land which they have pledged is forfeit. Now, I cannot take possession of the land, because I am not a Christian, but I am free to draw the rents or sell the crops until I have recouped the debt. However, you will appreciate that it is a great burden for me to have to manage farms here and there about the country, and the bailiff would surely cheat me, so when I see that there is little likelihood of being repaid, I sell the debt itself before it becomes due.'

'Like Sir John's debt, which the Abbey of Fountains bought last month?'

'Yes, everywhere the religious houses are buying up these debts and taking the land into their own hands. So you see, Benedict, how important it is for me to know what is happening in the country. There comes a time when I have to decide whether it is going to be worth my while to work an estate for many years in order to recover my own money, or whether to part with the debt and let the Church take the responsibility; for many of my debtors are still carrying debts which they inherited from their fathers.'

'So they borrow when they are already in debt!' said Benedict in surprise.

'When I was young,' said Josce, 'I was clerk to Aaron of Lincoln. Now, part of his business was in collecting the debts owed to the King.

For rendering this service he received a commission and it served the King well, for the animosity of the debtor was turned not against the King who demanded his money, but against the Jew who came to collect it. In this way I learned a great deal about the northern landowners. I need to know far more than the acreage they own or hold in fee. For instance, I must know whether they manage their land carefully, whether they keep one or many mistresses, how many bastards they support, and how they are related to the powerful men of this kingdom.'

'Sir Richard Malebisse is one of your debtors. Who are his connections?' asked Benedict.

'Ah, that question is interesting,' said Josce. 'Sir Richard Malebisse has connections with the Percy family and through them with a very important man indeed, for of the Percy family there are three sisters, who are aunts of Sir Richard Malebisse, and the youngest, Adeliz, is the mistress of Hugh de Puiset, Lord Bishop of Durham, and by him she has borne a child. In time of trouble, Malebisse would turn to a powerful man like Hugh de Puiset, and if de Puiset should fall foul of the King, then the whole complexion of affairs in the north would be altered.'

The boy nodded gravely before expressing his greatest fear in the matter of the debts.

'What happens, Master Josce, to the tenants on the land which the abbeys seize?'

'Sometimes they are left in peace, and the abbey merely extracts a rent, as did their previous landlord; but sometimes, as in the case of your own family, they are turned off the land, for the religious houses find it more profitable to use their lay brothers.'

'Then could you not charge a lower interest, so that the landowners could keep their land?' asked the boy.

'The rate of interest is fixed by the King,' Josce replied. 'It is lower than it was in the days of the Christian moneylenders, such as Cade, and Christians do still lend, although it is now forbidden, but the loans are disguised in different ways, and if you learn of such a loan, one being made by a Christian but in which the money is passing through Jewish hands to disguise the transaction, never speak of it!' Benedict looked anxiously at Josce and saw that it was indeed a matter which must be kept very secret. Then Josce went on, 'The rate of interest is of only marginal importance, Benedict. The chief issue is who it is who holds the land, and the Church accrues more with every passing month. Is it only I who see a danger in this? How it is all to end I cannot see, unless the Church becomes too powerful and the King himself confiscates its land. On the other hand, the Church may in the end become the greater power of the two, and with the help of the Pope overcome the King. The matter of this division of power almost came to a head with the murder of Archbishop Thomas at Canterbury, and the King was persuaded to do penance only after some years had passed. No, the struggle for power began long ago and will continue until long after we are all dead.'

'I feel no pity for the nobles,' said Benedict, 'but I do feel sorry for the people.'

'There is nothing I can do for them,' said Josce. 'How the Christians treat each other is beyond the range of my influence.'

'So,' said Benedict thoughtfully, 'the interest depends on the King.'

'Yes indeed, the King is behind everything. We Jews were invited here to perform the task of bankers, as the Christians are now forbidden, lest they tarnish their souls. We are under his protection, yet we are allowed to grow rich only in order to provide the King with the money which he would never dare to demand from the Christians. They have arms and can defend themselves, so there is always the danger that they might rise against him, whilst we are helpless.'

'Then why stay here?' asked Benedict. 'Would you not be better in your own country?'

'We have no country now. We live in order to survive, Benedict, down the ages, one generation following another, until we can come into our own again, until we are restored to Jerusalem,' and he remained silent and thoughtful.

Benedict watched him until he straightened himself and, smiling, said,

'And in the meantime to enjoy life, eh Benedict?'

Benedict smiled with relief and pleasure for he liked nothing better than that his beloved master should be happy.

'It is a fine day!' exclaimed Josce. 'Tell Aldred to saddle Belazzar and we shall go down to the river meadows to sport in the sun.'

The oppressive heat of August had culminated in thunder and torrential rain which had cleared the air, and now every leaf and blade of grass sparkled in the sun. The river had returned to its course, but it boiled along angrily between its banks, as though threatening to spill over on to the land again at any minute. The water was pale brown with the spoil of many fields and was bearing leafy branches along on its surface.

The meadows had dried to a damp softness, delightful to walk upon, and the citizens of York had come down to the riverside to stroll in the sun. Milk cows had again been sent to graze in the meadows, each animal with its small attendant, and some of these boys were sporting and splashing in the shallows where a stream fed the river.

Here Josce rode out that afternoon on Belazzar, surrounded by the men and boys of his household. The boys ran here and there on the grass, whilst their elders walked soberly beside the horse, deep in conversation.

Benedict kept an eye on Belazzar, for he had never seen a horse like him; indeed the animal was the talk of the town. Josce said that he came from Arabia and that this was the kind of horse on which his ancestors had ridden, the kind written about in the Bible. The horse's coat was a rich, shining, cream colour, but his lower legs were glossy black. The sunlight rippled over his coat and Benedict admired the high curve of his neck, from which the mane hung like a curtain of black silken threads.

It was a glorious afternoon. Above them the air was filled with the lusty song of the larks, and around them finches flitted, red, yellow, black and white, among the purple thistle heads, teasing out and tossing aside the downy seeds. In the distance, along the river bank, a small group of horsemen could be discerned, but at such a distance that it was hard to tell whether they were approaching or riding away.

A large branch was sweeping past the confluence of stream and river, and a foolhardy child set off through the water in pursuit of it but, realizing suddenly that he was being caught by the current, he panicked, striking out wildly. His head went under, and for a horrifying second only his hands were visible.

Josce had lifted his head at the shout and, turning Belazzar with smooth economy of movement, dropped quietly down the bank and into the water. A few strides only, the horse up to his belly in the fast-flowing river, and Josce bent, seized the boy, swung the horse round, and with a mighty heave the animal was again standing on the bank, water pouring from his sides.

Quietly, Josce deposited the child, gasping and retching, on the grass. All the people who had been disporting themselves in the sunshine, Josce's party included, had stood transfixed whilst they watched, and now, as though a spell had been broken, they began moving and talking at once, telling each other what they had seen, exclaiming on the boy's luck that a horseman had been passing and remarking on the beauty of the horse. One man ran off towards the town, calling to others as he ran, that the Jew had saved a boy from drowning.

Josce quietly turned Belazzar for home, and his people were beginning to follow him, when they became aware of the party of horsemen, first seen in the distance, and now about to pass them. Benedict started, and made a sharp intake of breath when he saw the formidable figure of Sir Richard Malebisse riding so close on a bay war horse. He had never before seen Malebisse close at hand. The man had a broad tanned face and a high hooked nose. His mouth was clamped shut, as though he rarely opened it except to issue an order. His eyes glittered darkly and, although he did not turn his head, Benedict saw that he eyed Josce as he passed and his look was fierce and cold, like that of an eagle. With him rode his squire, Richard de Cuckney, and after came Walter de Carton, Picot de Percy and Roger de Ripum. They had ridden through the crowd by the riverside and, if they had not seen the events, must have heard the discussion of what had happened. At that moment only Malebisse's broad dark face was surly; the younger men were laughing together and all seemed to be about to pass when de Carton turned his horse and, coming within hailing distance of Josce, called out to him, 'Keep that horse dry. I don't want him to catch a chill before he becomes mine.'

There was laughter among his friends and, perhaps to impress them further, he turned again to Josce as he rode on, shouting, 'That horse is too good for an infidel Jew. We'll have him yet, you'll see.'

Everyone had been happy, but now silence fell, both on Josce's party and on the people around. The sun still shone, but it was as though a dark cloud had passed over, chilling them all. Malebisse was not popular with the citizens of York. Subdued, Josce's party returned home, and while they were at their evening meal a neighbouring Jew, Leo the son of Hagin, entered the hall.

'What is this rumour that is going about the town?' he asked, as he took the place indicated for him by Josce, who replied,

'I haven't been about the town, so you must tell me.'

Benedict sat back, his spoon in his hand, the better to savour the pleasure of hearing Leo retell the story of the rescue. This, he felt, would wash away the bad taste which the squire's jeers had left behind.

'I was by a tavern door in Goodramgate and overheard some young gentlemen talking,' said Leo. 'They were saying that you had tried to drown a boy in the river.'

Benedict dropped his spoon with a clatter. Everyone else had stopped eating and all were staring open-mouthed at Leo. Josce's face grew white.

'Will they never stop?' he asked, rising to his feet. 'Whatever we do or do not do, they turn against us. Can there never be any peace? What is this Christianity, this strange new religion born of our own? What have we done that God should so punish us by creating these Christians?'

# 6

August of 1189, and the great King Henry was dead; harried across France in his last illness by his son Richard, whom men were calling Coeur de Lion.

Benedict had lived in the Coney Street house for four years; now seventeen years old and a valued member of the household, his admiration for Josce amounted almost to worship.

On a warm evening, all the household was gathered in the solar where there was an air of excitement. News had gone round the house that Josce and his partner, Benedict of Spen Lane, had been chosen to represent the Jews of York at King Richard's coronation which was to take place on the third day of September at Westminster.

'We must send Thurstan to London ahead of the party,' said Hannah, 'to make sure that everything at Catte Street is in order; for you will wish to entertain our London friends in style, Josce.'

But Josce, of all the company in the room, showed no enthusiasm for the prospect. Indeed, he had seemed preoccupied ever since it had been proposed. 'I shall take only a few servants,' he said. 'If trouble comes to York, this house must be strongly guarded. The old King was a firm ruler, for all his faults, and now that he is gone the nobles will make trouble. Everything, the realm itself perhaps, must be sacrificed to King Richard's passion for crusading. What pickings there are go to new men, and there is disquiet in the land. King Richard will leave almost immediately for the crusade and, mark what I say, there will be disorder.'

At his words the room grew silent and the sounds of the riverside drifted in through the open window. After a while Josce spoke again, and his words brought no comfort. 'You see how readily the poor of the town have accepted the rumour about the child in the river.'

'How is it possible?' Hannah exclaimed. 'You rescued the child; a crowd of people were witnesses to what happened!'

'Men believe what they wish to believe,' said Josce. 'Suppose I were to tell you that our good Doctor Abraham here had murdered a child, and that Sir Richard Malebisse had given all his land away to the poor. Would you be inclined to give each tale the same value?'

'Of course not!' she cried.

'Well, you will readily believe that it was Sir Richard who started the rumour that I had tried to drown the child,' said Josce, 'and, as the poor people of the streets have been taught by the Church to hate us, they readily believed it.'

There was a young chirographer present whose business it was to copy charters, and shyly he spoke. 'Is it the poor we have to fear? The small landowners, such as Malebisse, hate us because of the debts they have contracted. They are resentful, as you have just pointed out, because the new King does not hand out to them the lucrative offices which he gives to his courtiers, and the taxes he levies force them to borrow.'

Josce turned to him. 'Was it you, Solomon, who wrote Malebisse into the shetar which I checked today as Evil Beast?' The scribe's face reddened, but the room rang with laughter, for of all the lesser nobles in the north of Yorkshire, Malebisse was the most disliked. It had become known that he was building himself a fortress from oaks which he had felled illegally in the King's forest of Galtres. The citizens of York had protested against it, and their dislike of him was tinged with fear.

'Suppose one of them should see these words,' said Hannah.

'There is no fear of that,' replied Josce. 'Scarcely any, even among the Benedictines, read Hebrew, but the name was written only into our copy, so none will ever see it. It was well written, Solomon.'

'But that Malabestia is dangerous!' said Hannah. 'More dangerous than any wild boar.'

Benedict looked at Francisca and saw that she was nervous. She seemed to be making up her mind to something, and suddenly rushed headlong into the conversation, 'Father, you will be sure to take special care in London,' she said, 'to observe the costume of the ladies. You must note if there are any special colours worn, or any new kinds of headdresses.'

'And bring us presents!' cried Miriam.

'Are you not in bed yet!' Josce cried in mock horror, as he chased and caught her, lifting her as he had when she had been small, and catching up one plump little hand to examine the palm. She clasped his face between her hands and rested her forehead against his.

'At least those hands are clean today,' said her father, setting her down and pushing the protesting child gently towards Isabelle who had come to take her to bed.

If Francisca had intended to turn all their thoughts away from the dangers outside the house, thought Benedict, she had succeeded.

✳

Over the next few weeks there were many comings and goings at the great house in Coney Street. Benedict learned that the Jews of York were contributing to some costly gift for the King and arrangements were being made for the journey in the company of other merchants, most of them Christians, who would be going to London for the same event.

In the garden one morning, Benedict was seated on a stone bench set into the high wall, reading from a Book of Hours with which Josce had entrusted him. It was another of those Christian books, the pawning of which never ceased to amaze Aaron. 'Can you imagine our pawning any of our precious scrolls?' he had asked. 'We would starve first!'

Benedict handled the work with great reverence. The raised gold of the illuminations in this beautiful volume, which gleamed in the candlelight, blazed here in the full light of day. Benedict marvelled how the monks were able to raise the large capital letters, like cushions on the vellum, and he delighted in the miniature figures and tiny scenes which decorated the edges of each page.

The previous night had resounded with thunder and now the sun shone with extra brilliance. The grass was littered with leaves torn from the overhanging trees and Miriam was heaping the fallen leaves over her cat. For a while the animal lay still, tolerating her play, but suddenly it made a dash for freedom and, darting out a hand to catch it, the child was badly scratched. She howled, not so much at the hurt as at her cat, that it should scratch her so cruelly.

Benedict jumped to his feet and, for safety, pushed the precious book into his hood as he ran. Josce was also hastening to rescue his favourite, but Isabelle was there before them and scooped up the child to carry her, still crying, into the house. 'There, there my pet, my little love. Did the wicked cat scratch my Miriam?' and he heard the child's voice as she disappeared into the house, protesting now that the cat hadn't meant to scratch her.

Benedict retrieved the book from the depths of his hood.

'You take care of my possessions . . .' said Josce and he seemed, although he spoke to Benedict, to be speaking more to himself, 'But instead of leaving you here, I think I will take you with me to London. Aldred will look after the horses and, as my partner intends to take an army of servants, I shall borrow from him if the need arises.'

Benedict was delighted. Despite his father's bragging, they had never travelled further south than Stamford, and it was London above all else that he wished to see. Whilst the boy stuttered his thanks Josce, preoccupied with plans, strolled on towards the house, still deep in thought.

They set off on the tenth day of August. Josce, perhaps recalling the jibes of Walter de Carton by the river, decided against riding the beautiful Belazzar; instead, he and Benedict rode upon good but less attractive horses, with Aldred riding behind, leading a spare horse laden with changes of clothing. Benedict had been learning to ride for some months and was pleased to be able to test himself on a long ride.

It was a merry cavalcade, consisting in the main of merchants well known to Josce and his partner; merchants with whom they did business, and with whom they were on friendly terms. In a cart which carried the gifts destined for the new King, rode the elderly Benedict, as was fitting to his age, and alongside him on a smart white mule rode Prior William of St Mary's Church, a scholar of Hebrew who liked to discuss matters of theology with the learned Jews.

The journey was uneventful until they reached the hamlet of Bentley to the north of Doncaster. The track had been wide and sandy, passing through a sparse woodland of birches and gorse bushes. A short stretch of the lane, as it emerged from the wood, was squeezed between earthen banks and there they were overtaken by a group of crusaders, travelling at great speed. Without pausing to allow the travellers time to get through the narrow way, the knights and their squires crowded that part of the slow-moving convoy which was trapped by the banks, pushing them to one side, causing horses to shy and stumble. A pack-horse turned on its haunches and sprang up on to the left-hand bank, before plunging into the field beyond and losing part of its load. As the crusaders passed, Benedict caught sight of Sir Richard Malebisse and close behind him rode Roger de Cuckney and Picot de Percy. The latter recognised Josce and, despite the speed of his companions, pulled out of the throng, wheeled the great raw-boned bay he was riding and came back.

Josce and young Benedict were out of the narrow way, and had turned in their saddles to see how their companions fared when they were startled by the thudding of hooves in front of them. As he rode alongside them, Picot de Percy caught the shoulder of young Benedict's mare with his horse's quarters, almost knocking Benedict out of the saddle. De Percy showed no sign that he had noticed, although he must have felt the jolt, and, ignoring the boy as he struggled to retain his seat, he shouted across to Josce, 'We will have your Belazzar yet. He will carry me well I think; better than your daughter would!'

Josce's face turned white with fury, but de Percy spurred his horse into a half-rear, before it plunged forward and set off at a canter, rattling the pebbles on the track and causing young Benedict's horse to swerve and throw its head. The boy hardly dared to look at his master, but whilst he was still settling his horse, Josce's calm voice reached him.

'You ride well, Benedict; better than that young fool.'

Benedict risked a glance at his master's face and found that, apart from his pallor, there was no outward sign that he had heard the insult.

The merchants were angry. It took them some time to calm their horses, and two of the pack animals had got loose and had to be caught. During the delay the Prior rode up to Josce and, nodding after the departing crusaders, said, 'That young man will give trouble, I have no doubt. You must take care in London, Master Josce; I hope your house in Catte Street is well founded.'

'Thank you for your concern, Prior William,' Josce replied. 'The house is not as strong as mine in York, but it is stone built, with a roof of stone, so it would be difficult for the mob to fire.'

'I am glad to hear it,' replied the Prior, 'and there is surely no risk at the ceremony itself.'

'We are not to be allowed into the cathedral,' said Josce, 'But we will present our gifts at Westminster Hall afterwards.'

They saw no more crusaders on the journey and Benedict almost forgot the incident in his excitement at seeing London. He had thought York the finest city in the world, but here there were many more streets, and they were thronging with crowds such as he had never seen before. There were more stone-built houses than York could boast and the carved beams on the timber buildings glowed with bright paint of many colours.

At Catte Street they made themselves comfortable with the two clerks who conducted Josce's business in London and the two elderly men and a boy who attended to their needs and kept the house in order. Josce immediately sent out for peaches, pomegranates, grapes apricots and the finest French wines. With these he entertained his friends, both those who had travelled from the north and those who dwelt in London.

Benedict was in a state of rising excitement about the coronation, but still Josce did not seem to anticipate the day with pleasure. Benedict was to act as his page when they entered the hall to present their gifts at the banquet, but he wished to see the procession to and from the abbey as well. With Josce in his present mood, he feared they would not venture out in time. But his impatience was brought to an end by his elders. Old Benedict sent word by one of his servants that he and two other elderly Jews were going early, so as to see the procession. Josce hesitated, then, seeing the look of disappointment on the face of his erstwhile page, he smiled wryly and consented to go. Benedict thought afterwards that it would not have made any difference, even if they had stayed at home.

The crowd was much greater than any of them had expected. The country people had come flocking in to see the show, outnumbering the Londoners. There were merchants and knights in the throng, the crusaders distinguished by their surcoats which were decorated with the cross in red, and all eager to see the great ones of the land as they passed. Adding to the crush were the squires and pages of the lesser nobility, who had already entered the abbey church.

It wasn't as easy to see the procession as Benedict had imagined. At first they were almost at the front of the crowd and had a good view. They saw Sir Ranulph Glanville, a former Sheriff of York and now Lord Chief Justice, whom they recognised easily. There were no less than four archbishops in attendance, Canterbury, Dublin, Rouen and Treves, and then came bishops and abbots with lesser clergy carrying burning tapers and holy water. Other notables were eagerly pointed out to them by those beside them in the crowd. So Benedict learned that the man dressed in a fashionably short coat of brown and gold brocade, who bore the King's cap, was Geoffrey de Lucy and he was followed by John Marshall, who carried the spurs on a cushion. The man who followed, wearing a red surcoat edged with brown fur and with hose the colour of oak leaves in autumn, was the new King's half-brother, one of the late king's bastards, William Longsworth, Earl of Salisbury, and he carried a golden rod topped with a dove. Then Josce and Benedict found themselves pushed further back into the throng.

A big man in front of them, amused by Benedict's comments, pushed his neighbours to one side a little, and for a while Benedict again had a really good view. He clearly saw the King's younger brother, John, Earl of Mortain and Gloucester, and his behaviour puzzled Benedict. For as the prince passed with the sword of state, he smiled in a sardonic manner, turning this way and that to speak with the men around him in a way which the boy thought was not dignified; it was as though he mocked his brother's coronation.

The crowd chattered with excitement as William Marshall, Earl of Pembroke, strode by, serious of face, and carrying the sceptre, his surcoat of blue and red girdled with a belt of cloth of gold. Benedict looked upon him with awe, as he had heard the stories of his valour and courage. All these grand people were escorted by their squires and pages in splendid garments, and all the while the trumpets sounded high and shrill and the drums beat thrillingly, rousing the excitement of the crowd. Next came four barons, carrying aloft a chequer board as a sign of the Exchequer Royal, but after a while, the crowd pushing and swaying this way and that, it became difficult for Benedict to see and he caught only glimpses of the canopy, supported on four lances as it was carried over the head of Richard, Duke of Normandy, who would be King within the hour, and Benedict never saw the crown, although he could hear taller people commenting on it, as it was borne past by the

Earl of Essex. Benedict could not see the Earl, but Josce shouted over the noise in explanation, 'Essex is also Lord of Holderness where you were born.' He was disappointed not to have seen the most important people, for Josce told him that Hugh de Puiset, Bishop of Durham, was walking on the new King's right hand, and Benedict had wanted to see him since he was in some way related to the notorious Malebisse.

Eventually they became tired of the crush and the smell of some of the people who were pressed close against them. Even so, Josce went so far as to admit that he was glad not to have missed the show. It was time now to return home, for they must present themselves in two hours' time with the gifts for the new King.

# 7

After the royal procession had entered Westminster Hall the doors were closed, and an air of anticlimax fell upon the crowd. The royal guard found it impossible to shut the gates because of the crush of people and turned their attention instead to the youths who had perched along the rails, poking at them ineffectually with their staves in an attempt to dislodge them. The youths shouted and made rude gestures at the guards, and the crowd, eager for further entertainment, pushed forward to try to see what was happening. The elderly Benedict, some other Jews and their servants, who had been close to the open gates, were pushed forward into the enclosure, and at that moment, a voice from among a party of crusaders shouted that the Jews were trying to get into the hall.

Josce clutched at young Benedict's arm and a look of alarm passed between them. They were by now standing with Jacob, one of Josce's London clerks, on a slight rise some distance from the railings. Benedict cast an anxious glance up at his master's face and, with a nod, Josce acknowledged the need for haste. The three had begun to edge their way out of the crowd when behind them arose a tumult of sound, and loud above it there came a cry, perhaps again from the crusaders, of 'Kill the Jews!'

They had made but a few yards of ground when there was another disturbance away to their right and they hesitated, turning to see what was happening. A crowd of noisy apprentices, obviously out for mischief, was coming their way, but at the same moment there were screams and shouts from behind the youths and a wagon burst through the mob, scattering the apprentices to right and left. The wagoner was standing up and lashing his horses with his long whip, and as it passed Josce shouted to the others, 'Stay with the wagon.' They ran along beside it, clutching at the rim of the cart for support, until the crowd had been left behind and, allowing the wagon to roll away, they turned, breathless, into a lane which led down to the river. Now, towards them, hurried people who had left the precincts of the palace before the trouble began and who, on hearing the noise, had turned and were making their way back, crying 'What is happening?'

'A riot.' Benedict replied and then, as the advancing crowd thickened, 'Make way for my lord's steward!' This had the desired effect, for he had counted on there being so many strange noblemen and their servants in town that the Londoners would never be able to tell one from another, and with a respectful glance at Josce they gave way. Soon the three were free of the knot of advancing people and were alone with the old, the lame, and with women who clutched the hands of children, all of them anxious to get away from the mob and making the best pace they could. In this way, Josce's party came to the river bank.

The great grey expanse of the Thames stretched away to the dim green of grass and trees on the further bank, and they descended to the water with a sense of having escaped. Even the boatmen, usually scathing of any show, had been attracted to the coronation procession, and had left their boats in the care of a few of their fellows, so that it was necessary to climb across three moored craft to reach the first which was manned and ready to go.

'To the City!' Josce commanded, as they flung themselves on to the seats.

'What's amiss, masters?' asked the boatman, pushing off as he spoke.

'There's a riot outside the hall,' Josce replied.

'And I should think that it concerns the Jews, which bodes ill for you, master,' the boatman replied with a knowing look.

'Yes, it would be well to be out of this,' said Josce, his face grim.

'Will you give me a shilling over and above the fare if I get you home with speed? I am a strong rower, and I'll row up the channel which will bring us closest to your dwelling.'

Josce told the man exactly where to set them down, and agreed to pay him well in return for a speedy delivery. The oarsman pulled strongly, too strongly to allow conversation, though these men were usually very ready with news of the day, garnishing it well with their own opinions. The three passengers were glad to sit in silence, considering the implications of the riot and the friends they had left behind.

They were rowed as far as was possible into the City, and the boatman accepted his pay, saying 'I had best get back there and see if there are other Jews or men with broken heads wanting speedy transport home.'

On foot the three made all speed northwards, relieved to find the City streets still quiet. When they reached his house, Josce hammered at the door and when it was opened they hurried upstairs to the counting house and flung themselves down on the stools. Josce pushed back his hood and the clerks started to ask questions, but for some moments none of them had breath to spare for an explanation. Then Josce spoke.

'Jacob! As soon as you feel able, go round to Master Benedict's house and tell them that their master was trapped in the riot.' Then, turning to another, he said, 'Go down with Jacob and make sure that the bars are put up to the shutters and that the men keep the door.' But before either of them could move someone else was heard knocking and they exchanged an enquiring look. The clerk ran downstairs to find one of Master Benedict's servants who had already heard of the riot and wanted news of his master. They could give him none, and found it difficult to explain just how thick the crowd had been and how helpless they had found themselves. Looking out of the upper window, young Benedict was alarmed to see that the street was filling with excited men, and it was decided that old Benedict's servant should stay for a while until the crowd dispersed.

But the servant was not to return home that day, nor yet that night. The noise from the street grew in intensity and an attempt was made on the two weakest points of the stone house – the ground floor shutters and the sturdy oak door. Then, whilst those inside held their breath, there came the welcome sound of a herald's trumpet. Josce opened a little port in the shutter of the upper window and they heard the voice of the Chief Justice, Ranulph de Glanville, exhorting the crowd to disperse.

That brought a brief respite and Josce led his partner's servant out of the back yard and through a passage between the houses which backed on to Catte Street, but when they reached the stout door at the far end, they could hear a considerable din in the street outside. That escape route was clearly closed for the time being. Returning to the house, Josce showed young Benedict and Aldred the groom how to get out of the cellars. At the far end of the arcaded undercroft was a section of wall only one brick thick and held with very soft mortar. This had been made so that it could be demolished easily, and Josce told them that beyond it was an upward-sloping passage which would lead them to a yard and a timber fence which they could climb if need be, but he emphasised that this escape route was to be used only as a last resort.

Soon the mob returned and from the street came the sound of drunken voices shouting for the Jew's gold. A battering ram was used against the front door and with every thud of the heavy pole those inside shuddered. Then a cry went up for crowbars with which to prise open the shutters, but once again the mob was dispersed by the arrival of Sir Ranulph Glanville and a large body of knights who this time accompanied him. Those inside the house looked at each other with surprise and delight, but they were not to know that this was to be his last attempt to stop the riot, and that he would soon return to the coronation banquet only to report that he could do no more against the mob which was growing hourly.

No one slept that night, but they prowled the house, listening, and trying to interpret each sound which rose from the street. After a while, all seemed quiet and it was with the greatest difficulty that Josce persuaded his partner's servant to remain, at least until daylight. It was fortunate that he did, for only ten minutes later the mob was back, and a glimpse through the little port showed that they now had a handcart, half filled with loot. The listeners were alarmed to hear talk of fire, and Josce risked opening the whole of the shutter. After the briefest glance at the situation he snatched it shut again.

'They are dragging up brushwood to pile against the door and windows,' he said. 'Get to the kitchen and fill everything you can find with water.'

Then began the most intensive activity which Benedict had ever seen. The household servants, the clerks, and Josce himself, dashed to and fro, with everything which would contain water. The boy at the kitchen well became exhausted and Aldred had to take his place. For some time the rioters' brushwood wouldn't light, so that the defenders had marshalled their water containers at the upper windows with a few minutes to spare.

Josce ordered his men to wait until the last possible moment when smoke was creeping into the room before he gave the order. Immediately the upper shutters were flung wide and, two by two, his men poured water on to the flames below. Then the shutters were slammed shut, and they moved to the window above the front door. The operation was repeated, and as soon as each man had pitched water on to the flames, he rushed down again to the well. So efficient were they that the fire was not only extinguished but, although they couldn't know it at the time, the brushwood was soaked and could not be re-kindled.

The rioting continued all that night. Benedict, who had curled up in a corner of the room, dozed off during the early hours of the morning and awoke with a guilty start to find that Josce was awake and watching him.

'Go back to sleep,' he said. 'And in the morning, I will send you out like the dove from the Ark, to see if there is dry land.'

Benedict slept uneasily, disturbed at intervals by some patrolling watcher who stumbled sleepily against him in passing. He woke eventually from a nightmare in which, alone on a ship, he was surrounded by pirates who made constant attempts to scale and board the vessel. The pirate who came closest to success had the ferrety face of Picot de Percy, and Benedict awoke to find himself clutching, not a sword, but the rolled edge of a blanket which someone had thrown over him whilst he slept.

It was much quieter outside, and Aldred, thinking that the rioters had gone to their homes, opened one of the shutters. Immediately, from down the street, they heard the frightful screams of a woman. The rioters had broken into the house of a neighbour with dreadful results.

'Close the shutter,' cried Josce. 'There is nothing we can do. Don't let them see the open window. Pray that this riot is confined to London.'

So, this was the morning which should have brought relief! Benedict struggled to sit up and looked around him. He was in better shape than those who had stood guard. Jacob was red-eyed and coughing from the effects of the smoke. The others were no better, all pale, unshaven, and bone weary. One of Josce's elderly pensioners, a venerable man with white hair, was leaning against the opposite wall and breathing painfully, holding his hand at his heart with the grim concentration of one in pain. The smell of smoke was strong everywhere and began to irritate Benedict's throat. One of the clerks reported that he could see seven blazing houses from the back window.

It was decided that no Jew should try to leave the house and, after some debate, Benedict was chosen to stand watch, as being the one who had had most sleep, whilst Aldred was to be let out of the passage into the back street. His errand was to go first to Master Benedict's house; not to attempt to gain entrance, but just to ascertain how well it had stood the siege. If it had not, he was to find Prior William of York and report the condition of both houses to him. When the Church bells were rung, he was to be back at the gate, and to make a certain knock. If the opportunity was missed he was to return again whenever the Church bells rang.

Alone now, Benedict paced the house among the sleeping men, hastening to the front whenever the noise rose in the street. From the back windows he could see the spaces where houses had been. From the piles of wreckage smoke rose and swirled, and at times fire would flare up again. All around the house, the sound of the riot ebbed and flowed as the mob moved from street to street.

The night had been frightful, yet during all that time they had been sustained by the hope that the Chief Justice would come to their rescue or that the rioters would tire and disperse, but neither happened. After Aldred's departure, the mob collected again in Catte Street.

'Will it never end?' Josce groaned as his men pulled themselves wearily to their feet and returned to the well, filling every receptacle and hauling it wearily upstairs to set it once again in place. Benedict slipped away and made his way through the ground floor warehouse. The room was filled with smoke which set him coughing but the shutters, the only barrier between them and their enemies, held firm, with no chink of light showing through. With relief he turned to climb the stairs. Then, one sound, clear amid the hubbub outside, sent a thrill of fear through him. It was the scrape of a crowbar against the stone wall just outside. A voice above the rest called for greater effort, 'If we can get in here, lads, we shall find more, I promise you, than in all the rest of the street together.'

Another added, 'But there are no women here, boys!' Benedict darted back up the stairs to the comfort of his fellows.

'Did you learn anything downstairs?' Josce asked.

'One of them is promising great wealth if they can get into this house,' Benedict replied, 'and they have a crowbar.'

The attackers first tried fire, and were again foiled by the amount of water the defenders were able to send down. Then began another onslaught with rams and crowbars, but although the attackers seemed better equipped than they had on the previous night, they must have been tiring. After a while their efforts slackened and, to the amazement of the listeners, the mob fell upon the timber-built house of their Christian neighbours. There must have been brushwood to spare, for finding themselves barred, the rioters set fire to the door, and the house was soon ablaze. The crackle and roar of flames was loud in Josce's house and they could soon feel the heat. Running to the back windows they saw their neighbour, a chandler, his family and servants, dragging as much as they could of the contents out into the yard.

'Their cellars are full of candles and rope,' cried Josce. 'If that catches fire those people will roast even outside! Get ladders up to the garden wall.'

The neighbour's wife and her maid screamed when figures appeared on top of the wall but they were quickly reassured, and ladders were lowered for them. Josce came down to confer with the chandler and Benedict guessed his dilemma. They could all be led out through the undercroft, but they were sure to relate by what means they had escaped, and the route would then be lost to the house for all time. He watched, and saw Josce give orders for breakfast to be prepared for everyone. The chandler's family was utterly dejected and his wife was sobbing in the arms of her maid, but Josce rallied them and, choosing the strongest men from both households, set them to replenish the water containers.

Meanwhile, Aldred had returned several times to the passage door, but had either found too many ruffians in the street, so that he dared not approach, or had received no answer. He had almost despaired when he saw their neighbour's house blazing to the heavens, and had stood rooted to the spot, along with some householders who had ventured out to investigate the situation. As the fire raged the bells were rung, and Aldred tried the door again, but that coincided with the rescue over the garden wall, and his knocking went unheard. It was mid-afternoon before he attracted their attention.

'Master Benedict is taken by the mob,' he announced.

'Do his servants know where he is?' asked Josce.

'No, they learned this from someone who called up to them from the street during the siege, so I went, as you said, to find Prior William, and his clerk told me that he had been summoned away to baptize Master Benedict.'

'Where was this?' cried Josce, aghast.

'At St Margaret's Church close by Westminster.'

There was silence in the room, and Josce sank on to a stool. 'That means he is well,' he said. 'And a forcible conversion will surely not be held to be legal.'

'He is not well, master,' said Aldred. 'Some of his servants had to leave him and flee, I met them on the way here, but they say he is badly hurt.'

Josce groaned, then after a pause, he said, 'Prior William is a friend, and better a friend than an enemy. Now, where to look for my good old partner?'

'Shall we send to the Chief Justice?' asked Jacob.

'That would be our best policy,' Josce agreed. 'But we should also send again to Prior William, and it would be wisest to send our Christians, Aldred and Benedict.' Turning first to Aldred he went on, 'When you have eaten, go again to the prior's house and see if he has returned. He will give you what news he can.' Then, to Benedict he said, 'You, Benedict, have the more difficult errand. I wish you to go to Sir Ranulph Glanville and tell him of our plight. Remind him that the Jews are under the King's special protection and ask for an escort that we may leave London. While you are both away I will superintend the saddling and packing of the horses, for I would rather abandon this house than risk all our lives on a second night.'

'But the house stood when others didn't,' said Jacob.

'We were lucky,' Josce replied. 'If the mob had not found easier prey and had taken time and planned more carefully, we also would surely have been burned alive or killed as we escaped. London is too dangerous, we must return to York.'

Young Benedict set out with directions to the house of the Chief Justice, well rehearsed in his speech. He was relieved to be away from the confinement of the house, yet afraid of what he might find in the streets. Many houses had been burned to the ground, and here and there men were searching the ruins. Benedict stopped and shied like a frightened horse when he saw, almost too late, that the two blackened pieces of timber over which he had been about to stride were the charred bodies of two of the victims. Several houses which he knew to have been those of Jews were completely burned out and, ominously, nobody was searching there. He supposed that the houses had been despoiled before they were fired and that, of these families, there was no one left to do the searching. Wooden houses, he now saw, provided no defence at all and, perilous though their situation had been, the stone house had saved them.

He reached the Chief Justice's house where the servant took his message, but left him standing outside in the street. Returning, he brought him into the presence of his master. Benedict was glad to be out of the street, for he had spent the time glancing anxiously this way and that, expecting more rioters to appear at any moment. Glanville was not alone, there were several men there, all with stern and serious faces. It was with some temerity that Benedict began his address, but after a few words he remembered the gravity of his errand and his voice grew stronger.

'My Lord Chief Justice, my master, Josce the Jew, prays that you will relieve his sufferings and enable him to leave London as speedily as possible. He entreats you to provide for him and his household an escort to some safer place.'

Sir Ranulph glowered at him from beneath shaggy black brows. 'Your master is lucky to have his skin, and his house is still standing. I have no men to spare for an escort for a rich Jew when the city is in riot. Tell your master that the King is mightily displeased.'

Benedict could not understand why the Jews had to be told that the King was displeased, but it served to remind him of the rest of his message.

'My master begs leave to remind your worship that the Jews are under the special protection of the King and that their wealth, which is ever at the King's service, would be safer in this time of trouble outside of London.'

Before he could go on, he was interrupted again, 'God's teeth! Is there no end to the impudent demands of these people? Go boy, to your master, and tell him I have no escort to spare!'

Benedict, in desperation, tried one last throw. 'But, sir,' he pleaded, abandoning his pre-arranged speech, 'what of the Jews' presents for the King, which they were unable to present at Westminster?'

At this, the Chief Justice paused, and thought for a moment. Then he took Benedict through a door behind him into a small and private room. Benedict felt sure that it was mention of the presents which had caused this change in the great man's attitude, and he fully expected that Glanville was about to cheat the King in some way, but no. 'You go to York?'

'Yes, sir.'

There was a pause, and Glanville felt at his jaw and began to prowl the small room like a caged bear.

'Very well,' he said, 'I shall send a guard with you. Your master must leave this morning, calling here with the gifts, and I will give him sealed letters to take with him to Yorkshire. There will be no names upon them, you understand, and the letters must be delivered with the seals unbroken to the men I name. Furthermore, you and your master and all his other servants must say nothing of these letters.'

'If you give them directly to my master when he calls, and in private, then only he and I will know of their existence,' said Benedict.

'You are a shrewd lad and I suppose you have been trusted with your master's secrets before this. Tell him in secret then, and I will provide an escort for a distance of five miles beyond the City, no more.'

Benedict was relieved to get away and sped down the street, until he saw a group of figures approaching. They were carrying something and, fearing more rioters, he stepped into an alleyway. From its opening he saw two men supporting in their arms, as though he were seated in a chair, an old man whose head lolled helplessly and whom he recognised as his namesake, Josce's partner, the injured Benedict.

# 8

___

It was an evening in late February of 1190, and the family was gathered around the fire.

'There is some new trouble brewing,' said Josce, and they waited in silence for him to continue. 'This has nothing to do with the Christians and their animosity, but it could rebound upon us, nevertheless.'

'What is this, can we have no peace, not even in York?' asked Hannah.

'Trouble between the northern Barons and the King – yet I fear King Richard knows less about it than I do. Ever since the old King was known to be dying there have been rumours of trouble, but now it seems, even Hugh de Puiset is involved, and the new Sheriff of Yorkshire has been sending out to determine how many men can be mustered in the county.'

'What has roused them, master?' asked Benedict.

'The root of this new disquiet may lie in the report that King Richard has offered to sell the County of Yorkshire to Otto of Saxony,' said Josce.

'Aye, I have heard it too,' said Thurstan angrily. 'This King Richard, who harried his own father to the grave and, as soon as his coronation is over, hies it to France and the crusade, he would sell Yorkshire to a foreign prince!'

'Do not allow people to hear you speak ill of the new King,' said Josce. 'He has made himself a great favourite with the people, but he would sell the whole country to finance his crusades. It is said he jested that he would sell London itself, but I doubt it was a jest. No wonder the lords are troubled. The King's brother, John, despite the wide lands he has been given, is strengthening his castles, and if Richard should die on the crusade, John might succeed him. Then God help us!' and he stared into the fire for some time before continuing, 'I have been thinking that it would be better if some members of this family lived elsewhere so that, if anything untoward should happen here in York, they might be safe.'

At his words, Hannah clutched at the shawl she was wearing. Ever since the coronation and the death of Old Benedict, she, who had always been so proud and confident, had become nervous, and now she glanced uneasily over her shoulder at the rattling shutters. Sirich noticed her anxiety and, crossing to the embrasure, stepped up on to the seat and closed them firmly. All this time, Josce had sat gazing into the fire and although Hannah's lips parted once, as if to speak, she remained silent.

At last he said, 'Francisca is of an age to marry, and this is perhaps a good time for her to go to Isaac's family in Stamford.' Hannah made a little moan, so low as scarcely to be heard. 'And Aaron,' Josce continued, 'might go to our friends in Lincoln; I spoke to them when I was last there.'

Isaac of Stamford, an old friend of Josce and Hannah, had visited York with his son, Moses, during the early winter following the coronation riots, and Francisca and Moses had become affianced. She had been very serious ever since, and Benedict was reminded of Bella, who had ceased her childish games at the time of her betrothal. Perhaps this was natural to girls, but Francisca did not seem to be excited or even pleased about her planned marriage, in fact, she had been unusually subdued since that time. Sometimes Francisca visited Bella and her husband and their new baby, but she always returned from their house silent and thoughtful.

Josce had spoken of the separation as though it were something he was still considering, but they all knew as he spoke that the decision had been made. Aaron, now almost as tall as Benedict, had stopped winding the new string about the middle of his bow, and sat attentively, his eyes on his father. Benedict glanced across at Francisca, to see what she might be thinking, but found no indication. He had become more self-assured since the riot in London, but to sit with Francisca made him uneasy, for now she was betrothed she rarely spoke to him and he felt offended, thinking her too proud.

Ever since their return from London, the mood of anxiety among the Jewish households had deepened. The house in Spen Lane was in mourning. Old Benedict had denied his forced conversion and, on the return journey, had died a lingering death at his house in Northampton. His two elder sons were in London, appealing for permission to inherit their father's wealth and debts.

Benedict had never been able to like his elder namesake, for he had not forgotten their first encounter when it seemed to him that the old man would persuade Josce to return him to the goldsmith. Now he felt ashamed before the bravery of the old man. And he understood old Benedict's alarm that Josce had rescued a Christian child. It was an act which could have brought disaster on the whole community. He often envisaged with horror what would have happened to them all had he died in the Coney Street house; then the Jews would have been accused of his murder. Hannah too, he remembered, had been well aware of the situation, yet he had never seen in her a hint of fear or resentment.

During the following week, messages were sent to Lincoln and Stamford, clothes were sorted and packed, and presents procured for the families to which each of the children was going. It was decided that Thurstan and Benedict could be spared, and Isabelle was to go as Francisca's maid, but Hannah raised a great cry. What way was this, she asked, for the daughter of Josce of York to marry? Her bridegroom should have come to York, or Francisca should have been accompanied by her father, or some respected elder of the Jewish community. Josce tried to comfort her by reminding her that he was sending the children away for their safety, and that the usual ceremonies must be abandoned. His words, however, served only to increase her anxiety.

One of the difficulties they had to overcome was that of finding a safe means by which Francisca's marriage portion could be carried; for Josce said it was bad enough to send her alone to her wedding, without having her arrive penniless. He had smiled at his daughter as he said this, as though to make light of the separation, and she had summoned up a smile in response. It was decided that Thurstan should carry some of the money in a linen belt which he was to wear under his clothes, around his waist; that Benedict should have another such belt, and the rest of the coins and other valuables should be sewn under the braid around Benedict's new cloak. This was a very handsome cloak of closely woven wool, dyed a dark green, and the collar lined with fur. Josce had bought it for him as a present on his saint's day.

A whole evening was assigned to hiding the marriage portion. Heaps of silver coins, gold rings, a gold clasp for the neck of a cloak and a gold chain stood along the edge of the table, and Isabelle and Hannah stitched by the light of the fire. Benedict, when he tried on the cloak, was dismayed at the weight, and wondered how he would mount a horse without everyone noticing the heavy way in which the cloak swung.

'What you must beware of, lad,' said Thurstan jokingly, 'is not to fall in the water, or we'll lose both you and the money.'

In a surprisingly short time they were ready to leave, and the tension grew as they gathered in the great hall, wearing their travelling clothes. Then Hannah, usually so serene, began to weep and clung to her departing daughter, crying 'I will never see her children.'

This outburst surprised Benedict into the realisation of how things had changed since he had come to Coney Street. At that time it would never have occurred to Hannah that she would be unable to make visits to a married daughter, nor would she have behaved in this unrestrained fashion.

The rest of the household accompanied them to the river, and it was only then that the white-faced Francisca shed a tear. Benedict, as he settled in the boat, also felt a moment's unease, and shivered at the thought that this might be his last sight of York. He brushed the idea aside as they set off downstream, and was soon distracted by consideration of their fellow passengers. Towards the front of the boat were a master carpenter and his apprentice with a chest of tools, while an elderly Knight who travelled alone occupied the middle section. The Knight's horse travelled in the second boat, with those undistinguished horses of Josce's which had carried them to London for the coronation.

At first the company sat in silence, watching the passing fields. Benedict had carried the heavy cloak down to the boat and had chosen to sit on it rather than to wear it, but as soon as he felt the wind blowing across the open country he regretted his decision and began to wonder if he could stand up and swing it about his shoulders without drawing attention to its weight. The sail bowed to the wind, and sent them along at a fair speed. After another half hour of the chill wind he decided he must wear the cloak, and with great care he managed to pull it from beneath him and to put it on without displaying its full length.

Benedict found the boat ride interesting, for he had never seen the country from the river, and he looked out for familiar church towers which told him of villages he knew better from the road. He was not looking forward to their stay in Stamford, for he still recalled with painful clarity his family's ignominious departure from that town, and Lincoln held only the unhappy memory of Alyce's disappearance, sold, he wondered, into what kind of slavery?

At Selby they disembarked briefly, crowding into an inn by the dock, where, to Benedict's surprise, the Knight made room so that he could sit beside him on the bench and addressed him as though he were his social equal. Then he beguiled the company with his reminiscences of other journeys in those parts, so that the time passed quickly. On the way back to the boat, Thurstan drew Benedict aside and told him that the Knight was Sir Jocelyn de Birkhau who held a small manor, of the Honour of Richmond, for which he owed one knight's fee. The old man was known to Thurstan's family and was unfortunate, said Thurstan, in that his only son had died the previous year.

Benedict knew enough of such tenures to know that it was often difficult to find the money to provide a knight if there were not a young man in the house able to perform that duty. He looked at the Knight and assessed his age at perhaps sixty years, too old at that for much useful service in arms.

Again on the boat, the Knight made room beside him for Benedict, and surprised him by saying how much he resembled his dead son. He pointed out landmarks, and Benedict looked around at the country through which they travelled with interest. The sail was up and a north-east wind carried them forward at a good pace. Even so, Benedict soon wished that they were riding, for he began to tire of the cramped sitting, and glanced across at the two women to see how they fared.

Francisca's aloof manner still disturbed him. She was a good-looking girl by any standard, yet she seemed to him to lack the brilliance of her mother. Benedict thought Hannah so much more beautiful, and caught himself occasionally daydreaming about being married to a woman like her, but he would then tell himself not to be so foolish. It would be a miracle if he should ever find himself rich enough to take a wife, and to think of being married to such a grand lady was, he knew, the height of folly.

By early afternoon they reached the place where the Ouse entered the Humber, and he looked with amazement on the great stretch of water, five, no, six times the width of the Ouse. He began to be excited now, for had he not been born on the banks of the Hull, and might he not see the mouth of the Hull, where it entered the great estuary? He wished that he had asked Sirich for more information before they had left, but the Knight, when applied to, said that it was no use his hoping to see it, for the River Hull joined the Humber out near the sea, and they were to turn south again quite soon. Sure enough, almost immediately, there was a clattering and scrambling, and Benedict looked round to see that the oars were being taken out for their entry into the mouth of the Trent.

The Yorkshire Ouse flows southward, but the Trent drains the eastern midlands and runs due north. The current here, instead of carrying them along, became their adversary and the men had to row hard against it. Soon they could see to the east the low hills of north Lincolnshire, and away on their right, said the Knight, lay the Isle of Axholme amid its marshes. Somewhere past Owston Ferry the carpenter asked the boatmen where they were. 'Not far from Gainsbrough,' they replied, and at Gainsbrough the company disembarked again for food and rest, before the last stage which would bring them to Torksey.

At Torksey, they abandoned the river to go overland to Lincoln, and so did the carpenter who had been working on York Minster, and had been engaged to work on the half-finished cathedral at Lincoln. The Knight stayed aboard, for he was travelling, he told them, to his brother's manor at Tuxford in the Clay.

The horses were stiff after standing for so long in the boat. 'Stay you indoors,' Thurstan told the women. 'Let us walk these horses up and down to get the stiffness out of their legs. Sit inside and warm yourselves.' The carpenter set off on foot, and it was some time before Thurstan was satisfied with the horses and they were able to start, Francisca riding pillion behind her brother; Isabelle, considered too heavy to make up a double burden, rode alone, and Thurstan, who disliked riding, strode along beside them.

They approached Lincoln across the level land to the north, a direction from which it is impossible to see how the town tumbles away down the steep escarpment to the plain below, but Benedict remembered it well. When last he had come there, his family had climbed a steep hill to the alehouse, and his thoughts were now only of Alyce. The rest of the family was fading from his memory, but he could still conjure up at will the picture of a slight young girl dancing and spinning, with little cymbals on the palms of her hands and the bells on her wrists ringing merrily. Deep in remembrance, he had allowed his horse to go slowly and was now lagging behind the others. Before him, on a little knoll beside the road, stood an isolated building which was surely a leper hospital. He frowned with distaste as he recognised it, but his mind was still occupied with scenes of the past.

The others were already well beyond the building when Benedict became aware of a figure standing in the doorway; a young woman in a black gown, such as were worn by the inmates of these hospitals. He noticed at the same time that a narrow path had been worn in the grass of the knoll; the white limestone, smoothed by the passage of many feet, showing through the beaten earth here and there like bones. Then he realised that the figure was no longer in the doorway but was flying down the path towards him on bare feet.

He cringed from an encounter with the leper; afraid of seeing the deformities of hands, or worse, of the face, which the dread disease brought with it. Instinctively, he made to move his horse away, but his eyes were drawn irresistibly to the approaching figure. Her hands were held out in supplication, and her lips were about to frame the words of an appeal for alms, when suddenly she was still. It was then that Benedict snatched at the reins and brought his horse to a sudden halt.

Whatever she had been about to ask was never uttered. The two remained frozen, oblivious of everything but themselves. The monk who had followed her, and who took her arm and quietly bid her return, was scarcely noticed by either of them.

The silence was broken by a shout from the road ahead. Benedict tore his gaze from the girl and looked up to see Thurstan who was standing, waiting, legs apart, hands on hips. The others waited also, turning their heads to see what kept him. When he again looked round, the monk and the girl were climbing the path to the doorway. She looked back all the way, and hesitated at the door, still staring at Benedict.

Reluctantly, he pushed his horse forward. The others hadn't waited for him, but had carried on, expecting him to catch up. He moved slowly, and turned his head to look again at the doorway, only to find that the two figures had disappeared inside.

She hadn't looked like the Alyce he remembered, yet, when he tried now to reassemble the face he had just seen, it dissolved, as a dream does when the dreamer wakes. What had made him think it was Alyce? Already he was doubting. What had he seen? All he could now remember were the eyes, and a moment of – was it recognition? There had been a sudden change in the expression, and she had stopped then, the words frozen on her lips. He could not be sure . . . yet he found himself trembling.

They stayed at the house of Cresse, a Jewish trader and friend of Josce, who seemed to wish to make a celebration of their visit. At dinner he made a speech about Josce, in which he praised him and Hannah, complimented Francisca, and spoke with respect of the family into which she was to marry.

The food was good, the house was warm, and the others slept well that night, but Benedict was tortured by the idea that he had seen his sister and had left without a word. He had told the others why he had stopped; not confessing that it might have been the lost Alyce.

'Of course she stared at you,' said Isabelle, 'any girl would stare,' and she smiled then, 'Don't you know how handsome you are?' But Isabelle, he thought, had not seen that look of sudden, startled recollection.

The next day they said goodbye to Aaron. He came out of the house and stood on the step, tall and handsome, watching them as they descended the hill. Francisca looked back and waved forlornly several times until a turn of the street hid him from view. They rode on across the level land towards Grantham, where they were to stop for a meal at the house of Ephraim, before proceeding to Stamford. Francisca rode in a silence which Benedict ascribed to her sad parting from her brother, and gradually, she became more hunched in the saddle. Benedict recollected that she had never before ridden more than three miles at a stretch. At an inn where they stopped, Thurstan lifted her down, and it seemed to Benedict that he did so with some difficulty.

The night's rest had not eased Benedict's mind and he still pondered on the encounter at Lincoln. Inside the inn Francisca refused to eat and Thurstan ate very little, although Benedict remembered this only later. His thoughts still dwelt on his own problems. What could he do? He had no money of his own. If he had, he could have given it to Alyce on the return journey, but their only money was that which Josce had given them for their expenses; that and Francisca's marriage portion. But then, he wondered, had it been Alyce? His vision of her as he rode towards Lincoln had been so startlingly clear that he wondered now if he had imagined it to be her. Just because a girl had stared at him, like one mesmerised?

When Benedict helped Francisca to mount again, he noticed her flushed cheeks, and after some time on the road, despite his preoccupation, he became aware that Thurstan was no longer striding alongside the horses with his usual vigour. By the time they stopped at Barkston it was obvious that both man and girl were ill. The remaining miles to Grantham were a nightmare and their difficulties drove all thought of Alyce from his mind. He gave his horse to the reluctant Thurstan, and while Isabelle rode on one side of Francisca, he walked on the other, each of them putting out a hand to steady her whenever she swayed in the saddle. It was with a great sense of relief that they arrived at the house of Ephraim.

Their elderly host and his wife were dismayed to find that two of their guests were by now in a raging fever and, polite though they were, it was obvious that they were preoccupied with an unstated problem of their own. They brought pallets into the hall and put them near the fire for the invalids, and sent a messenger to Stamford. It was the sixth day of March.

On the seventh day the messenger returned with the news that the Jews of that town had been attacked and that the family to which Francisca was journeying had all been killed in their house.

# 9

'We are going to the castle at Lincoln,' Ephraim announced, as soon as he heard the news.

'But what shall we do?' asked Isabelle.

'You can stay here; no one will attack Christians, and you can claim Francisca for one of your own if you have to. We dare not stay; there were killings at Lynn and Norwich, did you not hear? We will be safer in the castle.'

They must have packed before their guests arrived, for they left immediately, taking their two servants with them.

Neither Thurstan nor Francisca was aware of what was happening, for they were both delirious with the fever, and on that first night Benedict found he could not sleep. He sat upright on his pallet in the firelight, his back against the wall, listening to the sounds around him, and deep in thought. He was brooding on their perilous situation, when he suddenly saw in his mind's eye the thickset figure of his father, dragging the heavy sled from fair to fair, with the two little boys riding on top of the bundles, making the load harder to pull.

For the first time, he began to wonder that his father had struggled on for so long. He knew now that many men in similar circumstances would have deserted their families. Every city had its share of destitute women and children who lived by begging, and when they had lived at home, he had had a rough kindness from his father; it was poverty and despair which had driven the man to drink. Neither was it any fault of theirs or their neighbours, that they had been driven from the land. The four bovates of good arable, and grazing for eight hundred sheep, which Robert of Meaux had granted to the abbey for the good of his soul, had done nothing for the bodies or souls in his hamlets. The fragile houses of wood and daub, with their earthen floors, had been torn down, and would leave little mark once the grass had grown. One family had stayed behind, hoping to live off the scraps from the monastery, but his father would have none of that. He railed against the monks who could turn families off the good land and then, of their Christian charity, give them in return only the broken meats from their evening meal.

Benedict's thoughts turned to Josce, who had saved his life, and apart from the calculating had taught him everything he knew. The respect he had been taught for the men of the Church was now in tatters; he reserved his admiration instead for the courage of the Jews, especially since he now understood that their wealth did not bring them security. He could not understand why Christians, so sure of their superiority in religion, possessed of their own land, and confident, they said, of the life to come, need bear such intolerance for any other religion. Why could they not be content to be saved themselves, without wishing to save others? The Jews felt sure of a place in Heaven without the intervention of Christ. Why not leave them to their own devices? Christ, it appeared, had been a Jew himself, so why did not the Christians honour the Jews?

It occurred to him then that the concept of life after death had been an exquisitely clever invention to ensnare all men into the power of the Church. In case Hell awaited him, the rotund and jolly Sir Robert had given his huge estate to the Abbey of Meaux, and all over England men like him, no more wicked than any others, were hastening to endow abbeys and to buy prayers for their souls. They even borrowed from the Jews in order to buy their way into Heaven. What would they do, he wondered, when they died and found that there was nothing but a long sleep which need have cost them nothing? He smiled in the darkness at his own folly. That was the beauty of the trick, for they would never know, one way or the other.

For fully nine days, they lay at the house in Grantham and Benedict almost forgot the episode at Lincoln in his anxiety for the invalids. He had little experience of dangerous illness, but Isabelle's obvious fear for their lives made him observe their condition with increasing intensity.

He and Isabelle took turns to watch the invalids and on the second day Benedict went out to buy food. He found what he had feared, that the suspicion of their neighbours was palpable, and he took every opportunity for conversation, taking care to explain that all in the house were Christians.

As the fever continued, and neither Thurstan nor Francisca had eaten for four days, his fear for them increased. What, he wondered, if Thurstan should die, what would he and Isabelle do here among strangers; to whom could they turn for help? Not until the sixth day did the two invalids show a marked sign of improvement and Francisca, as soon as she regained the strength to speak, asked when they were to resume their journey. Isabelle, glancing anxiously at Benedict, put her off with excuses, for although they both knew that the girl must be told the news from Stamford, neither of them wished to be the one to bear ill tidings.

While they hesitated, Benedict had to go out again to buy food, and this time he heard with alarm that the trouble had spread to Lincoln. He thought the matter over on the way back to the house, and was tempted to keep this news to himself. Once Thurstan heard it, he might refuse to return that way, and Benedict had a burning desire to call at the leper hospital, and to ask if the girl was Alyce. What he did not allow himself to consider, was what he would do if she were.

As he re-entered the house, passers-by stared curiously at him and he closed the door quickly, bolting it behind him. Isabelle was entering from the yard with firewood, and drew him aside.

'Francisca has been asking about Stamford again. We shall have to tell her what has happened, and then make for Lincoln as fast as we can.'

Benedict hesitated, but he knew in that second that he must tell her what he had heard.

'The riots have spread now to Lincoln.' He blurted it out, and then he thought of an excuse for going there, 'But we must go that way in order to return Ephraim's key.'

But Isabelle replied briefly and dismissively, 'The key might be the least of our troubles.'

Neither of them spoke about this new danger, but busied themselves preparing the meal, stirring the fire and the soup in the pot unnecessarily, until Thurstan became irritable and demanded something to eat. It was not until they sat down that Isabelle found the courage to begin.

'Francisca, my love, Benedict has been out into the streets, and he has heard that there has been trouble at Lincoln.' The girl started, and although their thoughts flew to Aaron, none dared mention his name. In the silence which prevailed there was only the tiny sound of a twig crackling in the fire, and the soft murmur of falling wood ash. Francisca said nothing, but stared vacantly into the fire, her empty bowl held so loosely that Benedict took it from her limp hand without her noticing, lest it should fall with a clatter and startle her. He felt a desperate need to protect her and he was wondering if Isabelle should not have softened the news, when she spoke again, and it seemed to Benedict, all too quickly, 'My pet, my dear one, we cannot go on to Stamford, for there has been a riot there as well, and the family of Moses has been killed, all of them, every one.'

Benedict expected Francisca to fling herself into Isabelle's arms in a torrent of weeping, but instead she threw a wild-eyed glance in his direction. It seemed to him that she tried to tear her eyes away from his face, but that she could not. Her look was riveted on him and a flush of colour swept up her pale throat and blazed in her cheeks. He could not disengage his eyes from hers and his own face reddened.

The realization came upon him in a sudden flash, that she was beautiful. He saw that now, though he had never been aware of it before. She was as beautiful as her mother! He was so startled that he could think of nothing else. He found it hard to breathe and he was burning hot, and still he stared, deep into her eyes, until she succeeded in turning from him. Then at last, her shoulders sagged and she fell against Isabelle's breast and sobbed.

Benedict was confused and troubled, and curiously elated. Why should Francisca look at him in that way? Thoughts began to stir in his mind which he suppressed with violence. He glanced quickly at Thurstan and saw that he too had been startled by Francisca's look, and over the girl's bowed head he saw that Isabelle also was regarding him with a curious look of concern. Francisca became quieter, and Isabelle sat her down gently and lowered herself on to the bench beside her, careful not to disturb the trembling girl, and holding her round the waist.

Thurstan, practical as ever, and perhaps wishing to break the tension in the room, thrust his bowl toward the pot and grasped the ladle, saying, 'Another helping of broth, let us eat for our health's sake. Just give us another day or two, then we will make for York as quickly as we can,' and as though he had read Benedict's thoughts, he added, 'As for Ephraim's key, we must take it with us. We can't risk our lives for the sake of a key.'

'Yes,' Francisca said quietly, staring into the flames, 'we must get back in time for the Passover.'

Benedict felt both disappointment and relief that they were not to go by way of Lincoln, and then his thoughts turned again to Francisca. It seemed strange and unfeeling that she said nothing about the tragedy at Stamford nor about the young man to whom she should have been married. He knew they had met only once, and whether she had wanted the marriage or not, he did not know. Still, even for appearance's sake, he felt she should have uttered some word of regret. He watched her. She was quiet now, and after a while she raised her face, pale again as a ghost, and looked at him coolly. This time she was able to withdraw her gaze almost immediately, and Benedict felt a sense of loss.

They left on Tuesday and as they rode away from the house a man ran up the street, calling to them, the words tumbling out of his mouth, 'There's a riot in Lincoln; is that where Ephraim went? Do you have business with him? It looks bad for the Jews.'

No one answered him. Indeed it would have been impossible for the torrent of words still poured forth. 'Have you heard any news? Did they take all their goods with them? Do you have the key?'

Benedict fingered the key which he was still clutching in his hand. He thrust it into his belt, and with a last look over his shoulder at the house he said, 'Yes, they took everything,' And as he spoke, he wondered for how long the massive door would stand.

They left the streets of Grantham as quickly as they could, conscious all the way of hostile faces, and of eyes watching them suspiciously. Glad to leave the town behind, they rode north again, down the steep hill which leads to Newark on the Trent, where they soon found room for themselves and the horses on two boats which were going as far as Gainsbrough. There they stayed the night, but next morning they were disheartened to find only one boat bound for York. It was empty, and it seemed to Benedict that there was no sensible reason why they should not travel in it, yet Thurstan hesitated, suspicious of the man in command. He said he had seen him in York, but though they questioned him anxiously, he could not remember what he had heard against the man. They discussed the matter in a huddle on the bank. If they allowed this boat to go, argued both Benedict and Isabelle, they might be delayed for another day or more, and they glanced at Francisca, pale and shivering inside her cloak, knowing she wished to be home that evening.

They embarked the horses, and settled on the seats. The crew, four men and a boy of about twelve, cast curious glances at them, but until they reached the Humber, the men were fully occupied and there was no time for conversation. The sail was tightly furled, for although they travelled with the current, the men had to row against a strong head wind which shifted frequently to the east, throwing them constantly towards the left bank. The wind served them better when they entered the wide waters of the Humber, veering to the east and blowing them quickly towards the mouth of the Ouse.

During this brief spell of rapid and easy sailing, Thurstan's suspicions of the boatmaster were confirmed when the man approached them.

'Do you wish to be set down at the Swinelanding?' he shouted against the wind, 'That will be nearest to your master's house.'

He obviously knew who they were, and this was confirmed when he went on, 'A pity that the Swinelanding is so near to the Jew's house; I hear that the pigs like to stand in front of his door.'

At the far end of the boat his men grinned and guffawed. Then they were occupied with getting the boat into the Ouse, and setting the oars to row hard against the current, but where the river took a westward turn the wind again carried them along for a short distance, and the boatmaster had time on his hands. Coming to them again, he said, 'Have you heard that all the Jews in Stamford and Lincoln have been killed?'

Benedict turned quickly to look at Francisca who, after one fearful glance at him, turned her face away to gaze across the cold flat landscape. When Benedict looked again at the boatmaster, he found that her look had not been lost on the man, who was smiling, and staring intently at Benedict's fur-lined cloak.

'Suppose they rob us,' Benedict muttered to Thurstan as soon as they were alone.

'They are too busy now, but we must escape at the first opportunity. Watch me carefully, and if I make a move, follow me as fast as you can.'

It was as they approached Selby that they found their chance. Before the town came in sight, they were surprised to find the boat pulling into the bank, and the crew tying up to a post, which was driven into the bank just before an isolated and disreputable-looking inn. Without a word to their passengers, as though they were no longer of any concern, the men made ready to disembark. Their casual disregard confirmed Benedict's fear that they were to be killed and robbed. The men knew that the four were helpless and in their power.

'How long are we stopping here?' asked Thurstan, keeping his voice very steady; not betraying any alarm.

'All night!' replied the boatmaster, grinning. 'You can stay in the boat if you wish, or come in with us.'

Thurstan appeared acquiescent, and replied in a resigned tone, bending as he spoke over one of the bundles as though he intended to follow them into this dreadful den, 'We'll follow you in.'

'Give us the fare now,' said the boatmaster, 'so that we can drink the health of your master.'

'I'll bring it in with our bundles,' Thurstan replied.

The men disappeared, an uncouth rabble, jostling, swearing, laughing and attempting to trip each other as they crowded all together through the inn door. Benedict looked up and down the river and found the banks were completely deserted.

As soon as the crew was inside and yelling for ale, Thurstan leaped ashore, dragging Jet, the most amenable of the horses, by its bridle. Isabelle saw what was toward and scrambled over the side to hold the horse. Meanwhile, Benedict had dealt with the second, and in a flash, Thurstan was back in the boat to grasp the bridle of the third, which was only too eager to join the others. The men bundled the women on to their mounts, and slapped the horses hard, to drive them forward. All this time no word had been spoken. Benedict threw himself, heavy cloak and all, into the saddle and set off after the women with Thurstan leaping along beside him and tossing a small purse of money through the inn door as they passed.

They made the best speed they could, and had covered a hundred yards or so before there was a shout from the inn door, but they wasted no time in looking back, pushing the horses northwards as fast as they could go, and bound for York.

# 10

Across the level land which stretched away on either hand, each coppice and clump of trees faded to a yet paler shade of grey, until the last one merged with the misty distances of the vale. The wintry sky showed no sign of the approaching spring. Cold enough for snow, thought Benedict, and ahead, as though to confirm his thought, in the direction of York, a column of cloud slowly gathered itself up, until it stood like a tower above the city.

He glanced across at Francisca, whose face he could scarcely see, for her hood was up and she sat, tense and miserable in the saddle, staring in the direction of home. They had travelled fast, giving themselves no time to consider what the boatman had said. Could it be possible that the Jews of Lincoln were dead?

No word had passed between the travellers, and perhaps to assuage his fears, Benedict had dismissed the boatman's words as mere spite, spoken with the intention of hurting. What Francisca felt, he could only guess, for she had barely spoken since they had begun their journey. He remembered now the look which had passed between them when she had heard of the death of Moses. He experienced a strange excitement at the recollection, but he refused to acknowledge the significance of his emotion, and turned his thoughts to events of the past. During their childhood, she had made him feel coltish and unsure of himself, but their journey had increased his confidence. The manner in which the elderly Knight had spoken to him on their journey down told him that he now appeared to others as an educated young man of some consequence.

He found it easy to distract his mind from the curious sensations connected with Francisca, for his conscience was troubled by the incident at Lincoln. Perhaps, when they were safely at home and this danger had passed, Josce would give him money to return and to discover whether or not it had been his sister.

The light was going rapidly now, and it seemed to Benedict that the cold must have driven everyone indoors, for they had seen not a soul for some miles past. They had passed some hovels, clustered at the edge of a common, but nobody had come out to see who was passing. Home! How he longed to be at home in Coney Street; with no more miles to travel, good food and a warm bed. He glanced at Thurstan, who was walking still, bravely and uncomplaining, on the far side of Francisca's horse. Benedict would gladly have changed places, but having been rebuffed so often, he held his tongue, amazed at the man's stubborn determination. Instead he called cheerfully, 'Nearly home, Thurstan, we'll soon be sitting at the fireside!'

But instead of replying, Thurstan came round to the nearside of Benedict's horse and, speaking quietly, said, 'Do you see the smoke?'

Benedict looked in the direction of York. 'That is cloud, I have been thinking that it's cold enough for snow.'

'No, it is smoke,' said Thurstan briefly. 'Let us approach with care.'

At his words, Benedict peered through the mist ahead, and his stomach gave a lurch. He remembered London, and began immediately to make plans for their safe entry into the city and to consider where they might stay, in case, though he hardly dared think of it, the Coney Street house had been attacked. The castle was the first refuge which sprang to mind, for there, under the protection of the King's Constable, they would be safe from attack.

Through the gloom they discerned a group of approaching figures and stopped their horses.

'Are they men-at-arms?' asked Thurstan.

'No, village people,' Benedict replied, standing in his stirrups and leaning forward over the horse's neck.

Soon it was clear that these were market women who must have left the city half an hour before. The women were still at a distance when Thurstan called out to them, 'What news of York?'

The women came close and set down their baskets, glad to rest and ready to talk.

'No good news, masters,' said the first. 'The city is in riot and you had best stay outside at an inn if you can.'

'When did this riot begin?' asked Benedict.

'It's been three days now,' she said, and then another spoke, 'We stayed late today to see what would happen, for some are still in the castle.'

Before Benedict could ask what this meant, Thurstan interrupted, 'Who is rioting, and what damage have they done?'

'Well, it's a puzzle,' said the first woman. 'All sorts and kinds. There's the Sheriff of Yorkshire with the county militia, and some knights, though they rode alone and did not arrive with him . . .'

but before she could go on, the others broke in, eager to give their accounts.

'There's Sir Richard Malebisse, William Percy, and others I don't know the names of . . .'

'. . . and shepherds from the country, brought in by the knights, and clergy of the town, and journeymen, and all kinds of ne'er-do-wells.'

'But who is this riot against?' asked Benedict, afraid as he spoke of hearing the answer.

'Why the Jews!' came the immediate reply. 'As soon as that Benedict's house was afire, and those inside had been killed, the rest of the Jews took themselves to the castle for protection, and much good may it have done them.'

Her eagerness and her obvious enjoyment in telling the news made Benedict feel sick. He dreaded to hear more, but the description went on inexorably.

'They've set fire to the castle. They might all be burned up by now.'

'Who has set fire to it?' cried Benedict.

'The Jews, of course,' and her voice rose with excitement. 'What can you expect from infidels?'

Benedict turned quickly to see if Francisca had heard but her head was turned away.

'Nonsense!' he said, searching the woman's face for any indication that she was exaggerating. 'They wouldn't set fire to it if they had gone there for safety, surely it is only some huts in the castle ward which have caught fire?'

'No, it's the keep on top of the mound,' the woman replied, seemingly sure of what she said.

Benedict looked at Thurstan in consternation, then turning again to the market woman he said, 'What has the Sheriff done to stop it?'

'He brought up a great sling, they'd been sawing and hammering all day to build it, and threw rocks at the castle, and would you believe, one boulder hit the timber, and tumbled back down the mound and killed a white monk that was raving and screaming to the people to kill the Jews.'

'What, the Jews are in the castle and the Sheriff is attacking it – the royal castle – are you sure you haven't been drinking too freely, wife?'

The women looked resentfully at him then and began to pick up their baskets.

'We know what we have seen, master, and you'll see for yourselves if you venture into the city. We've told you what we know,' and with that, they departed towards their home village, leaving the travellers confused and fearful.

'She said nothing of our house and that is the strongest in York,' said Benedict. 'We survived a riot in London, with shutters at the ground floor windows. The Coney Street house was built for a siege.' He turned to Francisca as he spoke, but she was staring grimly in the direction of the city.

'I don't think we should stop at all,' said Isabelle. 'Let's ride straight on to Langthorpe.'

'We still have to go through the city, sister, in order to cross the river,' said Thurstan. 'But I would dearly love to be home at Langthorpe this evening, and it would be dangerous to stay at an inn, Francisca might be recognised. It would please me well to go to our brother at Langthorpe and to return in a few days when this is all over.'

'No!' cried Francisca. Her voice startled them as it pierced the cold air. 'I must know what has happened. If they are in the house we might be able to help. We can't just ride by.'

Without a word, they pressed on, and as they came closer to the city, they could clearly see that the base of the column of smoke was stained red by the fire. Benedict was pondering all the while on the difficulties of entering the city and of getting through the streets which, he supposed, would be filled with rioters.

By common consent they avoided Fishergate Bar and took instead the little-used track to the left which would carry them close by the castle and provide a quick route to Coney Street. This lane soon took them along the top of the bank which dammed the River Foss in its southward flow, creating a huge lake within the city walls. The castle stood on two islands, close to the bank, and the mere served it as a moat.

Riding along the bank top was not easy. The fire struck fear into the hearts of the riders and alarmed the horses. It blazed high before them on the castle mound and was reflected in the water below, so that the fire seemed to be all about them. They dragged their eyes from the mesmerising flames above and, as they passed, from their elevated position were able to look down on the roof of the King's mill. On their right hand, they had a clear view of the castle ward which occupied the first and lower of the two islands. The ward was surrounded by a strong palisade and seemed to be filled with the Sheriff's men, whilst what they could see of the mob occupied the strip of land outside the fence. The massed men inside the stockade were relatively still, but those outside were running to and fro, black shapes against the firelight. Suddenly, a group broke away and, scrambling along the bank, crossed the causeway which linked the island of the ward to the high mound on which the keep was built. There they proceeded to run up and down the steep sides of the hill, in a seemingly purposeless frenzy.

The riders came to the point where a wooden stockade obstructed their line of approach; cutting across the triangle of land from the bank of the Ouse on their left, it formed a solid barrier until it met the edge of the lake, and their path was now barred by a high gate of solid timber. The roaring of the flames was so loud that they could hear nothing from the throng of soldiers out there in the lake, and Thurstan had to pound on the gate for some time before the barrier guards heard them.

Eventually, a man's head appeared above the timber, only to disappear again immediately. For a few seconds Benedict held his breath, wondering whether the guard had gone to fetch someone in authority. Then, to his surprise, the man opened the gate wide, making no enquiry as to who they were, and seemingly pleased to have company.

'Jack is down by the lake edge watching the show,' he shouted, above the roar of the fire. Then, recognising Thurstan, 'Aren't you a servant of that Josce the Jew?'

Benedict took advantage of the man's preoccupation with Thurstan to indicate to the women that they should ride on through. He followed them, then stopped, and turning his horse broadside across the path, attempted to prevent the guard from seeing the women too clearly. He, however, was still gesticulating animatedly and shouting above the roar of the fire, and seemed not to have noticed Francisca. '. . . Well, I reckon they're all dead by now, so you'll be wanting a new master. You shouldn't find it hard to get employment, a great fellow like you,' and he laughed.

The riders proceeded and Thurstan, as he hurried to catch them, thought for a moment that he heard someone calling his name, but the sound was so muffled by the roaring of the fire, and the sudden fall of more timber from the ramparts, that he dismissed it as imagination and did not look back. The wind tore at the flames, ripping them across the sky like ragged banners. The fire was scorching their faces now, and as the wind swirled the fire in their direction, the horses stopped in their tracks. Thurstan ran forward, grasped the cheekpiece of Jet's bridle, and dragged the animal along, keeping himself between the horse and the fire and shouting words of encouragement. It was not until they reached Castlegate and entered the dark and silent streets of the town, that the animals settled down.

There, all seemed deserted and Benedict was feeling thankful that the streets were empty when, rounding a corner, they came upon a group of drunken revellers; shepherds by the look of their clothes. The first stopped in the middle of the street and, tipping a skin bag, tried to drink from it. The beer ran over his face and neck, and most of what he aimed at his mouth was lost down his clothing. Another, more sober, snatched the bag from him, and managed it more successfully; then, catching sight of the riders, the drunkards made an unsteady advance towards them, crying, 'Ale money! Masters! Give us ale money to drink to Sir Richard. He has done great deeds against the infidels.' One leering, dribbling man made a snatch at Isabelle's reins but the riders sent their horses on at a brisk trot, leaving the men still staggering about the street in a futile search for largess.

Now the travellers were rounding the curve of Coney Street. Benedict, half eager, half dreading, what they might find, stood in his stirrups, leaning forward, ready for his first sight of the house. There it was! At first he thought that the house was sound, but then to his dismay he saw thin whisps of smoke curling up from the windows. He scanned the roof with frantic eyes, and by the light of the distant fire discerned a hole through which more smoke was seeping. He rode up to the doorway but turned his horse away immediately with a groan, for the door was charred and had been splintered and battered inwards.

'Where are they?' cried Francisca.

Benedict was in despair, and he felt a kind of paralysis creeping over him. 'They can't be in there,' he replied, as he sagged in the saddle and bent double with the pain of loss. Then, driving himself into activity for her sake, he looked quickly up and down the length of the street, 'But they might have taken shelter with neighbours.' His gaze raked the adjacent houses but all were close shuttered and silent. Even so, he had the feeling that there were people listening behind every window.

He dashed up to a merchant's house, and leaning from the saddle, beat upon the door with his fist. Immediately, above his head, a shutter was opened and the white face of a woman looked out.

'Where have they gone?' Benedict called, pulling his horse back to the middle of the street so that he could look up at her.

'They went to the castle. That was . . .' She had more to say, but Francisca had spun her horse and was dashing off in the direction from which they had come. Benedict was immediately in pursuit, for he remembered the London mob, and knew she must be stopped before she was recognised. He overtook her in Nessgate, and grasped her left rein, dragging both horses to a standstill. 'Why are you keeping me here?' she cried furiously, trying to snatch the reins from his restraining hand. 'I want to go to my family. I want my mother!'

# 11

The three horses stamped restlessly, throwing their heads in alarm, for they could plainly hear the roar and smell the smoke from the blazing castle. Thurstan held Isabelle's horse. There was a moment of complete stillness, which was broken by a voice which addressed them from the shadows under the houses. They started, and stared suspiciously into the gloom until a figure detached itself from the darkness saying, 'I've been out searching for you. Follow me.'

'It's Sirich,' said Thurstan.

'Didn't you hear me call at the gate on the causeway? The miller's wife saw you pass and sent me to fetch you.'

'But that means going through the gate again. The man knew me, and this time he might recognise Francisca,' said Thurstan.

'The gatekeeper will let us through, never fear,' said Sirich, but still they hesitated. There was nothing they wanted more than warmth and food, a cessation of motion, a place of safety where they could stay and take stock of their situation; but a house could be a trap as well as a shelter.

'You can't stay out here all night,' said Sirich. 'Come, the goodwife has some broth ready.'

They followed him back by the way they had come. At the barricade the guard again threw open the gate, saying eagerly to Sirich, 'You found them then, that's good!' He leaned hard against the gate to stop it blowing shut in the strong wind. 'The fire is getting worse,' he continued cheerfully and, indeed, it was. The two western towers had burned down almost to the level of the wooden walls. 'Where are you bound?' he then asked and Sirich, hoping to cover their tracks, replied, 'We will go down to Fulford for the night.' Then they rode away from that dreadful place.

Henry of Fishergate, who held the mill lease, was waiting in the yard and ordered them into the house while he led their horses away to his stables. The travellers were soon seated around the table, and the miller's wife clucked and crooned sympathetically while she served them bowls of soup.

'My goodman thought we would be safer here than in the house, but I wish we had stayed in Fishergate. Our men who keep the mill have run off to the riot.' Then, turning her attention to the two women, 'Oh, you poor souls, just look at you!'

Francisca, after taking a few spoonsful of the soup, pushed her bowl away, and, putting her arm down on the table, laid her head upon it. When the miller returned he exchanged a look of concern with his wife, and then sat silently, watching them eat.

Thurstan, as soon as he had finished the bowl, turned to Sirich and questioned him sharply.

'What has become of Josce?'

'I don't know,' Sirich replied, shaking his head.

'How did you come to be here?'

'The Jews went into the castle, and Master Josce told me to leave them and go home to Langthorpe.'

'How many went in?'

'A few were caught in the streets before they got there, but more than a hundred went inside.'

'And what word do you have of them?'

'No word,' was his only reply.

Thurstan looked enquiringly at the miller, who shook his head sadly, saying, 'No, we have no word.'

Benedict accepted the offer of more soup, and resolutely turned his thoughts from the castle. Somehow he felt that if he didn't think about what might have happened, all would be well, and while he waited for the soup he remembered what must surely have been another self, secure and happy, when he would visit the mill with Thurstan and Sirich. Then he had amused himself with innocent play, floating twigs on the mill leat whilst his elders had sat on a bench, talking, their backs resting firmly against the sun-warmed boards of the house.

'Now,' said the wife, 'you can all sleep here by the hearth. We have pallets enough for the women, but you men will have to sleep on the floor. You must be tired enough to sleep anywhere.'

'I'll wake you before dawn,' said Henry. 'You will want to be away before it's light, and I'll have your horses ready.'

'But we can't leave before we know what has happened,' said Thurstan.

Francisca lifted her head and sat upright, saying, 'I will not leave my family behind.'

The miller looked unhappy. 'You should leave the city,' he said, and then, addressing the room at large, 'you can come back when all is quiet again, but you would be better at Langthorpe.' Then he added, 'Shall I lend you my wagon to help you on your way?'

'Wake us, as you said, before dawn and we will decide then,' Thurstan replied.

The miller and his wife climbed the ladder to the loft, leaving the rest of the company to draw their cloaks around them and lie down as best they could near the embers of the fire.

Benedict woke suddenly and completely. Perhaps some hours had passed; he had no way of knowing. There was the soft scrape of feet descending the ladder and a quiet tapping at the outer door. His immediate thought was that they were discovered, and he sat bolt upright. The dying fire cast a light for only a yard or so around, leaving the rest of the room in darkness, and he could only sit, ears straining for an indication of what was happening. The footsteps shuffled towards the door; there were some whispered words, the bar was lifted and someone slipped inside.

'Who's there?' Benedict whispered into the darkness.

'My wife's brother,' came the quiet reply, and Benedict allowed his tense muscles to relax a little. He could hear the miller guiding his visitor to the far end of the room and then one of the shutters was opened a little, letting in a wedge of flickering light from the burning castle. Now Benedict could see the new arrival, who sat wearily down upon a stool. Henry returned to the hearth and, ladling out a bowl of the broth, took it to the man. Benedict rose and joined them as quietly as he could.

The newcomer was greedily drinking the tepid soup from his bowl and Henry turned to Benedict and whispered in explanation, 'He is a soldier in the castle garrison. He will have news.'

Sirich and Thurstan had risen quietly and came to see what was happening. The soldier put his empty bowl down beside his stool on the floor and leaned back against the wall with a sigh of fatigue.

'I've no good news,' he said. 'I've seen some things in my time but never anything like this.'

'Do you know what has happened to our master, Josce?' asked Thurstan.

The man rolled his head round and regarded Thurstan with lacklustre eyes. 'Aye, I know,' came the brief reply, but he added nothing and they waited in silence.

'These folk must leave in the morning before light,' said the miller. 'They were servants of the Jews. They ought to know before they leave whether their master is dead or alive.'

'Dead,' said the soldier, and there followed a longer silence. Then the man began to speak again and with greater energy. 'They came to the castle, after the murders at old Benedict's house.'

'Who was killed there?' asked Thurstan.

'The widow and the younger children; they say his two elder sons were away somewhere. They're probably dead now anyway; people say all the Jews are dead. Well, that was seven days ago, and most of them, those who weren't killed in the streets, got to the castle with their goods, and it seemed all would be well with them, until the Sheriff attacked.'

This tallied with what the market women had said on the road. Benedict felt a drumming in his ears and a wave of heat which almost stifled him. His immediate thought was that Josce had been killed by one of the Sheriff's missiles, and Thurstan must have had the same idea, for he said, 'But why did the Sheriff attack?'

'Well, it came about this way, as well as I can tell,' said the soldier. 'The Constable left with a few men, perhaps to go and fetch the Sheriff, but when he returned the Jews wouldn't let him in again. They thought he had betrayed them, and for all I know there might have been some truth in that, it was a strange business. All sorts of rumours have been flying around, because you see, the Sheriff had the militia raised, even before this riot began; now why do you suppose? Anyway, the Constable was in the right in trying to get back inside; after all he is responsible to the King, and to be shut out of his castle with nothing but six soldiers and a crowd of Jews inside was not to be born. The King would have had his life!

'So, the Constable asked the Sheriff to attack. That let the rabble loose, and at first the Sheriff tried to control them, but when he found he couldn't, he settled for trying to regain the castle. And all that time there was this monk, the one you will have seen preaching against the Jews in the streets. Well, he was ranting and raving at the foot of the castle mound like a mad man. He had respectable journeymen, and some of the lesser clergy – it is always a wonder how men will follow any ranter – and all sorts of wastrels gathered there besides. And that suited Malebisse and his followers.'

'What has Malebisse to do with it?' asked Thurstan.

'I don't know, friend, but he and his knights have been in it from the start and he has brought his serfs and villeins up from Wheldrake and Acaster. It may have been them that started the fire in Spen Lane. They say another house was on fire before old Benedict's house was broken into and set alight. There is more in this than I can understand.'

'So how did our master come to be killed?' asked Thurstan, in a hard, tight voice.

'Oh, it was a terrible business,' said the soldier. 'When they had held out for six days, that Jewish priest began preaching in their own language. I couldn't tell what it was all about, but there was a lot of crying and wailing. Then, they gathered all their stuff together that would burn, and set it alight. The wind was blowing strongly from the north-east and the two towers on the far side caught light. Some of our men only just scrambled out in time. You can imagine our plight, but we forgot our own troubles when we saw what was happening.' He took a gulp of water from the beaker which Henry offered him before he continued. 'First of all, that Josce took a knife – the priest was standing beside him, praying or something – and Josce cut the throat of a little girl. She had a green dress with a golden braid round the hem, I could see it plainly by the firelight, and then the blood spread . . .' The man, hardened soldier though he was, shuddered and lowered his face into the palms of his hands. There were some moments before he spoke again. 'Then he cut his wife's throat. I've never seen anything like it, and then the others did likewise and killed their families. Last of all, the priest went round and killed those men who had killed their own. I could have wept with the pity of it, and I thought of my children, at home with their mother . . .'

'So, they are all dead?' said Benedict, his voice rasping in his throat.

'Not all of them. Some couldn't or wouldn't do it. They're still inside, but we had no food left and we had to get out. We let ourselves out down the eastern towers with ropes. I must get back soon; if the mob see the ropes they'll try to climb in, but we had to have some food.' He rose as he finished speaking as if to depart immediately. Henry muttered something about finding him some bread and went to look for it.

Benedict realised then that tears were streaming down his face and seeping into his mouth. He covered his face with his hands.

'But what about those Jews still inside?' asked Thurstan.

'I don't know. I suppose the Sheriff will storm the keep tomorrow morning when it's light,' replied the soldier. 'I must get back to my post before anybody finds I'm missing.'

There was a sound behind them and, startled, they turned to see Francisca, silhouetted against the embers of the fire. Thurstan jumped up and went towards her, but she fended him off and began slowly to fall sideways. He caught her before she hit the floor.

'She must have heard everything,' he said softly, as he gently laid her down beside his sleeping sister.

Benedict didn't sleep for long and lay rigid in the dark, feeling sick and desolate. He waited until the first light, when he rose, crept out of the house, and scrambled on to the embankment where he was quickly joined by Thurstan and Sirich. All three stood silently for a while and regarded the smoking ruins. There was a light wind and the air was misty so that the smoke hung about, swirling around the mound and across the ward, from which came sounds of the soldiers, moving quietly about. Above, the dark scavengers, kites, buzzards, ravens and crows, flapped and glided in unhurried circles over the castle enclave, watching and waiting for the time when they would come down and feed. Benedict thought of his loved ones lying up there, inside the wooden walls of the keep, and he watched the birds with hatred. After a while Thurstan spoke softly, as though afraid of being overheard.

'We must leave this place. People in the streets last night saw Francisca, and the news will soon be about; some of them may come looking for her.'

'But where shall we go?' asked Benedict, drawing his cloak tightly around him as though to defend himself against the future. He remembered the days of his wandering and could see nothing before them all but homelessness and misery.

'There is only one place,' Thurstan replied with confidence. 'We must go to my brothers at Langthorpe.'

'We shall stick together then?' asked Benedict.

'Never doubt it,' said Thurstan. 'When we are safely at home we can discuss what is to be done next.'

Benedict's heart went out to him in gratitude, for it seemed that he still belonged to a family. Then he looked across at the smoking ruins and his heart sank again. There was the problem of Francisca and who would take care of her? Try as he might, he could not make himself believe that any of her family still lived. The soldier's story seemed incredible now, in the increasing light of day, yet the man had been distressed by what he had seen, and had no reason to lie. The pictures he had painted passed before Benedict's eyes, and he shuddered until his teeth began to chatter.

There was some activity over at the keep, and silently they moved forward along the bank top until they could see more clearly. A man was shouting over the parapet, words which they could not distinguish. At the foot of the steps there was a party of knights, some of them on horseback, some on foot, and surrounded by a motley crew of rioters. Among the mounted knights, Benedict was sure he saw Malebisse on his great bay horse, and he thought he recognised others of his followers. An answering shout went up from one of the horsemen, and there was more parley, followed by an expectant silence.

Then the gates of the keep opened slowly, and some figures began to creep down the steps, coughing and retching as they came. The watchers on the bank moved forward involuntarily, their eyes fixed on the people before them. They could distinguish a man with his arm about a woman; she holding a baby. A boy of about ten. Another woman alone, with a baby in her arms, and Benedict saw, as the light wind lifted the drifting smoke, that she was Francisca's friend Bella, but where was her young husband? She stumbled at the edge of a step, and he longed to rush forward to help her, but she righted herself, and continued her pathetic progress. She held the baby tightly against her shoulder and looked fearfully down at the crowd below. Two elderly men followed, one of them Benedict saw to his distress was the doctor who had attended him when he was almost dead from his injuries; and then Benedict recognised the Jewish butcher, his wife trying to hide behind him, and he saw that a child clung to her skirts and stumbled as it descended the steps. Benedict had never liked the butcher, but now he felt a terrible anxiety for the squat, ugly man and his family. Others followed, but it was on the first few that Benedict's eyes were fixed. They came hesitantly forward and two of the knights moved as though to shield them from the mob. There must have been fifteen or more smoke-begrimed people on the steps and suddenly there was quick movement, but not from the mob, at least, not at first.

What had Benedict seen? He asked himself again and again in the days which followed. Had he seen those helpless people hacked about and cut down by the swords which rose and fell? Had he heard the sickening sigh and then the joyous roar of the mob? Had he seen the blow which felled the butcher as he tried to shield his wife, and the child tossed to one side and left to the mob?

Some of the things which happened he saw with awful clarity, but there were other sights which he must have blotted from his mind, but which returned to him in waking moments, and in wild confusion in his nightmares.

The three stood, transfixed. Their attention was drawn to those still near the top of the steps, who had emerged last of all from the gates above and who now tried to return to the keep, but the gates were shut on them from the inside. Paralysed by the scene before them, they might have stood there longer, but a cry from along the bank made them start and turn about. Isabelle and Francisca had followed them out of the house and were a few yards away. Isabelle was holding fast to Francisca's hand and wrist in an attempt to prevent her from approaching further, but it was too late; she had seen it all and was struggling in a vain attempt to go to their aid. The men stepped quickly towards her. Thurstan swept her up in his arms and they scrambled down the bank to the shelter of the mill, the shouts of the rioters still reaching them across the water.

Henry had the horses ready and was drawing his covered cart out into the yard. 'What has happened?' he asked. Isabelle was sobbing quietly. The men remained silent and shook their heads. They all crowded into the house and Thurstan set Francisca down on the settle. She didn't faint this time, but stared before her like a blind woman. Isabelle put her arm about the girl's shoulders, talking to her all the time, and rocking her to and fro as though she were a little child, but there was no response.

'You must go,' said Henry. 'My horse is out at grass; will one of yours draw a wagon?'

'I'll try Jet,' Thurstan replied, and went out into the yard.

'The women should ride in the cart. Leave it at the Earl's mill and I'll fetch it back from there. The wife has some food for you. Now go, before the crowd starts to move about.'

His anxiety for them to leave was understandable, and they coaxed Francisca outside where she was lifted into the cart, still ghastly white and apparently seeing and hearing nothing around her. The spare horse was tied to the rear of the cart, Isabelle climbed in with Francisca, Benedict mounted his horse, and they moved off uncertainly. Sirich drove and Thurstan walked beside Jet, unsure yet whether he would pull steadily. It was full daylight now but misty, and the smell of burning timber still reached them whenever the breeze blew from the direction of the castle.

Benedict felt that all eyes must be upon them, but the gatekeepers at Bootham Bar hardly glanced at them as they passed. There were a great many people hurrying to leave, having spent the night behind well-barred doors. The road was almost as crowded as it would have been on a fair day. Some people, pushed close to them by the crush which spilled out of the gatehouse, spoke of the horrors of the night, but Benedict, Thurstan and Sirich were in no mood for conversation. They wanted only to put as much distance as they could between themselves and the city.

Benedict's mind was a whirl of conflicting emotions. Pictures flashed before him: little Miriam playing with her cat in the sunlit garden; firelight and candles flickering on the tapestries of the solar; Josce riding Belazzar down by the river. He repressed a sob and, try as he might, the sickening sights of the morning crowded out those of the past.

They moved slowly at first, because of the crowd on the road, but even when they had room to move they made slow progress, having to handle the cart carefully in and out of the ruts. At one point Benedict rode alongside the reluctant Jet, taking the driving reins in his left hand whilst Thurstan and Sirich pushed the cart from behind. They reached the Earl's mill after an hour of difficult travelling and, setting the silent Francisca on the back of the spare horse, embarked on the longer stretch of their journey to Langthorpe.

They had reached the common of Little Ouseburn on the Dere Street when a party of horsemen passed at a distance of a hundred yards or more. They were in some hurry. At the rear of the party was a groom riding one horse and leading another. His cloak blew suddenly into the led horse's face, making it pull back on the reins and jerking the man's arm. He turned and they saw that it was Josce's groom, Aldred, and there was no doubt about the horse he led, it was the beautiful Belazzar; they had him at last.

# Part II

## *1190*

# 12

They rode in silence towards Langthorpe; Benedict tormented all the way by conflicting emotions. Whichever way he looked and with whatever he tried to distract his mind, he could not escape the visions which the soldier's story had implanted there, nor the horrors which he had witnessed that morning. He shook his head violently from time to time, but the visions would not go away.

He could hardly bear to think of Josce and of what he had done. It was scarcely credible to him that Josce had stood, amid the swirling smoke, with the prayers and cries of his neighbours filling the air beneath the blazing towers, and had killed Hannah, beautiful Hannah with the slender white neck. He had taken a knife . . . Benedict shuddered; and Miriam, how could her father have taken a knife . . .?

Benedict remembered how her soft arm had curled around his neck when he had carried her about the garden to show her the apple blossom, and to set her down so that she could touch the hen's yellow chicks. How could her own father have killed that pretty, mischievous child? He thought of the delightful dimples in her elbows and on the backs of her plump hands. How could anybody kill such a child? But then he remembered the joyous howl of the mob, when the knights fell on the weary people who had not a weapon between them, and he remembered the child of the butcher; he saw again the small body, as it arched through the air and landed at the feet of that hate-filled mob. That could have been his beloved Miriam.

Thurstan spoke then, as though he had been reading his thoughts, 'You saw what happened to those who came out; you heard what happened at Master Benedict's house; what else could he have done?' Benedict knew he was right, what else could they have done? Escape was impossible; better that their own fathers . . .

Francisca rode beside him. It would be more correct to say she was carried, for she payed no attention to the horse beneath her, allowing it to go its own way beside Benedict's mount. Swaying slightly, she leaned forward in the saddle, the reins bunched uselessly in her hands which were clasped on the pommel. Her staring eyes were black in the stark whiteness of her face, and seemingly intent on the distance but seeing, he knew, only what he was seeing. He could say nothing to comfort her and when he touched her she recoiled, as though something had burned her arm, still staring ahead and never looking at him.

Benedict's thoughts turned again to Josce and Hannah. How beautiful they had been, how gentle, how learned. Yet, like his own tow-headed, ignorant family, they had been destroyed by men who had power; men who could give away estates containing whole hamlets and farms; by monks who preached destruction in the name of Christ; by knights who had dedicated themselves to the crusade and could not wait to start the killing. Then the spirit of vengeance filled his heart and he wished more than anything to get some of this power into his own hands. How then, and with what scorn, he would turn upon Sir Richard Malebisse, denouncing him in the courts of the King himself, and the King would surely punish Malebisse and all his followers, confiscating their lands and forcing them to make reparation! But what reparation could they make? Nothing they could give, and no punishment of the malefactors, would bring back his loved ones. Even at that moment, Benedict had a premonition that little if anything would ever be asked of Malebisse and his faction, they might never be brought to justice. Such men had their value to the King and were lightly punished unless they attacked the King himself.

A pedlar with a pack upon his back rose from the roadside bank as they approached and, settling his pack more comfortably, fell into step beside Thurstan.

'Are you from York?' he asked, and when they nodded, he went on, 'What a business that has been. They say its the end of the Jews in England, and for all I know in France as well. In all the towns of the south they have been killed and none of them live beyond York, as you must know, my masters. I have been recently at Grimsby on the coast where I met travellers from Flanders and from France itself, and they were agreed that in this great age of the crusade, we cannot suffer the infidel in our midst. This is just the beginning. Now that we are free of them, England can become a truly Christian land and soon all Christendom will be free!'

Benedict roused himself and opened his mouth to speak but Thurstan threw him a warning glance and turning to the pedlar said sharply, 'You say all of them are slain?'

'In Norwich and Lincoln, Stamford and Lynn, way down in Kent at Canterbury, and in London itself. Yes, all are slain. If there are any hiding out in the country, they will surely be found.'

Benedict pushed his horse forward, quickening the pace, grasping Francisca's left rein to make sure her horse kept pace with his. Soon the pedlar with his load and his ill tidings was left behind.

By mid-morning the sun had broken through the mist and was already uncomfortably warm. Thirsty and weary, they reached Langthorpe and rode into the farmyard with its high fence of wattle hurdles. The homely sounds around them would have been gentle and reassuring had not Benedict that very morning had a glimpse into Hell. Could this, he thought, be only twenty miles from the horrors they had just left? Were the bodies of the slain still lying on the blood-stained steps; were the crows and the buzzards still gorging? As they came to a halt before the door, Benedict looked up to see that the warm sun was raising steam from the thatch of the roof.

Their arrival had been unexpected and Askil, in a sleeveless leather jerkin, his browner arms folded across his great chest, came out of the house, his face beaming. He called out to them with exclamations of pleasure and surprise, and before he had registered the haggard appearance of the travellers, he was well into both questions and news.

'We heard you were travelling, for Sir Jocelyn called here last week and he was asking about you. Which way have you come? Did you know there was a riot in York?'

As he was speaking, his stout wife Maud came out, fresh from the fireside, with ladle in hand just as she had when Benedict had come there before, and smiling a welcome as wide as her husband's.

The riders dismounted stiffly, Sirich hastening to lift Francisca down from the saddle. She collapsed limply into his arms as though she were lifeless. Thurstan, his face grim, turned to his brother's wife and said, 'Take them in and feed them, sister, while I talk with Askil.' He took his elder brother's arm then, leading him off across the yard. The slow farm men, as they led the horses away, stared back curiously at the solemn travellers and Mistress Maud's happy face turned grave as she ushered her silent guests into the house. Sirich was carrying Francisca in his arms, and Maud pushed him gently in the direction of the sleeping loft. Isabelle followed as her brother carried the girl up the ladder, leaving only Benedict standing there alone. Mistress Maud motioned him to sit at the table. She bent and whispered, 'What has happened?' but Benedict could only shake his head, unable to speak. She muttered a prayer as she hurried back to her pot on the fire, where she stirred the contents vigorously, muttering prayers and imprecations under her breath all the while. Some time later, both Isabelle and Sirich descended the ladder and slumped on the bench opposite Benedict. Nobody spoke.

After one more glance at the stricken company, Mistress Maud refrained from further question or conversation. She stooped over the pot, but glanced at them over her shoulder from time to time, as the farm men had done, concern deepening the crease between her brows. Soon the two brothers returned and Askil took his wife aside to tell her, in a low voice and at the farthest end of the room, the fearful story which he had just heard.

Outhan, the youngest brother, entered then, and from the look on his face Benedict guessed that he had been told the news whilst he was still out in the yard.

'We heard of the riot at York the next day after it began, but we also heard that you were on a journey to Stamford,' said Askil, 'and thought you must be well away. We had no idea the mischief had spread to every place, and that you might be in trouble further south. Sir Jocelyn de Birkhau rode into our yard last week and said he had gone down river with you in a boat.' He looked curiously at Benedict as he spoke.

'Our journey was wasted,' said Thurstan, 'Francisca's betrothed was killed while we lay ill at Grantham and we never reached Stamford. Now we don't know what to do. We must rest a while, both I and the maiden are still very weak. What we need is a long rest in this quiet place, and some good food, then we shall be able to think clearly. If you will have us here for a while, brother, we can recover and decide what is to be done.'

They slept like logs and woke late the next morning to find Maud pounding herbs for a poultice and exclaiming over Francisca, whose fever had returned. The women fussed and bustled about, up and down the ladder. Benedict was stricken with fear lest Francisca should die and went out into the yard where he found Outhan, who asked, 'What will you do now?' and, jerking his head in the direction of the house door, he added, 'What will you do with the maiden? She has no kin left you say; all slain?'

'If she lives,' said Benedict, frowning. 'We shall have to make more enquiries; it is possible that some Jews have survived. Aaron, her brother, was in Lincoln where there is a royal castle. He may have escaped the slaughter and when the King sends an army to punish the murderers he may be found. Then he would be able to take charge of Francisca again.'

'You think the King will send an army, just because the Jews have been killed?'

'Of course,' Benedict replied, resenting Outhan's assumption that the Jews were not of sufficient importance to warrant the King's concern. 'The Jews are under the King's protection. He cannot ignore an attack upon them.' Then he remembered another circumstance of the relation between the King and the Jews. 'He will want his money too, for if a Jew dies the King becomes his heir. His sons must pay heavily before they can inherit a part of his possessions. The King also takes the debts and he is bound to send people to find out how much was owed so that he can claim it.'

'You sound bitter,' said Outhan.

'They were good to me. One day I will tell you the story of how my life was saved by Josce of York.'

At dinner the whole household, with the exception of Francisca, gathered round the table and ate in silence. Isabelle went, from time to time, to the pallet where Francisca lay, wiping away a tear when she returned. Benedict watched her anxiously.

Askil seemed to wish to distract them from their memories of the riot and, after a while, began to talk to them about Sir Jocelyn.

'He rode into our yard only last week and, strange it was, but he questioned us about young Benedict here.' Benedict didn't seem to hear what Thurstan had said, nor even to notice his own name. He was struggling to push a little food down his unwilling throat and he could raise no interest in the matter of the knight. They all looked at him, but he was now staring blankly into space and the conversation moved on.

'There was a farm-man with him, no squire, and I think that things are not going too well with him. He wants to sell me some oats and his man had a small sample to show; it must have been the best they could muster, but not very good at that. I don't understand why his manor does not produce a better crop; the weather last year was good. Even so, he seemed more cheerful than he was when he called in here on his way south, as though he had heard something to his advantage. He had been, he said, to visit his elder brother at Tuxford, but if he had heard good news it was not from Tuxford that he brought it.' He ate a little before continuing:

'What an unfortunate family they are! This brother of his has a barren wife and it may be his brother at Tuxford is barren, too, for I have heard tell he hasn't even a bastard to his name, and then, last year, Sir Jocelyn's only son was killed. The finest young man for many a mile. Did you hear about that in York? Killed in one of the mad tournaments they have these days. Trampled to death under the horses' hooves. Why these knights cannot be content with warfare I do not know, but they must imitate it for their pleasure.'

'And you say he was interested in Benedict?' said Thurstan.

'Yes, he wanted to know who he was and what was his parentage, but we could tell him nothing. We said he was a servant of the Jews and a very learned young man.' He turned to look at Benedict as he spoke, 'And then he wanted to know about the young woman who travelled with you. Well, from his description we knew it must be the daughter of Josce, although we had never seen her. Then he asked if she was travelling to her wedding, which seemed very strange to us, for why should she be travelling to her wedding with just servants for company?'

'I don't understand,' said Thurstan, 'why he should be interested in either Francisca or Benedict, but then,' and he turned to Benedict, 'he did say, didn't he, that you were like his son?'

Benedict roused himself and replied briefly and without interest, 'Yes, he said I reminded him of his son.' Why must they talk and talk? he asked himself, when he needed to think and be still. On and on they talked of this knight and his son as though nothing had happened in York, while Josce and Hannah and little Miriam lay dead, their corpses burned, and the crows picking at . . . he shuddered violently.

'He is like, is he not?' said Askil, seeking his wife's confirmation and when she nodded, he turned again to the others and resumed his tale of Sir Jocelyn's woes.

'Well, I feel sorry for the old man, I suspect he is so reduced in fortune that he can't raise the knight's fee, and with his only son dead, what will he do? Had his son lived he could have gone when called, but as there is no fighting man in the household, and as he cannot pay for someone to go in his place, he may lose the patronage of his overlord. Then he can only end his days in a monastery.'

'That would seem his best course,' said Sirich.

'But for some reason he dislikes the monks,' Askil replied. 'He said he was determined on finding some other solution, but what can he do, apart from borrowing money? Yet, despite it all, he seemed cheerful, as I think I said before.'

They had a disturbed night for Francisca woke the whole house, talking wildly and unintelligibly in her sleep. At dawn the others were glad to rise and go out into the spring sunshine.

They ate earlier than usual, sometime in the late morning, and as it was so fine a trestle table was set up outside, away from the smoke of the fire. As they began the meal, they were surprised to see Sir Jocelyn come riding in at the gate, a rough-looking man following on a mule.

Outhan and Sir Jocelyn's man took the animals away while Thurstan led the old Knight to the head of the table. Food was set before him, but he didn't eat at once and they waited to see what he had to say. For a time he said nothing, but looked with interest at Benedict, and he had a look of satisfaction on his face, as though what he had wanted to see was before him.

'I have been wondering what had become of my fellow travellers. You returned through York no doubt, and have seen the result of the riot.' There was a long pause during which no comment was offered. The Knight continued, 'I heard what had happened at Stamford and at

Lincoln . . .' then, picking up some food he said, 'When I have eaten, I will talk with Master Benedict.'

They ate almost in silence, the others looking sideways at Benedict from time to time, wondering what Sir Jocelyn had to say to him. When the meal was over, the Knight rose from his seat and indicated to Benedict that they should walk together.

'Let us walk in the sun,' Sir Jocelyn said as they crossed the yard side by side. Benedict couldn't think what to say and, tired as he was after the ordeal of the previous days, he hardly felt equal to whatever lay before him. His legs felt weak and he longed to sleep, yet sleep brought only nightmares. Something important was about to happen, of that he had no doubt, yet what the Knight could want with him he couldn't imagine. He cast a sidelong glance or two at his companion. Benedict had grown tall, but although age had caused the Knight to stoop a little, it was still necessary for Benedict to look up slightly to see Sir Jocelyn's face. Benedict judged him to be sixty or thereabouts, and he must once have been very handsome. He reminded Benedict of someone, but try as he may, he could not remember who it was.

At last the Knight spoke. 'We were three brothers; three, and now not a child to show between us! The elder, whose manor is near to Tuxford, had a barren wife and has bequeathed all he owns to the Church; nothing to help me at all! My younger brother took himself into the Church when he was young – a great waste. Anxious to save their souls – mine can take care of itself. I can always repent at the last, hey young man?' He sounded almost jovial, but his voice became serious as he continued. 'Then my son, as you may have been told, died before he was married, no heir, nothing . . .' They walked on in silence for some time until the Knight stopped suddenly, and turning to Benedict he said, 'I will speak plainly, young man. Your appearance has tormented me since you climbed aboard that boat in York. You are so like my dead son, and my younger brother the monk for that matter, that I could scarcely take my eyes from your face. Now tell me, how did you come to live among the Jews, and what was your parentage?'

Benedict hesitated. How much should he tell? But he decided to relate the whole story, exactly as it had happened; only omitting any mention of Francisca's marriage portion, thinking that no business of the Knight's.

'And where were you born?' Sir Jocelyn asked as he finished.

'At Aike, on the River Hull, near Beverley,' Benedict replied, and at that, the Knight gave a shout of surprise. Benedict thought he should explain, and had begun to tell about Sir Robert of Meaux and his gift of land to the monastery, when the Knight interrupted him.

'You have me amazed.' But instead of explaining himself, he turned, and they walked back along the lane in the direction from which they had come; then, without having said anything, he turned again and Benedict found himself pacing beside him in the opposite direction.

'You have an ability in calculation, not taught to you by the Jews, but by a monk; now would that monk have been Brother Aidan?'

'Indeed it was,' said Benedict.

'And did you resemble these people, your parents, in looks, and were your brothers gifted in calculation?'

'No,' replied Benedict, 'I talked of this with Josce one day,' and then he stopped, realising that for half an hour or so he had been distracted from thoughts of the disaster in York, and he felt ashamed that he had forgotten them, even for a minute. He was recalled by Sir Jocelyn, who had no interest in Josce but said eagerly, 'Brother Aidan of Meaux was my younger brother and my cousin, Robert of Meaux, was one of those fools who gives away his land to the Church, which is a thing I would never do, even if I were possessed of some, ha!'

It seemed as though he would laugh, but he fell silent and continued his pacing, looking down at the sandy lane beneath his feet. Benedict's mind was whirling now, for he had grasped the implication of what had been said and he realised at the same time why Sir Jocelyn was so interested in him. In the midst of this, he remembered suddenly who it was of whom the Knight reminded him and he knew that his suspicion about his parentage had been correct. 'The get of some cleric in holy orders,' had been an astute guess on the part of the goldsmith. The Knight's voice broke sharply into his thoughts.

'I have a proposition to make to you, young man, but first I wish to know what you mean to do about the Jewish lady you have in your company?'

Benedict hesitated. 'If she lives,' he murmured as though to himself, then, in a firmer voice, he added quickly, 'we have not decided.'

'They tell me,' said the Knight, 'that all the Jews are dead and if she has no kin you must decide whether to abandon her or keep her with you, and to keep a Jewish woman in a Christian house would be impossible. She may die, of course,' he concluded with an air of finality.

Benedict tried to swallow the sting of that remark, and braced himself to speak calmly. 'That is the greatest of our problems,' he said. 'The brothers could find work, and I could perhaps get a place in some great household, but we must protect Francisca. You must know, Sir Jocelyn, that I hold the Jews in great respect. Josce saved my life.'

'You are right to speak so. Gratitude in the young is rarely found, but do not speak so openly to others. As for finding a place for yourself,

I have a plan, but what I would like to ask you first is something you may not wish to answer. Will you tell me whether you carried her marriage portion with you?'

Benedict was startled at this new turn in the conversation and he stopped in his tracks, leaving the old man to walk on a pace or two. Turning, the Knight smiled and said, 'You have nothing to fear. I will not betray you, but you must understand that yours is a curious situation. You are encumbered with a young woman who is rich. You are poor and, apart from Askil's family, you are at present homeless and friendless. What are you to do?'

'We have hardly had time to consider our situation,' Benedict replied stiffly.

'You are correct in assuming that you could enter a great household; you have the necessary learning to earn a living, but why do that when you could . . .?'

They had come to a place where the bank beside the lane was overhung with elm trees and the Knight continued, 'Both your problem and mine might well be resolved if we can come to an arrangement. Let us sit here by the bowl of this elm, for I have a proposition to make to you.' They sat themselves down in the shade and the Knight continued. 'I have a manor in the hills above Fountains Abbey, which I hold of the Honour of Richmond. However, this is an isolated manor – isolated, that is, from other lands belonging to the Honour – and although my lord's constable would sustain me in it if I had an heir, he is now doubtful of his course. The time has come for my tenure to be examined and if my overlord decides against my continuing, he has two alternatives. He can let the manor to a younger knight, that is, to one who can render knight service, or he can sell to the monks of Fountains. They would dearly love to get their hands on the land, which is almost surrounded by their own. I am too old to fight. I have neither heir, nor money for the knight's fee, and I do not wish to end my days in the charity of the monks, their ways are not mine. What is needed is money and an heir.'

So, thought Benedict, he was to be the heir, and Francisca's money would supply the knight's other wants. But his mind still reeled from the shock he had sustained when he witnessed the massacre, and he recoiled from the idea of conspiring to spend Francisca's marriage portion in order to prop up a crumbling manor somewhere in the wild hills above Fountains. He felt still that he was a member of Josce's household, and could not countenance the idea of transferring his allegiance so suddenly to this stranger, kinsman or not.

If, however, he became the Knight's heir, there would be no need to seek employment as a clerk at some great baron's door. In one leap he would become a member of the knightly class. But he felt ashamed

*111*

that thoughts of his own future had prevailed over Francisca's. He tried to suppress all thought of himself and, in any case, the Knight was surely mistaken. 'I see the way you are thinking,' Benedict said, 'but how could I become your heir? The Church would not allow your overlord to admit a bastard to tenure of the manor, let alone that of your brother, a monk! As we walked just now, I remembered who it was of whom you reminded me, and it was Brother Aidan,' he blushed. 'I think you must be right in your surmise.'

'You are kin to me, of that there can be no doubt,' said the Knight, 'though we will not go into the matter too closely, hey? We need not bring Brother Aidan into the story; but I shall tell my lord that you are my bastard and he will accept you. He admired my son, and when he sees you . . .' Here his dialogue trailed away as he fell to musing again. Then he added briskly, 'The Church interferes wherever it can, but it does not yet control every aspect of our lives. As to the manor, it is not an hereditament, my overlord can sub-let to anyone he chooses. He need not let to you as my heir when I die, but to you as his fief no matter what your parentage. Until you can perform knight service, I will tell him that I have inherited money from a kinsman in the south and that I can now render to him money for my knight's fee.'

'But what of Francisca?' exclaimed Benedict. 'The money was for her. How can we in all honesty spend money which belonged to my beloved master?'

'And I ask you in return,' Sir Jocelyn replied sharply, 'how can you keep that woman in a Christian place?' Then it seemed he regretted what he had said, or else, thought Benedict, he wished not to offend, for he continued in a pleasant tone:

'You are honest, I admire you for it,' yet, as he spoke, Benedict felt instantly doubtful of the Knight's sincerity, 'but I ask you again, how can the woman spend the money and who will take care of her? It might be possible to find a place where none would ever discover who she is, but to present her to the neighbourhood as a Christian would be one of the most difficult tasks a man could envisage. As soon as she spoke with the neighbour women she would betray herself. Let us be thankful to God that her parents gave her a French name, but I still do not see how it can ever be accomplished.'

What was the Knight after? Benedict asked himself. Did he want an heir and the money, or just the money? If Aaron were found, and Francisca with her marriage portion were returned to him – would the Knight still want him at Birkhau?

There was no time to reflect on all the legal niceties which Sir Jocelyn had set out for him on the tenure of manors. It would be enough if the Knight allowed them to live at Birkhau for a month or so. Their problems were too pressing for any consideration of the distant future. The only real hope for them all was to find Aaron, and they needed a safe haven for Francisca while they searched. A month, perhaps two, might resolve everything. He stole a look at the Knight, who was smiling to himself, and Benedict decided to test him.

'First,' he said, making his voice strong and trying to sound bold and confident, 'we will accept your offer of a home at Birkhau, whilst we make more enquiries about the fate of the Jews. Then, if her brother still lives at Lincoln, he can arrange his sister's marriage to one of their own faith, and she can take the marriage portion with her.'

'Indeed,' said Sir Jocelyn, surprised, 'you must, I suppose, do everything to clear your conscience. However, I have only until the end of the month.' Benedict looked hard at the Knight's profile, but could discern nothing from his expression. 'When, or I might say if, you find this Jew, Aaron, you could say that you lost some of the money and give him only half of it.' He glanced at Benedict, who made no reply. 'My overlord requires a decision and I must have your answer before two weeks are out. Can you travel to Lincoln in that time?'

So, it was as he thought, the Knight could not be trusted; but the manor was their only hope of refuge, he must take a chance.

'Very well,' Benedict replied. 'I should surely be able to get to Lincoln, make my enquiries and return in that time. Give me leave to tell the brothers and Isabelle, for they will have to be party to the plan, and leave us to make enquiries about Aaron. Two weeks is little enough for all we have to do, but I will bring you an answer within the time.'

They talked for a while longer, and when Sir Jocelyn left Benedict re-entered the house to find everyone agog to hear his news.

'Did you ask him about us?' said Thurstan.

'Aye, you would be welcome at the manor. Indeed, the benefits are as much his as ours. He would be glad to have you. He said his servants were too old to farm the place properly, but I fear that the money weighs more heavily with him than an heir and fresh servants.'

'Well, it seems a good plan to me,' said Sirich. 'And he cannot claim the money for himself, it is Francisca's. We can take her with us to the manor while we make enquiries about Aaron.'

'Francisca is too ill to travel,' said Isabelle. 'But no one in these parts will enquire too closely about her for the time being. You men go off and search while I remain here to nurse her.'

'Are you sure, Isabelle? What of Malebisse, suppose he were to come seeking her?'

'He is too busy counting the plunder,' said Thurstan. 'And he does not know we have the money.'

'What if you find the Jews,' said Isabelle fearfully, 'and return Francisca to them. There may be another riot and she might be killed.'

'Do not rush to the river crossing,' Thurstan said, 'we will get to it soon enough. Let us overcome one problem at a time.'

Benedict had already shared Isabelle's fear, but he agreed with Thurstan. 'Isabelle may be right but still we must enquire, then if we do not find the Jews we shall have to face the difficulty of keeping Francisca in a Christian household. The Knight gives us two weeks' grace; shall Sirich and I go in different directions to seek the Jews while Thurstan and Isabelle take Francisca to Birkhau? Or should I go alone to Lincoln?'

'I will go to see the manor at Birkhau,' said Sirich, 'while Benedict and Thurstan go to Lincoln. I would like to see this place where we might live, so that I can judge how isolated it is and how difficult it would be to keep Francisca there.'

Thurstan spoke slowly, as though still mulling over what he was saying. 'I think I should go alone to Lincoln for, if Benedict is to appear as Sir Jocelyn's heir, I think it better that he is not seen again in the streets of York or Lincoln for some time. In York it will never be forgotten that I served Josce, but Benedict has hardly reached manhood; in a few years those who knew him will scarcely recognise him, and that is as it should be.'

# 13

The waiting was harder than Benedict had foreseen, and during their absence his brain was racked by three questions – the money, Francisca, and his own future. The problems chased around inside his skull until he felt feverish. Benedict had had no difficulty in persuading the Knight that the three servants should go with them, and why not? The Knight was penniless and no doubt expecting Francisca's money to pay for all. Sir Jocelyn knew what a good bargain he had made and had gone off in good spirits to York. In the brothers he had found honest servants who would put his farmland into good condition.

Benedict walked to and fro in the lane, and the matter of Francisca and how they could present her to their neighbours at Birkhau reasserted itself as their most pressing problem. The prospect was daunting and he hoped fervently that Aaron would be found alive and well so that he could take care of her, but what then of the money in her marriage portion? Would Sir Jocelyn still wish to stand by his agreement? Did he intend to cheat them? Once in his power at the manor they might lose everything. Benedict had no idea of the amount of money with which Josce had endowed his daughter. The marriage settlement was still divided between the lining of his cloak and the two money belts, and he wondered whether Josce had confided the amount to either Francisca or Thurstan?

He marvelled again at the speed with which the Knight had seen his own advantage in their difficulty. He tried to unravel the working of Sir Jocelyn's mind. All the Knight could have observed on the boat was a Jewish merchant's daughter travelling with three Christian servants. How, then, had he guessed that she travelled with money? Had he made enquires about them and heard of her prospective wedding? Then he must have remembered her when he heard of the catastrophe which had overcome the Jews and, putting youth and money together, he had seen the answer to his problems.

What was the Knight's most pressing need, money or an heir? Benedict considered for a while and decided that, even without the money, the prospect of having an heir might be paramount, for it would ensure that the Knight had young and healthy people about him in his old age. With money alone, he could still find himself in trouble – for who could be trusted to farm the land and not to steal the money when he was too feeble to know what was happening? By promising Benedict a stake in the manor, he ensured that someone would care for him.

Then, for the first time, Benedict boldly confronted another question which had been lurking in the back of his mind. Did he really wish to become a knight? His education as a clerk was useful in the management of affairs, no doubt, but not acceptable in the knightly class to which he would belong. He had not been trained to arms and, at his age, it would be an embarrassment to have to learn. He imagined himself in the fields below some castle, watched by others of his age already well-versed in the use of sword and lance while he struggled to learn what they already knew so well. He blushed at the very thought.

There was also the responsibility for managing this property, high in the hills and on land which might be unprofitable. The Knight had made little money out of it. Sir Jocelyn it was who needed the manor, not Benedict, who could exploit his skill in accountancy and sell his services to any great household in the land. He could perhaps enter the service of Sir Jocelyn's own overlord, with none of the burdensome responsibilities for the welfare of sheep or the winning of harvests in bad weather. On the other hand, if it could only be made profitable the manor would support his sons, and he had seen how easy life could be for those with an inheritance.

But what sons? For if Francisca had to be taken along with them to the manor, how could he explain her presence to a prospective bride? How could they explain her under any circumstances! The problems seemed to overwhelm him and he felt a pressing need to talk them over with someone.

He found Isabelle sitting on the settle by the fire, mending a skirt of Francisca's which had been torn at Selby in the scramble to get out of the boat. Years seemed to have elapsed since that episode and it had been almost erased from his memory by the events at York. It seemed to him now that he had been a mere child on the journey but that now he was a man and burdened with difficult decisions. Sir Jocelyn might think his dilemma resolved but the resolution depended upon Benedict's agreement and once that decision was taken there would be no going back. What was more, the fate of Francisca and the servants depended upon it.

'I need to talk to you,' he said, as he entered the room. 'There seem to be so many problems and I can't sort them out.' He sat beside her, and held his head in his hands.

'Now lad, what's amiss?' she asked, breaking off the thread with her teeth as she finished and laying the skirt aside.

'Francisca is our greatest problem, for how can we keep her in a Christian house? If all the Jews have been killed who can take care of her? If the pedlar was right, we could not even take her to France.'

'If, if, if! You have indeed a great many things to consider, but there's no problem unless Aaron is lost,' she replied, 'and we must hope and pray to the Blessed Virgin that he lives.'

'But if he doesn't?'

'Then will be the time to worry, but until Thurstan gets back you are troubling yourself for nothing. I watched you when we rode towards York, biting your lips and making plans but, you see, it was all in the hands of God and Sirich found us.'

Benedict wondered why Josce's family had not also been in the hands of God, but he knew that if he asked she would only say that they were not Christians and he did not wish to hear those words spoken.

'But we must make plans; we have so little time,' he said. 'If Aaron is alive, there will be no money and Sir Jocelyn might abandon us and decide to give up the manor.'

'He will be able to keep it with you there to perform knight service and our labour to keep the home farm in good order.'

Could she be right? Those had been his own thoughts, but he tried her with more of his doubts.

'The money is important to him; he asked outright if she had her marriage portion with her. Without it he might well change his mind and then what would we do?'

'You could enter the service of Lord de Lacy, at Pontefract, or at Chester. He is a great man and must need people like you. He would be glad of your skill in accounting and you might become his steward in course of time.'

It was reassuring to hear from her lips a confirmation that his own solution might well be realised, but . . .

'What would happen to the three of you?' he asked.

'We would manage, you must seek your own fortune first,' she said, but then she hesitated, suddenly seeming less sure of her ground. 'You are right about Aaron, if he isn't found, we shall have to take Francisca with us to the manor and I never heard of a Christian house which had a Jew in it.'

Askil's wife had been plucking a chicken at the far end of the room and now she came towards them, the naked hen swinging from her hand.

'Perhaps she will agree to be converted and the nuns might take her in,' she said, with the air of one who has found the perfect solution.

'No!' Benedict shouted, for he saw Francisca shut away from all she knew and wandering the cloisters of a convent, surrounded by alien people whose only interest would be in her conversion. What would Josce have thought? Josce, who had risked all their lives in order to rescue him. And quite apart from Francisca's plight, the thought of parting from her hurt him surprisingly.

Sirich returned after five days and Francisca, who still had not spoken, had recovered a little and been carried down from the sleeping loft. She was seated, white and sickly, on a bench by the hearth. She barely glanced at the door as he entered and gave no sign that she even recognised him, before resuming her contemplation of the flickering fire. Sirich looked at her and, seeing no change in her, he frowned and shook his head sorrowfully.

During the waiting time, Benedict had come to realise how disappointed he would be should anything prevent his inheriting the manor and was again ashamed that he had allowed himself to indulge in this ambition. He tried to hide it by at first feigning a lack of interest in Sirich's news. Isabelle, however, was eager for information.

'How is the house?' she asked, turning from the table where she was helping Askil's wife to prepare the dinner.

'The house is well enough,' was all he had to say.

'In what state were the sheep?' asked Benedict. 'Sir Jocelyn said they had the murrain last year.'

'Close on two hundred head,' Sirich replied. 'What were not taken off by the plague seem well enough, though they were not dipped last year and their feet need attention.'

'What like is the sleeping accommodation?' his sister asked.

'I slept by the fire in the hall; I know nothing about where the gentry sleep,' he replied.

'Is it hilly country?' asked Benedict.

'There are some gentle meadows by the stream, but the manor lies on the side of a valley, facing westwards, and beyond and behind it the hills are fierce. I climbed to the highest peak with a lad from the farm above and I could see how it was that the flock had been neglected. The old man who was shepherd keeps to the fireside now and last year, so the boy said, he hobbled out only to see the animals in the low meadows by the house. Nobody knew how many lambs there were on the tops until Sir Jocelyn's neighbours counted them for him.'

This was the longest speech Benedict had ever heard from Sirich and straightway Isabelle began again with impatient questions about the house.

'Is there no woman about the place?' But her brother had a mouthful of food to chew and kept her waiting for an answer.

'An old woman with little life left in her I should say.'

'Is there an oven as well as a hearth?' she asked next.

'We ate some bread, but I don't know where it was baked.'

'Is the place clean? Are the rooms wainscotted? Does it have an indoor staircase?' she went on.

'A stone staircase outside, I can remember that,' he said and his sister shuddered, but he did not seem to have noticed and continued, 'The place was clean enough I suppose and, as for panelling, I can't recall,' and he stuffed his mouth with more food, winking at Benedict across the table.

Isabelle turned to her sister-in-law. 'Isn't that the way with a man? They notice nothing so long as they have food in their bellies. I need to know what we must take with us, for I don't suppose Sir Jocelyn will be any more likely to take an interest in the house than my brother there. A knight's house with an outside stair; that shows how much he cares for creature comforts. What's that going to be like in icy weather? A neighbour of ours fell to his death on an icy stair when he went out one night to relieve himself. And only an old crone to keep house; we hardly need to ask what state the place is in. What shall we do with Francisca in a house like that? It's not what she is used to, nor me neither. I can't wait to get there and fettle the place, and I must have some comfort!'

'What are the fences like, are they in good order?' asked Benedict.

'There are some fine stone walls; fallen down here and there, but they will soon mend, and some stone-built sheep pens near the house; pig sty and barn, and a bit of a garden all grown to weeds.'

'Shall we need to take some plants and herbs with us then?' asked Isabelle.

'I suppose the neighbours would serve you from their gardens,' Sirich replied.

'Have they any corn planted?' asked Benedict.

'No, not an acre, all is lying fallow, and the neighbour boy was grieving over it for they have none too much food for humans let alone animals up there. The winters must be hard.'

'This is worse than I thought,' said Benedict. 'Thank God we have money with which to buy seed corn and food for the winter.' But he hesitated then, for there could be no certainty about the money. Until Thurstan returned from Lincoln, they could not know what the future held. He hoped Aaron would be found alive, but he wanted a prosperous manor as well. The wishes were contradictory. He dismissed the unwelcome thoughts and went on, 'Will there be any hay to be cut in the meadows?'

'Now there we might be more fortunate,' said Sirich, 'for the meadows which fall to the stream should make hay if we can get the sheep off them before another month is out, and the hill land on limestone makes very sweet hay.'

'And what like are the neighbour women?' asked Isabelle, anxious now about the company in which she might find herself.

'I saw no women, only the boy who'd been sent over to see if Sir Jocelyn had come back.' Then he remembered more, 'The boy said he was the eldest of three, so perhaps his mother still lives,' and Sirich winked again at Benedict.

'It's to be hoped she does, else there's only the old hag in the house for company,' said Isabelle. 'What of the nearest manor, did you ask about the household there?'

'Nay sister, I am not concerned about such things. I went to see the land and the beasts they keep on it, not to spy out the neighbours. You will see for yourself, soon enough, what gossips there are around.'

Isabelle sighed with impatience and rolled her eyes up at the roof timbers for the benefit of her sister-in-law who, by her expression, seemed to agree that men had no sense of the importance of houses or of neighbours.

The next day Thurstan rode into the yard with a serious face, and they brought him in and sat him down with concerned looks to match his own. Francisca had come down again and sat silently, as before, gazing into the fire.

'Well, brother,' said Sirich, 'How did you fare?'

'Well enough but I travelled slowly, the wind was against us and the boat was rowed most of the way down the Ouse; then at nightfall it ran aground on a sandbank in the Humber and we were delayed two nights and a full day. When I found myself at last on the road to Lincoln, Jet cast a shoe. The farrier was a fool and pricked him with a nail so that he went lame and I had to leave him at the forge and walk the rest of the way.'

'Did you ask after my sister?' Benedict asked, as soon as he could interrupt the narrative.

'Aye, I asked, but they had no Alyce there. The monk was new that week but he enquired among the lepers in the place and they could remember no Alyce.'

A conviction then fell upon Benedict for, although he had been doubtful at the time, he now felt sure that the woman he had seen had been Alyce and he frowned as he looked at Thurstan, who had risen and was pacing up and down the floor.

'I got to Lincoln with only two days in which to make enquiries,' Thurstan looked at the silent Francisca as he spoke. 'I went to the houses that had been Jews' houses, and I called at the house of Cresse where we last saw Aaron; all were deserted. The neighbours could tell me little but to say that since that evil night they had seen nothing of any of the Jews. I can only suppose that they were killed.' His voice dropped very low at the end, as though he did not wish her to hear, and they all glanced at Francisca who continued, as she had for so long now, staring silently into the fire which flickered palely in the sunlight shining in at the window.

'So you cannot be sure,' said Benedict.

'No, I cannot be sure.'

'And Sir Jocelyn returns tomorrow; did you see him as you rode through York?' Benedict asked.

'No!' he seemed startled at the question and hesitated, 'I did not know where to look for him and I wanted to make speed to get back and tell you what I had found.'

'So, tomorrow we must give him our answer,' said Benedict, knowing that Francisca must have heard all. She had still not been consulted about the money, and without speaking first to her how was he to speak to Sir Jocelyn? Where to begin? He went and sat beside her, and began boldly.

'Francisca,' he said, 'Sir Jocelyn claims me as his son and wishes us to go with him to his manor away up in the hills, and there we might be able to live well and far from . . .' he did not know how to go on.

'Well away from York and from those un-Christian devils!' said Isabelle.

'Your brother cannot be found, Francisca, you must have heard what Thurstan said.' Benedict stopped there, trying to see the girl's expression, but still, with face averted, she stared into the fire, motionless and silent as though she had heard nothing. He regarded her pale profile for a while before continuing, 'On the way from York, travellers were saying that all the Jews in England are dead, and in France as well. There is no place to which we can take you, for we know of no Jews. Will you consent to come with us to Sir Jocelyn's?' Then he corrected himself and for the first time he said, 'To my father's manor in the hills, away from towns and company?'

She did not reply, nor even move in her seat, and then, overcome with pity, he did something he had never done before; he took her hand in his, for he knew what it was to find oneself suddenly alone with no one to call one's own. He was amazed to find what he had done but she did not snatch her hand away. It was impossible to tell what she thought of the action for she merely allowed her hand to remain in his, still and unresponsive, whilst she continued to stare at the fire.

'If Aaron lives we shall find him, in time,' said Benedict; then, summoning up his courage, he broached the dreaded subject of the money. 'My father, Sir Jocelyn, is not a rich knight; he needs money to farm his land as it should be farmed and a son to perform knight service, for he does not love the monks and will not retire to a monastery. Francisca, you have money. Can we use it, for we must care for you and we must take you far away from any who might know you?'

Still she sat and made no response nor even seemed to hear him.

'Francisca,' he said again, trying to draw her attention to himself and to the matter in hand, 'we need the money and you cannot spend it. If Aaron is found, you can go to him.' She shivered suddenly and he hesitated. 'And we could still take our chance with Sir Jocelyn,' he went on. 'I would take up the knight service and the brothers would work the farm, but in the meantime, with your money, we can live with comfort such as you are used to. Can you speak to us, Francisca, we need to know before tomorrow? If your brother is not found we shall at least be able to make you comfortable for the rest of your life.'

At that she did turn and she gazed at him with eyes so sorrowful that he looked away and a sob rose in his throat. He interpreted her look as one of despair, and felt that no words of his could comfort her; it seemed to him that she cared nothing at all for what remained of her life.

He would have been startled to know of the conflict which raged in her poor head.

How I hope, she was thinking, that Aaron lives. Oh, my poor brother. How shall we tell him what happened in York? But if he lives I must return to him, and then I lose my beloved Benedict. Life is so cruel.

The household went to sleep that night with nothing resolved and the next day Benedict greeted the arrival of Sir Jocelyn with some diffidence. The Knight arrived as they sat down to eat, and as soon as he had taken his place at the table he looked hard at Thurstan. Benedict was surprised, for Thurstan looked down at his trencher and did not seem to wish to look the Knight in the face. What could be wrong with him?

Nothing was said of the affairs which concerned them most. Instead, they remained at the table after the meal and talked of other matters, for which Benedict was grateful. He had been afraid that Sir Jocelyn would broach the subject of the money while they were still in company, and he wished to speak to him of it in private. Eventually the Knight led him away, and again they paced up and down a short stretch of the lane in the bright sunlight.

'Have you spoken to the lady?' the Knight asked and Benedict was relieved to hear him speak of Francisca with respect.

'Yes, Thurstan could not find her brother nor any of the Jews of Lincoln, so last evening I put to her the subject of the money but she did not speak. I do not think she has spoken since the day we left York.'

'So, Thurstan found none of these Jews.'

The Knight sounded strangely satisfied. So, it was the money which was uppermost in his mind! Benedict felt a wave of depression sweep over him. His enthusiasm for the manor had waned since the previous day and he wondered why he felt so miserable at the prospect of this new life. He should have been overjoyed to be made heir to a manor, but then he realised that he had had no time in which to grieve over Josce and Hannah and little Miriam. Josce he had loved more than most men love their fathers. Josce had rescued him, and not as this Knight was doing, for his own ends. The rescue had been at grave risk to himself and to all his people. Even so, the picture he could not get out of his mind was of Josce standing with a bloody knife in his hand over the bodies of Hannah, whom Benedict had loved with a boy's uncritical worship, and of Miriam, that darling child, who had been to him like his own little sister. The conflict of emotions further depressed his spirits.

That evening Sir Jocelyn had Outhan unpack some of the goods he had brought from York. He did not say at the time that he had all these supplies on credit, though Benedict wondered where he had found the money. There was a pair of linen sheets, some printed woollen wall-hangings; poor stuff, thought Benedict, but it was such as hung on the walls of most manor houses, and then Outhan pulled out a bundle of clothes.

'Your clothes are good,' said the Knight to Benedict. 'But I thought you should have something particularly fine in which to be presented to my Lord Constable,' and out of the bundle there rolled a gown of red and blue silk. At the sight of it Benedict covered his face with his hands. Those who had come from York were pale and their eyes were fixed upon the garment as it lay across the table, but the Knight did not notice.

'Where did you find this gown, Sir Jocelyn?' Thurstan asked. The Knight looked up in surprise.

'I bought it from a trader in the Pavement who admitted that it was second-hand, but I have not seen so fine a gown since the time I journeyed to Paris.'

'I do not wonder at it,' said Thurstan, 'for this was Josce's gown.'

# 14

After a troubled night of dreams, Benedict woke to find Sir Jocelyn pacing the threshing floor, where the sun flooded in through the open doors, eager to discuss their future, and once again they walked in the lane where they could not be overheard.

'How long do we have before we must see your overlord?' Benedict asked with concern, and to his surprise the Knight replied,

'I have been considering whether it is advisable for me to take you with me; the King has appointed Alan as Constable again, he holds a castle in Wensleydale and was Constable in the time of Earl Conan. He is not the friend to me that Amalric was. He is less likely to accept you than Amalric would have been.'

Benedict was amazed for he had assumed all was well, and now this . . .

'As you pointed out to me yesterday,' the Knight continued, 'there are problems which I had not considered with sufficient care, and again, as you said yourself, the greatest of these is the lady and how she is to be presented to others. I shall have to explain to my lord how I have discovered my lost son, and he will no doubt ask whether you are married, or likely to be. That will be the first of my difficulties. Then, will the lady consent to be converted to Christianity so that you could wed her?'

'I am surprised, sir,' said Benedict, 'that you should consider such a marriage for me. Isabelle and I think that Francisca would never agree to conversion and, by the same token, she would surely not marry me, a Christian. But why should marriage to Francisca be necessary?' As he spoke, he was overwhelmed with a trembling excitement, his face flushed and his knees shook so that he longed to escape from the Knight's company. What was this sensation?

'Be sensible, young man. She is a Jew, an infidel. If her brother is found the money will be forfeit to the King. If she is converted to the Church and married to you, you will have control of the money.'

Benedict was suddenly sure of what he most wanted in the world. Francisca must be saved; he would not be parted from her. The need to make a choice had brought him to this sudden realisation of his feeling for her. 'Then it can never be. She must not be forced to convert and I shall find a place where no one will know her. When she goes to church, I will tell people that she is not quite right in the head!'

'Foolish youth! You cannot protect her. Where would you go? There is no hiding place for a Jew. You must come to the manor, but the lady must be converted. I cannot harbour an infidel.' With that, he crossed himself, something Benedict had never seen him do before. 'How else can you explain her presence in the house? She must be your wife. You cannot present her as your sister, she is not like enough, and I refuse to claim her also as one of my bastards!' He looked again at Benedict. 'The only alternative is to give some of the money to a convent of nuns. Explain that you found her wandering on the outskirts of York and leave her to them.'

That suggestion again! Benedict was horrified, for Francisca would be like one dead; and he, who owed his life to the Jews, could never abandon her to her enemies.

'No!' he said emphatically. 'We cannot do that; she would despair.'

'Then you must not only marry her but convince her also that she must at least appear to be a Christian. She must attend church and do all the accepted things, though how it can be accomplished, I cannot see,' and the old Knight shook his head in despair.

'But how do I speak to her about this?' asked Benedict. 'Last night when I asked her about the money, she did not reply. You have seen for yourself how she is; she has not spoken since she saw the slaughter on the castle mound.'

'Will she ever speak again, I wonder?' said the Knight, his voice brightening.

Benedict did not reply, for the thought that her silence might be permanent had never occurred to him. But suppose she were silent for ever! He saw that this could be their salvation. If she could not speak she could not converse with outsiders, and the story that she was not quite right in the head would indeed explain her condition. He felt a sudden qualm at the thought of lying so about Francisca but Sir Jocelyn was correct – she must appear at church. But suppose she were silent . . .? There was no point, however, in pursuing these ideas unless her silence indeed proved to be permanent, and for how long would they have to wait to be sure of that? No more of this! He needed time to think and he changed the subject.

'Will you tell me more about the manor, Sir Jocelyn?'

*125*

'You will have to learn to address me as sire,' the Knight replied, with a faint smile. 'Well now, the manor consists of three hides. You may think that a good provision but the land is mostly on the hill, moss and peat hag, poor grazing. I rent one bovate to a villein who lives in the village, he owes me two days' work for each month of the year and he also holds some land by free tenure. To another I rent two bovates of land on one of the hills. He owes me but ten days' work in a whole year. I keep the river meadows and the hill grazing in hand and it needs more workers than I can muster. I suffered a bad harvest in the year before my son died; so bad that I had to buy seed corn last autumn. We had a wet summer with very little hay and what we won was brought in in poor condition, so that I kept only a milk cow for the house and my sheep went short of food after Christmas. Then last year, as I think I told you, the sheep suffered the murrain, due perhaps to their lack of food during the hard months. I have a man and his wife living in the house, very ancient and barren of children, and I have no money with which to pay the villagers for day labour. However, I resisted the temptation to resort to your late master for money, so at least the estate is unencumbered.'

'Do none of the village men owe you labour?' Benedict asked.

'Nay, they are all freemen,' the Knight replied scathingly. 'My father wasted the manor. When he had no money he allowed the villeins to commute their service for cash, though what they want their freedom for I cannot see. However, when times are bad again and food is short, I may be able to turn the tables.'

Benedict looked at the Knight with distaste, but at the same time his mind was working fast. He had learned something of estate management from Josce and was quickly reckoning the prospects for restoring this neglected demesne. If they could only use Francisca's money ... It was too late to plant corn, but with the brothers' labour and that of the villein and the ten days which the tenant owed ...? This year they could get the hay in, Isabelle could help with that. Later, they would plough and sow some winter wheat, buy some hay and feed the sheep well, raise some pigs ...

Then another idea occurred to him. 'Is there any woodland?' he asked.

'There is, and that again has been neglected but the coppices are more than ready for cutting, all I need is labourers for the work.'

'If we can only use Francisca's money,' Benedict said aloud and looked up to find the Knight regarding him with amusement.

'You are enthusiastic to begin, I can see,' he said and smiled as he spoke.

'I have always been interested in the management of land,' Benedict replied very seriously. 'My master, Josce, sometimes took me with him when he visited the manors to buy corn or wool or to negotiate with his debtors.' He looked at Sir Jocelyn and found that he was frowning.

'What you say reminds me of another matter,' said the Knight. 'You are known by sight to those who owed money to your late master and you must never refer to him in that manner within the hearing of others. How many of these knights and their squires would recognise you?'

'I visited Sir Thomas de Warter but he is dead now, and Sir Richard Malebisse at Wheldrake; he and all those who follow him would know me.' He remembered the incident by the river; Malebisse and his followers had seen him there and also on the road to London.

'And they, of course, are the very ones responsible for the massacre at York,' said Sir Jocelyn.

'So, they were indeed the ones! I thought I saw Malebisse at the foot of the Castle mound,' then, after a pause, Benedict was able to continue. 'We saw them, but I wasn't sure at the time, travelling northward as we came from York and Josce's groom, Aldred, with them, leading the beautiful horse which Josce used to ride. Did you hear where they went?'

'Before I tell you anything more of what I know,' said the Knight, 'you must promise to give up any idea of revenge. These men are powerful and your best interest is to avoid them. If you serve the Honour of Richmond it can perhaps be arranged that you should be found service abroad for a while, at least until this trouble is blown over and forgotten. But you ask about Sir Richard Malebisse and his party. It has been said that they have gone to Scotland. I doubt it, however, for I have heard from a good source that Sir Richard is at his own manor in the forest of Galtres but that some of the lesser parties in this matter have scattered farther afield. What they did after the riot, on that last morning, is truly sacrilegious. There are rumours aplenty, but I went myself to the minster to verify the story about the charters.'

'What story is that?' asked Benedict.

'They rode off, it seems, with the blood still on their swords and dragged the monks out of their seclusion with oaths, threats and blows, demanded the chests which held the Jewish charters and smashed them open. These charters, as you know well, describe their debts and those of others in the neighbourhood; so they made a bonfire of them in the very nave of the minster. By that means, they let it be known, they were free of all their obligations. They must be mad to think it! The debts of Jews are the property of the King and although Richard is in France he will not overlook debts, he is mad for money!'

'What devils they are!' Benedict exclaimed. 'The King will surely send to find out what has happened. Not only the debts but the Jews themselves he regards as his property.'

'Aye, avoid Malebisse and his followers if you can.'

There was silence for some time while they walked, each preoccupied with thoughts of his own, until Benedict asked, 'How will you explain my upbringing and education?'

'I could say that your mother was the daughter of a rich merchant and that you were raised with the prospect of becoming a merchant, for you are only my bastard son and such a course would be reasonable. We might also be able to make men believe that Francisca is the daughter of a merchant of the Low Countries and that she is my ward.'

'But then we shall have to name the merchant with whom I was raised and if anyone asks questions abroad they might find us out.'

'I should merely refuse to answer,' the Knight replied. 'Then I can say that a friend of the rich merchant nominated me his daughter's ward at his death. That might serve us well.'

'Could you not say the merchant was a distant relative, a cousin's cousin perhaps?

'Not a relative. If you are to marry the Jewess she must not be a relative for that would be a prohibition against marriage. Even a cousin's cousin. The Church again interferes in our lives increasingly . . .'

'Very well,' said Benedict. 'But you are right to look abroad for my origin, and there is an advantage in a story of France for I speak French and so does Francisca. If she should ever speak again, it may be made to appear that she comes from that country. One thing is most important though, no one must know that I was raised in a Jewish household.'

'Your anxiety is understandable, though you must never forget that, infidel or not, he saved your life, of that there is no doubt. However, it must not be known and you must not be recognised. That is why I would like you to spend some time away from these parts. When you are fully grown and appear again, perhaps as a knight, it may well be that those who slayed your old master will have forgotten you.'

'So you think I should leave your manor for a while?'

'Let us wait, and see the result of my appeal to Alan the Constable, and when you have gained some knightly education you could perhaps go to France in the service of the King.'

'But would you be able to manage the manor?' asked Benedict, for he had begun to see himself as the one who would make it profitable and he did not relish the idea of leaving so soon all that he had just gained.

'With your servants I shall be able to do very well.'

The description of the brothers and Isabelle as his servants startled Benedict, for he had always thought of them as equals, even as his guardians, and now a gulf had opened between himself and these people who had been so good to him in his need. How could he give orders to them? Yet he saw immediately that in this new life he must do so, for if he treated them as equals people would wonder at it. Sir Jocelyn had increased his confidence in his ability to take his place as the son of a knight but he must come to terms with this new circumstance.

The next day he looked carefully at Francisca as she sat silently by the fire with a bowl of porridge on her lap, the spoon idle in her fingers as she stared into the fire. The rest of the household sat at table and, while they discussed the future, cast occasional glances over their shoulders to see if she gave any sign that she heard what they said.

Still she did not speak and Benedict allowed himself the new hope that she never would. He excused himself by arguing that if she did, all would be lost and she would be the one to suffer most; it was either silence for her or life in a convent. He knew that the religious life called for sacrifices even a Christian would find hard to make. He thought of the manor as it would be in the future and the improvements they could make if they used Francisca's money; he knew that he could have fine horses, perhaps one to rival Belazzar, and hounds, sleek cattle, and fat sheep. The idea of himself as lord of a manor was growing in importance and the prospect of life as a clerk in the service of a great lord receded correspondingly.

Already the King's messengers were active in England. Since the massacre at York, de Longchamps had arrived with an army and had replaced the Sheriff of Yorkshire by appointing his brother in his stead. The old Constable, Alan, son of Raold, had been re-established at Richmond and was reported to have arrived at the castle. Sir Jocelyn was to go there the next day. He had arranged for a load of seed corn and oats, a new ploughshare, an axe and a saw, to be brought to the farm by Henry the miller. He warned Benedict that neither he nor Francisca should be seen when Henry arrived, and that the miller should be told that they had taken her in search of her relatives. The goods could be thought to be for Askil, who would convey them to the manor some time later on his cart. The Knight had not asked Benedict for money for his journey – did he have some of his own, Benedict wondered, or had he approached Thurstan and received some of what he had in his belt? He had seen the two of them talking in the lane.

Sir Jocelyn took Benedict aside that evening but, instead of asking for money, he spoke almost fiercely to him.

'You should marry the maiden now, before I leave. A hand-fasted marriage will be sufficient and you have witnesses enough. If the marriage takes place at the manor, it will cause people to ask about her. There will be difficulty enough making her seem a Christian, but if the marriage takes place there the curiosity will be all the greater. The churchmen are trying hard these days to make men marry in church. You cannot take her to the altar, but a promise before witnesses and the union itself still make legal marriage. This may not be the case for much longer if the churchmen have their way.'

'Is it necessary?' Benedict asked, startled.

To Benedict, the thought of marrying Francisca at some distant date was one thing; to be confronted with it at such short notice was truly alarming. He had to admit to himself that he was still in awe of her, and he would have to broach the subject immediately if Sir Jocelyn's plan were to be carried out. Suppose she awoke from this state of bewilderment when they arrived at the manor and objected to the arrangement? She had proved on the night of the riot to be courageous and if the marriage were abhorrent to her she would be prepared to sacrifice her safety for her scruples. And for him there would be no going back. He would be bound to her for life. What if Aaron then were found?

With Francisca in the house, he envisaged other problems. She would refuse to eat the flesh of pigs. Then there were the Jewish rules about the keeping of food. Would she be content with their more haphazard ways? They could scarcely keep up all the careful ritual of a Jewish household. Then what of the Sabbath? Oh, the difficulties were truly insurmountable! Sir Jocelyn was eager for this marriage in order to get his hands on the money, with no thought for Francisca or for him. He went in search of the servants.

'It won't be easy,' said Isabelle. 'Marriage is never as easy for a woman as it is for a man.'

'Nay sister, what nonsense!' said Sirich. 'She was going to her marriage when we travelled south and she had seen her bridegroom only once. She should be glad to marry Benedict with a manor and all.'

'But she will not see it in that light,' said Benedict. 'She would want to marry her own kind and a manor is less to her than it would be to a Christian maid. Then there is the money and the chance that Aaron might be found. She may wish to wait a year, maybe two . . .'

'We might all be dead by then,' said Thurstan. 'Wed the girl now. Girls are fickle creatures and she will be satisfied enough when you have bedded her.'

Benedict blushed, finding the matter deeply embarrassing, but Thurstan was impatient.

'Speak to her now. We cannot leave her here and we shall have enough troubles on our hands getting the place into some sort of order, without having to conduct a marriage under the eyes of strangers. Sir Jocelyn is right, it will cause less of a stir and there will be fewer questions asked if you are already man and wife when we arrive.'

So he went to Francisca who was sitting in her usual place by the fire and, summoning up all his courage, he spoke to her of their difficulties and of their problem in having to explain her presence in the house. She turned from him.

'Francisca, where else are you to go? Thurstan tried to find Aaron and could not. We cannot just go and buy a manor – we need connections and some protection in case Sir Richard Malebisse should find us. We must take this opportunity. Then, if Aaron is found . . .' but there he stopped, for what would Aaron say about the marriage? Benedict did not wish to contemplate that problem. He looked at Francisca and found that she was staring again into the fire, but she turned and looked at him steadily and then, to his surprise, she nodded solemnly.

That evening they all dressed in their best, and gathered in the houseplace. Askil, as head of the family, spoke solemnly, saying that as Francisca had no family, he would stand in her father's place and that she consented to wed Benedict, son of Sir Jocelyn of Birkhau. Then Benedict stated that he was a free man and wished all present to witness that he wished to marry Francisca, daughter of . . . and there he stopped, for he was suddenly choked with tears and could not speak Josce's name. It was Francisca who moved, and she took his hand in hers as though to comfort him. The action surprised them all and Benedict pulled himself together and, to the sound of Isabelle's weeping, they were proclaimed man and wife. To his relief, no one suggested that they be bedded together and he fervently hoped that at the manor there would be a private place for them to sleep.

The next day Sir Jocelyn left and Benedict took the first opportunity to speak privately with Sirich. It seemed a strange thing to do, for nothing had ever been done but they had all discussed it together. However, Benedict was now convinced that at the manor Sir Jocelyn might prevent them from getting any access to the money and, for some reason which he could not at that time resolve, he was reluctant to speak to Thurstan. Making an excuse, he took Sirich off to the brook at the bottom of the pasture land and began as though asking his advice.

'What do you think of the Knight, Sirich? Is he an honourable man, can we trust him?'

'I do not know, I cannot be sure,' Sirich replied. Then, to Benedict's surprise, he went on as though he also had been giving the matter some thought. 'We have never counted the money. Now is the time and I think you should keep some of it secretly; do not even tell my brother.'

Benedict said nothing for a while. He was surprised to know that Sirich shared his concern. There had been a change in Thurstan's manner and it seemed that Sirich had seen it also.

'But how should I go about it?' Benedict asked.

'You have at least half of it hidden in your belt and cloak. If you can get some of it out today and hide it elsewhere . . .'

'But I can't take the cloak out of the house without somebody seeing me, and if I were to go up to the sleeping chamber where it is and pick away at the stitching, how could I sew it up again?'

'Isabelle and Maud are gathering fresh herbs. I know where my sister keeps her sewing things,' said Sirich. 'Take as much from the belt as you can without letting what remains seem too small an amount and I will get a needle and thread, then you must do what you have just described. Francisca can sew. Perhaps she will help and nobody will intrude on you. This is your moment, do just as I say.'

'But, when we get to the manor, it will be Isabelle who will take out the rest of the stitching and she will know in what way she sewed and will recognise that somebody else has been at work,' said Benedict.

'We can tell her later, she is loyal to Francisca. You must hasten. The more I think on this matter, the more sure I am that the money should be divided,' said Sirich.

'I will explain what I am about to Francisca,' said Benedict, 'but then, where shall I hide it?'

'Tie it up in something. Francisca will have some small piece of cloth about her, but don't leave it with her unless you intend to tell Isabelle for she will see everything that Francisca keeps. And don't fret about Francisca; she may be strange in the head just now, but she is her father's daughter and no fool. She will see that we must hide some of the money.'

'I shall have to find a hiding place for it when we get to the manor.'

'You can leave that to me,' said Sirich. 'I will find a place and then I will keep it for the time when you return from the castle, or wherever they send you. I will return it to you, never fear.'

'Where are the others?'

'Thurstan is helping Outhan to bring the cows in, they are still down in the water meadows and the women have only just set off, it will be some time before they return.'

They hurried back to the farm and Benedict went straight away to the sleeping loft where Francisca lay on the bed.

'Francisca, you must help me,' he said urgently. She sat up. Her back was to the unshuttered window, her face in shadow and she listened intently.

'Sirich and I suspect that Sir Jocelyn may steal the money. He agrees with me that we must hide some of it in case he cheats us. The money has not yet been counted; do you know how much there was?'

She nodded.

'Did anyone else know?' he asked.

She shook her head.

'Let us examine my money belt,' he said, 'and then we will look at the cloak and see if we can unpick the braid and get some of the money out. Sirich says he can get Isabelle's sewing things and thread a needle. Would you sew the braid on again, Francisca?'

Solemnly she nodded again and Benedict, with a great sense of relief, fumbled under his jerkin and untied the money belt which he had worn, day and night, since they had left on her wedding journey. He laid it on the bed and together they unwound it.

'How much was there?' he asked, but she said nothing. 'Are you sure that Thurstan didn't know how much there was?' he asked again, and again she shook her head.

'That is good,' he sighed with relief. 'Then he won't know that it's been divided. Sirich and I think he is under Sir Jocelyn's influence and we dare not trust him.' He felt miserable as he said it for he had loved Thurstan and had trusted him entirely until the day on which he had returned from Lincoln. There had been something in his description of his journey which had not rung true.

They removed each coin separately, careful not to tip them into a heap, for the chink of coins might have been heard by anyone who had entered the room below. Slowly, one by one, the coins were laid out on the blanket and Benedict's eyes grew wide. It looked to him like a King's ransom.

'How much of it shall I put back?' he asked, but she only stared at the money. He answered his own question, 'I shall put half of it back. Have you a piece of cloth in which I can tie the rest? I must give it to Sirich and he will hide it when we get to the manor.'

She rose and went to a bundle which lay in the space where the floor met the roof timbers. Kneeling down, she rummaged among the clothes and brought out a square of linen which she handed to him. In it he put half the coins, folding the cloth between each one so that the money would make no sound.

'Sirich says he will hide it for us when we reach the manor,' he explained.

They turned at a sound, only to see Sirich's head and shoulders appear through the hole in the floor, and in silence he handed to them the threaded needle.

'Now,' Benedict turned to Francisca again, 'do you have something which will unpick these stitches?' She produced a tiny pair of shears and with the points she began to unpick the braid along the edge of his cloak. It was backed with a linen strip and the coins were sewn independently, carefully separated one from another, along the length of the ten inches or so which she first turned back for his inspection.

'Isabelle will know how many she put in. Do you think we can trust her?' he asked. She nodded. 'Shall I take out half again?'

She looked doubtful now and he was unsure of what to do next. Then, remembering that this was their last chance, he decided to be bold. 'If we don't get it now, we never shall,' he said. 'Unpick the rest of the hem. That is where the gold chain and the rings were hidden. Some day soon Sir Jocelyn will demand to know how much we have and then we shall bring forth only what we have left here and what is contained in Thurstan's belt. We will have to tell Isabelle but she would not betray us, would she? Not even if she saw the new stitching she could never betray you!'

Francisca nodded again.

They picked away, he with his fingers, she with the shears and when they had half the braid undone, she produced a square of cloth and taking the coins, the chain and the rings, he carefully wrapped them. As they finished, they heard feet on the ladder and Benedict swept his cloak off the bed and stuffed the money belt, now much lighter, under the front of his jerkin. But it was Sirich again and he relaxed.

'Have you got the money safely?'

'We have hidden it in cloths, as you said.'

At this, Francisca, of her own accord, handed both tight bundles to Sirich.

'That's a good lass,' he said, and he lowered them into the flat satchel which he always had hanging from his belt. 'Here is the threaded needle,' and he handed it directly to her.

With more energy than he had supposed she could muster, Benedict watched as Francisca neatly sewed the lining back to the braid. Sirich produced a bundle of thread and she loaded the needle again, trimming the thread with her little shears. Then she stitched the braid to the front of the cloak and the men were delighted with the work.

'I doubt even if Isabelle would notice,' said Sirich, with great satisfaction.

# 15

When Henry the miller had driven away from Langthorpe with his wagon, they prepared for their departure. What had been a dream was suddenly reality, and Benedict was filled with dread. What hope could there be for them in this new life? How long would it be before their neighbours discovered that Francisca was not a Christian? They spent some time teaching her how to conduct herself in church, when to kneel and how to handle the rosary beads, but one small slip and someone might comment, and that someone might talk of it to another who would connect them with the Jewish community in York.

And what of himself? Would the neighbours accept him as Sir Jocelyn's son? They had known Walter, who had been killed in the tournament, and might reject him as an upstart. Isabelle, too, was fretting about the problems of living in what she always spoke of as 'the mountains'. She had checked their baggage over and over, sure that there would be some essential item missing when they arrived.

Benedict rode Jet. He had wanted to keep the mare so that they could breed foals from her but Sir Jocelyn would not hear of his riding a mare.

'Sir John Wickham was riding a mare in a procession at Rouen when one of the following stallions tried to mount her!' He laughed loudly at this recollection. 'You would be in a pretty pickle if that should happen, hey young fellow! With the money we have, we can always buy other horses when we need them.'

A chill ran through Benedict, for whenever Sir Jocelyn spoke of the money it was as though it were his by right. He began to wonder if Sir Jocelyn's troubles had come about through extravagance, but once again the Knight's opinion prevailed and it was decided that Jet and the bay gelding should be kept and the two mares be sold before the next winter.

Still Francisca had not spoken and none of them could tell whether she was content or not, though it seemed to Benedict that she sat straighter and held her head up higher. Isabelle packed their clothes, all repaired, cleaned and aired in the sun, but when she came to the red and blue silk gown which had been Josce's, the extent of their loss overcame her and she wept for the rest of the morning.

At last they were ready and it was the turn of stout Maud to weep, for she was sure that she would never see Isabelle again; Birkdale might have been at the end of the earth for all she knew of it. She had enjoyed their company and not least, Benedict knew, the drama of their situation. Such excitement was not often come by at Langthorpe.

They rode south for a short stretch, along the Dere Street, on a bright morning of blue sky, small white clouds and bird song. Benedict tried to see the fine weather as a good omen for their future and before long they turned westward, towards the purple mounds of the Pennine hills, the sight of which filled him with excitement and Isabelle with apprehension. They pressed on, then north a little and the hills loomed larger. Now, with increasing frequency, they passed lay brothers dressed in the clothes of the Cistercian order and knew they must be approaching Fountains.

They climbed steadily, with the loud bleating of sheep for company, until they found themselves on the lip of a deep gorge from which there arose a hum of activity. Below them, the valley floor was filled from side to side and along its length with the abbey buildings. It was as though a whole town was spread out beneath them. The River Skell gurgled beneath them busily clattering its mill wheels. At that time the church had a very low tower, but even then it dominated the farther side of the enclave. They paused, fascinated by the hive of activity below, and, riding further, they found themselves looking down into the cloister and then along the roof of the lay brothers' quarters which, even in their unfinished state, were already the length of a city street. Finally they were above the abbey's guest houses and the entrance.

Despite his antipathy to monasteries and their depredations, Benedict could not help but be impressed. This was so much grander than its daughter house at Meaux, the abbey of his childhood, and it dwarfed the Benedictine house in York from which it had sprung. On any other day they would have called at the abbey guest house for food and rest but they were afraid that there might be someone there from York who would recognise Francisca, and they were also unsure of her behaviour and of whether it might cause curiosity.

Isabelle had packed food for the journey and they did not stop until they were some way beyond Fountains where they ate in a little hollow, their riding horses tied to the wheels of the wagon, quietly cropping the grass.

Above them, the track continued to climb, until it disappeared out of sight over the brow of the hill, where it narrowed between high rocks. A flock was approaching along the track, they could hear the anxious bleating of many sheep and the thin piping of a shepherd. They looked up from time to time but the flock was still out of sight until, suddenly, the first sheep appeared, silhouetted against the light between the rocks. At the same moment, the slight figure of a boy leapt on to a boulder above the sheep. Then the sound of the sheep and the sheep-bells filled the air as the flock spilled through the gap and spread about the grass on both sides of the sandy track. Two monks followed the sheep, their sleeves rolled high and their habits tucked up to knee length. The sheep flowed on past them and the boy hardly glanced in their direction, but ran here and there to gather the sheep, leaping upon the rocks and stopping to play from time to time upon his little flute. It was the kind, Benedict could now see, which the shepherds made from the wing-bones of birds, and the sound of it was light, like the plaintive song of a bird.

Benedict felt cheered as they rode on, up the sandy track, which was deeply scored by last winter's heavy rain, and presently they came to the river crossing where there was a cluster of dwellings and a poor church of wood, hardly bigger than the houses. Further up the valley they found people who lived on rough common land, not in houses but under elder bushes, with camp fires nearby on which the women were cooking. The children ran towards them, crying out for alms, and Benedict began to fear what they might find in the high recesses of Birkdale. But he was pleasantly surprised when they came to the hamlet of stone cottages which was Birkhau, for the people seemed independent and had a well-fed look about them. They hailed the travellers cheerfully as they passed, and Benedict remembered that Sir Jocelyn had described them as freemen. With what strength of will and with what economies, Benedict wondered, had they kept their land out of the hands of lords and abbots?

The manor stood some distance beyond the village and they had still some way to go. The rapidly darkening hills enfolded them; the bleating of sheep surrounded them on every side and, issuing from the hilltops, seemed to fill the air itself. They entered a wood and when they emerged again into the open valley the light had faded so much that the manor house, which nestled into the hillside fifty yards beyond on their right, was barely visible. Benedict could just make out a stone-built house with an undercroft and, at the far end, an outer stair at the top of which was the dark shape of the door. The path ran on, past the house. There was no division of wall or fence between the manor and the road but a gentle rise of the grass and a beaten footpath leading from house to track. At the far end of the building, near the steps, a rowan tree had been planted to ward off evil, and the intricacy of its branches showed sharp against the remaining light. They drew nearer and he discerned a window halfway along the upper storey, a crude imitation of those in the Coney Street house but, even so, the place looked strong and the stonework was good.

Somewhere in the darkness on the left of the track gurgled the stream and above them the bowl of hills at the head of Birkdale was silhouetted against a pale yellow sky from which the last of the light was fast disappearing.

A very old man hobbled out of the shadows to meet them and grudgingly showed the brothers where to stable their horses in the undercroft. Benedict could see nothing of the man himself, but his movements had the lurching gait of one who suffered severely from the pains of old age.

The cart was drawn in through the great doors and left on the threshing floor while the women climbed the stone stairs and disappeared into the house.

Benedict wondered again about the sleeping quarters and whether this was the night when he should sleep with Francisca for the first time. He delayed his ascent of the stairs, making himself busy with unnecessary supervision of the work, until everything was done and he could delay no longer; then he and the brothers, carrying bundles and followed slowly by the old man, went up into the house.

The vast room would have been in darkness but for the glow from the hearth which was halfway along the opposite wall. Benedict saw as he closed the door that the end wall beside him was of bare stone. He could not see the far end of the room at all, as it was in deep darkness. He looked up but he could not see the rafters. The hall was like a great, dark cavern. A subdued muttering drew Benedict's eyes to the fireside where he could make out the figure of a gnarled old woman with a blanket wrapped about her legs. She made no move to welcome or to serve them, but the old man motioned them to a solid-looking table which occupied the centre of the floor at some distance from the fire and at which Isabelle and Francisca were already seated. There was bread and cheese but no smell of cooking and no sign of any meat.

Soon, grumbling to himself all the while, the old man brought from the recesses of the fireplace a large jug of cider which he placed upon the table. For a few minutes the dispirited newcomers waited for beakers or flagons from which to drink but none was forthcoming.

'What are we to drink from, old man?' Thurstan called, for the two old ones were now huddled by the fire and seemed to have settled for the night.

Sirich said quietly, 'In this house they drink by turns from the jug.'

'They all drink . . .!' began Isabelle, but she was interrupted.

'Bring beakers!' shouted Thurstan and the old man rose and shuffled towards them, empty-handed.

'There is only the master's cup.'

'Then bring it here,' said Benedict, 'and my Lady shall drink from it.'

'Sir Jocelyn wouldn't like that,' the old man said.

'Sir Jocelyn would not wish us to be served from a communual jug,' said Benedict. 'Better service than this can be found at any alehouse!'

The old man muttered something and it seemed he might return to the fireside, but he hesitated before disappearing into the darkness at the far end of the hall. They heard the sound of his hand feeling its way across a wooden door, followed by the click of a latch. Soon he approached, with his gnarled fingers stretched around four horn beakers, and, placing them on the end of the table, he gave the seated company a wide berth and painfully eased himself once again on to the bench at the fireside.

'There are five of us and he hasn't brought Sir Jocelyn's cup,' said Benedict.

'Perhaps he is mortally afraid of him and dare not bring it,' said Isabelle.

'Do not insist then,' said Benedict, remembering the fear which could be instilled in servants by a savage master. 'We will manage with these and see what Sir Jocelyn has to say when he arrives.' He wondered as he spoke what sort of master Sir Jocelyn was, yet the Knight had kept these decrepit people by him, instead of turning them out as some might have done.

'Begin as you mean to go on,' said Thurstan. 'That is my motto. Once they see they can disobey, you will never master them.'

Benedict felt embarrassed at being told how he should behave and concealed it by sinking his nose into his beaker. The wall at either side of the fireplace, he noticed now, had been wainscotted at some time with white Norway boards to a height of about six feet, but the boards had never been painted. What a pity it was, he thought, that the Knight had not employed a man to paint arms and mottoes upon them before the smoke begrimed the new wood. Then he wondered again how he was to discover where he and Francisca would sleep.

'Isabelle,' he said at last, 'find out from the old woman if there is a privy place where you and Francisca may go before we retire and then ask where the beds are to be put out.'

Isabelle went and spoke with the old crone and, returning, took Francisca by the arm and led her out of the house again and they were away for some time.

'Is there no guardrobe?' asked Thurstan.

'We went outside behind the house when I was here before,' said Sirich. 'There is a crude wattle place with a seat.' Benedict looked round about him and perhaps Sirich noticed how disappointed he looked in the place, for he added, with some enthusiasm in his voice, 'But there is a sleeping chamber for the knight and his lady up there,' and he turned as he spoke and peered into the roof-space at the dark end of the hall. How Benedict wished that he had said so before. All three turned and looked into the darkness, but could see nothing. 'It's up there, like the one over the solar at Coney Street, but narrower and more like a wide gallery. The old one fetched the beakers from a hutch that stands under it. They keep a chair there for the master and a stack of pallets.'

Isabelle and Francisca re-entered the hall, Isabelle still holding the girl's arm, and they sat down silently at the table.

'Sirich says there is a sleeping chamber up there,' said Benedict, indicating the far recesses of the dark roof, and speaking more from relief that there was to be some privacy than to give information.

'Then I wish he had said so when he came home,' said Isabelle in annoyance. 'I have been pestered with not knowing where Francisca would sleep.'

'Do not call her Francisca,' said Benedict quietly. 'Before these people you should call her my lady.'

They had finished eating and now sat silently, looking at the two old servants by the fire, whilst they in turn regarded the newcomers sitting round the table with an indifference which bordered on hostility. Occasionally the old woman would cackle with laughter, as though they had been sent for her especial amusement.

'There will not be much entertainment here this night,' said Thurstan loudly. 'Are you for bed?'

He seemed to address them all and Benedict hesitated again, not knowing whether to propose that he and his bride withdraw to the sleeping chamber, when Isabelle relieved him of the responsibility.

'I will go up and make the bed comfortable for my lady and master,' she said and, going to the fireplace, returned with a lighted candle in an iron holder. As she passed the table she said sharply, and loudly enough for the two old ones by the fire to hear, 'You men can get pallets out for us. I don't know where the old ones sleep but don't let them keep us too far from the fire, it's cold up here in these mountains,' and with that she proceeded to the room's end and carefully climbed the ladder, her light disappearing at the top and leaving them again almost in darkness. She returned shortly and Benedict thought she would say something but, ignoring them, she went to the fireplace and spoke again to the old crone. Then she lifted something from the hearth and, wrapping it in a cloth, climbed again to the upper chamber. After a few minutes she called for Francisca to follow her.

Still Benedict didn't know what to do; should he follow, or wait to be called? He kept his eyes on the table top not wishing to meet the gaze of his companions, until Isabelle returned and, approaching the table, said sharply, 'It's time for you to go to bed, master.'

Benedict almost laughed for she addressed him as she had when he had been a child and at the same time as a superior, but he went quickly and to his relief no ribald comments followed him.

Up in the sleeping chamber the lighted candle showed him a bed with ragged curtains about it. On the nearside they had not been pulled to and he could make out the shape of Francisca under the blankets, but whether she was awake or asleep he could not tell. He took off his clothes and was glad to get into the bed and cover himself against the cold air. His foot met something very hard and warm. He knew then what Isabelle had taken from the fireside. It was a warmed stone which she had wrapped in a scrap of blanket, as she had done when he was first at Coney Street and lying close to death. Below, he could hear the quiet voices of the servants as they made ready and the swishing sound as the pallets were dragged the length of the room. It seemed they were sleeping somewhere near the fire.

He lay still for a while, scarcely daring to take up more than the width of his own body. How, he wondered, would he ever dare to touch her? It was as though he lay beside one of the ivory statuettes in church. He wondered if Francisca's skin were smooth and pale as ivory.

They lay in the darkness, each stiff and separate as figures on a tomb, and when he eventually slept he dreamed. At first it was a happy dream of his childhood in Coney Street. He seemed to be playing in the garden but he could not see the other children with whom he played. He was shooting with Aaron's bow but he could never hit the target, let alone its centre. Another boy took the bow from him and, without being able to see who it was, Benedict knew that it was Aaron. He hit the centre with every arrow but Benedict felt no resentment. It seemed to him that it was a natural consequence of Aaron's superiority and he had no desire to equal him. Then he took up the bow again, and this time he shot wide and hit something in the grass. He ran forward and to his horror he found that he had killed Miriam's cat.

He ran in from the garden and was relieved to find himself standing in the beautiful solar. Calmly he looked around and could clearly see the pattern of golden lions on the red tapestry. Again he had a deep feeling of wellbeing. The room was warm and sweetly scented. Hannah was sitting by the fire with a lyre across her knees which she played with her long, pale hands.

He turned then, and to his joy found that Josce was standing close behind him. He looked up eagerly into his face, only to find that Josce's expression was grim. Something impelled his eyes downward and he saw with terror that Josce's hand held a bloody knife. Now all around them was swirling smoke which blotted out the glowing tapestry in wreaths of suffocating grey. He saw the knife again, dripping with blood, and tried to scream. There was a gale of icy wind blowing through the room yet nothing moved and Josce's pale face swam before him. The scream would not come out of his paralysed throat, yet he could hear himself screaming.

The sound woke him, frozen with fear and sweating, and he knew as he woke that it was not he who had screamed but Francisca. After a second or so he put out his hand and touched her, but she gasped and flung herself away from him across the bed.

'What is it?' called Isabelle's voice from the darkness of the hall below.

'Nothing, nothing,' Benedict replied. 'Only a nightmare.'

He rose quickly, not wanting Isabelle to appear in the sleeping loft. The candle had burned itself out. He cautiously crossed the dark floor to a chink of light and found a little window closed with a shutter. This he opened and moonlight flooded in. Returning to the bed, he knelt on the place where he had been lying.

'Francisca,' he whispered into the darkness, 'wake up, it was only a dream.' He lay down again and pulled the blanket up to his chin. 'You are safe here,' he said softly. 'Francisca . . .' and he felt in the bed and found her hand. To his surprise she turned to him. He put his arm around her and held her close, talking all the while. He could not have believed that her body could be so soft, so smooth.

She rested her cheek in the hollow of his shoulder and he caressed the silken skin of her back. His hand reached her neck and he lifted her long hair away, draping it across the pillow.

# 16

'Take those muddy boots off before you come in here!' Isabelle called, turning from the spit as they opened the door.

Benedict and the brothers grinned at each other, 'This is a farm, Isabelle, not a palace.'

'It's not a farm, it's a manor and I'll have some cleanliness if we can have nothing else,' she replied. She was proud of living in a manor, which amused them, and they obliged her by leaving their filthy working boots behind. A boy from the village came to the manor each day and helped generally about the place in return for his dinner. He would clean their boots. Isabelle had wrought wonders within the houseplace and she had done it all alone. Nothing would move the old crone from the fireside but the calls of nature. Isabelle maintained that if she could get up and down the steps she could do a bit of sweeping, but the old one just cackled with laughter and resumed her seat by the fire. During the day the old man would shuffle about the undercroft or around the buildings. He could be trusted to feed the pigs, to scatter some grain for the hens and collect their eggs, but he volunteered nothing else. The men didn't need his help with the sheep, in which he seemed to have lost all interest.

Sir Jocelyn, when compared with Josce, was overbearing and uncouth. This was the conclusion to which Benedict had come after a few months at the manor of Birkhau.

Isabelle had planted the overgrown garden which her brothers cleared of the ranker weeds and tree saplings which had set themselves there. She would soon be able to provide all the herbs for medicines and cooking which most manors had available. Thurstan had planted peas, beans, leeks, onions and kale for the table. The brothers, with occasional help from the two men who owed task work, had done wonders. They ploughed the land, herded the sheep, built another sheepfold of the white limestone which lay everywhere, and cleared out the accumulation of years of neglect in the undercroft, but Sir Jocelyn never praised the work they did. He would disappear for days on end, giving no explanation of where he was going or saying when he would return. Benedict remembered everything the Knight had promised and wondered constantly when his education as a knight might begin.

Sir Jocelyn must have returned to York on one of his expeditions and whether or not he had repaid his debts there he had certainly spent lavishly, for he came home with new clothes and a fine saddle and bridle for his horse. He had locked away all the money which remained in Benedict's cloak and in the money belts which they had worn, saying that it was safest in the chest beside the fire. There was no denying that the money should be locked away somewhere but no mention had been made of it since. Benedict thanked God for the secret hoard which Sirich had buried.

When he was at home the Knight never rode around his demesne or seemed to take any interest in his land, but sat opposite the old crone at the fireside, each of them wrapped in a blanket against the draughts of cold air which were a marked feature of the hall.

Despite the Knight's disparagement of such ungentlemanly behaviour, Benedict often went out into the fields and over the hills with the men. From them he learned the practicalities of farming and woodland management, and when no strangers were about to observe he would help with the heavy work. Although it was not dignified for him to occupy himself in this way, he enjoyed the exercise of his limbs and the work distracted him from his disappointment in Sir Jocelyn.

He learned the use of the billhook, with which he slashed the older trunks and branches of the hawthorn in the hedgerows. Then Thurstan showed him how to bend half the trunk, lay it down, and fasten it so that new growth would shoot upwards along its length to strengthen and thicken the hedge. He learned to mend the stone walls, looking carefully at each stone to see which would fit, and Sirich showed him how to lay long stones at intervals crossways in the wall to give it strength.

He was happy working thus but he had come there to be a knight and there were days when he gave up all hope of ever being recognised by the Constable of Richmond and of being trained to arms. True, Sir Jocelyn had been to Richmond but there he found, or so he said, that Sir Alan had gone to his own castle of Bolton in Wensleydale. Instead of following the Constable thither he had returned home with nothing gained and Benedict was left wondering whether or not they would be allowed to keep the tenancy. He enquired about this but the Knight seemed unperturbed and laughed off his concern. Benedict reflected that when he had been persuaded to marry Francisca in such haste the Knight had made him think there was an urgent need to get everything settled before he met Sir Alan. What had the urgency been? It seemed the matter could wait. Benedict felt cheated by the Knight, but he did not regret his marriage. He knew such joy that every night he recovered from the hurts of the day and woke again, determined that all would eventually be well.

But then Isabelle began to suggest that the Knight might wish to rid himself of Francisca. 'The Knight loves only money,' she had said. 'He could put ivy berries in her food and get you another rich wife; then he could squander another marriage portion.' Benedict had thought at the time that Isabelle was becoming fanciful but the idea had taken seed in his mind and, in conjunction with the Knight's curious behaviour and his possession of Francisca's money, it began to grow.

When supper was ready that evening the Knight bestirred himself, rose from the fireside and came to the head of the table. 'I hear Sir Alan is at Richmond again,' he said as he took his seat.

'But you were told so before,' replied Benedict, sharply, 'and your journey was in vain.'

'I was misinformed, but I shall go again and see how the land lies with the manor.' There was a briskness in the Knight's voice, as though he implied that on this occasion all would be well.

'Shall I go with you?' asked Benedict, but he did not receive a reply, for at that moment the dogs barked and, as Thurstan rose to see who was about, there came a knocking at the door. Thurstan admitted a squire who bore the royal badge on his sleeve; a tall youth who looked around in a haughty manner as he entered. He presented himself as squire to Sir Alan, the Constable, and Sir Jocelyn bade him sit and eat so that for some time there was no further conversation and they had no idea of his errand until the meal was over.

'Now, what message does Sir Alan send to me?' asked Sir Jocelyn at last.

'Sir Alan is at Richmond and bids you come soon if you would swear allegiance. He has heard that your fortunes have changed for the better,' at this the squire looked at Benedict and then at Francisca, 'and he wishes to know how you intend to provide for the knight service due from Birkhau.'

'I came to Richmond but Sir Alan was already away to Bolton,' Sir Jocelyn replied, and there followed a silence during which Benedict wondered what the squire made of this curious story and whether he would ask why Sir Jocelyn had not ridden on to Bolton. 'I shall be glad to accompany you tomorrow,' Sir Jocelyn added, still not indicating to the visitor that there were members of his family present. Benedict felt increasingly uncomfortable as he wondered if he was ever to be made known to the squire and, meanwhile, he observed the other with interest. The squire, in his turn, had been looking curiously at Benedict, who found it hard to keep countenance under the circumstances.

There was a pause, until the squire dragged his gaze from Benedict and, turning again to Sir Jocelyn, replied unhurriedly that he was not returning to Richmond but would like to sleep at Birkhau that night.

The next day, he said, he must ride on to York where he was to deliver letters to the Archbishop. Benedict thought it would be a fine life to ride the countryside, delivering messages from one important man to another. He remembered the pride he had felt when Josce had been entrusted with the letters of Sir Ranulph Glanville.

'This is my son, Benedict, and his lady,' the Knight said unexpectedly, indicating them with his hand.

'I am Philip de Lonsdale,' the squire replied, turning towards Benedict and Francisca.

Benedict inclined his head but said nothing, for he felt unsure of himself and did not know what to say. He knew that it must seem strange to the squire that Sir Jocelyn was so tardy in introducing him and that Francisca never spoke at all, but for the life of him he did not know what to say. He was painfully aware of the gulf between himself and this self-assured young man, the son, no doubt, of a Yorkshire knight of ancient family; skilled in the use of arms and knowledgeable about the affairs of the world.

Sir Jocelyn must have realised that the room was strangely quiet and that the visitor was not receiving due hospitality, for he broke the silence by calling out, 'Come, Thurstan, sing us a song and have Sirich play on the pipes.' So, while Isabelle put apple rings to float upon a jar of ale which she set to warm beside the fire, Sirich got out the small pipes and, setting them on his knee, played some old airs. Benedict watched the squire and saw that the haughty expression was leaving his face. Isabelle filled the drinking horns and Thurstan sang the ballad in which the jester, by his wit, gets the better of the king. The company was now more relaxed and the squire sang, unaccompanied, a sweet ditty about a maid and a rose. He had a fine voice and when he had finished he turned to Benedict and enquired if he was a singer. Benedict, glad to find something he could do without displaying his ignorance of affairs, admitted to having a poor singing voice, but instead told the story of The Fox and the Grapes which he had read in a book of Josce's and, while Isabelle replenished their drinking horns, Sirich played The Feast of St Canute and followed it with The Vigil which, the squire said, sounded very well on the pipes though it was usually played on the fiddle. Thus warmed by the spicy ale and well entertained, the company retired to bed contented.

The squire left next morning without Benedict having found an opportunity to speak privately with him, by which means he had hoped to learn something about the Constable's intentions. As soon as Lonsdale had disappeared into the wood below, Sir Jocelyn had Sirich saddle up for him. Benedict dashed down the outer stair and took hold of the bridle as the Knight was about to ride away, 'Why may I not come with you?' he asked angrily.

'And what would you say there? You know nothing of knightly behaviour. You were unable to make conversation last evening but sat there like some yokel. I must go first and prepare the way.'

'But you bought clothes that I might present myself to Sir Alan. You must then have intended to take me along with you.'

'You might say the wrong word and show that you are a scholar and not worthy to be a knight,' Sir Jocelyn replied.

At this Benedict's anger overwhelmed him. First he was described as a yokel, then as a scholar . . . 'How can I become a knight without help, and what help do you give me?'

It was then that he decided to force the issue. 'If you will not wait, I shall saddle up and follow you,' he shouted.

'You will not!' replied the Knight.

'There is some reason other than those you have given,' said Benedict, 'and I will go with you.'

The Knight wrenched his horse's head round so that Benedict lost his restraining hold on the rein and was left standing, watching helplessly as the Knight rode off. Benedict now felt sure that whatever was afoot he should know about it and to learn anything meant going to Richmond. He ran up the stairs and hurled himself through the house door.

'A saddle for Jet. Get me a saddle and bridle. Where is my cloak! Get me some clean linen and, Isabelle, some bread to eat on the way, for I will follow him to Richmond whatever he says to the contrary.'

The ferocity of his expression and the anger in his voice sent the servants scurrying to do his bidding. Francisca, who was sitting in a patch of sunlight near the window, rose and came towards him with a look of deep anxiety. Benedict was immediately sorry that he had caused her alarm.

'I must know what he is doing at Richmond,' he explained, taking her back to her seat. He stood for a minute or two, stroking her hair, Then he turned and took the saddle bag from Thurstan's outstretched hand and, swinging his cloak about him, said, 'I suspect that he did not go there last time but went off on some errand of his own. This time I will go and I will see Sir Alan. There is nothing to be lost. If he sees before him only a clerk, time will make no difference. Sir Jocelyn teaches me nothing about knightly arms. If Sir Alan wants a knight, then he must undertake my education himself.'

He kissed Francisca, then he turned to leave. It was the first time that he had ever caressed her in public but he did not wait long enough to see the flush of pleasure which came to her cheeks.

He rode up and over the hill behind the house and followed the pack-horse tracks to Jervaux Abbey. There he asked if they had seen Sir Jocelyn and the monk who served him with cider replied that the Knight had passed that way less than an hour before.

The day was dull and the clouds were low on the hills. As he rode towards Swaledale, his situation began to assume a more serious aspect. It was no longer a matter merely between himself and Sir Jocelyn. Should he turn back? The country before him was still obscured by the mist as over the deserted hills and through the woods he rode, but when he was thinking that Richmond would never appear, the sun broke through and there before him, across the valley and the swirling torrent of the Swale, stood Richmond Castle.

Even from this distance the castle looked forbidding. He remembered the White Tower of London, this must be its equal in size. It was then that he felt the first doubt about the wisdom of his errand and, as he drew closer to the mighty keep, his doubts grew stronger.

Yet he would not return home! Something must be done to bring things to a head. He had had some idea of announcing himself at the door and being escorted into a hall such as he had seen in many a manor house, but the size of the castle stunned him and he became afraid of what lay ahead. The nearer he came to the towering keep the less resolute he felt, yet to retreat was against his nature.

He was admitted to the outer bailey and found it lined with houses and workshops, their thatched roofs pitched against the high curtain wall. The ragged grass was criss-crossed with many beaten pathways and grazed by sheep and tethered cows. Outside his shop, a smith was deftly beating the dents out of a helmet and, in the darkness within, another was hammering more vigorously. Then came the hiss of hot iron as it was plunged into cold water and, after a little pause, the invisible smith began his hammering again. To the right was a dovecote tower and from it came the gentle cooing of doves; before him on the path, children were playing with a small, yapping dog. He looked up at the tower. Where to go now? One of the nearby houses was obviously an inn and he hesitated, thinking to go inside and so put off his errand, but he feared he might waver and resolutely turned his horse towards the gateway; above it the keep seemed to reach the sky. He looked up and up, until the tower seemed to be moving, as though it would fall on him.

He banged on the door and was admitted to the gatehouse, where half a dozen soldiers were leaning on their spears. They bestirred themselves, obviously glad of a distraction.

'My father rode on ahead,' Benedict explained. 'Has he arrived yet?'

'If that is Sir Jocelyn de Birkhau then he has arrived, sir, an hour ago,' said the sergeant, 'and he's now in the hall with the Constable. Here, lop-ears, stir yourself and take this gentleman to the hall. Your own name, sir?'

Benedict gave his name and, as he followed the soldier out into the great inner court, he saw how the man had got his nickname. The light shone red through the huge ears ahead of him and for a moment he was amused and distracted from his concerns. The walk across the green took some time and the soldier turned to him as they went. He had an extremely wide mouth which now spread in a smile and he said, 'Come to find you a wife has he, sir? He arrived in the company of Sir William de Sedley and they were discussing the details of a marriage portion as I escorted them to the hall. A fine wench, they say, and very well provided.'

Benedict was astounded and, without thinking, he exclaimed, 'I have a wife already!' The soldier seemed discomforted and hurried to say that he must have been mistaken, but what he had said had set Benedict's mind whirling. There was, however, no more time in which to think on the matter for they had already crossed to the farthest corner of the great enclosure and had come to the foot of a wide stone stair which led to the door of the hall. They entered the screens passage and stopped to allow a servant with a steaming dish to cross before them. Then, turning to the right, Benedict found himself standing in the hall, and what a hall! The shutters were open down both its sides and the sunlight flooded in through twelve or more huge windows. Far off was the raised dais, filling the end of the hall, and there was seated what seemed to him a fearsome assembly of strangers, but before he had time to try to identify any of the men he was startled by a loud bang and a voice beside him proclaiming his name.

'Benedict, the son of Sir Jocelyn de Birkhau!' and he turned sharply to find a groom of the chamber who held a long stave with which he must have struck the floor. Benedict looked again towards the dais to find that all eyes were upon him. At the centre of the table was a man with piercing eyes under shaggy brows and a fringe of dark grey hair. This, thought Benedict, must be the Constable.

Sir Jocelyn was sitting two places from him and Sir Jocelyn looked displeased. There were others at the table and Benedict wondered which of them was Sir William de Sedley, the father of the heiress, but his eyes were held by the man on the Constable's right hand. Benedict thought that this could not be the man. He was obviously a person of importance; a man of about thirty years of age whose face was tanned brown by the sun and whose haughty stare was fixed upon him. For a moment he thought there was something familiar about him but then he dismissed the idea.

He walked the length of the hall and bowed to the Constable, not allowing his eyes to flicker in the direction of Sir Jocelyn.

'So you are the long-lost son?'

'Yes, sir, my name is Benedict.'

'And where have you been all this time?' the Constable asked in a sardonic tone.

Here, he saw immediately, was the difficulty which Sir Jocelyn had foretold. His impetuosity and distrust had led him into a situation where he must pronounce on his origins in public.

'I was brought up by a merchant in the Low Countries,' he said, beginning on the story which he and the Knight had rehearsed.

'As you have been brought up to trade, how shall we make a knight of you?'

Perhaps, Benedict thought, if he could keep the conversation upon the subject of knighthood, the Constable might forget to ask any more questions about his previous whereabouts.

'I am eager to learn, sir.'

'You do not seem to have been smittled with the merchant's manner and bearing,' the Constable said with satisfaction and, turning to Sir Jocelyn, he went on, 'He is a fine-looking young man.'

Sir Jocelyn bowed his head slightly in acknowledgement.

'You ride well?' asked Sir Alan.

'Competently, sir.' Benedict answered.

'And you handle a sword?'

'No, sir, but I had some practice with the bow when I was a child.'

'That is no bad thing. King Richard is a great man for the cross-bow, but swordsmanship and practice with the lance are what is needed.' Turning again to Sir Jocelyn, he said. 'Do you intend to leave your . . .' he hesitated very slightly, 'son with us?'

Benedict coloured at the hesitation but Sir Jocelyn answered promptly and without the slightest trace of embarrassment.

'He can stay here if he wills.'

You are married already, I hear,' said the Constable. 'Did you bring the lady with you from the Low Countries, or was it France?'

We were married here in England,' Benedict said, ignoring the rest of the Constable's question. 'The lady was my father's ward.' That part of the story, at least, they had worked out well in advance.

'And did your lady bring a fine marriage portion?' asked the Constable, with the trace of a smile. 'I hear she is not in good health.'

'My lady brought a good portion,' Benedict replied, clenching his fists as he spoke. Isabelle's fear might not be imagination after all. Had Sir Jocelyn been putting it about that Francisca was ailing and might die? If so, the soldier had heard correctly and the Knight had been making betrothal arrangements. He fought for command of himself and returned the Constable a steady look, which served him well for the subject was not pursued.

'Sit you down,' said the Constable, indicating a stool on Benedict's side of the table. The Constable then began to converse with a short, fat man who sat between him and Sir Jocelyn, was this de Sedley? A page brought food and drink and Benedict began to eat.

'Have you ever travelled to York?'

Benedict looked up and was surprised to find himself being regarded keenly by the haughty man he had noticed as he entered.

'I have been to York,' he answered cautiously.

The Constable must have heard, for he leaned towards Benedict and said, 'This is my Lord de Lacy, young man.'

'I beg your pardon, my lord,' Benedict said. So this was de Lacy! His father had died on crusade and he had returned from the Holy Land to claim the Honour of Pontefract through his grandmother, Aubrey de Lisours. He had only recently, on the occasion of his inheritance, changed his name from fitzEustace to de Lacy, the ancient name of his ancestors who had long held Pontefract, and he was also hereditary Constable of Chester! Benedict had heard a great deal about Roger de Lacy.

'You have not been to Pontefract?'

'No, my lord, but I have heard the castle described and every man knows the fame of the great Honour.'

'And do you think Pontefract must be as fine as Richmond?'

Benedict stole the briefest of glances and saw that there was a trace of amusement in the eyes.

'Richmond is a fine castle, but I hear that Pontefract is its match,' Benedict replied.

'A very wise answer,' replied the other with a hint of satisfaction in his voice and then, to Benedict's relief, de Lacy turned his attention to the general conversation.

Benedict followed the talk with keen interest, whilst at the same time he tried to give every appearance of being occupied only with his food. He was eager for clues as to who the other men might be. They talked of the absent King Richard, of his brother John and of the Lady Constance, heir to the Honour of Richmond who had been married in early childhood to another of the King's brothers, Geoffrey, killed in a tournament four years back. They fell then to discussing her son and daughter, the Prince Arthur and Princess Eleanor, and the Lady Constance's present husband, the fierce Ralph de Blundeville, Earl of Chester, who now called himself Earl of Richmond and kept his wife a prisoner in France. And then they came to the Honour of Richmond itself.

'This Honour rendered one hundred and forty knight's fees of late, but with all these troubles it is sorely depleted,' the Constable said. 'Now, in the time of King William, the first of that name, there were four hundred and forty manors it is said, with one hundred and ninety-nine of them in Yorkshire and . . .' he hesitated, 'how many does that leave?'

Without a split second's hesitation, Benedict answered, 'Two hundred and forty-one outliers, sir.'

'Ha!' said a voice close to him and he looked up to see de Lacy regarding him with a look of satisfaction upon his face.

*151*

'That's his merchant's training, de Birkhau!' the Constable shouted, laughing, and banging his hand down upon the table.

Benedict flushed deep red, but the conversation had turned to other matters.

'Our Lord the King pursues the crusade mightily, but where shall we find the next instalment of taxes?' enquired one.

'The Jews of York will not be at hand to help,' said another, and the hair on the back of Benedict's neck stood on end.

'There are other Jews,' said the man next beyond Sir Jocelyn. 'I am in contact with Jews in Chester who may help if need arises. I can part with no more land. What I have left is barely sufficient to support the knight I must provide.'

In Chester! Then some have survived, thought Benedict.

'Every year that passes our money buys us less,' said a small, stout, red-faced man. 'There was a time when a knight's horse cost five pounds, and what do we pay now? Why, fifteen! And look at the cost of supplying the castle guard. My men are standing their turn now, six of them at a shilling a day. My land holding is not sufficient to stand the rising cost, but what are we all to do?'

'Let us hope the spoils of war will aid the King,' said another, and then the conversation stopped as there came the sound of a horse cantering across the castle compound and slithering to a halt. All taking ceased; all eyes were upon the door. They could hear feet hurrying up the steps and a messenger entered in great haste, his hair sticking to his forehead with sweat, and his face flushed. The messenger strode up the hall and dropped to one knee before the Constable.

'Here, give the man a drink. He cannot speak,' Sir Alan shouted, and a serving man ran forward with a leather flask which the messenger emptied at once.

'I have come with news of my Lord Bishop of Durham,' he gasped.

'De Puiset, what of him? Here, give the man more drink.'

The messenger emptied another flagon before he was able to continue.

'Sir William de Longchamp has arrested the Lord Bishop at Tickhill, sir.'

'He has, has he?' said the Constable. 'What had de Puiset to say for himself?'

'I was not privy to the conversation, my lord,' the messenger replied, looking towards de Lacy as he spoke.

'Have you anything more to tell us?' asked the Constable.

'No, sir, only that the deed was done.'

'You may go to your rest. Tomorrow you shall take messages for me . . .' He stopped there and thought for half a minute. 'Does he lie at Tickhill yet?' he asked.

'Aye, sir they say he will stay until Wednesday.'

Benedict was all attention. Hadn't Josce said that there would be a conspiracy against King Richard and that de Puiset, who kept as his mistress an aunt of Richard Malebisse, might be party to it? Would Malebisse be arrested too? Now the country was splitting; some nobles were loyal to the absent Richard, and others, fearing he would never return from the crusade, were flocking to support his brother, Prince John, Earl of Mortain. De Puiset must have conspired with John. Why else should de Longchamp arrest him? Whatever anyone might say of de Longchamp, he was loyal to King Richard in everything.

'Young man,' the voice interrupted his thoughts and he found that de Lacy was leaning towards him across the table. 'We shall go into the Constable's solar to discuss this news but I would like to speak with you before I leave.'

'I will attend you, my lord,' Benedict replied, rising and bowing. He took care to bow to the Constable, although the man's back was towards him. Sir Jocelyn noticed his good manners and looked a little happier.

The Constable and his guests rose and disappeared through the door behind the dais, and Benedict looked about the room, unsure of what he should do next. Near to him was a table at which a squire of about his own age was playing Nine Men's Morris with a young boy.

'Damn it, Robert, pray attend to the game.'

'I am attending, Hugh, I intend to win this time.'

'You could no more win than fly out of the window,' the squire replied, moving one of his counters and sitting back to regard the board with satisfaction. He looked up then and found Benedict's gaze directed at the game.

'Do you play?' he asked.

'I have played in the past,' Benedict replied.

'Very well. As soon as I have beaten young Robert here, he can go and fetch us some ale and we shall have a game or two.'

That settled what Benedict was to do until Lord de Lacy claimed him and, as he was not required to play for a little while, he went over what he had said about himself and checked it off. How well should he admit to knowing York? he wondered. Could he claim to have been there several times between his arrival at the manor and now, the end of May?

He caught sight of Philip of Lonsdale who had called at Birkhau. He seemed just to have entered and was standing inside the screens looking around, and after a moment or so he caught sight of Benedict. He nodded but did not approach, although he did not seem surprised to see him there and Benedict thought he looked friendly enough.

There were other young men about the room, a group was rolling balls along the planks of the floor to knock down some skittles they had set up at a distance, and others watched idly, commenting on the play, until a jongleur entered, tapping on a little drum which he held in his left hand and humming to himself.

'Give us a song, Bernard,' someone called, and the singer looked up and grinned. He spoke then for the first time and his accent was French.

'I have a version in English of Hervis de Metz, who complains of the transfer of land to the monasteries; will you hear it in the English?'

'Why have you changed it? Who wants to hear a poem in the English? You cannot write poetry in English!'

'I did it to amuse myself and so that I could sing it in the market place,' and with that he began his rough version tapping out the rhythm and singing to a well-known dance tune.

> *Harken to me, my masters all,*
> *These times are ill begotten,*
> *For when a man lies dying*
> *His friends are all forgotten.*
>
> *Around his bed the black monks crowd*
> *To shrive him of his sin,*
> *He wills to them his lands, his wealth,*
> *Forgetful of his kin.*

'This is true, it is true indeed!' cried one of the squires. 'Sing on man!'

> *His sons have no inheritance,*
> *To foreign lands they journey,*
> *His daughters with their dowers bright*
> *In convents waste their beauty.*
>
> *When Church takes all, the manors fall!*
> *Old families are broken,*
> *And when the Church has taken all*
> *Their fame shall be forgotten.*

At the end of the song the young men cheered the singer, and the squire looked up at Benedict and raised his voice above the hubbub to say, 'That is my case. I have no manor and no hope of one.'

Then the solar door opened and Lord de Lacy led the way into the hall, followed by the Constable who turned his head as he walked, still in conversation with those who followed. Benedict began his game of Nine Men's Morris, but took sidelong glances at the company, expecting Sir Jocelyn to approach him and trying to ascertain his mood. But it was not his father who left the throng and came to him, it was de Lacy.

'Come, young man, let us walk in the cockpit, for I would like to hear more of your history.'

# 17

Benedict excused himself to the squire and followed the great lord out of doors, conning over the story which he and Sir Jocelyn had worked out beforehand. Yet the story of his origins was not put to the test in the way he had expected; de Lacy began instead with a story about himself.

'I asked you about York,' he began. 'I was there for the first time in my youth, in company with my father, John fitzEustace, at the time of the spring fair.'

Benedict began to feel uneasy. De Lacy continued.

'We were riding through the crush of people when we heard some oaf calling out about his boy who could calculate, and my father, who loved to find out a charlatan at his tricks, stopped to see.' He looked sideways at Benedict. 'Well, this boy was inside a poor sort of booth and a woman was putting questions to him, and he could calculate, or so it seemed. Yet my father thought that perhaps the man had trained the child to answer certain numbers by rote and, if the truth be told, there was nobody there who could have caught him out had he been wrong.'

Benedict knew now where he had seen the great lord before.

'So my father bethought himself to give the lad a try. We rode up to the place and had a look at him and, do you know, it was an extraordinary child, not like the parents in any way, no, a very fine child, and my father bid the man bring him out and then he set him such a conundrum. You would have laughed if you had heard how it went on and on, but the child answered up, quick as a flash, just as you did a while ago inside there, in the hall.'

Benedict's face turned red, he dared not look at de Lacy.

'That was seven years ago. How old are you, Master Benedict, the son of Sir Jocelyn de Birkhau?'

Benedict stopped and, turning, he looked directly at the great man.

'I was twelve then and I am almost twenty now, my lord,' he answered with great dignity.

'Good man. You are not afraid.'

De Lacy strolled on and Benedict walked beside him, and for a long time there was silence between them.

'You are married, I understand,' de Lacy said.

'Yes, that is so.'

'You are very young to be married, but do not tell me about that. What I wish to know is where you have been since that day in York, for it would be a strange thing indeed for a ragged child to find himself taken up by Sir Jocelyn and sent to Flanders, or was it France? How did this come about?'

Benedict was at a loss. If he told the truth, he would leave Sir Jocelyn looking an arrant liar, and then there was Francisca to protect. The story had been concocted for her sake as much as for anyone else's. He decided upon a bold strategy.

'May I ask you some questions, my lord?'

'Ask away young man,' de Lacy said, looking somewhat surprised.

'What is your opinion of Sir Richard Malebisse?' asked Benedict.

'What? What is all this? What has this to do with you, or York, or Flanders?'

'I am sorry to surprise you, my lord, but the answer does have a bearing on what I may or may not be able to tell you.'

'May or may not, hey!'

'I have a duty to Sir Jocelyn and to others. You would not have me dishonour promises?'

'Nay, you have a right in this. Yet the mystery teases me and I would like an answer.' He considered for a moment and said, 'Malebisse is an evil man.'

'And what do you think, my lord, of the killing of the Jews in York?'

'It was a wicked thing, an un-Christian thing to do. They wished to be converted and he sent their souls straight to Hell when they could have been saved.'

'And if I were to tell you more of myself would you do me the honour to keep it a dread secret?' asked Benedict.

De Lacy gave him a curious look. Benedict's face was now white and tense, and de Lacy must have seen that the matter was of great moment to him.

'Yes, you have my most solemn word,' he replied with great gravity.

Benedict decided to trust him. 'The very day on which you saw me at the fair, the man who was with me and who I thought at that time to be my true father, sold me to a goldsmith. After a year the goldsmith beat and kicked me until I was near to death and . . .' he hesitated. The first part of the story was easy enough to tell, but what he had to say now could cost him dearly and perhaps Francisca her life.

'But you did not die, so someone rescued you. However, I do not think it was Sir Jocelyn, not at that time. Something tells me that you have had the influence of cultivated society. Your bearing does not speak of a small manor in the hills, so who was it, young man, who saved your life?'

Still Benedict hesitated, but then he looked again at de Lacy and what he saw was a very honest look. The great lord might be severe but Benedict felt he could be trusted so, with his heart in his mouth, he replied, 'It was Josce the Jew.'

'And you lived with him for a year or so?'

'I lived with him until just before the massacre, when he sent me on a journey.'

As soon as he had said it, he realised he had made a wrong move.

'So you went on a journey to Flanders and brought back a wife with a portion which, from the manner of Sir Jocelyn's spending of late, must be large indeed. For a man who didn't have a farthing to bless himself with three months ago, his spending is prodigious. But explain to me, young man, how you left the Jew just before the riot in York and had time then to go to Flanders, become apprenticed to a merchant, woo his daughter, become so beloved of the man that he allows you to leave with a fortune, and return to England all within three months! You are not the only man hereabouts who can calculate!'

'Forgive me, my lord, if I answer no more of your questions.'

'I will forgive you if you will come to Pontefract and serve me for a year. I will keep your secret and I will give you some advice – whether or not you come with me.'

'What is that, sir?' asked Benedict.

'If your father, or should I refer to him as Sir Jocelyn? If your father has possession of the woman's marriage portion, you should take it from him before you leave his house.'

'But how can I? He has the money in a chest in his hall and he has the key. How can I ask him for the key or take it from him?'

'What does your lady say of the matter?'

'She cannot speak.'

'I hear she is not right in the head,' said de Lacy.

'That is not the case. She had a severe shock and she has not spoken since, but I think that she will do so, given time.'

'And the severe shock which was felt by this lady from France, or was it Flanders, occurred in the city of York I suppose? Another curious occurrence. But your life must have been full of these curiosities, for you have by no means told me the whole story.' His voice was stern but Benedict stole a look at him and saw that he was almost smiling. Then Benedict sighed with relief, for he knew that de Lacy would never press him for more of the story, having the gist of it already.

'Will you serve me at Chester?'

'I would do so gladly, my lord, if the Constable will allow it, but one further question from me if you please.'

'Ask away.'

'Does Sir Richard Malebisse or any of his men frequent your lordship's halls?'

'He stops at Pontefract if he is passing, as everyone does, but he is not a frequent visitor. I see the difficulty you are in. He would recognise you. Does he suspect, I wonder, that you have some of the Jew's money?' He considered for a minute or so, and then he said. 'Therefore, I shall make arrangements that you shall be warned if he or any of his people should be in the vicinity. And now another thought comes into my mind. If Malebisse is your enemy – and if he suspects you harbour the Jew's daughter and have some of the Jew's gold he will be your enemy and will seek for you – then you should remove yourself from his neighbourhood. It may be that I shall hide you in some out of the way place, my little calculator, where you can be useful and can learn to be a knight.'

'That is what my father . . .' he hesitated, 'Sir Jocelyn, hoped for me. He thinks it would be better if I were not seen until I am older and that these people would not recognise me then.'

'It may be so and yet I recognised you. Now, whilst I think of it, there is one thing which I must command and that is that you will leave your lady at home in Birkdale. I can hide one tender child who has escaped the wrath of God, but I fear I may not be able to hide two.'

Benedict hesitated before he said, 'I will leave my lady at home.'

# 18

Well might Benedict have hesitated. So elated had he been by the connection he had made with de Lacy and his new feeling of independence from Sir Jocelyn, that the problems of leaving Francisca at home had not been uppermost in his mind. Now they reasserted themselves as the most urgent priority. How could he bear to leave her?

As he rode home, Benedict reflected on what he had heard at Richmond. Certain it was that the Knight had nothing to lose by Francisca's death and everything to gain.

The Knight's moods were changeable and Benedict now saw more significance in Sir Jocelyn's behaviour. Although he treated Francisca with a reasonable degree of courtesy on those rare occasions on which he had anything at all to say to her, for the most part he ignored her. That in itself caused no alarm, but there were times when he would sit and glare at her as though she were his worst enemy. Benedict had challenged Sir Jocelyn about his surly manner but the Knight had merely laughed and chided him for imagining he had seen him frown. But the servants had been watching and had become increasingly suspicious of their master. Apart from Isabelle's warning, which Benedict had at the time dismissed, Sirich had said only the previous week that the Knight would be glad, now that her marriage portion was secure, if Francisca died in childbed.

Benedict had observed that Francisca avoided the old Knight's company, difficult though that was in a small manor of only two rooms. Perhaps she, too, had become suspicious of his intentions and Benedict regretted that she could not tell him all she felt. Only the previous week, while they were sitting at dinner, Benedict had witnessed the Knight's unfriendly behaviour and, swiftly rising from his place, went round to where Francisca was sitting, placing his hands on her shoulders and looking Sir Jocelyn in the eye. He remembered now how thin her shoulders were and how fragile and vulnerable she had seemed. He had faced the Knight boldly until he had put the old man out of countenance. Sir Jocelyn had glanced away towards the fireplace, then down at his plate. There was silence in the room until the Knight suddenly laughed to himself and, carefully avoiding any contact with their eyes, had resumed his meal. Only then had Benedict returned to his own seat.

If he were to serve de Lacy, thought Benedict, he would give orders for a bower to be built for Francisca. It could be done without altering the interior of the hall, for they badly needed a dairy. The two end walls of the manor faced west and east. The hall window faced south. The dairy could be built on the north side of the hall, which was close under the hill, and the bower could be built above it with its own internal stair at the west end of the hall. Francisca could retire there during the day and, while the dairy could have its door facing northwards into the curve of the hillside, the upper chamber could have westward and eastward-facing windows to catch the sun at morning and afternoon. The window slits could be narrow so that no enemy could gain access there. The idea had occurred to him when they had first come to Birkhau, and a private retiring room was now a necessity. The urgency was such that Benedict determined to dig up some of the reserve of silver coins for this purpose.

But would she be even more vulnerable in a private room? Isabelle was often about the garden enclosure, gathering herbs or attending to her beehives. At such a time, with the menservants about the fields or working in the yard, Francisca could find herself alone with Sir Jocelyn.

When the servants had first mentioned their fears, Benedict had replied, 'Then you must watch carefully. Never leave the food which Francisca eats where it can be tampered with between the fire and the table.'

Isabelle had replied: 'I already do that, but suppose I were ill, or should die?'

Benedict had scoffed at her fancies for he didn't wish her to know that her words had left him ill at ease.

It occurred to him then that the safest place of all for Francisca would be with their neighbours at Hopestones. The little manor stood a mile or so up the valley from Birkhau and Sir Philip and Dame Beatrice had proved kindly in their attentions to the young couple. But upon what excuse could she be left with them? She had her own serving woman and two devoted menservants, so that there was no excuse which Benedict could give without accusing Sir Jocelyn of evil intent.

Suddenly, he had a vision of the pale and distraught face of the girl at Lincoln. Had it been his sister Alyce? Perhaps it was the contrast between her plight and the pleasant life in Birkdale which brought Alyce to mind. He had been troubled ever since that day, and he determined there and then that before he rode off in the service of de Lacy he would return to Lincoln and discover once and for all if the girl had been his sister. If she were indeed a leper, then he would leave money for her. If she were not? Ah then, what could he do? Sir Jocelyn would not be pleased, of that there could be no doubt, and if Benedict acknowledged her as his sister then Sir Jocelyn would have to include her among his bastard children. The thought brought a broad grin to Benedict's face and he straightened his shoulders. If he found Alyce, he would bring her home and defy Sir Jocelyn. She could be the one who would help to guard Francisca.

How happy he would be to have his beloved sister in his care. He thought of the happy times they would have, walking up to the rocks on the hillock, sitting beside the stream or under the apple trees. Then he remembered that he had promised to serve de Lacy and he realised with a pang how he was going to miss Francisca.

His mind was awhirl with both pleasure and pain. He had failed to acknowledge to himself that his promise to de Lacy meant an absence of months, perhaps a year! How he would miss the pleasure of watching her, the delight of lying with her, warm and yielding in his arms at night. Now the prospect of months of days and nights without seeing or touching her threw him into a mood of deep despondency. It was customary, he knew, for young men of good family to seek their fortunes far from home, particularly when their wives had conceived, but how many left a wife as vulnerable as Francisca? Other ladies had kin to whom they could turn in time of trouble.

He had remained for three days at Richmond discussing his future with de Lacy and Sir Jocelyn had ridden off the day before, though where and on what business he had not disclosed. The thought that the Knight might be at Birkhau before him made Benedict urge his horse into a fast canter over the moorland.

He slowed his horse, for he was approaching the lip of the valley. His thoughts returned to Alyce. How happy everyone would be when he brought her home; how they would welcome her! Isabelle would be like a mother to her. But he stopped his horse and sat for a moment quite still, for he had realised that nobody at Birkhau had ever known Alyce. She would be a complete stranger to them and would they love her? He could think only with pain of the life his sister must have lived since their parting. She had been nine years at the time and now she was a woman. Had she been sold into prostitution and, if she had, did she have a child somewhere? If she had a child, he would bring it home as well.

His thoughts returned to Francisca. She had been brought up like any lady in an aristocratic household and might not wish to acknowledge as a sister someone whose manners and speech might be crude. Surely she would be kind to Alyce?

Now the shadows were long across the hills before him and he turned towards his home. Should he tell the family about his promise to de Lacy as soon as he arrived, or should he delay the news? He would like to speak privately first with Francisca, but he knew how the servants would clamour for a description of Richmond and his adventures there.

He lifted his head to look about him. The usual bleating of sheep was intensified at this season, for all along the dale there were pens full of newly shorn sheep waiting with their lambs. He looked eastward down the valley and, with a feeling of pride, picked out some of his own sheep pens. Soon the lambs and ewes would be put into newly mown hayfields to eat the first flush of new grass – 'mist' the dalesmen called it. That would provide the sheep with a tasty bite before they were turned again on to moss and moor to seek their food where they could. On the opposite hillside he could see two brothers carting the last of the hay into their stackyard and, far off though they were, he recognised them. They were Swain and Erik, the one with a curious straddling walk, the other always with his head slightly to one side.

Benedict felt a swell of affection for this land and its people. He delighted in the vantage points from which it was possible to see what was going on everywhere. Down in the Vale of York, or on the low-lying land of Holderness where he had been born, a man's view was restricted by the nearest hedge, whilst here, from every hillside, a man could look into a village or farmyard and know exactly how the work of the season was progressing. The hay at Birkhau had all been won two weeks ago. The day before Benedict left for Richmond Sirich had thatched every stack but one, secure in the knowledge that neighbours would see and say to each other, 'We must get on and finish, Sirich has finished his stacking!'

But now he turned his gaze westward, and higher up the dale he could see the soft greeny-brown of hay fields where the grass was still standing. He looked up at the sky. Would the good weather last? Up and down the valley floor were squares and strips of oats and barley, some of them showing signs of approaching ripeness. He felt a pang of anxiety for his neighbours at the head of the valley, for if rain set in between haytime and harvest the work of one season might run into the next and all could be lost. Harvest demanded labour from every man and woman, and from every child old enough to walk. There was no time then for catching up on the hay. Grain was needed to feed men, oat straw and hay to feed cattle and horses. Both crops were essential.

For the labourers at Birkhau whose work was well in hand, there would be a brief respite until the grain was fully ripe, and the men would be looking around for all the small tasks which could be accomplished before the demands of the next great onslaught. Up and down the dale, every man, woman and child shared the same anxiety; would the weather hold until harvest time and, if it did, would it then break just as the grain was ready? These had been the concerns of the husbandman since time immemorial and Benedict felt a comradeship with his neighbours, was glad that these were now his concerns and that he was going home to his manor, his household, his wife . . .

He smiled to himself. He would soon be in bed with his lovely Francisca, warm, soft, gentle Francisca. Perhaps next year they would have a child, a boy. He felt warm with pleasure and pride at the very thought of the child. Then it occurred to him that they might have several children and he laughed aloud.

As his horse plunged into the tree-filled cleft which led down to the valley bottom, the evening bells began to ring from the church of Middlestead high up the valley. They were more musical, but they chimed in with the toneless clatter of the sheep-bells. He could still hear them as his horse sank over its fetlocks in the deep leaf-mould and the spicy smell of it rose about him. The trees closed above his head for a while until, emerging from the darkness of the little dell, he turned his horse eastwards on to the sandy track which lead along the valley bottom and proceeded gently downhill, first to Hopestones, then to Birkhau. Some of Sir Philip's men had left the sheepfolds and were wading across the stream. Soon they would be at rest, or tending their own little plots. One called a greeting, and the sound of activity outside brought the household crowding to the door.

'How did you fare at Richmond, Master Benedict?' cried Sir Philip from the steps.

'Very well. Come down to supper tomorrow and I will tell you my adventures.' Benedict's spirits lifted at the very sight of his friends.

'Come in, come in,' cried Dame Beatrice, peering over her husband's shoulder from the doorway.

Sir Philip turned to her, 'Nay woman, he wishes to get home as soon as he can. He has a sweet wife awaiting him. Let him go now, we can contain our curiosity until later.' Then, raising his voice to address Benedict, 'Your invitation is for my lady as well?'

'Of course, you must both come, for Francisca will be glad to see you and by then I shall no doubt have remembered things I shall forget to tell this evening.'

He waved his hand again to them as he rode on.

Below him, he could see Thurstan walking towards Birkhau, carrying a scythe over his shoulder. But Benedict did not hail him, for he was pondering on Thurstan's loyalty. Only when the horse's shoe struck a stone did Thurstan turn, shading his eyes against the setting sun to see who rode behind him. Benedict waved a hand but continued at a walking pace, for the sight of the once trusted servant had set him wondering again about Thurstan's visit to Lincoln.

163

At the high table in Richmond Castle, he had heard for the first time that some Jews had survived and again he pondered on the strength of Lincoln Castle and on the strange tale which Thurstan had told, of delay after delay in getting there, and of no survivors at all. Was there some threat which the Knight held over him? Had Thurstan been told to stay away from Lincoln? Then, Thurstan had said he had not encountered Sir Jocelyn in York on the return journey, but something the Knight had said one day made Benedict suspect that they had indeed met on Thurstan's return. Thurstan's 'return', thought Benedict. Had he even been to Lincoln? In no respect had Thurstan shown any diminution in his love of either Benedict or Francisca, and he certainly seemed to harbour no love for the Knight, yet Benedict could never think of the day of Thurstan's return without being overcome by a feeling of unease.

'How went it?' Thurstan asked eagerly. He patted the animal's neck and the horse rubbed its forehead vigorously against the big man's shoulder, pushing him backwards a pace or two.

'It went well, better than I could have imagined,' Benedict replied.

'And what of Sir Jocelyn, where is he?' asked Thurstan.

'Ah, he has not returned to Birkhau! Then he must be off again on some secret errand. Let us hope that he does not hasten back,' said Benedict with a rueful grin.

'Will you tell me now?' asked Thurstan. 'Or will you save the whole story for the fireside?'

'For the fireside!' Benedict replied. 'Tell me about the demesne land and what you think of the prospects for wheat and oats and barley.'

'We've had the finest of weather since you left with never a drop of rain, although on Tuesday it threatened and it was sileing, I heard, on the far fields of the grange and on all the land at the head of the valley.'

'Aye, I saw some hay not yet cut. Let us pray there will be fine weather for all of us until the end of August. What of the orchard and of the nuts in the hazel coppice?'

'Oh, they are plumping up nicely, and of apples and pears I have not seen promise of so good a crop for some years. The graft you got of the Blaundrelle has taken and will bear three apples in its first season, as good as any I ever beheld. The Bur Knot will crop well and of the Costards, by My Lady, the branches are already covered with buds.'

'Lord de Lacy wishes me to go down to his manor of Woebly, it lies in Herefordshire. Have you ever heard of that?' Benedict asked.

'Herefordshire.' Thurstan sounded surprised and, as he spoke, Benedict regretted that he had mentioned the subject of his journey for he had intended speaking first to Francisca. 'No,' Thurstan mused, 'it must be a long way from here. Is that the new Baron fitzEustace's son, who takes the name of Lacy from his great grandsire?'

'Yes that is he,' Benedict replied. He saw Thurstan begin to frame another question and interrupted him by saying, 'I was thinking that perhaps I could get some imps of fruit and other trees whilst I am there, for it must be a rich county. Could we extend the impgarth further up the hill do you think?'

'Perhaps we could – should we do some digging do you think, to see what depth of soil there is? But then, would it not be wiser to make another garth, well sheltered within a coppice clearing?'

'I am jealous of the coppices, for the hazel is so profitable and I dare not sacrifice any arable field space, we have little enough of level land,' Benedict replied. 'If we make a new impgarth we can protect the young slips of trees from the deer with a wall of six feet or so. When the trees are big enough to transplant we can always reduce the height of the wall and turn the place into a paddock. I have always had a mind to breed horses.'

'It is a good thing to have an eye always to improvements,' said Thurstan, with satisfaction. 'But if you bring grafts of fruits from so far south, will they ripen here?'

'On that we would have to take our chance, or offer prayers for our trees,' Benedict replied, glancing ahead at the manor as he spoke.

'How long are you to stay at this place in Herefordshire?' Thurstan asked next.

'I will tell my adventures to the whole household after we have dined,' Benedict replied and swung himself from the saddle, for they had arrived at the foot of the stone steps.

The door above them opened and Sirich hurried to take charge of Benedict's horse. Behind him, Isabelle and the servant boy appeared in the doorway, and Isabelle turned to call to Francisca.

Benedict bounded up the steps and grasped Isabelle by both plump elbows, kissing her soft, downy cheek as he squeezed past her through the doorway and almost bowling the boy over in his eagerness to enter the hall. And there was Francisca, crossing the floor to meet him. She looked so like her mother that he stopped, amazed. Benedict saw Hannah now, as she had approached in her pink gown on that first evening on which he had entered the Coney Street house. Francisca's face, since the massacre at York and her long illness, had lost the softness of childhood and Benedict had not realised until that moment how much she resembled her mother. She blushed as he came forward to embrace her and he took her to the settle and sat her down, bending to look closely into her face and ask after her health. She smiled and nodded, and he wondered again not only how he could leave her behind but how the subject of leaving could ever be broached. 'Come up to the sleeping loft,' he said, taking both her hands in his and leading her to the foot of the ladder. He climbed first, turning to see how she followed him and catching a glimpse of Isabelle's upturned, smiling face as she arrived at the fire with two capons for the spit.

Benedict held Francisca against him for a few moments, stroking her hair, before he sat her beside him on the edge of the bed. He pushed her gently until she lay on the coverlet and then he kissed her mouth and stroked the delicate line of her jaw. He lay beside her for a while, not speaking, just contented by her presence, and it was some time before he sat up and, with eyes sparkling, eagerly began his story.

'I had a great adventure. The Lord de Lacy wishes me to serve him and the Constable of Richmond made no objection. To have a friend as powerful as de Lacy would be of great benefit to us in the future and the Constable seemed to wish me well.' It was dark in the sleeping loft and he could see only the pale oval of her face. What did she think? 'He wishes me to go to one of his manors for a time,' he added hesitantly, looking closely at her all the while but unable in the dark of the loft to see her reaction. She sat up and, taking one of his hands in hers, she placed it against her stomach. She held it close against the gentle curve and he answered by increasing the pressure of his other arm around her shoulders. They were perfectly still for a while, and then he realised that she had never made this gesture before and in an instant he knew that she was indicating that she was with child.

'Francisca, Francisca, is it true? Is it a child?' he asked.

He could tell she nodded in the dark and she pressed his hand more firmly against the place where the child lay and laid her head upon his shoulder. 'Oh, Francisca, I am so happy!' He was silent for a while and then he said more solemnly, 'This means a grandson of Josce's. He and Hannah live in you and will live again in this child. I am so happy, Francisca, so happy.' And he laid his head upon her shoulder and wept for joy. Then she held him in her arms like a baby, rocking him to and fro, but after a while he stirred and sat upright, for the matter of his proposed absence now assumed another dimension. She was more vulnerable than before, and the child! It must be protected. How could he go to Herefordshire at this time?

'Before we go down I must tell you something else,' he said quietly. 'You remember that on the journey to Lincoln I saw a girl who was in the care of the hospital there?' Francisca nodded. 'It might have been my sister, Alyce. She might be a leper, but if she is not I must fetch her home. Would you welcome her, Francisca?'

Francisca threw her arms about him and held him very tightly. She raised her face and brushed her cheek against his. She kissed his forehead and then his mouth, tenderly at first, and then with passion.

'Oh Francisca, how I love you,' he said.

'The dinner will go cold,' Isabelle called. The lovers were still, listening, and then Benedict felt Francisca shake a little and there was the tiniest of laughs in the dark. Then he laughed and raised Francisca to her feet, and they went together, down into the hall.

Isabelle was beaming with pleasure when they turned to face the company at the foot of the ladder and Benedict knew that she must know about the child. They took their places, Benedict sitting in the carved chair at the head of the table which Sir Jocelyn usually occupied and feeling for the first time that he sat there as master of the house. He felt a glow of importance and pride which had nothing to do with his acceptance by the great men he had met at Richmond and he could scarcely keep his eyes from Francisca.

At the end of the meal Thurstan ventured to ask Benedict to relate his adventures, but before he began Benedict dismissed the boy to his own home in the village, for what he had to say concerned only the immediate household and must be discussed before Sir Jocelyn returned.

'You have, I know, been suspicious of Sir Jocelyn and fearful for Francisca's safety,' he began, glancing all round the table as he spoke. Sirich rose and bolted the door. 'I do not wish to alarm Francisca, particularly at a time like this, but my own suspicions of the Knight's purpose have been aroused by what I have heard at Richmond.'

He told them what the soldier had said, adding 'The man may, of course, have misconstrued the conversation.'

Isabelle had placed herself beside Francisca on the bench and had put her arm about the girl.

'I have been puzzled as to what should be done,' Benedict continued and he paused then, wondering whether to say anything about his proposed trip to Herefordshire, when Thurstan broke in.

'We will protect her, never fear. No drop of drink and no morsel of food shall pass her lips but one of us will taste it first. She shall not be left alone, no, not for a minute.'

Benedict looked at Francisca, who had grown pale. 'Suppose I had to go away for a while, could you really protect Francisca for every minute of the day and night?'

'Why should we not be able?' Sirich asked.

Francisca had buried her face in Isabelle's shoulder.

'Suppose Sir Jocelyn should send you all away,' Benedict asked, rising as he did so and placing himself on the bench at Francisca's right hand. 'How could you refuse him?' As he waited for the answer, he put his arm around Francisca's shoulders so that she was held fast between him and Isabelle.

'If that were to happen,' said Isabelle, 'we would fetch Sir Philip right away, without any delay. I was up at Hopestones the other day talking to Dame Beatrice, and it is my opinion that she also has her suspicions of Sir Jocelyn. She said to me that he did not treat his own lady well and, though he always speaks with such pride of his son, there was something Sir Philip said which made me think that the poor lad was happier when he was with them, God rest his soul.'

'If that is the case then I will tell you the rest of my news,' said Benedict. Francisca had laid her head on his shoulder and he held her tightly.

'I have already told Francisca that the Lord de Lacy, Constable of Chester and now lord of Pontefract with all its great lands, wishes to be my sponsor. He knows, of my origins and also, and again I feel sure of this without his having said anything, he has realised Francisca is Josce's daughter.'

There was a gasp of shocked surprise from Isabelle.

'He knows my skill in calculating for he recognised me. He had seen me at the Lenten Fair in York on the day on which I was sold to the goldsmith. He knew me and when he had talked with me he wished for my services. However, he knows that I must keep away from Malebisse or any who would recognise me and he wishes to send me to Herefordshire.'

'Wherever is that?' asked Isabelle in alarm. 'Is it in Christendom?'

'Somewhere down in the south-west,' Sirich answered, eager to show his knowledge of the country. 'It is near the country of the Welsh.'

Isabelle crossed herself.

'There he has four manors,' Benedict continued, 'one of which is in the keeping of a dishonest steward. What he wants of me is that I should go there on some pretext and see how the man is defrauding him. I must report to de Lacy and he wishes that I then become steward in the man's stead for one year. After that time I shall be able to make it known to de Lacy how much stock the place will carry and what weight of corn and hay the land should produce.'

'But how can you assess that in one year?' asked Thurstan.

'It will not be too difficult with the help of the advices which I have written down. Josce saw how I was interested in the management of land,' and there he stopped, for at the mention of her father's name Francisca rubbed her face against his shoulder to brush away a tear. 'Yes, my love, I know.' There was a pause before he went on. 'He advised me always to ask questions and to make notes of land measurements and quantities of produce. This I did on every journey, for I had thought that Josce might take the management of a mortgaged farm into his own hands at some time and then my knowledge would have been useful.'

Isabelle crossed herself, as she always did when the dead were mentioned.

'I took his advice and I have the notes with me still,' Benedict continued. 'I have noted and written down how much fodder is needed by both horses and oxen, what yields of grain should be got from each acre, and what level of stock can be kept on different kinds of land. The figures must be used judiciously, for the land may be light or heavy or sick for some reason, as it is here in the hills wherever lead is found. Then the condition of the season must be taken into account, if the rain be light or heavy and how much the sun shines. I must allow for these things, but with the notes I have and the good practice of husbandry which I have learned from Thurstan and Sirich, I should make a fair steward.'

'You would, to be sure, and you have the accounting skills,' said Sirich. 'Would that I could go with you, for I would dearly love to see the rich land of the country of Hereford.'

'But you must stay, all of you. Francisca's safety is to be your chief concern from now on. I would take her with me but de Lacy is adamant that I must go alone. I know, without his having to say so, that he fears Francisca would be noticed and denounced if she were taken away from the safety of this place.'

'I have a duty to perform, however, before I leave to serve de Lacy and that is to seek my sister. She may be the girl I saw as we passed through Lincoln and I cannot rest until I know. If she is Alyce then I must bring her home to Birkhau.'

'Indeed you must,' said Isabelle. 'Why did you not tell us before this? Poor child, poor little waif,' and Isabelle wiped away a tear.

'We were in such trouble, Isabelle, we could not go back through Lincoln at that time,' Benedict objected.

'You are right, but now is the time to make amends. Go and fetch her home,' said Thurstan and Benedict's heart warmed to him as it had in the old days.

They heard a horse approaching at a canter and Sir Jocelyn's voice called for Sirich to mind his horse.

'He canters up to the door and I shall be all evening long trying to get that animal dry. Can he not walk the last mile home?' grumbled Sirich as he rose to go down.

Benedict remembered then what de Lacy had said about his being firm with the Knight over the marriage portion. Now, with the prospect of a long period away from home, it was time to deal with this matter. When Sir Jocelyn had finished his meal he broached the subject.

'As I shall be away for so long, it is time that my wife had charge of her marriage portion.' The Knight began to go red in the face. 'I wish her to have her money in a chest in her sleeping place and to keep the key.'

'And what shall I do for money? I clothe and feed you all. Do I not have a right to order the money and the purchase of what is required?' The old Knight was furious but Benedict no longer felt afraid of him.

'You shall have a share of money for your own use, but do not forget that before we came here you had no money, none at all. You shall have a share, as I said, but when you have spent it all, you must ask Francisca for more and I am sure she will allow you what you need.'

Sir Jocelyn rose from his chair. Benedict glanced at his face, and thought the Knight would have a fit, but slowly he gained control of himself and sat down again. Benedict realised then how easy it would have been to manage the matter before and he swore that he would never allow such a situation to arise again.

# 19

Benedict repeated the journey by boat down to Torksey and he rode across to Lincoln as he had done before, alone this time except for Jet, and on the road he spoke to the horse as though it would understand.

'Will we find her, do you think, eh Jet? Will she come with us?' He ran his hand down the crest of the horse's neck and patted the glossy shoulder. 'Shall we take her home with us, Jet, home to Birkhau?'

With trepidation, he approached the little hospital on its grassy mound, half expecting the girl to appear again, just as she had before, but there was nobody about. He knocked at the door, which was opened after an interval by a young monk.

'I passed by here, during Lent, and there was a young woman here then, her name is Alyce. Is she here yet?'

'We have no Alyce, but I will ask Bertrand who has been here for some time now.'

The monk disappeared inside, leaving the door partly open behind him. It swung wider so that Benedict could see the interior. There was a central hearth, and some benches. A child crawled towards him over the beaten earth of the floor and a man appeared, picked the child up and looked curiously at the doorway. Just then the monk returned, leading a blind man by the hand.

'Bertrand says there was a girl called Alyce. She was stolen away and I remember hearing the story before I left the abbey. A squire who rode by in the company of crusaders saw her, just there at the foot of the path. He lifted her onto his horse and carried her off. There was no one here who could help.'

'Did she go willingly?' Benedict asked, his voice gruff with emotion.

'No, my lord,' said the blind man in a quavering voice. 'She cried out for help and the riders were laughing. There was nothing we poor creatures could do.'

'What was her history?' Benedict asked.

'She said she had a brother who would rescue her one day. She had been sold into prostitution when she was yet a child. These things happen sometimes, my lord,' the old man said, and the tone of his voice was meant to comfort Benedict and apologise for the sad state of the world.

'Does anybody know who it was who took her,' asked Benedict, 'and where she was taken?'

'There was one here who had been in the service of de Tanquerville and he recognised the badge of one of them. The name was Mala – Mala – Malebisse, that was the name!'

Benedict's face flushed crimson. 'Was it this Malebisse who took my sister?'

'No, but one of the company wore his badge of the fox's head,' said the old man.

Just then there was the sound of hoofbeats along the road, and a squire came up on a little brown horse. The monk called out to him. 'Geoffrey, do you remember that a girl was stolen from here?'

'Aye, I remember,' said the youth, stopping his horse sharply, so that it danced about on the road with impatience. The youth looked up at them.

The monk turned to Benedict, 'This is my brother, Geoffrey,' then to the horseman he said, 'And who was it who captured the girl? Do you remember his name and where they said he came from?'

'Oh, there was plenty of talk about it at the time,' the horseman replied. 'I am not sure of his name, Stutville perhaps, something of the sort, and his hall is at Riccal, on the Ouse.'

'But I passed it on the way down here. Oh, what a weary journey, and I could have . . .' But here Benedict stopped, for he would have discovered nothing if he had not come to Lincoln. 'I thank you. I shall go in search of her, and will you accept alms from me, brother monk?'

'You are kind and I wish you well, but take care for yourself. If this man still has her, he will not let her go easily.'

'An adventure!' cried Geoffrey, jumping from his horse and leading it up the path to the door. 'Do you want a companion, my friend?' Benedict was startled. The affair did not concern this Geoffrey.

'I see you are surprised,' said the monk. 'My brother is always looking for adventure and his ideal of courtly love is the rescue of maidens who fall into the hands of evil men.' The monk's eyes were smiling as he spoke, but he managed at the same time to preserve a reproachful look.

'My brother is right,' agreed Geoffrey. 'I seek always for adventure and take it whenever I have the chance. The knight I serve does not share my love of valour and prefers to sit by the fire. My last adventure did not please him and so you see me now, a free-lance, left to wander at will and very short of money!'

'So you would go with me? I must warn you that I am not a rich man,' said Benedict.

'I do not look for a fee,' said Geoffrey. 'A bed at nights and food during the day will content me. Your name, sir?'

'Benedict de Birkhau, the son of Sir Jocelyn de Birkhau,' Benedict replied. 'I am shortly to enter the service of Roger de Lacy.'

'I am honoured to meet you,' returned Geoffrey. 'My father holds a manor in Derbyshire.'

'I know no one in that country,' Benedict replied.

'It is a fine, rocky, mountainous . . .' began the squire.

'Barren, cold and wet country,' his brother the monk added.

'Then come with me,' said Benedict, 'I shall be glad of your company if you do not mind the risk you take in this venture where there is little to be gained.'

Without any more introduction than that, the two young men turned their horses for the north, taking ship at Torksey. As they sailed, Benedict told Geoffrey some of his story and of their escape from the boatmen.

'Where is the inn where you escaped?' Geoffrey asked.

'A little further I think, perhaps round the next bend,' Benedict replied, and there it was, just as he remembered it. He shuddered, not at the memory of the escape from the boat, but at the thought of the events in York which had followed so closely. This time they sailed on into the town of Selby and took to the saddle again after a meal of leg of mutton with onions and beans.

They asked the way to Riccal and made further enquiries about the people there.

Benedict stopped a traveller. 'Is it true,' he asked, 'that Stutville has a mistress, a woman with golden hair?'

'Aye, he keeps some whore,' the man replied and Benedict had to force himself to remain silent. 'But he keeps her well away from the village, in a house in the woods to the west of the place. I should think he is ashamed. His wife is a fine lady who brought him a good portion and he keeps her shut up in Riccal so that she is a poor, plaintive creature.'

Benedict's heart leaped at the news. So, Alyce might be rescued after all! He had feared she would be surrounded by a multitude of people, but a house in a wood sounded much easier of access.

'Well now, that was interesting,' said Geoffrey when the man had trudged away down the road.

'Yes, we might be lucky. Shall we stay at an inn, if there is one, and ride about to view the district before we make a move?' Benedict asked.

'That sounds as good a plan as ever I heard,' Geoffrey replied.

The inn they found was in the village of Riccal, and a poor place, so that the people there asked why they did not seek hospitality at the hall. The two protested that they were perfectly pleased with the inn and too tired to move another yard. They made themselves agreeable to the company, dull though it was, and spent their time in singing and storytelling, though never revealing their names. Very early next morning they left, saying that they were heading east for Garton in the wolds and as soon as they were out of sight, turning west, they made for a large area of woodland which lay on the horizon.

A few peasants were about in the fields, but they met no one on the track. The path led them to the edge of a large clearing. There were haphazard patches of vegetables here and there, some poor huts and a wooden house. Sounds of someone chopping wood came from among the trees beyond and, from the house itself, the sound of a woman scolding. Whoever it was, Benedict knew it wasn't Alyce. He dropped to the ground and gave his reins to Geoffrey signing to him to ride away a little distance. Then he strode over towards the house.

'Hey there! Is there anybody there?' he called.

The figure of a woman filled the door. Stooping under the lintel, she emerged rubbing her hands on her drab apron. When she stood upright on the path outside, Benedict saw she was a woman of about forty years of age, missing most of her teeth and with scrawny hair escaping from her cap in all directions.

'What do you want, master?' she asked suspiciously.

'Do you have clear water? I would like a drink,' Benedict replied.

'Sit down there,' she said, indicating a log at a little distance from the house. Benedict sat down on it, looking round about as much as he could without appearing to be curious. The sound of axe on wood still came to him through the trees.

'Is it your man who is chopping wood?' he asked as she brought him a skin bag filled with water.

'My man! Nay, but what business is it of yours?' she asked.

'I thought your man must be a charcoal burner, or a woodward, or some such,' Benedict replied. A child crawled out of the hut and sat upright with one leg tucked under it. 'Is this your child?' he asked.

'Nay, it is one of his bastards. Get back inside you little brat!' she called, and the infant scrambled away into the dark interior.

'Whose child did you say?' Benedict asked and put his mouth to the flask immediately, so as to seem not very interested.

'Someone, you would not know him, and now he has left a whore of his here, though he leaves a penny every week for her food.'

'The water is good,' said Benedict. 'I have tied my horse up over there,' and he pointed in the direction in which Geoffrey had gone. 'Is there a spring nearby so that I can give the beast a drink?'

'Do you have a penny for me, sir?' she asked.

Benedict took a groat from his purse and offered it. She looked at it disdainfully, but took it readily enough.

'There is a spring in the woods over there,' she said, pointing a little distance away from the place from which the chopping sound came.

Benedict made himself walk slowly back to the horses. 'Geoffrey, I think I may have found her, but we must go carefully. Skirt round the clearing and meet me over there,' Benedict indicated the place where the woman had pointed. 'There is supposed to be a spring there. Wait for me.'

With that he took Jet's reins and led him across the clearing. The woman came to her door. 'Do you have another groat? I need a new dress. A penny would be better,' she called.

'I'll give my horse a drink and I may ride back this way,'

Benedict entered the wood, but the sound of chopping had stopped and he feared that he might be too late. Then there came the sound of thick twigs being snapped, so whoever it was was still busy. He made sure he was well out of sight of the house, when he veered away to the right and made for the sounds.

There, in front of him, was Alyce. He was sure of it now, quite sure. She looked up suddenly. She was holding a stick by the ends, her hands about two feet apart, and she had raised one knee over which to break the stick. She stopped and stood quite still, staring at him in disbelief.

'Alyce, Alyce. It is me, Benedict. I have come to take you home,' he said quietly.

She dropped the stick and ran to him silently. She threw her arms around his neck.

'I knew you would come back, I knew, but I thought you would never find me. Oh, Benedict my brother, at last.'

'Speak quietly, I have a companion and we must go to him now,' said Benedict, leading her away towards the spring.

'Geoffrey, this is my sister,' said Benedict, his voice full and rich with happiness and excitement.

'Now,' he said to her. 'Will you ride pillion behind me? Can you hold on tightly, for we had better hurry away from here.'

'Oh my brother, I will hold on never fear,' she replied, and a smile of pure happiness lit her face.

'Westward, and then towards Cawood. We'll cross the river there!'

The three made the best speed they could and reached the river crossing before noon. The river was low and the horses waded across.

Then on they sped, along the banks of the Wharfe to Ulleskelf and thence to Wetherby. The vale gave way to low hills and Benedict breathed a sigh of relief, for they were almost in his own country again.

There was a clothier in the street of Wetherby, and from him Benedict bought a green wool dress for Alyce. They stopped among the trees of a well-grown coppice so that she could shed the drab, brown dress she wore, and she emerged from among the hazels, pushing back her golden hair with both hands, and radiant with happiness. Then she frowned a little and approaching Benedict, she put her hand on his shoulder. 'Who lives at your house? Will they love me do you think?' she asked.

'Who could fail to love you?' Benedict replied. 'There is my wife, Francisca, and Isabelle her serving woman, and Isabelle's two brothers and,' here Benedict hesitated. Alyce was looking doubtful again. 'There is Sir Jocelyn, who claims me as his son.'

'I am afraid,' she said.

'Let us ride on and find some shelter and food,' said Geoffrey. 'We are hungry and tired and it is surely safe to rest now that we have come so far.'

There was a little inn at Pannal where they sat outside in the sun, eating bread and cheese and drinking cider. They spoke quietly among themselves.

'My fortunes have changed,' said Benedict. Then he glanced quickly at Geoffrey, who said, 'If you wish to be private, I will take my bread into the glade over by the stream.'

Benedict felt ungracious. Geoffrey had come with him willingly, but the matters he had to speak of could bring trouble to his beloved Francisca. 'I do not wish to be discourteous,' he replied, 'but my history is a strange one.'

'Say nothing. I understand and will leave you with your sister,' and with that, Geoffrey walked off, leaving them alone.

'Where did you go after Lincoln?' she asked.

'To York, where I was almost killed, but of that I will speak later. The important thing is to tell you about Josce the Jew who rescued me. He and all his people were killed, except for his daughter – and perhaps his son, who knows?'

'His daughter?' asked Alyce.

'She is now my wife and you must be most careful, sister, never to give her away. If it were known that she is a Jew, what do you think might befall her?'

Alyce threw her arm about her brother. 'I will serve you always and love your wife for your sake.'

'You must love her for her own sake. She is beautiful, but she saw the end, the murder of her people on the steps of the castle. Since that time she has not spoken. However, this misfortune has proved her salvation.'

'How is that?' asked Alyce.

'She is taken for a Christian. No one bothers her, do you understand?'

'Yes, I can see how it must be, but who is this knight, Sir Jocelyn?'

At that moment Geoffrey came racing out of the bushes. 'Get the black horse and hide in the glade. Quickly, man, there are horsemen coming at a gallop.'

'Go!' said Benedict, pushing Alyce in the direction of the stream. He dashed behind the inn, unfastened Jet, and ran with the horse, catching Alyce by the hand as he caught up with her and racing into the shelter of the thicket.

Geoffrey stood before the inn, a piece of bread in his hand as four horsemen galloped up and slithered to a halt.

'Have you seen a man on a black horse with a woman dressed in brown?' the first horseman gasped.

'No. There hasn't been a soul who has passed here since I arrived,' Geoffrey replied and took a bite of the bread. 'But when I was at Cawood I saw a man on a black horse. He was leading it. I think it had cast a shoe and he had a woman with him. She was following some yards behind.'

'How long ago was that?'

'A couple of hours or so I would guess,' Geoffrey replied, taking another bite.

'Go back. Go back to Cawood and we will begin again there.' The man spun his horse round and seemed about to put spurs to it when he hauled on the reins and said, 'A black horse came this way, a cottager told us he had seen one.'

'I have not seen such a horse,' Geoffrey replied, putting the last of the bread into his mouth and affecting a lack of interest in the matter. The horseman gave a frown and let his restive horse have its head.

Geoffrey untied his little brown horse, mounted and rode down to the stream. 'Come, let us get away from here. Others on the road behind have seen us.'

Benedict mounted. He removed his foot from the stirrup and Alyce used it to climb up behind him. 'Hold on!' he cried, and they set off for the western hills.

They stayed the night at Fountains, though Benedict would have liked to go straight home. He needed time to tell Alyce more about the manor and particularly about Sir Jocelyn. 'If he will not allow you to stay with us, then I am sure Sir Philip and his wife at Hopestones would look after you.'

'But they would have to feed me. Are they rich?'

'No, but I am rich and I will see that you lack for nothing,' Benedict replied.

She wept at that. 'Oh, Benedict. I thought I would never see you again. I told the people at the hospital that my brother had passed on a horse, but they didn't believe me. I began to think it had been a dream.'

'I could not come back. We have had our troubles, too. Try to forget, for there is a new life before you,' he said, holding her tightly and brushing the tears from her cheeks.

The next morning they rode on up the length of Birkdale. The village people came out of their houses, hailing Benedict cheerfully and asking who the lady was.

'This is my sister. She has come to live among us,' he replied. Despite his cheerful aspect, however, he was afraid of what Sir Jocelyn might say.

One of the village boys saw them coming up the rise from the wood and ran on to the manor. Francisca was running to meet them across the grass. The brothers were following her and Isabelle was still descending the steps as they rode up. Benedict could feel Alyce's arms tightening around his waist.

'Francisca!' he said, as she ran to him and grasped the rein. 'I have her here. This is Alyce!' He turned in the saddle, disengaging himself from Alyce's clutching hands, and giving her a gentle push, so that she dropped from the horse and stood, face to face, with Francisca. There was a moment's hesitation, then Francisca held out her arms and clasped the weeping girl in an embrace.

'Is this Alyce? Oh, Heaven be praised,' said Isabelle, gasping a little as she hurried to greet them. 'Here, let me look at her. The poor child, she must be fed. Come to the house, do not linger here.'

'Come Geoffrey,' said Benedict, turning in the saddle to look at his neglected friend. 'This is Sirich, he will take your horse, and this is his brother, Thurstan.' Geoffrey grinned, threw a leg over his horse's neck and the reins to Sirich.

'Giants they are indeed. I thought you were spinning me a yarn,' he said.

They followed the women. Isabelle was holding Alyce fast by the arm and Francisca, on the other side, had her arm around the girl's waist; they had to disengage themselves in order to climb the stone stairs. Benedict was so glad that they had welcomed her so warmly. He hastened after them and when he entered the hall he was in time to see Sir Jocelyn rising from his seat by the fire, the woollen blanket falling from his knees to the floor as he stood.

'So, this is Benedict's sister!' he said. 'Another from the same union I see. A bonny girl,' and that was all he had to say. He resumed his seat and ignored them for the rest of the day.

Alyce was very quiet during that first week at Birkhau. She was afraid to be too happy, in case she lost everything again. The contrast between her former life and this was such that she could not, as yet, comprehend it. She moved about the hall, touching the table, then walking to the hutch under the sleeping loft and running her fingers over the carving on its doors. She would move then, trance-like, to the fireside where she watched, wide-eyed, everything which Isabelle did. On the third day, she took from Isabelle the heavy pot and carried it for her down the steps to the undercroft.

When Isabelle brought a broom, and made to sweep the old rushes from the floor, Alyce took it from her and, despite her protestations, swept the floor herself. She even managed to communicate with the old crone by the fire, whose filthy clothes stank, to the deep distress of Isabelle. Alyce had been taken on the second day to visit Sir Philip and his family at Hopestones, and now she went there by herself and begged an old dress from Dame Beatrice. Then, by what means nobody knew, she persuaded the old woman to undress behind the curtain which was fixed when the women needed to bathe. She washed the old one and laundered her filthy smock, wrapping her in a blanket the while. When the family assembled in the evening, the old woman was crooning contentedly to herself beside the fire, cleanly dressed in the old red dress, her shoulders draped with Alyce's shawl.

'I looked after the old ones in the hospital,' she explained. 'You just have to be patient and show that you care for them.'

'I should never have believed it possible!' said Isabelle.

The next day, Alyce went down to the undercroft with Isabelle who ventured for the first time to ask, 'What happened to you, child, when you were sold in Lincoln?'

'A pedlar bought me, and for a year or so he took me about with him, until he returned to Lincoln and exchanged me for a bolt of cloth.'

Isabelle made a clucking noise of commiseration.

'I was left there as a servant of the clothier who threw his wife out of bed and dragged me in. You can imagine how I was treated, and the wife would beat me the next morning. I was kept there for three years, until I had sores all over my body and the clothier's wife persuaded her husband that I had leprosy. That is why I was sent to the hospital.'

'And Benedict saw you there. Wasn't that like a miracle?'

'It was. I knew him as soon as I saw him, but I was so miserable once he had gone that at first I wished myself dead.'

'Oh, that is a terrible sin, my dear. Have you confessed?'

'Yes, Isabelle. Then after a while I was filled with hope for I thought he would come back the next week. I took to waiting at the foot of the mound on which the hospital stood. That was a mistake, for people grew used to the sight of me and a squire who had ridden past with his friends one morning, snatched me up as they returned in the evening filled with wine.'

'Again, it seems like a miracle that Benedict found you,' said Isabelle, putting down her chopping knife in order to make the sign of the cross.

'I was thinking of running away and was trying to make a plan when Benedict appeared before me. You are right, it was like a vision.'

'The Saints be praised,' said Isabelle.

'The monks at the hospital had been so kind to me. They cured my ills and told me that I did not have the leprosy. Do you know, it is not so catching as people think. The monks do not catch it from their patients.'

'Perhaps that is because they are holy men,' said Isabelle. 'But how could that wicked clothier treat you so! I wish I could rescue all little children who are beaten and bring them here.'

'When Francisca has her baby, shall I be allowed to care for it?' asked Alyce.

'Do you not wish to marry and have children of your own?' asked Isabelle.

'That is impossible,' said Alyce, hanging her head. 'I am no longer a virgin. No honourable man would want me.'

'Pray to Our Lady. You are a beautiful girl. Some man might want you and you are kind and good, I have seen that for myself.'

'Can I tell you something?' asked Alyce, blushing.

'What is it my dear?' said Isabelle, putting down the knife again.

'I like Geoffrey. He is very merry, is he not?'

'Aye, but we do not know much about him and he has neither hearth nor home.'

'You are right. I should not hope for so much,' Alyce said in a very quiet voice.

'Take heart!' said Isabelle. 'So many good things have happened to you that you must have a special angel guarding you. Now, look, here comes your brother with Francisca.'

The young couple were returning from the garden. Despite the separation which hung over their lives, the two managed to be happy. He talked to her of the child and of how it would tumble about on the grass and lie on a sheepskin, among the new lambs. She clung to his arm and walked about with him, looking at him when he talked and reaching up to touch his fair, waving hair, or to smooth his cheek or touch his lips gently with her fingertips.

Geoffrey spent much of his time up at Hopestones with Sir Philip who still had no son and loved to talk with young men about his past adventures. He had travelled in his youth and knew the valley of the Derwent where Geoffrey's father had his manor.

'I remember Padley,' he had said with amazement. 'I was there in my youth. It lies on the hillside, facing south, and near it is a deep dell with a watermill. Then, just along the hill, going westwards, there is a place called Hethersedge. Yes, I remember it very well indeed. Does your father still live?'

'Aye, but he is not very proud of his son I fear,' Geoffrey replied ruefully. 'My elder brother is gone into the Church and my father wishes me to marry and settle down.'

'But you have seen no young woman who suits you. It is the way with young men. You have visions of some damsel like those in the legends and can settle for nothing that is human.'

'Until last week,' said Geoffrey.

'It is a mistake to cast one's eyes on the wife of a friend,' said Sir Philip sternly.

'Oh, you mistake me, sir. It is my friend's sister that I love. She is so beautiful I could swoon when I look at her.'

'Alyce! Ah, you are right. She is fair indeed. Would your father approve of her?'

'Would she approve of me?' asked Geoffrey.

'Well, Benedict is going away soon, so you should speak your mind before it is too late. Youth does not last for ever!'

Philip de Lonsdale arrived to tell Benedict when he must appear at Chester and that he was to ride by way of Peveril with de Lacy, and then to Clungford Lacy in Herefordshire.

'Peveril is near my home!' said Geoffrey, but he dare not speak to Benedict of Alyce. He plucked for her a bunch of flowers and said farewell, blushing and stammering so that it made Benedict smile. He left them without speaking his mind.

# Part III

## 1190–1191

# 20

When the day came, Benedict rode down the valley, turning to look back until he could no longer see the manor or the village, and away to Pontefract with a heavy heart. Not until he sat at table in the great hall of that castle did his spirits lift at the sight of the company.

Knights, squires, pages, clerks, men-at-arms, thronged the lower tables, and he with them, whilst upon the dais sat de Lacy with his lady beside him, his younger brother, Richard, and a visiting baron, Robert de Bosco one of the lords of Holderness, on his right hand.

Pages served the great people on bended knee, by turn, according to their importance, and there was a fanfare whenever the Groom of the Hall entered to usher in a new silver platter laden with food. Above the dais, as a mark of its importance and to keep the birds which flew about the rafters from leaving their droppings on the table, was an awning of red and gold brocade. Benedict appreciated its value, for it was such cloth as they had had at Coney Street and its quality bespoke great expense.

A clerk sat beside Benedict, a man of mature years with a look of wisdom and rectitude about him. He was travelling in company with Robert de Bosco. His own name, he said, was Isaac of Skeffling, and he held lands also in his own right near the Priory of St Bees on the Cumberland coast.

'Where is Skeffling?' asked Benedict.

'In Holderness, near to the Abbey of Meaux, close by Beverley. The little manor I hold of the Priory of Birstall lies on the banks of the Humber. If you ever travel in that land, young man, you should visit me and see my books. I have four and they are my pride and joy.'

Benedict almost jumped with surprise. This was the first man he had met who came from the land where he had been born and, without revealing anything of his origins, he kept the old clerk busy all evening, describing the land of Holderness.

As soon as the sun rose next morning, Benedict was out at the stables with his saddle bag and inspecting Jet for the ride south.

'You are ready, Birkhau?' asked someone who strode across the yard behind him and, turning, Benedict saw de Lacy's brother, tall and chestnut-haired, wearing a coat of mail. He wore a surcoat of green decorated with the de Lacy knot. Benedict had seen the design carved on a church wall as he had approached Pontefract and had been told that the device appeared on the reverse of de Lacy's seal. It was said that the name of de Lacy had derived in France from the lacy pattern of their device.

Benedict looked up from his brief consideration of the intricate pattern and answered that he was indeed ready.

'Here's my horse and here are our men. Mount up. My brother sits his horse already, let us be off!' and Richard de Lacy threw himself into the saddle, impatience in every movement. He was turning his horse for the gate almost before he was seated and ramming his feet into the stirrups as men ran to open the gates before him. Benedict waited for Lord de Lacy to precede him and rode out in his train among five horsemen, two of them men-at-arms, two squires and a page who kept his pony at a distance from the horses. Benedict learned from the warnings given to the page that this pony would kick at any of its kind that came too close.

'Pray keep that little brute away,' called one of the squires. 'If he kicks my animal, you'll rue the day, my lad.'

They stopped for refreshment at Wakefield and for their rest that night at the neat little Priory of Ardsley. Next morning, after a night of heavy rain, they were off early and rode over the hills until they came down into the flooded valley of the Don where they were obliged to go upstream to the village of Sheffield in order to cross by the bridge. Then they climbed south-westward steadily, always heading towards the high moors, until Benedict saw that the country began to resemble Birkdale but that the rocks were darker and more gritty. They kept to the high land, where pools of standing water gleamed among the green and purple.

'It is well to stay up here on the hill tops,' called Richard de Lacy, to those who rode behind. 'We should be bogged down in clay if we took the low road.'

'And we can see all around us,' replied one of the squires. 'No party can surprise us up here.'

'I am not so sure,' Lord de Lacy replied, riding forward at that moment and hearing what the squire had said. 'Men could lie among the heather and bilberries. I have been on the high moors in the border country, between us and the Scots, and there brigands are known to lie where you would think there was no cover and spring out at men on horseback, unseating them before they can draw their swords.'

'Our path lies through the heather beyond,' replied the squire. 'Shall we draw our swords now?'

'Nay, this is not the Scots land,' de Lacy replied. 'Just over this hill and we shall be in the valley of the Derwent, and soon we shall arrive at Peveril.'

As he spoke, there was a rumble of thunder in the distance and the wind seemed to turn towards them from the south-west.

'Shall we get there before the rain?' someone asked.

'We had better, for there is little shelter in these parts,' an anxious voice replied from the rear.

They trotted their horses up the long slope before them, single-file along a narrow path, while the distant thunder continued to reverberate and the dark bank of cloud loomed nearer.

'Where now?' the leader called as he reached the top of the rise. Coming up with him they looked across the hills, as fair, thought Benedict, as Birkdale. What was the weather like in Birkdale, he wondered? Had the heavy rain flattened the grain to the ground? What was Francisca doing now? He hoped she was not weeping for him by the window.

Far away, a river wound its course along the valley bottom and the trees along its bank were already bending before the wind.

'The Derwent lies ahead!' Lord de Lacy announced. 'But we must descend into this narrow valley which will lead us there. Now go carefully down this ravine, the ground is very broken, keep to the right to avoid the steeper part of the descent, I remember it well, but be wary of deep bogs among the peat.'

Just then the first flurry of rain hit them. The horses tried to turn their backs to it and tucked their long tails between their legs. The men struggled to turn the horses again into the wind and rain, clutching at the same time with their free hands at their cloaks to pull them tight at the throat. When all was settled they could not make any speedy progress, for they passed down between rocks, where they lost sight of the river and found themselves heading down a narrow gorge, with a hillock under the moors on its northern slope, just visible for a second before the rain blotted everything out. There seemed to be buildings there, huts at least. Soon the track levelled a little and grew wider so that they were able to jog down uncomfortably, two abreast, as the gusts of wind and the bursts of blinding rain soaked their cloaks and blinded their eyes. The descent of the hill had taken but a few minutes and now before them the leading riders were just able to make out the figure of another horseman, riding towards the place where they had discerned habitations.

Jet, pulling hard, had barged his way almost to the front of the company and Benedict saw that the stranger stopped and turned his horse broadside across the path as he peered to see who followed him.

Richard de Lacy was still leading the party and called out to the horseman before him, 'Is there shelter at hand?'

'Aye, my house is near. Follow me,' came the reply, and they trotted on behind the stranger in single file where the path narrowed again between rocks. The stranger turned his horse suddenly uphill and they scrambled after him for a short way. Blinking the rain out of his eyes, Benedict saw a wooden church surmounting the hillock, and a curious earthen bank about twelve feet in height which had been thrown up from the excavation of the dry moat surrounding it. The strange horseman rode through a gap in the bank, and Benedict was fully occupied in preventing Jet from crashing against Richard de Lacy's horse in the gateway.

There was a grassy hollow two hundred feet across inside the ring of earth and a grove of ash trees which sheltered a long house of wood. Two cows stood close together in the lee of the bank. A number of sheep lay in the shelter of a hawthorn tree. Rough servants ran out to take their master's horse and through the sound of wind and rain Benedict could hear orders being shouted. An uncouth man with wild ringlets of hair blowing wetly in the wind grasped his rein, and Benedict slid to the ground, unhooking his saddle-bag as he landed and looking anxiously after Jet as he disappeared with the other horses. Turning, he caught a glimpse of firelight through the doorway, before his companions, hastening to get out of the rain, filled the entrance.

When he was at last inside and able to look around, he smiled to think that only two days ago he had sat in the noble hall of Pontefract. Even the little Priory, where they had slept the night before, had been neat and orderly, but this warm and crowded place, seething with activity, looked as though it had grown out of the ground and must have stood since the time of the Conqueror. The wattle walls leaned and bulged this way and that, so that the place resembled the interior of a gigantic, overturned basket.

The central hearth had an iron reredos and a tripod held a pot which steamed and bubbled over the logs. A crude spit, the end of it bent to make a handle, was being turned by a boy dressed in sheep's skins. Benedict looked around and saw that his host was attended by another rough servant. He also was dressed in sheep's pelts; the leather on the outside, and the rag-taggle wool sticking out at arm and neck holes and hanging down from the bottom of his coat. Benedict's companions were hastily divesting themselves of their cloaks and two women came forward and took the heavy garments and threw them over a rail where they dripped, shining with rainwater.

He had time then to regard their host and a merrier man he had rarely seen. Out of a round and jovial brown face shone twinkling blue eyes. The man's head was bald at the front but a fringe of white hair, which continued into a short white beard, framed his whole visage. The fire shone on the raindrops still glinting in his white hair, giving their host the appearance of having a halo. The two women hastened back to the fire, the fronts of their garments wet from the cloaks they had carried. They stooped over the fire and began with great speed to ladle out the broth into bowls of dark brown clay, shiny with a black glaze on the inside. Then they hastily distributed the broth, bustling about among the standing company, not inviting them to sit but seeming to think their first duty was to fill the travellers with something hot. So, standing around the fire, some turned towards it, some roasting their backs, the travellers raised their bowls and drank noisily while the rain dripped from their wet hair and ran down their necks.

'Sir Godfrey de Hethersedge, at your service,' said their host to de Lacy, as the latter lowered his bowl from his mouth and swallowed the last of his soup.

'De Lacy of Pontefract,' replied the other.

On your way to Peveril, I should think,' said their host. 'And then on down to Chester?'

'Aye, but glad to find you en route. We would have been drowned if we had continued any longer in that downpour. Listen to it now! By God, does it always rain like this in these parts?' de Lacy replied, laughing as he spoke.

'You are familiar with the Welsh Borders, I have no doubt, for you are Constable of Chester are you not, my lord?' their host replied, and Benedict saw that he was a man not unused to fine company. 'And I think you will agree that the rain here is no worse than Welsh rain.' He laughed uproariously as he finished and, turning to the hearth, commanded more broth to be served. One of the women protested that there was insufficient to go round for she had not expected so many. 'There is a sheep carcass hanging in the larder. Go you and fetch it in, Thomas. Cut it up small enough and it will soon be cooked. You boy, don't gawp at the company, fetch some kale leaves and leeks and herbs and such stuff. These gentlemen need feeding, for they do not often see rain such as ours!' He laughed heartily again and bade his guests take seats. Benedict pushed back his wet forelock with his sleeve and looked around. There was neither table nor stools, but all around the wall was a narrow platform. He was loath to leave the fire and so, he saw, were the rest of their company, but they backed away to the wall and sat themselves down. The floor was probably of beaten earth, but Benedict could only guess at that for it was littered deep in dried bracken which served to keep the draught from their feet, and they felt no chill. The heat of the fire reached them, even at the wall,

They slept on the narrow bench that night. The page rolled off it into the bracken and perhaps others did as well, but the child was the only one to admit next morning that he had. Still, they awoke refreshed to find that the women were warming ale and tearing up loaves with which the guests were to break their fast. A brief visit to the outside of the house to relieve themselves and then they were round the fire again, with fists full of bread which they dipped into the ale. It was remarkably good.

Now he had time to look round there were, Benedict saw, no windows, but the door was left open and, by the light which came through it and the glow of the fire, Benedict saw that the walls were made of thin boughs of hazel wedged between the heavier timbers which had built the hall. The hazel had been left unplastered, but the daub which covered the hall was showing here and there where it had squeezed in from the plastering of the outside. A mere hole in the roof, set to one side so that no rain should put out the fire, allowed some of the smoke to escape and further examination showed that the hall was surprisingly large, forty or fifty feet in length, with a curtain draped roughly across the far end to form a bower for the women of the house.

Having broken their fast, Lord de Lacy's party was eager to leave.

'How far is it to Peveril, Sir Godfrey?' asked de Lacy.

'Why, no more than a hop and a skip,' and, as he answered, the young men smiled at his curious speech, more like that of a boy than an old man, but he did not notice the amusement he had caused and continued. 'You should keep along this northern edge of the valley and do not descend until you see, far below and still some way before you, the river coming down from the northern hills. You will need to bear left and go up the side valley to a bridge. Now that will be your best place after such rain, for making a crossing.'

'Unless last night's rain swept it away!' said de Lacy.

'Nay, the bridge is builded well and will stand a summer flood. Go you across it and down the further bank if you can. Then turn westward and follow the salt road which some say was built by the Romans! Would you believe that now? Follow this road, I say, along the valley, passing a hamlet but not taking any tracks you see either to left or to right. Keep out of the valley on your left, it is Edale, the valley of the Noe. You will see two peaks. Keep them on your right hand. In that way you will come to the valley's end, where the hills rise all around you like a bowl. Take note of Mam Tor, a hill with the rocks and shale all fallen away from the face of it. You will see that it seems to block the end of the valley. I should send a man with you to show you the way,' Sir Godfrey added as he finished.

'And how shall we find the castle?' one asked.

'Why, there it is! You will not fail to see it unless the cloud be very low. Perhaps I should send a man . . . Handsome it is, and the keep faced with fine sandstone. Some liken it to Richmond!'

Again, some of the young men could scarcely conceal their amusement, but the knight pressed on with his description.

'High, and perched on top of a limestone outcrop so steep that you had best dismount and walk your horses to the top lest you should slide off over the cruppers.' At this one of de Lacy's company let out a guffaw and the old man turned to rebuke him.

'You may laugh, young man, but you have not seen how this castle sits above deep gorges and with a huge cave at the foot of it on the western side, such as you will never have seen before, the biggest in England. I think I should send a man, this mist may lie thick in the valley.'

'We thank you,' de Lacy said, loudly and firmly so that none in his company doubted that he was determined to stop the outpouring of words. 'We thank you for your hospitality, sir knight, and we leave you in the hope that you will prosper and live long to rescue benighted travellers.'

His companions commended his words and stepped outside into the misty green enclosure. Their horses were being brought out to them ready saddled and their host bustled around, still protesting that he should send a man with them.

Rough though the place was, Benedict was ashamed of his companions, that they had mocked the old man. The hospitality could not have been more welcome had they found themselves in a palace. He strode across to where a servant was holding Jet by the bridle and had begun to fix his saddle-bag when he looked down and saw that the clenches on the near fore were standing up like a row of church candles. Jet had but two faults. He had been used in the light plough and his mouth was toughened at one side by constant jerking of the bit to turn him to the right, which made him hard to stop in that direction, and his feet tended to be shallow, so that his shoes needed replacing frequently.

'My horse will cast a shoe before we have gone a mile,' he called and, as he spoke, he bent to pick up the horse's foot and found, as he had thought, that the shoe was already loose and could almost have been pulled from the hoof there and then.

'Get it shod and follow us. Sir Godfrey says it is "Only a hop and a skip"' de Lacy called, his face almost breaking into a smile. Then turning to the old knight he asked with every courtesy, 'Will my companion be safe, travelling alone?'

'Surely, surely,' the old knight replied. 'The smith in the village will shoe the horse all round, within the hour. One of my people can take the horse down to the forge.' But Benedict protested. He was particular about the way his horse was shod and determined to supervise the work himself.

'If this mist has not lifted, I will send one of my carls along, all the way to Peveril if need be, to see that your friend arrives safely.'

Benedict reflected on the old knight, as he led Jet down the hill towards the ringing sound of hammer on steel. He had been surprised to hear the Norse word carl, for it was little used nowadays, and he thought how fitting it was that the old knight should use old ways. He compared Sir Godfrey's honest joviality with Sir Jocelyn's greediness and devious ways and wished it had been this good old man who had claimed him as his son.

And thus it was that de Lacy and the rest of the party rode off into the mist without Benedict, and had they not left him he would not have met with the adventure in Jaggers' Clough and made another new acquaintance that day.

An hour later, and satisfied with the farrier's work, he emerged from the forge into a mist which lay even more thickly over the land. He decided to ride back to the hall in the enclosure to ask that the route be described for him a second time. He hoped also that the knight would indeed send someone with him, for to attempt to find Peveril alone in this weather was not a task he relished.

'In this mist you would be better going with my man, Segwen,' said the knight. 'You will travel faster and will not make any mistake which causes you to go back on your tracks. Here, Segwen,' he shouted, 'go you with this gentleman and take him safely to Peveril.'

'Before I go, can you tell me about your earthen circle?' Benedict asked. 'I have never seen the like of it before.'

'Perhaps it was built by the Danes, I like to think on the Danes,' the knight replied with enthusiasm. 'It was certainly here when the Conqueror came. A timber castle was built within it at that time. How long ago would that be now?'

'Over a hundred and twenty years,' Benedict replied.

'As long ago as that!' exclaimed the knight. 'All gone now, and some of the timbers were used to build this place in my great-grandfather's time. The castle here was no longer needed once Peveril was built and, as you will see, that is stone, like Richmond, all stone!' He spoke with awe and Benedict wondered whether Peveril was going to be a surprise or a disappointment, for like Richmond it could surely never be.

With more farewells, he set off with the house carl running at his stirrup. The mist, instead of dispersing, seemed to become more solid and the air oozed water. Benedict understood the man to say that they should not take the highest ground but ride along under the craggy wall of rock which showed now and then on their right. It was quiet all around them, for what sounds there were were muffled by the mist, except when pairs of grouse shot like arrows from the heather near the track and flew off with their warning cry 'Goback, goback, goback.' The tracks were surprisingly good and, despite the mist, they did not have to seek their way, but made a good pace.

The man's speech was strange to Benedict, but even though some of the words were quite unintelligible he was able to get the gist of it. After a while they began a steep descent and Benedict asked if the bridge were near at hand. The man nodded energetically, pointing away to his right. This was the place where their host had said they must go north to find the bridge. He had said that it was necessary to go upstream to the crossing place. From somewhere before them in the mist, a roaring of water reached their ears and they were soon riding upstream beside a torrent of brown and white water.

They were riding now across a place of level grass and there they came suddenly upon the bridge or, at least, to the spot where the bridge had been. On each side, the water swirled savagely round what remained of the bridge and spilled over the banks, flooding the meadows on either side with a brown and roaring torrent. The man grasped Benedict's stirrup leather and they plunged into the water. But when the man found himself waist deep he reached up to grasp the pommel of the saddle and a handful of the horse's mane, shouting something as he did so. Benedict turned the horse away and towed the man out of the water. As soon as they had struggled back to dry land, the man ran on ahead with unabated energy, upstream still, turning to beckon at every few yards. Reaching a place at a distance from the rushing water where he might be heard, the man cupped his mouth with his hands and shouted that they must go up along the left-hand bank.

Benedict's thoughts were all with his companions. Had they tried to ford and been swept down the Derwent to their deaths? Now, silent drenching rain began to fall and to soak its way through his clothing. How long would it be before they reached a place fit to cross this dangerous river? Here and there they crossed brooks rushing to join the river and swollen to the height of a man's thigh. At each one the servant hung on to the saddle and leaned against the horse to keep his footing.

Always, his guide tried for higher ground, and Benedict felt, though he had no means of judging, that they were still proceeding northwards when he thought they should have been going west, and the ground was not only rough with heather, but scattered with rounded boulders and set about with an ever-thickening cover of birch trees. The guide was saying something which Benedict could not understand.

At last they found a place where it was possible to make a precarious crossing, but Benedict's relief that they were now over the river was dashed almost immediately by the sound of another torrent somewhere in front of them. Then he realised that the man had been trying to tell him that there were two rivers. The stream before them was not so fierce, but the crossing was made almost impossible by the crush of tumbled boulders on either bank. His guide turned upstream, northwards again, and led the way into a cleft of the hill.

There were alders here which afforded a little shelter from the rain. The little valley levelled and widened suddenly. They entered a small clearing deep in bracken and a little to the right of the stream, and it was just then, in the quiet of the glade, that Benedict heard a sudden, terrible roar, which he had heard but twice before and which he recognised with paralysing terror. The man before him leaped for a tree and with frantic agility clambered towards the lower branches. Benedict's eyes darted to either side, and then he saw it. A huge wild boar was dashing towards him through the bracken, its little eyes blazing with malice. The horse whinnied with fear and, even in that second of time, Benedict knew that somewhere near was a sow and its young. He did not need to assess the danger for he knew he was facing death. Even then he clearly saw the long, coarse bristles standing like a mane along the ridge of the beast's spine as it came rushing onward, and the wicked white tusks. Benedict had never known such fear.

The horse half-reared and swung to get away, but among the bracken there were boulders and Benedict's eyes opened wide with panic at the realisation that the horse was going down with him. He reached up for an overhanging branch of alder, but it was too thin to support him and slid uselessly through his clenched fist. Down went Jet, and Benedict, falling sideways, found the presence of mind to thrust with his right foot and push himself away so that the falling horse did not pin him down. As he fell clear, the beast roared again; it must be upon him! He wasted not a second in looking round, but scrambled frantically on hands and knees over the nearest rocks, knowing that the boar could disembowel horse or man, or chop through a man's arm or leg with its vicious teeth. He wrenched himself upright and flung himself at the slender trunk of the nearest tree, but as he did so he found himself immobilised. His left foot was caught in a cleft of the rocks and he fell heavily, face down in the sodden undergrowth. In that moment he gave himself up for dead.

To his amazement, instead of feeling the pain of the boar's tusks biting into his leg, he heard a command.

'Get up, man, you will live.'

Benedict twisted round, his eyes searching desperately for the boar. It lay dead, no more than a couple of yards from his outstretched leg. Over the beast stood a giant figure whose spear still quivered in the boar's heart.

'Get up, I say,' the giant commanded again, wrenching his spear loose and casting a fierce glance about him. 'The sow is still to be reckoned with. Get you up into a tree!'

Benedict cast one anxious look at Jet, still prone among the rocks and struggling to rise, then he did as he had been told and scrambled up into the tree which had grazed his cheek as he fell. The giant was ready with his spear. Benedict regretted he had no sword and that his bow lay somewhere beneath the struggling Jet. 'Lie still, Jet,' he said in a voice intended to steady the animal. 'Lie still!'

'Quiet!' the giant commanded, and Benedict saw that he was listening intently as he searched the undergrowth with his eyes. Benedict set himself to search the bracken as far as he could see. Even so, the sow surprised him. She rushed out of cover so fast that he saw only a blur of movement, but the man was too quick for her. His spear was raised and he brought it down between her shoulder blades, killing her upon the instant.

The man left his spear where it was, shook his head, and straightened his back. 'Have you any weapon?' he asked without looking up at Benedict.

'A bow under my horse somewhere and a knife at my belt.' Benedict replied. At that moment Sir Godfrey's man descended from his tree. 'Ah, it is Segwen I see before me,' the giant said. 'Use the gentleman's knife and gut these two beasts, then cut us a couple of poles so we can carry them home.' He took a hunting horn from his belt and turning to the north, blew two notes upon it. There was an answering shout from above and the sound of men breaking through the undergrowth.

'You have him, Sir William!' said the first, beaming with pleasure and wiping the rain and sweat from his face. He took the knife which his master had taken from his belt and was holding out to him. A second man then emerged from the trees, 'What is this?' he asked, surveying the fallen Jet.

'This stranger's horse. He had a narrow escape.' Then, addressing Sir Godfrey's servant, the giant asked, 'What are you doing up here with this gentleman?'

The man Segwen replied rapidly in a dialect which Benedict could not penetrate, but which the hunter seemed to understand perfectly. Benedict climbed down and went to the horse, bending to examine the way he lay. Segwen came to the horse's head and they coaxed the animal to its feet.

'The bridge down!' said the giant. 'That will cost my lord a mighty sum to rebuild. I didn't think last night's rain sufficient to bring it down. Now, Segwen,' he continued, 'go you with my men and find the small pigs, while I show the stranger the way. Your name, sir?'

They had begun to walk together, a little way further up the ravine, Benedict leading the horse which was slightly lame.

'Benedict, son of Sir Jocelyn de Birkhau,' Benedict replied.

'Forgive me, I do not know the name of Birkhau. In what country is that?'

'In Yorkshire. Birkdale is almost due north of here and near to the Abbey of Fountains,' Benedict replied.

The giant turned then and leaped across the stream at a place where the banks were grassy and Benedict quickly followed, leaving plenty of room for the horse to make a safe landing without trampling him.

'And does your sire hold his manor of the abbot?' the giant asked, turning slightly, then plunging on through the wood.

'No, of the Honour of Richmond,' Benedict called after him, hurrying to catch up.

'A royal tenant, as I am myself,' the giant replied, scrambling up on to a rock and indicating with his hand a place where Benedict might lead the horse in a more level place. 'Sir William de Bagshawe, at your service.'

'I must be ever at your service, for I shall never be able to repay the service you rendered me today,' said Benedict, looking with admiration at the ease and strength with which his companion covered the ground, never seeming to look at the rough terrain, yet never making a false step. 'At my home in Birkdale we have twin brothers, giants like yourself.'

'So, this Birkdale breeds such men as me!' Sir William replied, laughing as he turned and showing white teeth among the black whiskers of his beard. 'Do you wish to go straight to Peveril? Or shall I take you to the manor of Ollerbrook, which is no more than a couple of miles ahead?'

Benedict looked down at the sorry state of his clothes. He had torn a sleeve in his scramble into the tree and it flapped wetly at the level of his knees. He had been wet before, but now one side of him from shoulder to ankle was thickly smeared with clay, and bits of leaves and bracken were plastered on his sodden clothing. His saddle-bags were soggy and he feared for his change of clothes inside them. His left boot was scraped, he regretted that particularly as the boots were new and he had been proud of them. It might be wise to rest, for now that he had time to examine his physical condition he realised that his back had suffered a wrench and that his knee was also damaged in some way and paining him severely. In any case, he did not wish to be separated from his companion until he found out more about him. 'I would be glad to stop on the way,' he replied and, as he spoke, the rain subsided and the air began to brighten a little as though the sun, given time, might break through.

Just then, Segwen and Sir William's two men passed them at a brisk trot, the family of wild pigs slung on poles.

'Get you on home. We shall eat well tonight!' Sir William called as the running men disappeared again among the trees.

Sir William and Benedict emerged from the wood on to gentle pasture which seemed to lie in a shallow valley. Benedict could see for the distance of perhaps a hundred yards.

'Is this the valley where Peveril stands?' he asked.

'No, that valley lies over yonder hills on our left,' Sir William replied, waving in that direction of the still-invisible hills. 'This is Edale and we are not far from shelter.'

At Ollerbrook, while they ate a good dinner, they regaled their elderly hosts, Sir Gilbert de la Brook and his wife, with their adventure and Benedict's narrow escape from the boar. Benedict wore some of Sir Gilbert's clothes while his own dried before the fire, and the old lady provided hot, stinging ointment for his painful knee. The knight leaned towards him.

'You were fortunate indeed, young man, to meet with Sir William. What was Segwen doing to lead you into that cleft in the hill?'

Benedict thought, from the way his host shouted, that he must be a little deaf, but before he could answer Sir William replied, emphasizing his words, and looking hard at the old knight, 'Do not blame the man. Have you been abroad today? The brooks are raging torrents and dangerous to ford and, besides that, the bridge is down!'

'Down! You say the bridge is down? Did you hear what he said, wife? Then last night's storm was worse than it sounded.'

'You were snoring so loudly, husband, that you heard nothing,' said his wife, smiling, and turning to Sir William she added, 'He has not been out of the house since Christmas, and that was nearly the death of him.'

'What did you say your name was, young man?' asked Sir Gilbert, turning towards Benedict, who repeated his name slowly and clearly.

'I was once at Lancaster. Have you been to Lancaster?'

Benedict thought of the apprentice in the goldsmith's shop. 'My father is a goldsmith of Lancaster,' he had said, 'do you know where that is, boy?' Benedict smiled at the recollection and, shaking his head so that the old knight would be certain to understand him, mouthed the word, 'No'.

'He knows York better than Lancaster,' Sir William shouted.

'Lancaster and Chester. I have been to both cities in my time.'

'That is where he is bound, Chester! He is going to Chester with de Lacy!' Sir William shouted across the hearth.

'Yes, I was in Lancaster when I was a youth like this one here,' the old knight said, and Sir William exchanged a look of mock exasperation with Benedict.

'We must be going,' he said to the lady. 'We must reach Peveril before night and the weather has lifted, I think.' He went to the window and opened the shutter. A brisk flurry of wind blew in and Benedict caught sight of the opposite hillside before Sir William closed the shutter again. The old knight had nodded off in his chair. 'Get your own clothes on, Master Benedict, and let's be off, the mist is all blown away,' said Sir William.

Jet was sound again, so Benedict rode and Sir William walked beside him, which reminded Benedict of Thurstan on their journey south. They crossed the valley and climbed its green southern wall. Then, slipping through a col in the sharp ridge, Benedict found himself looking down on to a plateau of white limestone. The contrast was startling.

'This we call the White Peak,' said Sir William. 'My home is over yonder,' and he pointed westwards. 'Peveril is below us, come, follow me.' Benedict looked all around and saw that they were riding along a ridge, with Edale on the one hand and another wide valley before them, into which they must descend, more or less parallel with the one they had left. He was thankful that he had a guide, for he felt he would have become lost among these peaks.

They dropped down from the escarpment. 'Look behind you now,' said Sir William after a short while and Benedict saw that the hill over which they had ridden was cut away, as though by a giant's saw, revealing a cliff of brown shale. 'That is Mam Tor, the shivering mountain,' said Sir William and they rode down into the valley.

'Now you can see how flooded the Hope valley is, and had you tried to cross lower you might have been drowned. Segwen did not lead you astray, though he did lead you into the boar's den.'

'I am anxious for my companions,' Benedict replied.

'Hardened travellers such as your lord and his men will not have come to grief so easily.'

As they reached the valley floor Benedict looked about him for the castle, and then he saw it, perched above, on a high peak of white rock with whisps of cloud around the top of its keep. It was indeed a fine castle, not, of course, comparable with Richmond, but Sir Godfrey de Hethersedge had not exaggerated; it was surprisingly handsome for such an out of the way place and its situation pleased Benedict. He dismounted and led the horse up the hill and into the castle enclosure, and there Benedict found his companions. With the exception of Lord de Lacy, they were disporting themselves with archery in the shelter of the curtain wall.

'Here he is!' shouted one of the squires. 'Here's Benedict,' and they ran towards him. 'We thought you were lost.'

They stayed for only one night at Peveril. Sir William de Lovetot held court there on behalf of Earl Ferrers, the King's Constable. There was talk of King Richard's brother, Prince John, who had sworn to his brother never to set foot in England whilst Richard was away on the Crusade. But their formidable mother, Eleanor of Acquitaine, had persuaded Richard to relent. Some there said that John would cause trouble, others said that he might make a more able ruler than his brother, for he at least was in England whilst the other had hardly set foot in the country. The two nobles who had been left in charge of England in Richard's absence were at loggerheads and Benedict knew, for he had heard at Richmond, that William de Longchamp had arrested the other, Hugh de Puiset, Bishop of Durham, at Tickhill.

The nobles were dividing, some for John, some for Richard, but though he was the King's Justiciar and ruled in the King's name, de Longchamp was almost universally disliked, even hated.

'It would not come as a surprise to me,' said de Lovetot, 'to learn that some of Longchamp's actions have been ordered by King Richard. It is typical of the Angevins to be moving men like puppets and it will be Richard who pulls the strings which jerk de Longchamp this way and that.'

'And John Lackland lacks land no longer,' said another. 'By his marriage to Hadwisa of Gloucester, he holds Marlborough and Luggarshall, Lancaster, Nottingham, Derbyshire and the Honour of Tickhill.'

'Aye, he is our lord now,' said de Lovetot. 'But though he holds these Honours he does not hold the castles in every case, not Nottingham, nor Tickhill for that matter, and not Peveril. They are still in the hands of the Crown.'

'And the situation could change at any time,' said Sir William. He had been sitting quietly beside Benedict, but his words had drawn the attention of the table to him. 'King Richard has named his nephew, Arthur, as heir, but only because the child is no threat to him. Prince

John is a threat. See how he is spending on the defences of all his castles. See how he rides the country perpetually with a retinue of a thousand, equal to that of de Longchamp. You, de Lovetot, as you stand for Earl Ferrers at this castle, are answerable in that to the King, but you have other lands, some your own and others in fealty. Like you, I paid a heavy fine to Richard for my post as keeper of this forest. Should King Richard not return and John become King, your words, all our words, might be remembered and held to our disadvantage.'

There was an uncomfortable silence, broken by de Lovetot who took a deep breath and, leaning towards Benedict, said,

'You do not perhaps realise how lucky you were, young man that such an expert hunter was close by; Sir William Bagshawe is an officer of the royal forest here. But did the deed take place,' he asked, turning to Sir William, 'in the royal forest?'

'On the edge,' replied Sir William, looking somewhat uncomfortable.

'Did you sound your hunting horn?' asked de Lacy, and when Sir William replied that he had, de Lacy continued. 'If there is any enquiry at the next Forest Court, your witnesses may testify that the boar was killed for my entertainment. For it is permitted, as you all know well, for archbishops and barons when they are travelling to take one or two beasts in places where food is not plentiful. They must take the game in full view of the foresters or else they must sound the horn so that it shall not seem to have been done illegally. It seems, Sir William, that we have conformed to the law!'

It was obvious from the good-natured laughter which followed, that Sir William was popular among his neighbours.

Sir William seemed to have taken a great fancy to Benedict and, before de Lacy's party left the next morning, took him to the top of the keep to see the country all around and to look down the cliff into the deep gorge behind the castle and into the cleft in the rock on its western side. Down this the two then scrambled, so that Sir William could show him the huge cavern which lay beneath the castle on its western side. From there, Benedict looked up, but from the cavern's mouth it was impossible to tell there was a castle above. It was a strange, quiet and formidable place.

'Do you have brothers and sisters?' asked Sir William.

'I have a sister, she is called Alyce,' Benedict said with great pride.

'She must be a beauty,' said Sir William.

They returned to the castle. 'Now, you will visit me on your return,' Sir William insisted, when the party was ready to leave.

'Sir William, keep this young man by you whenever you can,' de Lacy called. 'He has the devil's own luck, or else the Almighty has some purpose for him. This is not the first time he has been rescued at death's door. Good fortune follows him.'

'Perhaps Heaven had a hand in it,' said Sir William, 'for I do not often hunt so far from home and I had picked up the print of that boar's hoof only a minute before he attacked. I must have been guided!' and he crossed himself as he spoke.

Benedict descended the steep mound of rock and, with his companions beside him, turned uphill on a precipitous track which twisted through a gorge confined between pinnacles of stark, white limestone and hillocks of sheep-nibbled turf. 'This is the Windgates pass,' Sir William explained and there was scarcely need for explanation, for the wind, funnelling up behind them, caught his words and whipped them away.

Sir William left them at the head of the pass and, giving firm promises to visit on his return journey, Benedict turned his face for the south-west and thought of Francisca with longing. He suddenly felt very lonely and longed to turn and retrace his steps.

They rode over Axe edge and, leaving the hills behind, skirted the Cheshire plain. Here Benedict found a different world, of fat, flat meadows dotted with rich farms. Cheshire, like Richmond and Pontefract, was a huge Honour, created as a bulwark against the Welsh, and the men who held these Honours were powerful.

It was a great adventure, thought Benedict, to be riding into the city with the Lord Constable of Chester. If only he could have foreseen this as he struggled through the wind towards York so many years ago, how much less bleak would his future have seemed!

He did not stay for long in Chester. De Lacy was leaving for Wales and he was eager that Benedict should set off for his manor of Clungford Lacy, far away on the borders of Herefordshire. It was one of a group of de Lacy's own manors which lay close by two others which he held of the Bishop of Hereford. Isolated from his other possessions by the length of a county, this one in particular had proved difficult to manage and, before he left, de Lacy again explained what he expected of him.

Companions were found for the first part of his journey; a knight and his son who were riding to Whitchurch in Shropshire and, on the morning of their departure, Philip de Lonsdale appeared, heading north for Richmond, and greeted Benedict as an old friend. Benedict grasped him by the arm and told him to wait. He raced back into the castle and found a clerk.

'Do you have a piece of parchment? I wish to send a letter to my wife!' Then he hurried into the town where he found some beads for Alyce and a little scented box of sandalwood. He stroked it lovingly, opening the lid to enjoy the spicy smell. He imagined Francisca's pleasure in it, and he held the little box close to him for a few moments. He entrusted the presents and the letter to de Lonsdale, together with his greetings to all the family.

Sir Walter de la Reye and his party, with whom he left at noon, had been acquainted with the purpose of his errand and had heard something of the steward whose mismanagement had occasioned this journey.

'I am surprised that de Lacy sends no man to stay with you there; without a companion, you will be vulnerable. You should have a stalwart man who will stand your friend.'

'So, you think this steward, Leofstan, might kill me?'

'I have never met the man, but if he suspects that you are sent to spy upon him he might well think of getting rid of you. Why should he not?'

Benedict had to agree, 'I know no one in this land to which we go and you are right; an accident could easily be arranged.' He began to feel anxious; not only had he left Francisca at a time when she needed protection, but he might himself be riding towards danger. What would happen to her if he were murdered in this strange place? Why had he ever agreed to serve de Lacy so far from home?

'I will give the matter some thought as we ride along,' Sir Walter said; then, observing his young companion's despondent face, he fell to telling stories of the neighbourhood in which stood his own manors, until he had distracted Benedict from his worries. Benedict looked far away to the west, where he could see the hills of Wales, and was impressed, even at this distance, by their great height. Would the manor of Clungford Lacy be surrounded by such hills as those? Sir Walter paused in his narration and Benedict took the opportunity to ask for more details of the place to which he was bound.

'No, there are hills to the west of it, but the manor itself lies in the vale. The land is bosky and the view is everywhere restricted by trees and bushes. You will reach it through the pass called Ape Dale between the Long Mynd and Wenlock Edge. You will pass by Stokesay Castle, one of your lord's holdings. See what they have to say there about this man Leofstan, and from there it is but an hour's ride. Like most of the holdings in that part, it is merely a clearing in the forest. Then, if you should travel south from there, you will find yourself crossing Bringwood Chase, with the Black Mountains of Wales never far away. The manor lies between the Rivers Clun and Teme; it would be a good place to farm, if it were not so perilously close to the Welshmen.'

'Are they very dangerous?' Benedict asked.

'Not organised fighters, but yes, they are dangerous and they hate de Lacy; you have heard their name for him? Roger of Hell! So do not venture into their country. They are divided among themselves and you must learn who they are and how they are related one to another, for the Welsh of Archenfield fight for the English, providing the vanguard when they go forth and the rearguard on the return. They are at odds with their kin, the Welsh of Ewyas.'

'Are these two places, Archenfield did you say . . .?'

'Aye, Archenfield and Ewyas,' the knight answered.

'. . . Are they in Wales?'

'Nay, in England, but they are settlements of the Welshmen. Ewyas lies west of the Golden Valley, that is, south-west of Bringwood Chase, and Archenfield also south-west, but more northerly, and nearer to Clungford Lacy.'

'That is something in its favour then,' said Benedict with relief. 'The enemy Welsh are further away than the friendly Welsh.'

'I would not be so ready to see them as friends. Keep you always alert. I wouldn't trust the Welsh, even when they appear as friends and allies. You will find the manor well guarded, it has, no doubt, a strong stockade; we protect ourselves in the Welsh Marches.'

'So, you consider Shropshire to be a Marcher county also?'

'It is not so troubled as Herefordshire. We have not had raids for some time now but the whole of Herefordshire is plagued with raids and skirmishes. Agriculture cannot flourish and it is well know that it is poorer than its neighbours. How are you to spend your time, Master Benedict?'

'I have not been trained in arms, but to the merchant's trade. The death of my elder brother has left me heir to a manor. My lord has ordered me to act as clerk at his manor courts and in all other matters which require some scholarship, but I am to spend some time learning the arts of war.'

'You are late indeed. My sons began their education riding at the ring when they were no more than nine years. I bought for them a couple of the good bay ponies which are running wild in the hills of Wales. Then I had little lances made for them and before the year was out they were tilting at the ring. You will need to develop the strength of your arms and shoulders.' He looked closely at Benedict as he spoke. 'The lance and the great sword are weighty. Spend as much time upon it as you can and as little on the clerking as you have to.' He shook his head as he finished speaking, as though he thought Benedict's efforts might never be sufficient.

Benedict wished he were at home with Francisca. What was she doing now, he wondered?

# 21

Francisca was sitting alone at the hall table with parchment and pen, writing a letter to Benedict. She had put aside her sewing – a little jacket which she wished to have ready for her baby. There was plenty of time yet, for after its birth the child would be swaddled and would not need clothes, but the work gave her some purpose and seemed to bring the baby nearer. She had chosen to sit where a patch of sunlight fell through the window and made a warm place. Isabelle's voice rose from the undercroft below as she gave instructions to the boy about preparing the meat. Francisca felt comfortable so long as she could see or hear someone.

Sir Jocelyn had cancelled the order which Benedict had given for the new dairy with the arbour above it as soon as Benedict had disappeared into the wood below. She had been angry when she had seen the look of satisfaction on the Knight's face as he proclaimed his own wishes but, strangely enough, for herself she cared not, now that Alyce was here and slept with her at night, and thus she felt secure from any plot which Sir Jocelyn might hatch against her.

Now she left her writing and rose slowly to take the three steps which brought her to the window. From there she could see the sky and assess the prospects for a fine day. Alyce had gone out on to the green before the manor. She was spreading some linen over a bush to dry. Francisca returned to the table and took up her pen and wrote:

*Thank you so much for the little box, it gives me such pleasure, and greater pleasure still to know that you touched it just two weeks ago. I am sitting in the hall. It is still too cold to go out, but the sun is shining across the grass and making the dewdrops glitter. Later, when it is warm I will sit by the rocks for a while and in the afternoon, if Alyce will go with me, I will visit Beatrice and watch her children play. The month has been unusually warm but Isabelle says I should not sit on the hillside. I never go far from the house but she enjoys making a fuss. She frets already that the baby will be born during the winter.*

*Ah, the baby! How I long for the baby, though I hope it is not a boy for the Christians will not allow Jewish rites. I do not blame you for this, my love, but I hope it is a girl, and surely when it is born they will allow you to come home. I long for the baby because it will be part of you and I long for you both day and night. But I must be sensible.*

*It is good fortune for you to be taken into Lord de Lacy's household. I know I should be glad for it will keep you well out of the way of Malebisse and his following. The face of that man haunts me still, like an eagle with his brilliant dark eyes and his hooked nose like a cruel beak.*

*If you serve the Lord de Lacy well – but of course you will, did not my father train you in accountancy? – the Lord de Lacy will give you a more important post. Even so, it is fortunate that we have money of our own. This Honour of Richmond has long been beset with problems. I often wonder about the Lady Constance and whether she is happy or not. What is the use of being the heiress of an Honour as great as Richmond if you have no freedom? Two husbands, and both of them chosen only for the King's convenience. Now who will protect her and her small children? They are at the mercy of their uncles. I do not envy her. They say that she and her new husband, the Earl of Chester, are now at odds and if he divorces her, as I have heard people say he will, then the Honour might change hands yet again. What will happen to us? I hear that Alan the Constable is a just man, but he is old now and who might his successor be?*

She stopped writing, for there was no more room on the piece of parchment. She must find another, and meanwhile she heard Alyce talking to Isabelle below and Isabelle was saying, 'Sir Jocelyn should have built the bower, as Benedict told him. Then you and Francisca could have sat there. She will be wanting to go up the hill and sit on the damp grass. Oh, he should have built the bower.'

Francisca smiled to herself and thought, Sir Jocelyn will never change, he will soon have spent everything which Benedict gave him. Then he will have to come to me for money. I do not look forward to that encounter. But even if the old Knight were a skilful manager, this manor, being so isolated and surrounded as it is by the lands of the monastery, could be sold or exchanged at any time. Then the money we have hidden could be our salvation. I wonder whether we might buy some land of our own? However, I think there is an even better solution. When Benedict returns – and I must believe always that he will return safely – he must be persuaded to ask the Constable to make this manor an hereditament. I have a good understanding of business and government, learned from my father. These matters of land can be arranged with the help of a little money. I should have been a son for my father. My head is more inclined to business than my poor brother Aaron's ever was! Poor Aaron, how he would waste his time dreaming of horses and of archery, whilst I took an interest in whatever Benedict was learning. But what is the use of all these plans? Supposing some accident should happen to Benedict!

She gave a shudder then, straightening her shoulders, she moved to the table and pushed the stool before her across the floor until she came to the door, which she opened so that she could sit and look down the length of the sunlit valley.

Judith appeared and waved to her. She must have come down from Hopestones with Alyce. Francisca thought she intended to come up to the hall door, but the child turned and wandered across the front of the house towards the garden. Francisca was glad, for she wished to continue the letter and she rose and went to the shelf where, after some searching, she found another piece of parchment with which she returned to the table. Taking up the pen, she wrote:

> I shall continue to pay visits to Beatrice. That is my chief pleasure until you return, and she is so cheerful that the visits must be good for my health. The little ones come and put their heads on my lap while I sit. Then I stroke their beautiful, fine, silky hair, until they run off again to play. Beatrice will come down to Birkhau to attend me when I have the baby, which is a great comfort to me, and Isabelle will be here, of course; how could I have existed here, without her?
>
> You do understand, my dearest Benedict, that I must not speak. Perhaps I can no longer speak. I have no wish to do so and silence has served me well, for I do not have to explain anything to strangers. I understand that Sir Jocelyn has told people I am not quite right in the head. Did he believe that? I could not speak at first, no matter how I tried, but I knew everything that happened and now I not only do not wish to speak, it is imperative that I do not do so. This silence prevents the neighbours and the priests from discovering that I am not a Christian. I do everything you taught me. I dip my fingers in the holy water as I enter and leave the church, cross myself, and remember to kneel at the elevation of the host and they all take my Christianity for granted.
>
> Silence serves me best in this matter of the confession. What an extraordinary thing it is! Do you not think so? Instead of talking to the rabbi as one would talk to any sensible, well-educated person, there is this formula. Well, I am spared that, but I was reading one day when the priest called and luckily I put down the book before descending to the hall, for if he had seen me reading he might have asked me to write out my 'confession'. What then? I could, I suppose, have claimed only to be looking at the pictures. As far as the neighbours are concerned, I am illiterate as well as silent. They, I

*am sure, think that I gaze on the pictures and that the books are read only by you, my dear, and you pass here for a great scholar. Now, if they had seen my father's library . . .*

*They are killing a pig again, that terrible squealing as they cut its throat! The smell of pigs hangs about the place all the time. I do not wish to complain, but I can scarcely bear it. Please forgive me, my dearest, for I know how fortunate I am. It is just the pigs! I will be patient, we cannot have pleasure without pain.*

*If I had not lost my family I would never have been able to marry you. What a dreadful thing it is to have to live with this sense of guilt. As we rode away from the mill on that fearful morning, I was so weighed down with grief that I thought it would have been better if I also had been killed. It was my love for you, torn this way and that though I was, which kept alive a little spark in me.*

She moved again to her seat by the open door and closed her eyes for a while, and when she opened them her attention was attracted by a movement near the garden enclosure at the far end of the house.

There is the robin again! she thought. In the spring it had a nest in the ivy on the tree-trunk. Every so often it dropped down, like a leaf which falls in autumn, and took food back to its mate in the nest. Even the birds have their mates. Oh, I wish Benedict were home . . .

They were surprised when I allowed them to marry us. I suppose they had no idea that I had always loved him; how could they know? I took such care to hide it. I used to watch Benedict without his knowing, for I loved the bright pale gold of his hair and the curve of his neck as it rose from his collar. His eyes are blue, like the sky, but I was so careful to show that I had no interest in him that they were all deceived. Bella was right. Poor Bella! What would everyone have said? He has told me that he thought me proud and cold. He reminded me that once, when he first came to my father's house and couldn't read, he looked over my shoulder and I spoke crossly to him. I was pleased at the time that I had deceived them all, but my father was angry and poor Benedict was hurt by my words. I will write some more of the letter.

She moved again to the table, easing her aching back as she walked. She dipped the pen in the ink well and wrote:

*When I recovered in the house at Grantham, I was filled with dread at the thought of having to travel on towards Stamford. I have thought since that you must have wondered at my strange behaviour. Isabelle mistook my question about leaving and thought I was eager to go, and when you told me that the Jews of Stamford had been killed I didn't know what to say. Between horror and joy I was at a loss; afraid for my brother and my family, filled with sorrow and guilt about Moses whom I had never loved, but knowing that there was hope again – that I could stay near to you for just a little while longer. Just a little while, that was all I hoped for.*

    *That return journey to York was a nightmare, but it is amazing from where one finds the strength when there is a need and when one is going home. And it was better by far than continuing in that boat with those terrible men. I still feel sure they were waiting for dark, when they intended to cut our throats. Then, as we rode nearer to York, I became fearful again, for I saw clearly that if I admitted my love for you my father would send you from the house and we would be parted forever.*

    *And those market women with their dreadful news! I could not believe my ears and I remember staring hard across the darkening plain, concentrating my thoughts on a distant church steeple which I could barely see in the dusk. It helped me to keep my composure. I was sure we were facing death, and so near to home when all should have been safe. I have never told you this, and all the time while we were passing the blazing castle I was thinking of my parents and the children up there, where the timbers flared and fell.*

She put down the pen and pushed the parchment away from her. She was too weary to write any more and sat there, thinking over the past . . .

    But still I did not give up hope, I despaired only when we found the deserted house, the family gone, the battered door! And even then the horror wasn't over, for I heard every word the soldier spoke. I still do not know whether to believe him. Perhaps the soldiers had let the rioters into the castle during the night to murder our people. Perhaps those who survived until the next morning had been hiding. It was the sight of my dear friend Bella descending the steps with her baby in her arms which almost drove me out of my senses. The baby was born just before we left for Stamford and her husband was so pleased and proud. 'You will be the next to have a little one, Francisca,' they said to me. It seems impossible now that we did not know what would happen so soon afterwards . . . They lived near to Old Benedict and his house was in mourning. Had her husband gone there to pay his respects? Was he killed when the house was attacked? To have seen her walking alone, down into that crowd of howling savages, and the baby hardly a month old . . .

    The old Knight looks at me sometimes as though he wishes me dead. If I were, he would be able to marry Benedict to an heiress and gain another fortune. Fathers choose wives for their sons only for their money and the Knight would be glad to search the countryside for another wife for Benedict. I heard Isabelle warning Benedict, but it was some time before he saw for himself that she was right. How thankful

I am that we hid some of the money, for the Knight would have spent it all by now. My money is only for Benedict, I care for nothing for myself, only that he shall be safe and happy. Benedict was very wise to trust Sirich. The old Knight may be hoping that I shall die in childbirth, but I shall not die! I shall survive to welcome Benedict home. Sirich and I, alone in this house, know where the money is hidden. When I go up to the rocks and sit there in the sun, it pleases me to know that behind me, under the ground and now overgrown with grass, is more money than any Knight in the shire can boast. When the old man is dead, even if he has spent every last penny that he has in the chest on horses and clothing for himself, we shall still have a fortune for our children. In this manor there will never be any need to borrow, and certainly no need to go hungry.

She was restless and moved again to the door, from which she could see the branch of an apple tree hanging over the garden wall. Then she turned her gaze to the hillside beyond the stream.

There are times, she thought, when I think that I begin to love this valley. It was at the end of that first week here, when Benedict took me to walk on the hills, that I first began to feel I could be happy here. He told me that he, too, had felt lonely and homesick when we arrived, but that he had gone walking the hills with the brothers and, when they had come to the crest of that hill over there, he had looked down on Birkhau and suddenly felt at home here. We walked a long way that day, then we sat on the grass and he stroked my hair and, when we had rested, we walked back and it was just as he had said. I saw the house, so small below us in the valley, and thought of Isabelle and the brothers waiting for our return, and I also felt at home for the first time since . . . but I must not think of that! Despite all my best intentions, I feel my loss intensely on the Sabbath eve. Benedict thought at first that we might at least be able to light the candles, but then he realised that if we were to do so every Friday someone might notice.

I would be more content if I were a man, for they go abroad all the day long and it seems not to matter to them whether there is rain or sun, for they have so many things to do and they love their sheep! It surprises me that men love sheep, I had supposed that men loved only horses. The orphan lambs which Thurstan brought in to nurse by the fire last April were a delight, for I loved them like children. I was so pleased when Isabelle cleaned a bladder and filled it with milk, so that I could feed them. Their tails go whirling round as they feed. I had not observed them before and the sight was so funny that I almost laughed aloud. That would never do!

When it is spring again, in the month of May, I shall sit by the rocks and watch the lambs climbing upon little hillocks and playing the children's game of 'king of the castle'. Then they race, oh, how they run, down the hills and back again, what a joy they are! And, if God is good to me, I shall have a baby lying on a sheepskin by my side as I watch them.

She smiled briefly, and then her face became serious.

There were lambs in the fields last March, when we rode towards Stamford and I had no mind for the lambs, nor for anything else but the thought that I was losing Benedict – my beloved Benedict. I wonder what he is doing now and what opinion Lord de Lacy has of him? I once saw his father, the old lord, riding past my father's house. He looked very fierce. Perhaps the young one is kind, if these lords are ever kindly.

She moved uneasily on the stool then she stood and straightened her back, and placed the stool nearer the door so that she could rest her back against it. As she took her seat again, she thought: Will he forget me when he is far away? Will there be a woman there who will entice him? It is women who wait, and men are distracted by activity. He will see new places and meet people, while I sit here and wait and wait . . .

But here is Isabelle, out of breath from climbing; how she hates that outside stair, and Alyce, dear beautiful Alyce, is going down towards the stream and calling to Judith. Perhaps we can all walk to Hopestones in the sunshine.

# 22

Benedict was writing at a table near the window. The wall beside him was of solid timber, branches of four inches in diameter were laid horizontally. He had been at Clungford for a fortnight and it was harvest time. The shutters were held wide open to the balmy air. He sharpened his quill, dipped it into the black ink, and hesitated. Someone was creeping round the side of the house. He waited for the man to appear. That it would be a man was certain, for this was a household of men with no woman nearer than a mile off. There were small sounds, the scuffling of feet, but the expected head and shoulders never appeared at the opening. Benedict stood up carefully and quietly. He moved to the window and looked out to left and right. Then something made him look downwards and he found he was looking into the upturned face of Leofstan the steward.

'What are you doing, man?' he asked sharply.

'I am searching for the pin of my cloak,' the man said in his whining, pleading voice, a voice which had come to be the most irritating aspect of Benedict's life here. Benedict frowned at him and Leofstan tried an ingratiating smile, but still Benedict frowned.

'Can you not walk upright like a man? Why do you crawl around the house like a beast of the field!'

'My eyes are not so strong as yours, my master . . .'

Benedict turned away in disgust, there was a scuffling sound and again he turned quickly to look out. The man was gone. Three times Benedict had caught him, three times this week alone, trying some trick! What was it this time? What was the man up to?

There had been no accounts to be seen when he had arrived. The man held everything in his head, or so he said. Benedict tried him twice. He asked each time what weight of grain the place had produced, what labour was due from the villeins, what cattle had been overwintered, what timber had been felled and carted. The man had given quite contradictory answers.

Benedict inspected the barns and the ricks, to find only the most meagre quantity of threshed corn and half a barrel of beans. There was one small stack of hay which, upon inspection, proved to be mouldy.

'How did this come about?' he had asked sharply. 'Four men on the place and nothing to feed the animals through the winter.'

'Oh, this is an unlucky place, master. Nothing ever thrives here,' was all the reply he had.

So he had ridden over to Mansell Lacy, where he found a good store of both hay and corn. The steward there had hens, hives, a duck pond, a dovecote and a well-ordered coppice of hazel with oak standards above it. It was not therefore the case that famine was inevitable. It was possible, even in this lawless, Godforsaken place, to farm the land at least well enough to provide for the manor.

Gloomy and irritated, he returned to Clungford Lacy. With nothing left from the previous harvest, Benedict regarded the standing barley with incredulity. If there had been a crop of this quality in the previous summer, why was there no surplus? There was sufficient grain only to feed his horse, nothing for the plough bullocks. They were tethered here and there at the edge of the field strips, and were grazing the baulks. They needed better fodder than this with the season of ploughing before them. The hay was useless. There were enough beans to sow two furrows, but the strip to be sown would be ten furrows wide! The weather could not have been worse here than it was only three miles distant. He decided against writing his report to de Lacy. First of all there must be a plan for the recovery of this destitute manor. Benedict could not bring himself to write of nothing but defeat.

He went out to look round the manor enclosure again. It did not please him. At Mansel Lacy there was a ditch and stockade, and strongly shuttered windows on all four sides so that defenders could shoot in every direction. Here there was only one window and that was beside the door and faced southwards towards the gate. Any attack from north, west or east would be impossible to see, let alone repulse. There were ducks and geese, but the moat around the enclosure was dry most of the time and the poultry wandered away to a pond in the scrubby woodland nearby, a prey to foxes. There were no hives and no dovecote. De Lacy had never visited the place, but surely he must have known it was in a parlous state. Why had nothing been done before this? Benedict sighed and straightened his back. It was of no use to sink into despair. He had been commissioned to rectify matters and there was no time to be lost.

The steward of Mansel Lacy promised him some labour at harvest, for he had two men he might spare. There were four field strips at Clungford. They lay to the south-east and were sheltered from the east by woodland. The first supported the standing corn, golden now, and waving in the breeze; almost ready for the sickle. The second lay fallow, a riot of red, yellow and blue flowers, swaying among the long grasses. The third had been cut for hay, and twenty sick-looking sheep were grazing the new growth of grass. They had been enclosed on the strip with hurdles, many of them, Benedict saw, old and ready soon to disintegrate. The fourth strip had such a growth of weeds that at first he had thought the steward had left two strips fallow. On closer inspection, he found sufficient bean plants to signify that the strip had been intended to support a crop.

Benedict stood at the door of the manor, surveying the land. Beside the manor, across the ditch to his left and north of the field strips, was a wide area of heath land, broken with clumps of bilberries, ling and broom, and on a long bank of gorse, a hundred yards or so off, stood pale spindly birch trees. The heath stretched for perhaps a quarter of a mile and, beyond it, the forest. Two cows and their calves and the four pigs wandered about this heathland during the day.

Behind him to the north was dense woodland, level, and with a good track from Stokesay. Dense woods again and hilly to the westward, and to the south-west, between the wooded hills and the edge of the fields, lay the neglected coppice area. He looked across it now and determined that it would soon feel the woodsman's axe.

Apart from the steward there were four men about the place. Two were unmarried and lived in the barn. They were poor-looking specimens, thought Benedict, unkempt and weedy, not promising much in the way of strenuous labour. The other two were peasants and had their abode in a clearing in the woods where they raised some stock of their own, grew an acre of oats, and kept their hens and a vegetable patch. Benedict had ridden that way to inspect the clearing. Each of the men owed to the manor two days labour weekly. When he compared their achievement with that of Thurstan and Sirich, who must work the fields and woods and a huge area of sheep-walk and who had the help of a boy and a little customary labour from two men only, he felt nothing but disgust at the sight before him.

His first concern was the harvest and he had bought some barley from the steward at Mansel Lacy. This, he ordered, should be soaked and fed to the bullocks in the weeks of harvest time so that they would be fitter for the ploughing. The weather held good and, to the surprise of the labourers, Benedict went out himself to sweep double armfuls of the barley into sheaves, to tie and stook and to lift on to the sled until he was as grimy, sore and tired as they themselves. No man would willingly harvest the barley!

Isabelle had given him pots of salve and he was glad to smooth the ointment on to his forearms that night. The awnes of the barley had grazed his tender skin and pierced it like tiny splinters. The palms of his hands and his fingers were blistered and raw. But the next day he helped with the stacking of the sheaves and he sensed the men's resentment. They were not able to speak freely in his presence, so that the day was not enlivened with song or jest but the work must be done, and done it was, in record time.

He woke while it was still dark and turned over with a groan. There was no sound from the bed at the far side of the fire and he hauled himself into a sitting position and levered himself upright. Where was the steward? He dragged on his hose and jerkin and went outside. He was just in time to see one of the villeins heading for his forest clearing with a half-filled sack over his shoulder. Looking round, Benedict saw no sign of the steward and he set off in pursuit of the disappearing figure.

He entered the clearing in the wood and it was now light enough to see that the man had what seemed to be a new strip of land beside his hovel and he was bending to examine a good crop of beans. Then he entered the hovel. Benedict stood and watched for a few minutes and, while he watched, the door of the hovel opened and the man's wife appeared with a duck in her left hand. She was plucking it and stuffing the feathers into her apron which she had tied up round her waist by its corners to form a pouch. Benedict almost started forward, but then he thought better of it and returned quietly to the manor.

'How many ducks do we have?' he asked the steward who was emerging from the barn as he walked into the manor close. Leofstan scowled at him, and trudged over to the eastern ditch and looked down.

'Ten ducks and four geese,' he replied.

'Were there not twelve ducks yesterday?' asked Benedict.

'I do not count them every day,' Leofstan replied irritably.

'Then you should! So today there are two ducks missing.'

'They wander off and the fox kills them in the night,' the man replied.

'Come with me,' said Benedict, and led the steward off through the wood. They arrived to find the enclosure smelling of a good stew and one of the children was playing by the door with the severed foot of a duck. The man came from his hovel with an anxious expression on his face and Benedict strode over to the strip. The beans were indeed a fine crop.

'This is how you care for the manor,' he said to Leofstan. 'And it is the fox which takes the ducks from the pond, is it? You are lucky that I need labourers or you would all have been dismissed today. From now on you will account for every bird, on every day, and you,' he said, turning to the villein, 'you have a fine crop of beans, yet those in the manor fields have been sorely neglected. If you had done your work

well last year, the manor would have had beans to spare. Would you
have us all starve next year?'

There was no hay but that which was mouldy, and he ordered it to be
scattered like manure and ploughed into a new strip on the edge of the
area of heathland, which he intended to use next spring as an extra field.
Then, leaving more than a full day's work to be done to keep the men
from mischief, he rode north to Stokesay, where he bought from its
thrifty steward enough wheat to sow one strip and on his return he
did something which brought alarm and consternation to the men. He
had them plough the fallow. Nobody, they said, had ever ploughed
the fallow strip. Then, setting them to work, Benedict rode around
the neighbouring manors – a circuit which took him on a journey of
forty miles in that sparsely inhabited region. From each he bought a
small quantity of winter wheat and he arrived home two days later with
enough seedcorn to sow the fallow.

'That strip could have been allowed to lie fallow if you had only
done your work,' he said in answer to their complaints. 'But you shall
all do your share of the labour from now on. Go you, Godwin, and turn
the sheep on to the heathland, then use those old hurdles to enclose the
bean field. Pick what beans you can from among the weeds then fold the
pigs upon it. They shall spend a week rooting there and manuring the
strip before they go into the woodland for the pannage. Then you shall
dig in the weeds and what is left of the bean plants, and in the spring we
will plant it again with beans and put our trust in God.'

The next morning, as Benedict and the steward were rising from
their beds, Leofstan said in his whining, wheedling tone, 'You are
married, I believe, Master Benedict. Do you not miss your wife?'

'Of course I miss her!' Benedict looked angrily at the man, who gave
a faint smile and looked quickly away.

That afternoon, when Benedict was writing near the window, a
shadow fell across the parchment before him. He looked to see what
Leofstan wanted and, to his surprise, found himself looking into the
smiling face of a young woman. Her eyes were dark and brilliant. Her
hair was a reddish brown and tumbled about her head and shoulders.

'Good morning, Master Benedict,' she said, tilting her head to one
side.

'Who are you?' Benedict asked sharply.

'I am Gwynneth,' was all she replied, and she continued to smile
at him and to turn slightly, this way and that. His eyes were drawn to
her body, to her narrow waist, her breasts, her rounded hips, and he
could see she was beautiful. The sight roused him to excitement and he
looked quickly again at her face. She was smiling with amusement now

and suddenly he was angry. He remembered Leofstan's words that very morning. What was this? Was Leofstan behind it?

'Who are you?' he asked again, almost shouting.

'I have told you, I am Gwynneth. Can I come in, Master Benedict? You must be lonely.'

Benedict's face flushed bright red and he shouted at the girl, 'Go away, go back to where you came from. Go away, I say!'

She turned slightly, but hesitated, smiling at him over her shoulder as though she thought that he would change his mind and call her back.

'Go! Go from here!' He was clenching his fists and leaning heavily on his knuckles which were pressed painfully down on the table top. He looked out again and she was still lingering, a few yards away now, but still smiling back at him. He reached out and slammed the shutter closed. Then he sat down and buried his head in his hands. He was hot and trembling; he acknowledged that he had felt desire for the woman and was overcome with guilt. How could he have been tempted by that brilliant, vacant smile? Who had sent the girl and where had she come from? How could he have allowed his thoughts to stray, even for a second, from his beloved Francisca?

# 23

Winter drew on and, as soon as the sap had ceased rising, he set the men to work in the woodland, coppicing the hazel. 'For what do you need more hurdles, master?' one cried.

Benedict surveyed the woodland with satisfaction. Now, where strong clumps of hazel, six feet and more in height, had stood, the ground had been cleared. There were stacks of the branches, some two and three inches in diameter, others very thin, whippy stems which would weave easily into hurdles. One of the men had already begun, by setting a piece of wood five feet in length on the ground. It was pierced at intervals and he was thrusting strong, upright stems of the hazel into it. Another man was bearing some of the thinnest of the hazel in his arms. Next, the hurdle-maker would begin to weave the weak stems in and out between the uprights, banging them down hard to keep them close, and continuing until he had a strong length of woven fencing which would serve many purposes.

'You will see for what I need the hurdles when you have made them,' said Benedict, and after walking some way among the hazel stumps, to judge the condition of the great oaks which grew here and there about the coppice, he returned to his work in the house.

De Lacy had arranged that he was to do all the accounting and any necessary writing for his four manors. This work had previously been done by a monk of Hereford who walked from manor to manor, acting as the clerk to each manorial court and doing any writing which might be needed. Nothing had been said about payment for this service and as Benedict returned to his stool, still fuming at the idleness of the men, he decided that the other manors should pay for his labours with feed for his horse and the house cow for the coming winter.

There were days when Benedict seethed with resentment at his separation from Francisca. He longed to see her, especially now that the baby was due, and sent a letter to her bearing his greetings and telling her that he was safe. He found sufficient space at the end to tell her to call the child Jocelyn, for he still felt at times that people might ask questions about him and wonder from whence he had come. If the child were called after the Knight, it would reinforce the idea that he was the legitimate descendant of the line.

'I have never seen such a mighty stack of hurdles, master,' said the steward grudgingly, after two weeks of steady work on the overgrown coppices.

'Guard them well,' Benedict replied and rode off again on his rounds of the neighbouring manors.

'You do well to watch him, Master Benedict,' said Acaris, the steward of Mansel Lacy, sitting back in his chair of woven rushes and stretching the soles of his boots to the blazing fire. They had spent the day in conducting the manorial court, settling matters of land tenure and collecting the fines for entry to various holdings. 'A craftier, shiftier, more dishonest rogue I never knew. If Lord de Lacy only saw the half of what that one gets up to, he would have driven him away two years ago. I suppose Lord de Lacy has great concerns in the north?'

'With Chester and Pontefract, he has more than enough to keep him occupied without having to concern himself with one miserable knave like Leofstan,' Benedict replied. 'And the matter might have gone unresolved had he not wished to do me a favour. Does Leofstan have a kinswoman called Gwynneth?' he then asked. 'A woman appeared some time ago at my window while I was writing. Sh-,' he hesitated, 'she was sent to tempt me, I feel sure. I would be glad to know whether Leofstan sent for her.' There was silence for a while.

'Ah yes, Gwynneth. She was kept by Mortimer at his castle of Wigmore but he discarded her recently. It must be she. You have left a wife behind, Master Benedict, it is hard for you. Why, might I ask, does the Lord de Lacy send you here from so far away?'

'My family has an enemy who might try to kill me. De Lacy wished me out of his way for some time. Then it so happens that I was never taught the arts of war and, as you know, he wishes me to learn the use of lance and sword whilst I am here.'

'Indeed, it puzzled me that a knight's son should be such a good clerk and have no training in arms, but I suppose you were raised to be a monk?'

Benedict did not reply.

'Are you a younger son, Master Benedict?'

'My elder brother was killed in a tournament,' Benedict replied.

The steward nodded sagely. 'Then you will go from time to time up to Stokesay, Master Benedict?'

'Aye, they will teach me there, I have no doubt,' Benedict replied. 'Now, can you advise me? What must I do about this knave, Leofstan?'

'You should watch him, but you cannot watch him all the time. Even so, take particular note of his comings and goings in the direction of the south-west. His mother was a Welsh woman and it has crossed my mind that he is too friendly with the Welsh of Ewyas, who are no friends to the English.'

To give advice obviously pleased the old steward, but of what use was it?

'And if I take note of his comings and goings, what then, Master Acaris?'

'I do not know, Master Benedict,' the older man replied, sighing.

'I could follow him, I suppose,' said Benedict. 'But when he reaches the land of the Welsh of Ewyas, what shall I do then?'

'I do not know, Master Benedict,' the steward replied dolefully.

'Then I shall stay at home and mind my lord's business,' said Benedict. 'And perhaps I shall find out why the crops were so poor last year and I might even make a small profit for my lord by the autumn. That is my task here and an excursion into the lands of the Welshmen will achieve nothing.'

'You must watch your back at all times, Master Benedict,' said the steward of Mansell Lacy.

'I will endeavour to do so,' Benedict replied.

'It has been on my mind to say it ever since you came here,' the steward said, easing himself in his chair, then leaning forward to grasp the end of a stick and push it further into the fire. 'It has been on my mind indeed and I have something else on my mind also.'

'And what is that, Master Acaris?' asked Benedict, eyeing the good man sideways and repressing a smile.

'I wish that you had a companion at Clungford Lacy, someone to help you keep watch, for I do not trust that man Leofstan.'

'Sir Walter de la Reye said the same thing as we rode away from Chester,' said Benedict. 'In fact, we had hardly left the city gates but he raised the subject.'

'Do you not have a kinsman you could send for?' asked the steward. 'Or a friend, a young knight, even a scholar?'

'Sir Walter said he would be on the lookout for a companion for me before the winter set in, for I have no kin that I could ask,' Benedict answered.

'Then let us hope Sir Walter finds someone soon, for there is winter in the air and we could find ourselves snowbound. I would not wish to be snowed in with a man like Leofstan,' said the steward.

On his return, Benedict walked out to the ditch which surrounded the manor. It was deeper now, for he had had the men dig it out and spread the rich mud from the bottom on to the vegetable patch. The ditch was small protection he thought, as he looked down into it, and could even provide cover for an enemy who reached it unobserved. The water filled it only during the winter when the Welsh were least likely to attack. At other times there was often only a thin layer of mud in the bottom. There was no stockade and Benedict wondered what Sir Walter would say if he saw the place. Beyond the ditch the land had been cleared for a distance of only fifty feet or so and he knew he must clear more of it before the winter was over. Security demanded a distance of two hundred yards of clear terrain, but how long would it take to clear so much? More space would be needed if they were to see any Welshmen lurking near, and what he needed most was a strong stockade, but that would have to wait until next year.

He called across to the men who were dragging more hurdles from the wood's edge. 'Two more, and that will be sufficient. Has Godwin enough of the clay and lime mixed yet?'

'Aye, master, he has enough to plaster the manor as well as the cote,' replied a weary voice. Benedict thought he heard some curses, but they were muttered low. He smiled to himself and turned and walked round to the other side of the manor house. Two men from Mansell Lacy had been sent over to help as the good Acaris had promised, and already the four great posts for the corners of the dovecote had been set in place. The cote would not be as large as many which Benedict had seen, it might reach eighteen feet in height when its roof was in place, but it would serve for the time being.

He noticed that the men from the neighbouring manor kept to themselves and avoided his people. Had they been told not to talk with his men? Or did they avoid them of their own accord? Two of his men were now nailing some lighter timber in place between the corner posts, spacing it at the distance of a hurdle's depth.

'Plaster the hurdles when you have nailed and tied them, until you can no longer reach. Then, tomorrow, you must plaster them while they are still on the ground and haul them up with ropes.'

'They will be too heavy, master.'

'You need do only two more courses. Then you will need ladders to put the thatch on, can you make ladders?'

'Aye, we will do that on the next day and the day after that we will cut reeds,' the man said in a weary sing-song. 'And the day after that we will thatch the roof, master.'

Benedict turned away so that they would not see him smile to himself. He was pleased to see them working hard. They had neglected the place not only to the detriment of Lord de Lacy, but to such an extent that they had no feed for the animals and precious little for themselves. What would they have done during the winter, he wondered?

He heard a horse approaching and looked up sharply. Then he ran forward joyfully, for he had recognised Geoffrey.

'What do you here?' he cried, laughing, patting the horse's neck, and taking his friend by the hand. He had not realised how lonely he had been until he saw a face he knew and a man he felt he could trust.

'What do I here indeed! The knight I served will not take me back, so my honoured father has sent me to take care of you, though what I have done to deserve this exile I know not.'

'For how long?' asked Benedict.

'My imprisonment is to last the whole winter,' the young man replied. His pretence at a scowl was belied by the twinkle in his eyes. 'I hope you have good hunting, for it seems there is no company for miles around but the wild Welsh.'

'We shall find some hunting if we can avoid the foresters and perhaps some hawking,' Benedict eyed the hawk on his friend's wrist. 'And you may be surprised to hear it, but my neighbour at Mansell Lacy is a decent, humorous fellow and we can ride to Stokesay and take a turn at jousting practice.'

'Then we might make a merry winter of it!' Geoffrey replied, jumping down from his horse.

Until Christmas had come and gone there were many days of brilliant sunshine. The two young men laughed and joked together when Leofstan was not there to see. They rode several times to Stokesay, where they stayed the night and Benedict began to master the heavy lance and gain some control of the great sword which was used only from horseback.

They returned to Clungford Lacy very early one morning, having set off while it was still dark. As they approached on the track through the wood, Benedict reached out to catch Geoffrey's reign. They stopped, exchanged a glance then, turning their horses, they rode in among the trees on the right of the track.

'What do you make of that?' Geoffrey whispered.

Six or seven figures, none of them recognisable to Benedict, were leaving the manor by the door which was itself out of their sight on the far side of the building. The first of them had reached the gate which gave access to the enclosure and he turned as he opened it. The words he used were unintelligible at that distance, but there was no doubt that he spoke in Welsh. Then Leofstan came into view, bringing up the rear of the party, so that it was obvious that he had been the last one to leave the house. There was more conversation among the group of men and the leader pointed towards the west, into the bushes which

Benedict had not yet cleared. The man swept his arm to the north and the south, as though describing a half-circle of attackers, or so Benedict imagined.

As the Welshmen left, Benedict saw that over their shoulders they carried well-filled sacks. He spoke quietly, 'Wait until Leofstan is back in the house, then retreat and we will approach again after a while.' This they did and when they swung the gate open with its usual creak and their horses' hooves struck the stones of the enclosure, Leofstan emerged, rubbing his eyes as though he had just woken.

After breaking their fast, the two young men wandered down to the fields in order that they should not be overheard.

'What was in the sacks?' asked Geoffrey.

'What indeed? For there is nothing here except the beans and the seed corn, and I have looked into the barn and all that I bought is in place.'

'Was it something they brought with them or something they had stolen from another manor?'

'If any of our neighbours had been robbed we should have heard the hue and cry by now. Surely, the Welsh would not have brought heavy sacks here from their own country merely to take them back again.'

'The only answer . . . No, that cannot be . . .!' Benedict hesitated. 'What I am thinking is surely impossible, and yet . . .'

'What is it?' asked Geoffrey.

'When I arrived, the place was so bereft of food for men and fodder for the animals that I could scarcely believe my eyes. How could anyone leave himself so short of food? How was it possible that, in a good summer like the last, they had won neither hay nor corn? The strangest thing was that they did not seem to be concerned about their plight. Can you imagine what you would feel, isolated here in this place with winter coming on and food to last for only a month? What did they expect to live on after Christmas?'

'Perhaps they had intended to hunt for their meat in the forest.'

'This bunch of fools! They couldn't shoot a deer if it stood on the threshing floor and they haven't the wit to set a trap for a bird. It is almost as though they had been chosen for their stupidity and idleness.'

'Perhaps Leofstan did choose them for their stupidity,' said Geoffrey. 'Or else they are in thrall to him for some reason.'

'That might be so, but I do not think they intended to hunt their meat. They had warning that I was coming, and I suspect that they hid the food. That was what the Welshmen were carrying away and maybe Leofstan intends to join them when the food runs out here. But where has he hidden it?'

'We will search for the hiding place when he is not about, but why should he wish to join the Welshmen? And would he have left the villeins to starve when he went?'

'Perhaps he has been selling the produce for the past three years,' said Geoffrey.

'Aye, that must have been the case, for whenever de Lacy sent for the revenue this man had excuse after excuse. First the deer had eaten the corn, then there had been a sudden lightning flash which had set fire to the dry shrubs and thence the corn. There is no end to his ingenuity.'

'Is he planning to aid the Welsh in a raid? If that is the case we must take precautions.'

'I have been remiss,' said Benedict. 'The scrub beyond the ditch on the western side must be cleared for twenty yards and I will set the men to work today. It looks as though it will snow and there is no time to be lost. Such is our need that I will help in the work myself.'

Geoffrey protested, but Benedict quieted him. 'You must watch my back, as Master Acaris said. I will maintain that I am exercising my sword arm, which will be true enough, and exercise it will need if the Welshmen return.'

'Very well, let us return to the manor and set them to work.'

# 24

Benedict and Geoffrey kept Christmas on the food which their neighbours kindly provided for them. There was not one among the knights and stewards in the neighbourhood who was not sympathetic to their plight. The two friends had not yet found the secret store of food and Benedict began to think that he had allowed his imagination too slack a rein.

Two days after Christmas the snow began to fall. From mid-morning, when it had begun with a flurry of the finest, powdery snow which would not lie, but blew about the yard like a mist, until dinner time, when it began in earnest. Then the intense cold gave way to a slightly warmer wind and the snow fell like goose feathers, big and soft and smothering.

Benedict eyed the three hams which hung inside the smoke hood as he sat beside the fire. The clearing of the land beyond the west ditch had provided them with some small firewood and under the eves on the northern side of the house was a prodigious stack of logs. The cockerel and his hens had been brought indoors and roosted on the wicker shelf beside the fire, crooning softly.

'Eggs and ham, but little else,' thought Benedict. 'How long will it last? Shall we dare shoot one of the King's deer?'

Geoffrey came in from the yard with the snow thick on his shoulders. He turned quickly and barred the door behind him with a heavy piece of timber, resting it in the iron brackets which were fixed to either jamb. Benedict rose in alarm.

Geoffrey looked quickly into the dark corners of the room. 'Where is Leofstan?' he asked. Then, beating the snow from his arms, he hurried to the fire and hanging his head, he shook his hair vigorously to dry it. 'When did you last see him?' he asked as he stood upright and swept his hair back from his forehead.

'I have seen nothing of him for an hour or more,' Benedict replied.

'Beware,' Geoffrey said quietly. 'There are men on the western hill above, hidden among the trees. Leofstan came down from the hill and I thought he came into the house. He must have gone into the barn where the other two are milking. I did not let the watchers know that I had seen them, but there are at least a dozen up there.'

'He must be in the barn, he is not in here,' said Benedict, looking round again. The manor had but the one room. Outside, the north wall was sheltered by a lean-to which served as a dairy and occupied half the length of the manor. It could be entered only by a door from the yard. Against the rest of the outside wall was the huge stack of winter firewood.

Benedict had wasted no time. Even while Geoffrey was talking, he had fetched both their swords and now he brought three quivers of arrows and set them ready, against the wall, just under the window. Though the window faced south it would be possible from there to see the hill. He regretted that he had not made an arrow-slit in the western wall and now he opened the shutter an inch or so and applied his eye to the narrow opening. The snowflakes were so thick that it was barely possible to see beyond the ditch. He could make out the shadow of its far bank where tufts of long grass had stopped the snow from sticking evenly to its steep side. There was no possibility of seeing into the woods from here.

'Will they wait until nightfall?' he asked, drawing back, with snowflakes flecking his eyebrows.

'What would you do?' asked Geoffrey.

'Stay there for the time being,' Benedict answered. 'They are sheltered in the woods, and if they come close in daylight they know we will see, and shoot them from here.'

'They will wait,' said Geoffrey. 'But although the moon is thin and new, the snow will reflect what light it gives. We may be able to see them as they approach.'

Outside it was eerily silent. There was no sound of bird or animal. Benedict closed the shutter. 'Let us get some sleep now while we can,' he said. 'The dogs will bark if they approach, but what of Leofstan?'

'His job will be to open the gate, and do not be so sure of the dogs, Leofstan will have muzzled them,' Geoffrey replied casually, going over to Leofstan's bed and lying down.

They settled down to rest, Benedict on his own pallet. Soon there was a knocking at the door and Leofstan's voice was heard. 'Let me in, master, I have come from the barn, let me in.' The two inside sat up and exchanged a look, the one of anger, the other smiling.

'Oh, is it you, Leofstan?' called Geoffrey. 'Here I am, nice and warm in your bed. Have you seen your kinsmen on the hill?'

'Let me in, masters,' came the pleading voice from outside. 'I have no kin out here. Let me in or I shall freeze.'

'We can't open the door, man,' Geoffrey was almost laughing as he spoke, 'or the snow will drift in. Get you back inside the barn with the others. You can snuggle close with the cows!'

There was no further sound from outside and Benedict crossed the room and, kneeling by the window, eased the shutter open the merest crack. Leofstan was not walking towards the barn, but towards the gate. Still Benedict could see nothing beyond the far bank of the ditch. The snow continued to fall heavily and the light was going. It was quite silent outside. Then he saw the first of them, a dark shape through the snowflakes, and then another, and now half a dozen, skirting the ditch and making for the gate.

'Here they come!' he said, reaching for his bow with his left hand and for the first arrow with his right.

'The dogs made no sound, did you notice?' said Geoffrey, as he came to the window. 'Never mind, you are a good marksman. Concentrate on the fight and I will hand you your arrows. Wait until they are close enough and you will be sure to strike true.' Benedict carefully fitted the first arrow. Geoffrey hung a quiver around his neck and took up his stand just behind Benedict, where he could hold the shutter with his left hand and draw the arrows with his right.

'An inch wider,' said Benedict and Geoffrey eased the shutter open a little more. There were three men in sight, walking forwards cautiously and looking about them, but Benedict waited. A few seconds later he counted seven men inside the gate following each other, but not in single file, so that at least four of them presented a target. The first had already drawn his bow, the arrow's tip was pointing to the ground as he walked steadily towards the door.

Benedict shot the third raider, took aim and shot the second. He had resisted the impulse to look at the leading man while he shot, but now he fitted the next arrow and darted a quick look. The man was close, he must have heard a sound from behind him, but whether he had turned and seen that two of his companions had fallen, Benedict did not know. The leader was now aiming at the window. He had only a two-inch wide target and, as he raised his bow, Benedict dropped him where he stood. Less than a minute had passed, from start to finish. Benedict saw three enemies dead before him.

Geoffrey took the bow from Benedict and pushed him gently out of the way. Only two Welshmen were still in sight and they were making for the western side of the enclosure to take refuge below the rim of the ditch. Geoffrey hit one in the leg as he disappeared over the side. 'Three dead and one injured,' he said, 'and if I am right in my estimate of a dozen, we have still eight enemies out there and they won't come straight towards the door again. From now on our task will be harder.'

Benedict was sitting with his back to the wall beside the window and he was shaking. Geoffrey looked down at him and grinned. 'Never killed a man before? Well, I'll say this for you, you're a cool one. It is rare to see a man's hand so steady for three shots in a row at close quarters.' He closed and barred the shutter. 'Now, where will they attack next? They could easily set fire to the place and then where will we go, my friend?'

'There is nowhere to go,' Benedict replied, dejection in his voice. 'And we could be smoked out. They could keep the house intact and shelter here themselves when they have killed us both.'

'Why so despondent?' said Geoffrey. 'There are only eight, nine if you count Leofstan, but I would not stop to consider him and there are two heroes within the house! Now, what plan can we make?'

Benedict looked at him in amazement. They were trapped in a house of wood, and how he had learned to dread such a predicament! Did Geoffrey really think there was any possibility of their escaping with their lives?

Benedict stood with his back to the window and surveyed the room by the little light which came from the hearth. At night the two friends slept on pallets on a bench to the left of the central hearth. The steward slept on the other side of the fire, on a bench which stood a couple of yards or so from the eastern end of the house. Geoffrey had gone over to the place where Leofstan's bed stood.

'I lay here and thought about those men who left with sacks over their shoulders,' said Geoffrey, and then he bent and lifted the bedframe and stood it on its side at the length of his arm. He looked down and moved the loose rushes with his foot, and then he laughed.

Benedict couldn't imagine what there was to cause laughter and he began to think Geoffrey would never stop laughing. He rose and went to him, thinking some madness had overtaken him. Geoffrey turned to him, gasping for breath. 'Here is the hiding place,' he said. He crouched, and seemed to be pushing his fingers into the earthen floor. Then he began to rise and lifted a large wooden door. It hinged on the far side and Benedict found himself looking down into a dark, rectangular space. Geoffrey placed one foot on the floor at the window end of the hole and reached over to lean the trap-door against the bedframe. 'Now look here, Benedict,' he said, the laughter still in his voice. 'Have you been living here since last summer and have you never seen this before? No wonder the Welshmen were heavy-laden.'

There must have been twenty bulging sacks, neatly tied at the neck. He knelt and untied the string of the nearest and, as he opened it, they could see by the faint light from the fire that it was full of rich golden

227

grain, dry and good. Benedict dug his hand into it and brought out a fistful. The grain escaped from his fingers and cascaded back into the sack.

'May God forgive him,' he said. 'This is where it was all the time!'

'And is there more than grain down here?' asked Geoffrey, bending to peer into the recess. 'I feel a draught of cold air.' He turned to the fire and extracted a thick piece of wood from the blaze, holding it aloft above the hole. 'Yes, let us pull out the sacks at the end. I think there is more space beyond them.'

The two of them struggled with the first sack. It was difficult to grasp it and, gasping, they dragged it out and laid it down on the floor. Then Benedict got down into the space and, as he lifted from below, they were able to remove the second more easily. The depth of the hole was only six inches more than the filled sacks and beyond the sacks was darkness. Benedict bent double and ventured into it for a step or two. Then, turning, he said, 'Let us lift out another to make more space here.'

This they did and Geoffrey sat on the edge of the hole with his legs hanging down and, reaching for another light, he held it high. Benedict peered once more into the hole and again he ventured into the darkness.

'Ten steps and, when I feel before me, I am touching the rock,' he reported.

'Keep your voice down. If there is a way out they will be preparing to enter by that way,' Geoffrey said quietly. 'Here is the little lamp, try with that,' and he handed the clay lamp down into the hole.

Benedict disappeared this time for a few minutes. Returning, he said, 'A wooden door at ground level and fresh air coming from between the planks, but how is it I have not seen it before?'

'Is the passage straight?' asked Geoffrey.

'It must come out in the middle of the wood pile,' said Benedict.

'That is it! The wood pile covers the exit! We can keep this end open, for even if they manage to demolish the wood pile silently, we shall feel the blast of cold air and know they are approaching along the passage.'

'And my job is to mind the door and window, for you can easily hold them off as they come through the passage,' Benedict added as he climbed out of the hole.

'In fact, my friend, you can get some more sleep and I will watch for a while,' said Geoffrey, lying down on his bed. Benedict sat by the wall under the window and had closed his eyes, when Geoffrey said, 'Before they come, I must ask you something.'

'What is it?' asked Benedict, sitting upright.

'I love Alyce. Would you give your consent? Could I marry her?'

Benedict grinned. 'I wondered when you would ask. This is a fine time! Yes, if we survive, you shall marry her.'

He leaned back against the wall, smiling to himself, but almost immediately there was a creaking sound and a blast of cold air made them both start and sit up.

'They're here,' whispered Geoffrey. Benedict shivered with fear and excitement and put his hand down beside him on the floor to grasp his sword. It wasn't there. He felt around and couldn't find it.

'My sword's gone!' he whispered into the darkness. Then he realised that the fire had gone out on the hearth.

'I have mine here, keep searching,' Geoffrey replied, his voice coming from the direction of the hole in the floor. Benedict rose carefully and felt for the bow and quiver which he had hung on the inside of the shutter. They at least were there and, slinging the quiver over his shoulders so that it hung behind him, he gently removed the window bar and fitted an arrow. He kept the shaft of the arrow tight in place with his left hand, whilst with his right he eased the window open a crack. It had stopped snowing and two of the Welshmen, clearly visible in moonlight which shone brilliantly on the snow-covered ground, were conferring with Leofstan only five or six yards off. Silently he took aim and the nearest man dropped to the ground, the arrow squarely in his back. Benedict was already fitting another arrow, whilst keeping his eyes fixed on the enemy. The second Welshman had leaped sideways but was still in sight. Leofstan had dropped to the ground and was crawling away to the left. He was quickly out of sight, hidden by the partly opened shutter. Benedict shot the second Welshman, who fell and, injured, dragged himself away behind the right-hand corner of the house.

Benedict grasped the shutter, but before he closed it completely he looked round and by the light from the window saw that his sword was only a yard or so away. He glanced towards the hole and saw the whiteness of a face peering out from the darkness of the passage. He had time to see that Geoffrey was standing facing him, above the far end of the hole, and hoped that the light had not so affected Geoffrey's night vision that he would not see the Welshman emerge into the cavity below him. The intruder must scramble over the sacks in order to climb into the room, thus presenting Geoffrey with a good target. And Geoffrey was listening as well as watching. Benedict saw him move slightly and look down as he heard the slight scuff of a foot on the ground beneath. Benedict closed the shutter, plunging the room into darkness.

The Welshman must have been able to see him, Benedict thought, silhouetted as he had been against the window, so he moved to the right, picking up his sword, and stood perfectly still in the dark. As he did so there was a thud against the shutter. It was either an arrow fired from the mouth of the passage or someone trying to break in from the outside. Benedict waited, his ears straining for a further sign. Everything was silent. He could not believe that there were at least three of them in the room and more of the enemy – six perhaps, he could not know – approaching along the passage. He seemed to wait for ages and then, suddenly, there was a movement at the far end of the hole. A bump, someone muttered a short word, then a little tap. What was that? Silence. He strained again for some clue, but had no means of telling whether Geoffrey still stood at the end of the hole and whether there was still a Welshman down there, ready to climb out. He dare not move an inch, for to do so might give away his position, and he could not move to any purpose.

A whisper came from somewhere down in the passage; a tiny scraping sound, and then a flurry of noise and hot breath near his face. It might be Geoffrey! He could not tell friend from foe, so he used his hands to push the man away. He had touched a leather jerkin. Benedict took a step backwards so as to confuse the enemy as to his position and stabbed forwards with his sword. But the enemy had moved also and he felt no impact. He crouched down and above his head there was a bang as a sword-blade struck against the wooden wall. There were sounds from the place where he had last seen Geoffrey, but he wrenched his attention back to his own plight. Where was the enemy?

He put out his left hand and felt the wall, so close that he could almost lean against it. So, he was looking now towards the door, and had the hole on his right at about two swords' length. Another small sound, just before him and to the right. He struck again with his sword in a stabbing motion, restricting the possibility of striking his opponent, but reducing that of hitting some object and revealing his position. The darkness was impenetrable. For a split second he wondered if he had lost his sight, so impossible was it to see anything at all. Then there came a mighty blow on the outside of the shutter and one of the planks splintered. The room seemed to be flooded with light, though what came in entered through a split no more than one inch wide. Before him, just beyond sword's length, stood the previously invisible enemy. Benedict made one stride and lunged forward.

He took the intruder in the middle of his body. The feel of his sword going into the man sickened him. He looked straight into the eyes of his enemy and the man stared back at him, unable to comprehend that he was dying. Benedict wrenched the sword out and, turning, set his back against the door. The Welshman, still staring before him, crashed face downwards to the floor. Benedict looked to his right. Geoffrey needed only to stand where he was. Now that there was light in the room none of the enemy dared emerge from the passageway, and after a moment or so they were heard retreating.

'Back to the shutter!' said Geoffrey. 'They can shoot at me blind from there. Take command of the position!'

Benedict stepped past the body on the floor, careful not to touch it with his foot, and, ducking below the split in the shutter, took up his bow and fitted an arrow with shaking hands.

Just then they heard shouts from outside and a yell. Benedict felt a sudden release of the dreadful tension. Help had arrived.

He lifted down the bar and pushed the shutter open six inches or so. Then he turned as Geoffrey let the trap door fall with a loud bang and leaped across the floor to stand beside him.

'Philip de Lonsdale!' Benedict shouted with joy, and they watched as, across the moat, three horsemen set off in pursuit of the flying Welshmen.

Lonsdale had brought news of a son, born to Francisca in early December. Benedict was delighted.

'If married life brings so much pleasure,' said Lonsdale at sight of him, 'I must make my fortune and get myself a wife!'

'As Geoffrey will do shortly,' said Benedict. 'He is to go courting my sister!'

'And I have no fortune, so first I should go and court my father's blessing,' said Geoffrey, assuming such a doleful expression that the others roared with laughter.

With the Welshmen had gone the steward Leofstan and the two men who slept in the barn. Benedict had reported the affair to de Lacy and received word from Stokesay that de Lacy had arranged for some land in the woods to the north to be cleared and let to men who would perform labour service to the manor.

After Geoffrey had ridden off towards his home at Padley, the snow began again and, for a time, Benedict and Philip were almost imprisoned in the manor. They dug a tunnel through the snow so that they could get to the animals in the barn, and lived on oatmeal porridge and milk for a couple of weeks.

At the January court, Benedict fined the two who had been stealing the ducks and pilfering from the barn. Then the matter was forgotten. Benedict did not wish to alienate the men, for it was difficult to find men to till the land in this inhospitable region and, when he remembered the croft at Aike near the River Hull he felt sympathy for them.

Now that there was less to occupy his mind, Benedict's thoughts ran on his wife and the son he had not yet seen. He had done his duty by de Lacy and now he wanted, more than anything else, to return home to Birkdale. Two weeks after he had sent his letter, he received two letters in reply. The first he opened quickly, knowing it to be from de Lacy. He was disappointed to read that his lord, who was riding into Yorkshire, wished him to stay until the end of May.

The second letter was written on a very small piece of parchment, carefully sealed, and impressed with Sir Jocelyn's ring. He hoped it contained good news of Francisca which would cheer his depressed spirits, but when he opened it he found it had been written by Francisca herself. He was delighted and, after having read the first line, he hurried away to the garden patch and, leaning against the trunk of an apple tree, he gave his full attention to her words.

> *My dearest husband,*
> *The baby is well and growing. We have called him Jocelyn as you bid us. Geoffrey is here and will wed with Alyce. All are merry. I am well, but wish to see you.*

Here she had written something which she had then scribbled out.

> *Do not be afraid, but we have been spied upon. From the window I saw Aldred, my father's horseman. I am afraid and do not go outside the house with the child. Please come home soon. All else is well here.*
> *Francisca.*

Benedict hastened back to the house, and searched around for a piece of parchment. He kept edge cuttings, and pieces which had been cut from the bottoms of longer scrolls, rolled up on a shelf, but he could fine nothing large enough. He took up a scraper and with it he erased the words written by Lord de Lacy's clerk on the letter he had just received. Then, upon it he wrote the following:

> *My Lord,*
> *I fear that my wife and son are in danger. Pray give me leave to return to Birkhau immediately.*

This he signed and sealed, and rode off with it that afternoon to Stokesay where it was likely to be picked up by someone going in the direction of Chester. While he waited for a reply, he distracted himself from his anxiety with work. He and Geoffrey had become heroes in the neighbourhood for their stout stand against the Welshmen, and de Lacy sent workmen from Stokesay and a wagon load of timber for a stockade. Benedict was glad to see it finished.

He looked around at the place and was satisfied that he had done de Lacy good service in reordering the manor. All he wanted now was to ride north as fast as he could.

He planned his route, remembering his promise to visit Sir William

Bagshawe in the High Peak. It would have to be a short visit. He began to give Jet a feed of oats each day in preparation for a long and fast journey.

In early March Philip de Lonsdale brought the reply.

*Master Benedict de Birkhau,*
*The Lord de Lacy sends his greetings and gives permission for*
*you to visit Yorkshire for one month, provided that everything is in*
*order and well defended at the manor of Clungford.*

It was signed by the steward of Chester Castle, perhaps an indication that de Lacy was away.

'Good news?' asked Lonsdale.

'You must know well what is in it. Is my lord from home?' Benedict replied.

'He is riding up to Tickhill to meet de Longchamp. Prince John is trying to capture some of his brother the King's castles, and de Lacy remains loyal to the King.'

'His steward bids me put everything here in order and see to it that the place is well defended. What am I to do? It is in far better order than it was, but the stockade is only half-built and there is very little I can do to defend it when I am away. The Welsh could come down again at any time.' Benedict looked about him as he spoke.

'Hire a free-lance to take care of the place. You must have some money in hand.'

'I have the manor fees and the produce for which I must account to my lord, and a little money of my own, surely not enough to pay someone.'

'I have a younger brother. Eighteen years maybe. He has no occupation, as our father is hale and I am the heir. Give him something on your return and provide him with good food while he is here. The responsibility would be good for him, as it has been for you!' Lonsdale finished.

'I feel twenty years older,' said Benedict, making a wry face.

'You appear very little older, but certainly changed. The beard suits you and is darker than your hair, as is often the case, and your hair is losing its gold and turning brown. You should grow your moustache long. You told me once that de Lacy wished you out of the way of your enemies. Malebisse might be hard-pressed to recognise you now. You are broader as well,' he said approvingly, 'and you are skilled at the sword and lance.'

'Skilled enough I suppose,' Benedict replied. 'But the arts of war are not for me. I do not relish killing other men. I want only to manage my manor and live quietly.'

'Then hire my brother in your stead and get you home to Yorkshire,' said Lonsdale. 'I will stay here until my brother arrives.'

Benedict rode to Chester and told his story to eager listeners. It appeared that the raid on Clungford had been only part of a bigger disturbance further south. In the quarrel between Prince John and de Longchamp, Mortimer had taken a hand and had raised the Welsh against de Longchamp who, ruling with an iron rod in the absence of his King, had punished Mortimer by destroying his castle of Wigmore, only a few miles south of Clungford. Deep in the woodlands, Benedict had known nothing of the disturbance to the south and conjectured now on the part he had played.

# 25

Benedict left Chester and set off on the road, but he had not gone far when he saw a rider galloping towards him at great speed. He called out to ask why the man rode so fast, but the messenger scarcely looked at him or slackened his speed. A little further on and Benedict met another rider, travelling at a canter and wearing de Lacy's badge.

'What news?' Benedict called to him.

'Prince John is riding into Yorkshire and de Lacy has hanged the two castellans. John will get his revenge.'

'Who has de Lacy hanged?'

'The keepers of Nottingham and Tickhill castles. They plotted to surrender them to Prince John.' The man's horse was restless and, without relating any further news, he cantered off in the direction of Chester.

Benedict wondered what this would mean, but after a moment's hesitation, he decided against returning to Chester. If he did so, de Lacy might appear and forbid him to go north. Would there, he wondered, be trouble from Prince John and would he attack de Lacy's lands in Yorkshire? He rode on, thinking deeply, and decided to go by way of Peveril and to seek out his friends.

Apart from a handful of soldiers there was no one at Peveril, so he rode to seek Sir William Bagshawe who greeted him warmly. 'I hear your sister is to wed the son of our neighbour at Padley. This is great news and I hear she is a beauty. Will you visit Padley before you leave?'

'No, I must make haste. Geoffrey will be at Birkhau before me for the betrothal, and I have a son, Sir William! Tomorrow I must leave early for I am longing to see him.'

'You must tell us of your adventures tonight then and go carefully on your way. The country is disturbed. I admire de Lacy's loyalty to his King, but what are men to do? I am a tenant of the Prince in my little manor here, but an officer of the royal forest of the Peak. All I can do is to keep as far as possible from the troubles which beset us. Hunting is my delight, but warfare I avoid. I would advise you to go by quiet ways into Yorkshire. Do not go straight to Pontefract, and ask all the way what news there is of the situation there. You say your father holds his land of the Honour of Richmond? Good, you might be left in peace to enjoy your wife and son.'

Benedict rode via the hills near the village of Barnsley. He remembered well the route they had taken south and found his way to the Priory of Ardsley where he spent another night. And it was after he had left that place that he saw a group of people in a hamlet, lingering around the green, and talking excitedly. He stopped and asked what was amiss.

'Nothing amiss, master. A messenger rode through here this morning and he says Prince John is coming this way with a retinue of a thousand men. We have never seen the Prince, so we wait here, as you see.'

'Is he riding north or south?' Benedict asked in bewilderment, for this was the first he had heard of any movement by a large body of men, though he had asked at every village. Like all the Angevins, John was capable of moving fast.

'He comes from his castle at Lancaster and he will camp here this night,' was the reply. Benedict thought he would hasten away, but first he asked for ale at the inn and, while he was drinking, the sound of a multitude on the move came to their ears from no great distance. Benedict decided to stay and watch.

Riders and a horse-drawn cart stopped at a little distance from the hamlet. Brightly coloured tents were erected, and the baggage wagons came up next. There followed a long delay and to the disappointment of the villagers, there seemed to be no sign of the Prince. Then there came a sudden shout and a sound of trumpets. Some of the servants who had been making the camp ready ran towards the heralds who emerged from the woodland. Benedict was drawn towards the crowd, but he remembered how little he had been able to see at the coronation and he skirted round the excited people and took up his stand on a hillock at a short distance.

And there was the Prince. Benedict would have known him anywhere. He looked just as he had seen him at the coronation, talking animatedly to those who rode beside him on either hand and turning to call to those who followed. His eyes seemed to dart everywhere and he laughed readily. As he came within the area of the camp, he began to give orders to all around. The people scurried here and there, either eager to please or anxious not to incur his displeasure. Then, one of the servants, in lifting down a saddle-bag from a horse close by the Prince, dropped the bag on the ground. The Prince had been looking in his direction and, although the man was very quick to lift the bag again, the Prince had seen the small accident.

Benedict had never seen such a transformation. At one moment the Prince was smiling and affable. The next he was like a devil. He raged at the man, not as anyone Benedict had ever seen before, but as though he were possessed. His face was white and contorted. He spat out words of venom in the direction of the hapless servant, who had been seized by two of the men-at-arms. The Prince was standing in the stirrups and had turned to vent his anger on the hapless servant.

Perhaps the Prince's spur caught his horse sharply, for the animal leaped forward. The Prince did well to keep his seat for, twisted round as he was and standing, it was a wonder that he wasn't spun clear of the animal's back and dropped on the ground. But the Prince was agile and supple. Within a few yards he had stopped the horse and turned him back in the direction from which he had come. Now he bore down on the servant, still held between the two men-at-arms, and without hesitation he rode them down, all three of them. Benedict stood transfixed. There were shouts and groans, but nobody went to the aid of the fallen men. All stood back, afraid to move, as the Prince's horse cantered on and stopped and turned again. Benedict left his hillock and ran to the village. He got his horse out of the barn behind the inn and rode quietly away.

He made his way towards Pontefract by way of Ackworth, and now he began to find the villages strangely deserted. Before him on the road in the fading light he discerned a slow-moving party, a wagon, a horseman and people on foot. Hearing his horse's feet on the road, the horseman turned back and approached Benedict with drawn bow.

'Do not fear!' called Benedict. 'I am de Lacy's man.'

'Have you seen Prince John?' the horseman asked, lowering the bow, putting away his arrow and taking up the horse's reins again, which had been tucked behind his knee against the saddle to leave his hands free.

'He has camped for the night near Barnsley,' Benedict replied.

'We are bound for Pontefract. My house is not defensible and I had to scatter the cattle and sheep to the four winds. Let us hope that we find them on our return.' He jerked his head round to look after his departing household, chewing his lip with impatience. 'Still we move slowly! Ride on fast, tell them at the villages ahead to do as we have done and to go to Pontefract!'

Benedict cantered away, glad that he was a tenant of Richmond and not, for the time being, under Prince John's displeasure.

Benedict had been back in Birkdale for three days. On the journey home he had imagined how he would rush up the steps and into the hall to hold Francisca in his arms. He would conduct her to the sleeping chamber and he had filled his mind with the delights of lying with her again. But at the sight of the hall, crowded with servants and neighbours come to bid him welcome home, he found himself able only to take her by both hands and to kiss her cheek. She looked well and he teased her, asking if she had invented the story of Aldred in order to get him home again, but she instantly became pale and clutched at his arm. He made enquiries, but everything in the valley seemed normal and none of the people in the village could remember seeing a stranger who fitted Aldred's description.

He wondered now how he had managed without her for so long, and the very thought of leaving her again caused him such pain that he declared he would stay at Birkhau for ever. Francisca had shaken her head and smiled knowingly when he proclaimed this intention, for young men had to seek their fortunes at the courts of others.

Benedict had, several times, related the stories of the wild boar's attack and of the fight in the manor house at Clungford but, despite having told his adventures so often, they now seemed almost unreal to him.

Alyce and Geoffrey were so enraptured with each other that Benedict felt no anxiety about her leaving them. The two lovers wandered everywhere hand in hand, so that it was difficult to recognise in Geoffrey the cool defender of Clungford Lacy. The neighbours from Hopestones came down to Birkhau for the betrothal with everyone dressed in their finest clothes. The agreement was made before all these witnesses, with many congratulations and good wishes. Benedict declared that, as soon as it could be prepared, he would give a feast to celebrate the birth of his son and the betrothal of his sister, declaring that all the village would be invited.

Within two days of his return it seemed that he had never been away. The only change at Birkhau was the advent of the new baby and he went constantly to the cradle to see that the child was still breathing. Despite Isabelle's protestations he would often take the child out of the cradle and carry him to the window to show him the view, talking foolishly to him and thrilling at the feel of the tiny creature in his arms.

'That child will catch his death,' Isabelle called. 'Bring him back to the fire.'

On a sunny morning, when the air was filled with the song of birds, Benedict took Francisca by the hand and led her to the orchard. Sirich had made a flowery mead in imitation of the one at Coney Street. It was sheltered by an old box bush and the sun had warmed the grass. Here and there, above their heads, the white pear blossom was breaking into bloom. Benedict looked longingly into her eyes and she into his. He held her hand and stroked her hair, scarcely able to believe he was really with her at last. 'Why do you not speak to me, my darling Francisca?'

She closed her lips and shook her head sadly.

'You could speak when we are alone,' he said gently.

Again she shook her head and then she placed her fingers on her lips.

'Perhaps you are right. If you spoke at all, it would be harder for you. Oh, my dear love, how I have missed you.'

She lifted her hand to caress his face and then she laid her soft cheek against his. He trembled at the gentle touch and felt her tremble in return. 'Oh my dear, my dear!' he whispered in her ear and so they sat a while. Then he looked into her eyes again and held her face between his hands. 'You shall have a garland, my dearest,' he said, falling on his knees to pick the little flowers. She took him by the arm and, smiling, shook her head, but she could not induce him to stand, so she knelt beside him and together they picked daisies and primroses. Then they each made a garland and she hung hers around his neck and he placed his in her hair, twisting it in among the long red-gold tresses. He stood back to look at her, holding her at arm's length, but she broke free and flung her arms tightly around his neck, crushing the garland as she kissed him fiercely.

They eventually returned to the house, smiling and hand in hand. As they entered the hall, Thurstan, Sirich and Sir Jocelyn were sitting around the fire and Thurstan was forcefully expressing his usual opinion on the general decline of the country:

'Aye, there was a time they say when monks were merry and most of them married. They hunted and lived a lusty life, more like real men. In those days there was more life in them and not so much religion. Now they have these new customs, to shave their heads and wear their habits, and all of them, monks and priests, are forbidden wives, though we all know they have them and keep them hid . . . '

'The Church interferes in all manner of things these days,' Sirich agreed. 'It should mind the affairs of God and leave alone such ancient customs as marriage and the wills by which property is left within a family. These are not matters for religion. Why, they say the Church is the greatest landowner now, as great as the King perhaps, and what has all this property to do with the saving of souls?'

Benedict was listening from the far end of the hall. They felt safe, he knew, to talk thus in front of Sir Jocelyn, for he was no lover of the Church and, sure enough, he joined in enthusiastically at this point with his own particular grievance.

'Even the dubbing of a knight,' he said, 'has become a matter in which the Church must dabble its long fingers. In the old days, a lord would give the buffet with his own fist and knight a good fighting man in hearty fashion. See, now, how the Church must make of it a religious matter. How many are knighted on the field of battle these days? Instead, the ceremony must take place with prayers and night-long vigils.'

'They say,' said Sirich with an air of wonder, 'that before Duke William came from Normandy, there were peasants made knights!'

This change in the direction of the conversation was, however, too much for Sir Jocelyn and his face clouded over. 'That,' he said, 'is where the Church is in the right. Knighthood is not suitable for base men. Even the highest in the land are now becoming knights'.

The servants exchanged a wary glance. They had never before heard Sir Jocelyn defend the Church, but they knew they had gone too far. If the Church made common cause with the landowners in this, then Sir Jocelyn would make common cause with the Church.

Sir Jocelyn turned to the young couple and raised the matter of the feast.

'You are determined to have the villagers in the hall here!' The Knight was clearly aghast at the idea. 'And who, I ask again, is to pay for this hospitality?'

'My wife and I,' Benedict replied. Then he began again, 'Francisca and I wish to spend some of our money.' He had gained confidence in his absence and now felt no fear of the Knight.

'Little you'll have to live upon when I am dead if you spend in this profligate way!' Sir Jocelyn pronounced. There was no response and he scowled at the assembled company.

Nothing the Knight said could dispel Benedict's happiness and he merely smiled and turned to look again, deep into Francisca's eyes.

'Have you made a fortune in Herefordshire?' the Knight asked him truculently. Benedict was suddenly resentful.

'No more than the amount you have already spent from my wife's portion.' The Knight's face coloured and he glanced at the locked chest where his own money was kept; then, without a word, he rose and unlocked it, snatched from it a purse of money which he stuffed into his belt and strode from the hall, calling for the boy to saddle his horse.

Where Sir Jocelyn went, nobody ever knew, but he stayed away for almost two weeks and the celebrations went ahead unhindered.

Benedict strode the hills with Thurstan and Sirich. They gathered in some of the castrated tups and a couple of ancient ewes which they decided to sacrifice to the celebration. Isabelle was bidden to cull her poultry, and Benedict visited his neighbours at Hopestones to ask for some of the birds from their dovecote.

'You will have to build a cote at Birkhau. The place should have had one years ago,' said Sir Philip, while they waited for his man to raid the perches. 'The doves are wonderful good meat in the winter time.'

'I had one built at Clungford Lacy and it is one of the things I plan to do when I come into my own,' said Benedict, but he stopped then in confusion. He had always avoided mentioning his relationship to Sir Jocelyn, for Sir Philip must know he was not the Knight's legitimate son. He glanced quickly at the older man and Sir Philip smiled.

'Yes, you are of the blood of the family and the place is yours by right, or would be,' he added hastily, 'if your . . . if Sir Jocelyn would persuade the Constable of Richmond to convert his lease to an hereditable one.'

'My Lord de Lacy is of the same opinion,' said Benedict. 'It seems that this is becoming a widespread custom now. I have seen it for myself.'

'I have secured the hereditament of my own land,' said Sir Philip, 'and if my wife ever gives me a son,' he looked to the far end of the hall where his wife was playing with her three daughters and he sighed. 'If that happy day should come, I shall feel that my son will be safer.'

'Bring your wife and children to the feast and some luck might rub off,' Benedict said, smiling, and the older man smiled, too. Just then one of the farm men pushed through the outer door with a basket of white doves and received his own bidding to the feast.

# 26

Three days later, Benedict leaned back in the great chair and surveyed the happy company. The great hall had never seen such a crowd. The high-backed settle on the other side of the hearth held Sir Philip and his wife, the latest child on her knee and the two older girls at her feet. Francisca with the baby in her arms sat beside her. She had roses in her cheeks and looked extremely well in the glow of the fire. Benedict thought he would burst with the joy which welled up in him at the sight. Beside him sat Alyce, leaning her head against Geoffrey's shoulder, her beautiful golden hair shining in the firelight.

'Is the wedding to be here at Birkhau?' Sir Philip called to Geoffrey over the clamour of the crowded hall.

'No, my father has created a chapel in the hall at Padley and wishes to hold the ceremony there,' Geoffrey replied.

'A great pity,' sighed Sir Philip. 'I dearly love a wedding.'

Benedict looked round with satisfaction at the happy ring of faces which glowed in the firelight. Benches had been brought up from the undercroft, along with a stool from the sleeping loft, and Sir Jocelyn's chest had been dragged over to the fireside. There was a row of chickens on the spit and the servant boy was kneeling beside the hearth, keeping the spit turning.

For the first time since they had come there the house resembled Coney Street at the time of a festival, when Josce would invite numbers of the Jewish community to celebrate feast days. Now, seated on the benches, the elders of the village held out their hands to the blazing fire and the younger people leaned forward over their shoulders to hear the conversation and to watch the great logs burn and crackle Behind them stretched the long table, empty as yet, but under it the village children played, sitting astride the low stretcher, crawling under it, and climbing on to the ends of the table itself until their elders scolded them down again. For this was not one of those tables which stood on trestles, but a great, solid piece of furniture, of such a size that it must have been built in the room. The oak was dark from long exposure to the smoke and, since Isabelle had come to the manor, the top gleamed from her polishing. Josce's house had held a smaller version, the one covered to the floor with a rich cloth on which Benedict had placed the chequer set on his first visit to the great house in Coney Street. He remembered it now and how excited Aaron had been that evening, to see the chequers. He glanced again at Francisca and at the miracle of the baby in her arms. These had survived and again he felt a glow of gratitude and satisfaction.

Benedict asked Sirich first, as a mark of respect, to play on the pipes. Sirich sat on Sir Jocelyn's locked chest, over which he had draped a sheepskin, and lifted from the floor beside him his small pipes. He laid the bag across his knees as Benedict remembered his doing in the days of his own childhood and, as Sirich began to play, Benedict looked again at his son and wondered what his life would hold. He would protect his child from all harm, he would leave him the hidden hoard of money and the child would never know poverty.

After two of the old tunes, Sirich paused to refresh himself with cider, and Benedict called for food to be brought up from the hearth in the undercroft. Sirich went to help and there was a murmur of excitement as he and Thurstan, with straining arms, brought in the first basket. From it arose the smell of boiled and roasted mutton which now mingled with the smell of mulled ale which rose from the great pot, set on the hearth to warm. The basket was put down near the hearth and Isabelle brought in next a basket of apples. Some of these she hung on a string which was then stretched across the chimney opening and, when they were roasting with a hissing and splitting of skins, she quickly snatched them down and dropped them, white and frothing, into the pot of ale. Then she dipped a huge jug into the pot, down through the white and foaming top. She first filled the gentry's beakers with steaming amber liquid. Then the jug itself began passing round the company from hand to hand, returning five times, until the pot was empty. Some crab-apples had been put near to the glowing logs and were now splitting and hissing. One of the men picked them up with his work-hardened hands and passed them to the children. There were squeals and exclamations as the children dropped the hot fruits, but the little, bitter apples were soon cool enough to eat and, with wry expressions, the children munched. Two of the village men were pressed into service to haul up more logs, and then the two servants appeared from below, one holding each handle of another basket of meat, while Isabelle followed behind with a basket filled with hazelnuts and walnuts.

The hunks of meat were distributed, and to the ladies on the high-backed settle were passed pieces of the fowls from the spit. Francisca laid the baby in a wicker basket and picked morsels of the birds for Beatrice's little girls. The boy who turned the spit sat, alternately gnawing at his fistful of meat and leaning back to rest his head against the stone of the fireplace to keep some of the intense heat from his scorched face.

Never had the village beheld such a feast. Isabelle brought in a basket of bread. Another pot of ale, thick with spices and covered with more of the frothing, rosy apples, was set to mull before the fire. Some of the children in the dark behind the crowd of villagers were crying that they had no meat so, until more could be roasted, they were given the almost empty ale pot which they dragged under the table so that they could mop up the remains of it with their bread. Then two of the dogs began fighting over some scraps in a corner and, for a while, all was yelping and confusion.

In the middle of the din there was a loud knock at the door and what appeared to be a shambling mountain of furs entered. A murmur of excitement went round the room, for it was Lok the fowler, with his peregrine on his wrist. The laws of the forest forbade him to use the bird, but for his skill in finding and taming wild falcons he was honoured and his activities had been tolerated since before the memory of anyone present. He struggled through to the hearth and laid before them four grouse, two partridge birds and a hare. There were shouts of delight, for not only was it a contribution to the communal feast, but Lok was a hero. His poaching was a symbol of lost freedoms and he was known to provide the destitute with food when times were hardest. A drinking horn and a place were found for him and, while another basket of meat was handed round, he told the news from the neighbouring dales.

Now it was time for the story-telling and, to the sounds of the dogs crunching bones by the door and the crackle of the fire, old Mary, the widow of Guthrum the smith, embarked on the tale of the Dragon of Middlestead. A dish of hazelnuts began to circulate, but although the story was known by heart, even to those as young as seven years, there were times during the telling when the dish stopped in its journey, held by someone tense with anticipation. At each escape of a dalesman from the fearsome jaws of the monster, there came a great and universal sigh of relief and the dish would begin its rounds again.

Lok the fowler began then on the events of the battle of Stamford Bridge. This was another story oft times told, yet still welcomed, for the men of the valley were all of Scandinavian descent. Those who lived at the lower end of the dale were of the old Danelaw. Their ancestors had come from the high reaches of the dale to fill the places of those killed by Duke William of Normandy when he sent an army with orders to slaughter every man, woman, child and beast throughout Yorkshire. For some years after this the land had remained waste and so it was when the Conqueror sent men to write down the details of his new country. Then, from the higher hills of Westmorland and Cumberland, came the descendants of the Norwegian Vikings to populate the deserted holdings at the head of the valley.

It was natural, therefore, that Harold Hardrada should be their hero and his defeat by Harold Godwinson, the usurper of the English throne, was almost as great a tragedy to them as the victory over Godwinson three weeks later, when William the Bastard, Duke of Normandy, triumphed at Hastings. And so the familiar tale rolled on, of Hardrada's rightful claim, of the might of his armada, and the reasons, real and unreal, for his subsequent defeat.

Guthram the smith, whose grandfather had lived on the sea coast, then began a tale of the reiving ships which sailed the northern seas, raiding the islands of the Scots and the Irish. As he finished, one of his neighbours began the song of the Reivers, which begins:

> *Heeya Ha, Hirrum Ho,*
> *Early sails she to the reiving*

... and the song was taken up by others of the Norsemen, singing with bright, flashing eyes:

> *Heeya Ha, to Isles of daring*
> *In the Dawn she goes a reiving*

... and a great chorus shook the rafters, for the people from the head of the valley all knew the song:

> *Heeya Ha, Hirrum Ho-o-o-oh*
> *Early sails she to the reiving*
> *Heeya Ha-a-a-a-ah!*

Benedict had not been listening for some minutes. As he had looked on the ring of happy faces, the picture of a peasant with a sack over his shoulder came into his mind. Because he was de Lacy's servant at Clungford, he had fined the man for stealing beans. Now he asked himself what he would have done here in his own country? He knew that here he would have enquired into the man's condition. Was it the Clungford peasant's fault that the land had been neglected? The steward had been to blame. Benedict asked himself why he had not taken Leofstan to task for the state of the farmland, and knew that he had felt threatened by the steward and guilty for that momentary temptation when the steward had sent Gwynneth to his window. After the Welsh raid, when Leofstan had vanished with the raiders, the peasant, fixed to his place on the land, had been the only one on whom he could vent his anger.

He remembered the days of wandering, the hunger, the lack of clothing. And why had his family been wandering? Because a powerful landlord had been able to turn them off the land . . .

Another huge pot of the mulled ale was dragged across the floor and placed at the fire, and as the choruses came to an end the jug went its rounds again, whilst the old blind shepherd, readily acknowledged the wisest man in the village, forebore to tell a story, and Benedict was startled from his reverie to find that the shepherd was asking him.

Benedict's mind, occupied as it was with justice and tyranny, thought of Prince John, and he asked if they had heard of the strange descent of the Angevin Kings.

'It is a tale which has long been told, and I would not repeat it if the King and his brothers had not often told it themselves. As you know, these Kings are descended from the Counts of Anjou and Saint Bernard himself declared that they came from the Devil and that to the Devil they would return.'

At this there was a muttering of prayers and imprecations and a rustling of clothing as arms were extricated from the crush of bodies and raised to make the sign of the cross.

'It is said,' continued Benedict, 'that there was once, long ago, a Count of Anjou who journeyed far from his own home. He took none of his people with him. Where he went and with whom, therefore, none of his own people ever knew, and he was away, it is said, for three years, three months, three weeks and three days.' There was a sage nodding of heads at the precise information which, for them, verified the truth of the tale.

'When he reappeared,' said Benedict, 'he came with no attendants, but with him was a beautiful lady. Not one of his courtiers dared ask about her. She had no servants of her own, and whilever she lived with the Count of Anjou no kin came to visit her and no kin were ever heard of. The Count's own mother, when she asked about her new daughter, was told to hold her peace and ask no questions.

'The Count might have been content, for the lady bore him four fine sons who were strong and wilful, brave and daring and never ailed anything. They rode and fought and swam and climbed, longer and harder than any of their companions. Had it not been for her behaviour in church, as I say, the Count might have been content, but this behaviour it was which caused a scandal and eventually even he decided that he must do something about it, for the lady would never stay for the whole of the mass. Before the elevation of the host she would make some excuse and leave the church.

'So, one day he asked three of his knights to stay close behind her and to make sure she stayed. This the knights did and when the time came she again attempted to leave, but the knights stepped forward and stood upon the long train of her cloak so that she could not move. The lady uttered a shriek, and finding herself held fast she quickly unfastened the cloak and, grasping the hands of her two younger sons, she flew, still shrieking, through the church window. The glass shattered and rattled on the paving outside and, dragging the children through the air and still shrieking most eerily, she vanished from sight.'

'Master! Who was she?' cried a voice.

'Was she ever seen again?' asked another.

'No, she was never seen again, but all there knew who she was by the manner of her going.'

'Who? Who?' they cried, pushing forward and leaning upon those who sat on the benches in their eagerness to hear the story out to its end.

'She was Melusine, who is the daughter of Satan,' Benedict answered, and again there was a howling and groaning and the people were crossing themselves and praying.

'I won't dare go home this night!' said one woman.

'You must hold my hand all the way home, husband,' said another, and some of the children squirmed their way through the crush to the comfort of their mother's knees.

'Some cheerful music please!' cried Dame Beatrice and Sirich began the old Wassail song:

*Wassail, wassail, all over the town*

... in which he was immediately joined by one and all:

*Our toast it is white and our ale it is brown*

A child had brought some sheep-bells and clashed them noisily, whilst above the music rose the sharp, bright notes of the little bone pipes, played by the young shepherds.

# Part IV

## *1194–1211*

# 27

It was three years since the fight in the manor at Clungford. Benedict had recently been back to Herefordshire and had spent some months at Clungford Lacy, fretting all the time about Francisca.

A new steward had been appointed. The fields were well-managed and there were new shoots in the coppice. On his return journey he arrived at Chester to find that de Lacy was in residence.

'Could you support the estate of a knight?' de Lacy had asked. Surprised, Benedict had replied that he could. 'Then before you return to Birkhau, I will arrange the matter. I might have use for you, for if your manor of Birkhau is sold, I could enfeoff you in one of my own, and if you prefer to pay a free-lance, I should be satisfied. It is becoming more and more necessary that the matters of the manor court be well supervised, and there are so many knights' sons at large in the country that it is well to make use of them when there is fighting to be done. Peter de Lonsdale, who kept Clungford when you returned home, is now a member of my household.'

That night, before a host of people in the great hall, de Lacy dealt the blow on Benedict's shoulder in the old fashion and dubbed him a knight.

The journey had been a pleasure to Benedict, for he had visited his friends in the High Peak. Sir William Bagshawe entertained him in his little stone manor house, deep in the wood from which the knight took his name, and it was there that they celebrated Benedict's knighthood. The next day he strode over with Benedict to see Sir Godfrey de Hethersedge at Camp Green, who was looking older but was as jovial as ever in his dilapidated manor.

Then, still with Sir William beside him, Benedict rode down to Padley to see Alyce. He had visited her twice before in her new home and each time had found her blithe and beautiful. The two children she had borne had made her somewhat plumper and more matronly, but he could still see the glorious girl who had stepped out of the thicket wearing the new green dress he had bought for her in Wetherby on the day of her rescue, pushing back her mane of golden hair as she came towards them smiling.

Her children were bonny, fair and good-natured. Giraldus, the elder, took Benedict by the hand and led him across the yard to show a new lamb which was to be his own.

Geoffrey's father had retired to a little place nearby on the same hillside, and Geoffrey was now lord of his little manor. With pride, he showed Benedict the candlestick of polished boxwood, mounted in silver, which he had bought for their chapel. The chapel, which had seen their wedding, served as a sleeping chamber for himself and Alyce and their new baby, but it could be arranged at a moment's notice. Then the embroidered cloth was draped over the table for their altar, and the table stood under small a window into which Geoffrey had had a piece of engraved and tinted glass inserted which showed the Passion of Our Lord.

Geoffrey took him down into the deep and thickly wooded dell where he had his water mill. He shouted above the sound of roaring water and clattering wheels. 'You should ask permission to have a mill, it is a fine thing. Not only does it make a handsome profit, but I love to come here and see the wheels spinning,'

On their return, they found Alyce feeding the younger child, Richard, beside the fire, and the sight made Benedict long for his home where Francisca was expecting another baby. The next day he made his adieux and rode off towards Birkhau.

Now it seemed Lord de Lacy would not need his services for some time to come. He might have a manor in mind, but Benedict had long determined that he would ask the Constable of Richmond to make Birkhau an hereditament, and he rode home in time for the birth of his second son.

At sunrise on a day which was to prove momentous, Benedict rode down from the manor through a country so green and fresh it could have been the first morning the world had ever seen. The sun sparkled on the dew, the short turf was sprinkled with the earliest flowers and the new leaves were still crisply folded. The sky was blue and the air was full of the thrilling, bubbling notes of curlews.

As the years had gone by, he had begun to loose his dread of seeing York again and to feel some small excitement at the idea.

In the fields along the road, men and women sang as they worked, and he found himself humming the tunes they sang as he rode along. At Fountains the monks were going briskly about their work when he stopped for food and drink at the guest house. He sat outside on a bench against the wall, enjoying the first warm day of spring after a cruel winter.

Down into the flat land of the Vale of York he rode, and at the sight of the stout, square shape of Bootham Bar he remembered – how long ago it seemed – the day he had first entered the city. It might have been only yesterday. Now, as he passed through the gate, he answered the guard with his name and that of his manor and, glancing down at the fine cloak which spread over his horse's sides, marvelled at the change which the years had wrought. He had defended a manor of de Lacy's and had grown in confidence during those three years, yet still he could not face the prospect of seeing the great house in ruins and had determined beforehand not to ride down Coney Street.

He was thirsty so, along Goodramgate, he looked into the alehouse doors and returned to one which looked better than the rest, calling for the alewife. A stout and once handsome woman came to the door. She made a small boy take the horse round to the yard at the rear and asked Benedict what he needed.

Entering, he was pleased to find the place clean and the earthen floor well swept, but the fire made the room too hot for his comfort and he chose a bench near to the open door. The clattering and pouring sounds from the back room meant that he would soon be served and he was glad to sit and rest. The place was empty and would have been quiet, except for a gossip of the alewife's who sat on a stool by the fire and kept up a loud conversation with her invisible friend. Benedict, meanwhile, gazed out through the doorway down the length of the quiet street, only half conscious of the one-sided conversation behind him. It was hardly more than a long series of complaints about women of their acquaintance, none of whom, it seemed, could do anything aright. Only the alewife and her friend matched up to some unstated standard of excellence. Presently the alewife emerged from the back room and set a flagon and some pie before Benedict, asking, in a voice lacking energy, 'Have you ridden far, master?'

'My manor is in the hills above Fountains,' he replied, pre-empting any further question about his status. Her curiosity satisfied, she left him and joined her friend at the fireside. He ate and drank slowly, gazing out at the sun-drenched street and remembering times past, until his thoughts turned to Will, the goldsmith's servant, and it occurred to him that these women might be able to tell him what had happened to the old man.

'It is some years since I was in York,' he said loudly, so as to attract their attention. 'Can you tell me anything of a servant of Master Peter the goldsmith, his name was Will.'

'Will . . .' the alewife mused, but the other said sharply, 'Fancy asking about that miserable old creature, I never had much to say to him.'

'Oh, that old man,' the alewife joined in. 'Now you come to mention it, I haven't seen him for two or three years.'

'Five years at least,' said her friend. 'Wasn't he turned out by Master Peter over some trouble they had with a boy?'

'Aye, you're right, that was years ago. He's been at the hospital since then; I saw him sitting outside the door on a bench, but he's probably dead by now,' the other replied, casually dismissing the old servant.

'You say he was turned out?' Benedict said, inviting more information.

'Yes, the master beat his boy and that foolish old man went and told the Jews about it. Then they stole the boy away for their own practices and that's when Master Peter turned old Will out of the house.'

'I think it was later than that,' added the other, but the rest of their discussion was lost on him. He was amazed to hear this account of his own fate and soon broke in again, eager for more information.

'What happened to this boy?'

'Never seen again, sir, from that day to this! Disappeared without a trace, not that he was missed. Everybody knew that the goldsmith had bought him in the market from some wanderers who had him at that time. He didn't belong to anybody.'

Benedict asked again, 'And what of the goldsmith?'

The answer was delivered with such relish that it belied the woman's pretence at concern.

'Oh, he's dead, poor man. He died of a fit when they came to take him away.'

Benedict's mind leaped to some act of violence against yet another boy.

'Why, what crime had he committed?'

'He had done nothing! He was always well respected . . .' she hesitated, then added, 'and rich!'

'Then why was he taken away? And by whom?'

'They were going to take him with the others,' she began, 'but he died when they knocked on the door and they took that fine son of his instead.' She seemed to have finished, leaving Benedict little wiser, but then she exclaimed, 'One hundred of the finest citizens of York!'

He could see no connection between the two statements, until he realized that she was describing the King's retribution on the city.

'Was this following the murder of the Jews?' he asked.

'Murder!' she exclaimed. 'Those wicked limbs of Satan killed themselves. Just fancy, killing themselves like that and bringing so much trouble on this city. One hundred citizens of York!' She seemed to have finished, but then she added, 'Taken off to Lincoln and kept for ever so long . . . how long was it, Joan?' but before Joan could answer she went on, 'And the fines! They say the fines would have paid a King's ransom . . .'

The women's voices filled the room, rising and falling in indignation as they recounted the city's grievances and the harm done to its people by the mass suicide of the Jews, but Benedict wasn't listening. He was gazing along the length of the street but what he saw was little Miriam playing with her cat in the garden, and Hannah reading among the flowers and, best-remembered of all, Josce, riding in magnificence on Belazzar down by the river with his household beside and behind him, the boys running and laughing in the sun. But the querulous voices imposed themselves between him and his reflection. The women had returned to the subject of the goldsmith's family –

'. . . and the good woman, his wife, turned out of that grand house . . .'

'And those lovely children . . .'

'Were the citizens of York guilty?' he asked sharply. The startled alewife was indignant, 'That's just it, sir, they had nothing to do with it!'

'But we know who did,' said the other, and the alewife's expression changed from annoyance to amusement as she glanced at her friend. Benedict looked from one to the other with keen interest.

'Sir Richard Malebisse,' she said, with admiration in her voice, 'Now there's a fine man! Have you heard of him, sir?' she asked, turning to Benedict, but she went on without waiting for a reply. 'He has been in here and sat right where you are sitting now.' Benedict stiffened in his seat. 'Now, he is what I call a fine man. Do you know, sir,' she was warming to her subject, 'I had some money saved – Joan and I were laundresses in the old days – but Sir Richard gave me the rest of the money to set up in this alehouse – yes, gave it to me!'

'Not for nothing though, Betsy,' said the gossip, and she turned and winked at Benedict.

Then Benedict knew them; these were the two young laundresses who had been washing in the goldsmith's yard on the dreadful day on which he had been sold. They had cared nothing for his fate; he remembered their callousness and their desire only to escape to the fair. There was an ignorant dullness in their faces which had been obvious, he remembered, even in youth. How could they hold the goldsmith in such respect and Sir Richard Malebisse . . .?

The alewife was still speaking.

'That's the kind of man he is and they took his land away, just for killing those Jews.'

'I thought you said they killed themselves,' Benedict said, angrily throwing down the money for his food and ale.

'They did, the wicked heathens,' she replied hotly and, as she did so, she pounced on the money. 'And threw their money in the moat and burned all their fine things, which could have done a bit of good to the likes of us,' and, as she turned to her friend for approval, Benedict left without another word.

He called for his horse and rode on towards the house of the merchant, for his appointment was at noon and the sun was almost overhead. That morning had been so bright and beautiful that he had almost forgotten his fears as he rode down from the hills but now his spirits had sunk. For so long now he had held back from visiting York, fearing that just such an encounter would open up old wounds. He struggled with tears of sorrow and anger and, without realising it, he came to the end of Coney Street. He halted and stared along the curve of it, seeing nothing and deep in thought of times past until he was surprised out of his reverie by a childish voice and, looking down, he found an urchin who was asking if he needed a guide.

'No, lad, I knew the city well when I was as you are now,' he answered and the boy shuffled away through the dust, turning to look curiously at the fine gentleman who still sat on his patient horse, staring along the length of Coney Street.

There was a fat man who, unseen by Benedict, lingered at the mouth of an alleyway, watching. It was John, the son of Peter the goldsmith. He narrowed his eyes and looked hard at the man on horseback. Could it be the ragged boy they had almost kicked to death in his father's shop?

Had he not been sold, thought Benedict, he might have run about the city streets like that ragged child until starvation or fever had carried him off. Or would he have grown up to be one of those hangers-on down by the river, eager to earn a bare sustenance by casual labour? What a miracle to have been rescued by Josce . . . He gazed, unseeing, the great house still obscured by the curve of the street and, hardly knowing that he did it, he touched the horse with his heel and slowly rode forward, impelled by the past, yet fearful of what he would see.

What he saw made him stop in his tracks. The walls of the house could be glimpsed between a myriad of wooden scaffolding poles and new roof timbers spanned the place where, on that fearful Passover night, he had seen smoke seeping up through a gaping hole. Then he had known that all was lost. That moment was so fresh in his mind that he could recall the sensations, the smells and sounds of that night, even in the sunlit street. He moved forward again, his breath harsh in his throat, sadness and pleasure fighting inside him, for the house lived again!

At the corner of the building he stopped and looked up through the scaffolding at the windows which had been such a delight to him as a boy. The two sets of twin arches were plain to see and the new stone of the ornate pillars was startlingly white. The broken carving had been replaced with loving care, exactly as it had been before.

Men were clambering about, and standing in the road, looking up at the work in hand, was one who must be the foreman. Benedict called to him,

'Who is repairing this house?'

'Aaron of Lincoln,' the man replied, before turning back to the scaffolding and calling up to the nearest man to leave what he was about and get up to the roof.

To Benedict the name was familiar, but the Aaron of Lincoln whose name had been so illustrious in the house of Josce had died many years before. Could this be Aaron, Josce's son? His throat contracted. Had he survived in Lincoln after all? Were they misinformed all along? And had Thurstan really looked for him? The questions tumbled into Benedict's mind.

If it were so, his own future was immediately in doubt. Had they known of Aaron's survival in the summer of 1190, they would not have dared touch a penny of the money. Sir Jocelyn had been spending freely for years and Aaron, even as a child, had been proud and severe. What would he say or do when he knew? But, was it Aaron?

'Can I help you, sir, are you a stranger in York?' It was the foreman and Benedict was startled to see that the man was standing at his horse's head.

'This Aaron,' he asked, 'what age of man is he?'

'Why, about of an age with yourself, sir.'

'What does he here?' asked Benedict.

'This was his father's house, sir. He was the son of one of those killed in the siege of the castle in the first year of King Richard's reign.'

The blood had rushed to Benedict's face and he found himself sweating.

'It's a warm day now, sir,' the foreman commented, mistaking the flush on his face and neck. Benedict unclasped his cloak and, swinging it from around his shoulders, draped it across the front of his saddle.

'Yes, the sun's strong now,' he replied. 'When is this Aaron coming to York?'

'We're supposed to have this place all set to rights by the Feast of Saint Patrick, but we shall be hard pressed. The rain has held up the work. Those roofing stones have been stacked and waiting upwards of a month now, and I hope we shall not be delayed by rain again. What a wet winter it has been, and following on a wet summer, but the weather seems to be changing for the better!'

'Does this Aaron come alone or does he have a large household?' asked Benedict.

'Oh, I know nothing of his household, sir, but I hear he is very rich indeed, one of the richest men in England.'

Benedict had heard enough.

'It will be hot work on the roof,' he said and handed the foreman some money. 'Buy some ale for your men.'

'Thank you, sir,' then, looking at the coins in his hand, 'Thank you again,' he said, surprised at such generosity from a passing stranger.

John, the goldsmith's son, had followed Benedict down the street. He stood at a little distance but near enough to catch a few of the foreman's words, and he waited until Benedict had ridden off before he shuffled over and stood where the criss-crossed shadows of the scaffolding lay across the road.

'What's his name, the man on the horse?' he asked and the foreman saw with distaste that the man's jerkin was bespattered with the remains of his last meal.

'I do not know the gentleman,' he replied, turning away. 'Godwin!' he called to a man on the roof's edge, 'how goes it?' The workman answered that they had almost finished, and the foreman turned as a voice behind him asked, 'What did he want to know? Did he ask about the Jew?'

'Be off with you, I know nothing of the horseman. It can be no concern of yours,' the foreman answered sharply.

John set off along the street at a slow and clumsy trot, but he was soon out of breath. At the street's end he looked this way and that but could not see what he was looking for. He stopped and thought for a moment, chewing at his thumb, before hastening down the street in the direction of the Lendal Ferry. Soon he disappeared into the passage leading to a large and imposing house.

'Is Sir Richard indoors?' he asked at the kitchen.

'What do you want with him, fat John?' asked the cook, his fist, gripping a long wooden spoon, on his hip.

'I have some news for him,' answered John.

'Will he wish to hear your news though, that is the question is it not? Do you have news? Or are you after a feed, fat John?'

'I have news I tell you. I have seen someone today.'

'Oh, you have seen someone. Well, I have seen a great many people and you are one more that I did not wish to see. Tell me what you have to say to Sir Richard and I will send someone to relay the message.' The cook, grinning, licked the spoon. The sight made John's mouth water and he put one foot over the kitchen step.

'Out with you, say what you have to say from the yard. I can do without your fat carcass in my kitchen.'

'Tell him, then, that I have seen Benedict.'

'Benedict who, for God's sake?' and the cook licked the back of the spoon.

'Benedict, my father's shop boy who ran off with the Jew's gold.'

'Never heard of him,' said the cook, extending his hand and with great dexterity pinching between finger and thumb a crisp radish. He popped it into his mouth and crunched it noisily between his teeth.

'Well, he will have heard of him and he will want to know about it. Sir Richard Malebisse is a friend of mine. We were in the riot together. He will reward me, you will see.' John the goldsmith's son was sweating now and beginning to be angry. The cook decided that more teasing might prove dangerous and called for one of his scullions.

'Go tell one of the men that fat John is here and has news of a Benedict who ran off with the Jew's gold,' he said, grinning as he did so, and implying by his tone that he gave no credence to the story. A few minutes later, a man-at-arms came to the kitchen door.

'Sir Richard says that unless you know where he lives he has no wish to know merely that you have seen him.'

Fat John looked dejected. 'Can't I have a bite to eat?' he asked, trying to see past the man and attract the attention of the cook, but there was a guffaw of laughter from the dark recesses of the kitchen.

'Get out of here!' said the man-at-arms.

Benedict rode on towards the house of Galien the wool factor, pondering upon the new situation and, during the afternoon, his business was conducted with only half his mind on the affair, for he was preoccupied with the arrival in York of his brother-in-law.

On the journey home, he wrestled with feelings of guilt about the money and his marriage to Francisca, and he rehearsed all the excuses he could think of. To Aaron, he must be able to present a sound case for what he and the servants had done. It had, of course, been the only possible resolution of their difficulties, but would Aaron see it in that light? Above all, what would his reaction be to the marriage of his sister and the boy whom his father had rescued from the gutter? What did it matter to him that Benedict was the adopted son of a knight?

Despite the fact that they lent money at interest the Jews were proud people. Josce had told him how they had been scattered about the world after a great struggle with the Romans, a mighty race who had conquered England. Now the Jews had to live as best they could, but their lineage was noble and ancient. Benedict had no doubt that Aaron would not look lightly on his sister's marriage. Then, what of the children? That matter was even more difficult, for they had not been circumcised nor had they been brought up in the Jewish faith.

Perhaps there was no need for a meeting. Aaron would suppose his whole family dead and need know nothing about an obscure manor in the northern dales. Then it occurred to Benedict that Aaron, as a Jew, had no power over him. To whom could Aaron appeal? If he claimed that Benedict had his money, he would lose the money to the King and his sister would no longer have a refuge. But Benedict remembered Josce, as the brothers of Joseph in the Bible story had remembered how they had sold their brother. He dismissed the ignoble thoughts which had entered his mind. It was his duty to confront Aaron and tell him the truth. In Josce's house, he had been sheltered, fed and educated – treated, in fact, like one of Josce's own children. No matter what the cost, he must never betray any member of Josce's family and, remembering the dreadful price which the whole Jewish community would have paid if he had died when Josce took him in, he knew that the debt he owed was to all the Jews of York.

Although he could have reached home by late evening he chose to stay the night at the guest house of Fountains. As he had ridden out of York he had given alms to a beggar boy.

The child had been sitting by the roadside, weeping bitterly, and when questioned had sobbed out a sorry tale about his parents having gone off and left him. Benedict had asked a few pertinent questions and it seemed the child was telling the truth. Benedict knew too much about destitution to be easily fooled. Then, no matter how often he had turned and told the boy to leave him, the child had followed and after two miles on the road, Benedict had turned back.

The boy had cringed as he bent towards him, and Benedict spoke kindly, remembering how the stones of the road hurt a boy with bare feet, then he had hauled the child up behind him on the saddle.

Now he asked the monks if they would take the boy into their care, but they seemed reluctant. They feared, they said, that the bad winter would force many of the hill people to seek charity and suggested that Benedict keep him. Benedict wondered then if the child had been put in his way as a test of his charity. With the ragged child beside him, he attended vespers and the music moved him as never before. Afterwards he sat in the twilight, gazing down the valley as the sun was setting, thinking over the story he had to tell when he arrived home.

It was mid-morning when he rode up to the manor. Francisca was nursing the infant in the sleeping chamber. She rose when he came to her and looked at him anxiously. They sat down on the edge of the bed and he held her hand as he told her that her brother was not only alive but returning to York. He watched her carefully as he spoke, holding her hand tightly, seeking to sense her reaction through the touch. She looked away from him, then stared down at the floor for a while. Then she pressed his hand and looked straight into his eyes. He asked her to come down to the house, but she shook her head and he carefully disengaged himself and left her sitting there.

Thurstan and Sirich were called in from the yard, and he waited until all were assembled before he broke the news.

'What did Francisca say?' asked Isabelle, using the term as they always did, but meaning only to ask what her reaction had been.

'She was calm,' he said.

'The shock might have made her speak,' said Isabelle, regretfully.

'It is a blessing that she does not,' said Benedict.

'What will you do about this man?' asked the Knight.

'I shall have to tell him. I shall go to York when I get news that he has arrived.'

'Is that necessary?' Sir Jocelyn asked with obvious disapproval.

'Yes, it is,' said Benedict.

'And suppose he asks for his money?' said the Knight.

'Then we shall have to give it to him,' said Benedict, turning as he did so and looking straight into Sir Jocelyn's eyes.

The Knight shrugged and looked away in disgust.

'What about Francisca, will you take her to York?' asked Sirich.

'The shock might turn her mad,' said Thurstan.

'I do not think so,' said Benedict. 'It was almost as though she had expected it.'

'We must not let it be known that there is any connection,' said Sir Jocelyn. 'If you visit this man it must seem that you go there on business, we cannot let anyone suspect the truth. As for the lady going to York, I think it most unwise. People will see her enter the house and will remember who she was and who she now is. As for returning the money, I forbid it.'

'My respect to you, Sir Jocelyn,' said Benedict, 'but the money is not ours to keep.'

'The Jew cannot claim it, he dare not!' Sir Jocelyn exclaimed.

'How can I not offer it to him?' said Benedict, grasping the edge of the table.

'It was his sister's, and is hers still, or yours,' the Knight replied.

'The manor is prosperous now. We have enough, we must offer the money to her brother. I cannot see . . .'

'It is Francisca's money,' said Isabelle. 'Ask her what to do.'

\*

Thurstan had been looking troubled ever since Benedict had revealed that Aaron was alive and this had not been lost on Benedict, who wondered when Thurstan would speak to him.

It happened the following morning. Benedict walked up the hill and when he turned at the accustomed place to look down on the house, he saw that Thurstan was following him.

'I came to tell you . . .' Thurstan was out of breath.

'About Aaron?'

'Yes, about Aaron.' He looked miserable, but Benedict was angry and made no attempt to help him in his difficulty.

'Sir Jocelyn made me swear I wouldn't tell you. Perhaps he knew that some of the Jews survived, but he said that if Aaron lived all would be over between you; that he could not continue with the bargain if Aaron were alive. What could I do? You needed somewhere to hide Francisca and you needed the manor. He suggested that I go to Lincoln and stay there for a day or two and then return without asking any questions. I couldn't do that! Suppose I had found that the Jews of Lincoln had survived; suppose even that I had seen Aaron in the street, how could I then have returned and said I had not found him?'

'So you didn't go to Lincoln at all, and the story of the boat on the sandbank and the lost horseshoe . . .?'

'If I didn't go to Lincoln I could say that I had not found him, but if I had learned that the Jews survived then how could I bring back the story he wanted of me? You must understand that.'

'So you did not ask after my sister either?'

'No, I am sorry. I am very sorry for what I did, but he made me swear.'

'You do not mind breaking your oath now?'

'Nay, what oath! How could I keep up the story when Aaron lives and breathes in York?'

Benedict remembered how hard he had found it to argue with Sir Jocelyn, and for how long had the Knight kept Francisca's money?

'I forgive you Thurstan,' he said. 'The Knight is not an easy man to deal with.'

# 28

On an April morning in 1194, Benedict again sat in the Coney Street house he had loved so well. As he told Aaron his story, his boyhood friend toyed with a quill pen and regarded him in silence. It was as well for Benedict that he could not read his thoughts . . .

I can hardly believe this. He sits there, across the table, telling me that he has married my sister, that Thurstan couldn't find me in Lincoln and that they heard that all the Jews were dead! Does he think me a fool? Then he tells me he has two sons. Is that intended to win me round? What do these people take me for?

My father brought him here to Coney Street when he was at death's door, covered in blood and with broken bones. I remember everyone creeping about, trying not to disturb him while he lay overhead, regaining his health. No more could have been done for him by his own kin, if he had had any, nor if he had been the son of some great lord. If we had been Christians the matter would have been a simple one, but for a Jewish family it was madness. To call it charity is to underestimate the risk we took. We might all have been killed. The people would have rioted if he had died in our house.

I didn't allow my father to see, in those first few weeks, how angry and afraid I was, and I was always polite to the boy, even friendly, but now see what has happened. My father was a very pious man, what he did was just, but he risked all our lives to do it and then they killed him. What evil people they are! We must never trust them, they are uneducated and eat dirty food, and when we show them kindness they turn on us like savages.

But let him talk on. What excuse is this . . .? Oh, I see, they did it all to save my sister, and no wonder with a fortune to be gained. Now he tells me that he is not even the son of this knight – a man as bad as Malebisse I shouldn't wonder – but that he is the son of a monk. Even their holy men are immoral, begetting children of the peasant women! They took my sister away to this manor without making proper enquiries. He says that Thurstan went to Lincoln so that he, Benedict, should not be recognised. That seems strange – and what is this he is saying now? His sister was sold and he found her in a leper hospital! She must have been a prostitute, and my sister is married into this family. Not only that, but my nephews are of the blood of this bastard with a prostitute sister – it is not to be tolerated – what can I say to him to express my anger?

Benedict watched Aaron carefully, as he sat back in his chair looking very wise. He thought that Aaron must understand the predicament that they had been in. Meanwhile, Aaron had taken a long look at Benedict and was thinking:

He looks tired and confused, I'll say that for him. He isn't brazen, in fact he looks exhausted. Perhaps it took courage to come here to see me.

'Moses, bring some food and drink for our guest.'

Ah, he wishes to know how we escaped, I will tell him my story.

'We would have been safe,' said Aaron, 'even if we had remained in the castle, but we were not to know that and Cresse had arranged for us to leave when it was dark. He had had his own boat rowed down river when trouble threatened and arranged that it should be brought back the following night. Sure enough, we met them at the appointed place and sailed down to Boston where Christian friends helped us. The next day we took ship for Flanders.

'It was fully four weeks after Passover before we learned what had happened at York. The news reached King Richard in France much faster. I could scarcely believe what people were saying. They tell you things, you hear the words, but the reality doesn't come to you until some time later. I could not believe that my whole family had been butchered by Malebisse and his following, and not only my family but the whole community. I had thought that such things happened only in France. What a fool I was to suppose the English were different.'

He looked up sharply at Benedict then. 'But you saw this? You saw the killing of the survivors, but you say my father and the rest committed suicide. That I can never believe. You got the story from a soldier and they are great tellers of lies. My father could never have killed them, no, it is not possible. Once, long ago in the time of the Romans, my people had to do this at a place called Masada, but it could not happen now, not again!'

Aaron turned his face away and there was silence for a while. 'It is just the sort of excuse these people would make to cover their crimes. Backward people will do anything rather than face up to the result of their own actions. Everything which happens to them is somebody else's fault. If they have no money, it is because we have stolen it from them!

Yet they waste their resources in every conceivable way and come to us for money as though it were a right – to spend and spend, and to ask others to replenish their treasure chests. Then they complain about the interest we charge, as though they have a right to use our money to our own detriment.'

Benedict was speaking again, but Aaron was not listening. He was remembering the market place in a French town, where he had seen books which he knew to have come from Old Benedict's house and, worse than that, he had seen, draped over a stall, a gown which had belonged to his father. He remembered how Cresse had led him away, his eyes blinded with tears.

Now, thought Aaron, he has finished eating and leans back in his chair. I will not say too much to him, but sit quietly for a while longer and see what else he has to tell me. Now he remains silent, but I can wait. When he has considered for a while he will no doubt begin again with the excuses. He must have come to ask for some favour. He will not have eaten food of this quality since he lived here before. What do they eat up there in the hills? Sheep's meat, I suppose, and pig meat! I suppose they have very little fruit, apart from the wild berries they can gather in the autumn. He cannot have eaten grapes for a long time.

What does he think of the house, I wonder? It is more magnificent than it was in my father's day. Soon I will tell him about my London house. He seems to know very little about me, if anything at all. Does he know that I shall soon be one of the richest men in England? And he was the one who was the good scholar and studied accounts and the merchant's trade with my father. Now he is a knight and I, well, I am a merchant and a lender of money when, if I had been a Christian or if we had our own land again, I would be the one to ride and fight ... I will show these creatures that they cannot defeat us. We are not a race of savages to be beaten down. Has he noticed the new tapestries and the carved furniture from France? Or is he too preoccupied with his lies and excuses?

He offers me the money! Ah, but wait, he is offering me what is left of it – it appears his 'father' has been spending liberally. But now, what is this? They hid some of it! These people do well not to trust each other. This one cannot even trust his own 'father', but I mustn't let him see that I am amused. They hid the money in the ground, I see, but what is he offering back to me? Will it be all of what is left? Or is it going to be only a fraction so that he can live in luxury and idleness?

He says I must have it all and that he can work for his living. Yes, he can use the skills he learned in my father's house, but he admits it. He knows that my father taught him the skills which will allow him to be independent. He has earned money already in the employ of Lord de Lacy. Ah yes, there must be money to be made in the service of an Honour the size of Pontefract with manors under the stewardship of ... well, the English. Shall I take the money? But it isn't mine, it is my sister's. But how do I know that she lives and is well? I have only his word.

There was silence in the room, Aaron was thinking over what he should say, and he reached for a little scroll which lay near the end of the table. 'On this scroll,' he said, 'is one of the lamentations for the Jews of York which was written by Menahem ben Jacob of Worms.' He pushed the scroll towards Benedict who opened it with care and, as his eyes scanned the Hebrew writing, Aaron added, 'Of course, you copied the Hebrew but never, I suppose, understood it.'

'I learned some of the signs, naturally, as the same words were repeated constantly in the starrs, but poetry is beyond my understanding.' He placed the scroll in Aaron's outstretched hand and Aaron began to read:

> *Sword, wherefore turnest thou in all directions,*
> *Consuming all around thee?*

... and Benedict's head sank on to his open hands, for he had seen the swords and he wept and heard no more.

They sat in silence for a while, until Benedict asked Aaron if he would visit them at Birkhau. Aaron answered guardedly and all the time he had to struggle now to maintain the feelings of antagonism which Benedict's story had at first aroused in him. He was determined not to give way too easily.

Now he wishes me to visit this manor of theirs. What does he take me for? Some yokel who will go struggling over the hills in out of the way places, neglecting my business? Let him bring my sister here. But he says the Knight recommends that she should not come to York in case she is recognised. What does it matter? I live here in York and am recognised. But, of course, they are passing her off as a Christian. I am surprised at my sister, but then I suppose she had to suffer this in order to survive at all.

What is this he is saying? That my sister is happy but that she does not speak? Now he contradicts himself! She is happy, but she hasn't spoken since the massacre. Then how do they communicate with her? So, she hears perfectly well and nods or shakes her head. This is strange, but then she witnessed the killing of the last of our people. I was spared these sights, and was that the worst of her suffering, I wonder? What must it have been like to find herself alone with these, our servants, and not a single person of the Jewish race to turn to in her despair? I have heard of people being struck dumb with sorrow or fear, and she suffered both. Poor Francisca, who was once so bright and lively, now she says nothing at all.

What is this that he is telling me? That the Constable of Richmond will allow him the fief when his 'father' dies. I would not trust in a promise made by the Constable, but he says the Constable is to be trusted. He is a man called Alan, of a great age he says, and butler to Earl Conan in the reign of King Henry. He must indeed be a great age. I remember there was one called Amalric made Constable. He must have been one of those who bought a position from King Richard. There were plenty ready with their money as soon as he came to the throne. What was it that was said at the time? 'He relieved all those whose money was a burden to them!' That was the truth. I wonder what happened to Amalric? It must have been de Longchamp who recalled the old Constable . . .

When he has finished, I will ask him about this manor of his. I never travelled up into the hills. It is said the people there are wild men.

So, just as I thought, he did not take too readily to living in squalor after a luxurious youth spent in this house. It is not to be wondered at. Very few of the English have lived as we did, not only amidst luxury but in such a cultivated household. My father always made a great pet of him. Was I jealous? Perhaps I was, but he owes more than his life to us.

He is asking me again to go to his manor of Birkhau, but I must return shortly to London, I have business matters there. Seeing him again I remember now how once I hated the money business, but now I think of little else!

What shall I do? I would like to see my sister again but it would take almost a week of my valuable time to go up into the hills. He says it is beyond Fountains . . . one day to travel up, stay one night perhaps and return on the following day? It could be accomplished and there is business to be done at Fountains. The Abbot is Ralph Haget, a soldier from a great family in Yorkshire and he is no man for business. Perhaps he wishes to borrow. I have heard he is considering clearing a couple of hamlets . . . the way in which these people treat each other . . . it is as though they were two nations, and one exists to pillage and ruin the other. The rich do not seem to recognise their fellow Englishmen as a people, bound together like a family.

What if I go to Fountains, what excuse can I make for riding further into the hills? Perhaps I could say I was going to buy wool from the manor of Birkhau, yet they would think it strange that I should deal in wool with such a small manor when I can buy in huge quantities from the monasteries. They must have heard of the wealth of this family. If the old Knight has been spending in this profligate way, the news will have travelled. There is no end to their stupidity. It would not surprise me if they conjecture that all the money at Birkhau has been borrowed from me. But will a visit endanger my sister? Would she speak, I wonder, if she were to be alone with me? Does she live in fear of these people? Yet he speaks of her with affection. Would she recover or would the shock make her condition worse?

He is asking me again about the money.

'No, I thank you, but the money is my sister's. I ask you only to keep it safely and to continue to care for her.'

I had intended being severe with him, but here I am, almost thanking him. He is looking about the room now, shall I ask him to stay?

'Will you stay the night? It is too late now to travel and you will be more comfortable here than you would be at an inn. Moses, show this gentleman to the upper chamber, over the solar, and make sure he has a comfortable bed.'

He can sleep where he slept on the first night on which he ever entered this house, Aaron thought, smiling, and turning the ring on his finger.

When Benedict left next morning, he was noticed by a groom who was leading a horse along the street. The groom hastened to a house down by the Lendal Ferry.

# 29

The manor house had been swept as it had never been before, and Benedict was pacing the floor, waiting impatiently for his guest. He had been looking forward to showing off his manor to his brother-in-law, but now he glanced again at the hall and felt less sure of winning Aaron's approbation. Isabelle heaved herself off the bench beside the fire, the same bench on which the old crone had been used to sit. Her hips were giving trouble, but she had been determined that the house should do them honour in Aaron's eyes and had exerted herself mightily to see that everything which could be cleaned had been cleaned. She must have forgotten, thought Benedict, just how splendid the Coney Street house had been – if she were to see it now!

Thurstan and Sirich, also stiff and slower in their movements, had given the undercroft an equally thorough cleaning and this year's calves had been turned out of the building and put into the fold which Sirich had constructed. Benedict employed boys from the village to help with the work, and one of these had been sent to graze the pigs in the little wood on Hinderbank. In their absence, the sties had been swept and swilled until no smell of pig remained.

The old Knight had not been pleased at the prospect of this visit and, partly to Benedict's annoyance and partly to his relief, had ridden off that morning without saying where he was going or for how long. But Benedict wasted no time in considering Sir Jocelyn's affairs; he was preoccupied with the arrangements and was hoping that the weather would turn mild again so that Aaron's people could be lodged in the undercroft. He smiled wryly when he remembered that Sir Jocelyn had been annoyed and surprised to learn that Aaron would bring with him two servants, a groom and a clerk. As for himself and Francisca, they would give up their private room and their bed with the fine new red hangings to Aaron. The old Knight had never reclaimed the sleeping chamber, but seemed content to sleep in the hall beside the fire with the rest of the household.

The ancient man and his wife, who had crouched by the hearth for so long, had died two winters before, and now there was the boy, Peter, whom Benedict had brought home on that day on which he had discovered that Aaron still lived. The boy was learning to be useful in the house and about the farmland. He was learning to feed the pigs and poultry, and in the evenings he mended harness or plaited straw; he even helped Isabelle to spin wool. He was a good boy and a salve to Benedict's conscience, for he had always felt he must repay Josce's kindness in some way.

Benedict had considered what the neighbours might think of this forbidding young man, Aaron of York. They knew that he would be arriving but had been left to conjecture the reason for the visit. It amused Benedict to think that they might suppose him in debt to the Jews, a supposition he was almost inclined to encourage for he was anxious that it should appear he was no richer than his neighbours. Benedict hoped that Sir Philip and his lady Beatrice would not come down from the manor of Hopestones to see the visitor. It would be difficult enough for Francisca, without having an audience to gape at her first meeting with her brother. Benedict hoped Aaron would be gentle with her for, although he had been polite, he seemed a hard man.

What, he wondered, would Aaron think of young Jocelyn? He was now three years old, a beautiful child with the gently curling black hair of his grandfather Josce. The likeness pleased Benedict and he felt that Aaron must notice it. The children resembled neither of their parents and Dame Beatrice had teased them, he so blonde and she with a mane of auburn hair, about the black-haired children they had produced.

Francisca looked well, and he glanced across the room, admiring her. She no longer stared into the fire all day, as she had after the dreadful events at York, but stood erect and walked gracefully. Her complexion was pale, as her mother's had been, and she resembled her more as she grew older. He tried to see her as Aaron might and hoped once again that the meeting would not prove distressing to Francisca, for she was still very nervous, and subject to fits of shivering when anything upset her.

At last Sirich hobbled in.

'I can see them coming, they've reached the wood. They'll be here in five minutes.'

Isabelle went to the fire, to stir the pot and turn her capons on their spits once more. 'Peter!' she called to the boy, 'go up again, and make sure the shutters are closed. I don't want sparrows getting into the sleeping chamber.'

But the child was impatient, 'I've been three times. Let me go to see the strangers.'

Thurstan had been eager to be the first to go down the hill to escort the company to the door. Benedict wondered if he had taken the opportunity to speak to Aaron and ease his guilty conscience.

Now they were below and getting down from their horses. Benedict went out to greet Aaron, who had alighted from a fidgety black palfrey of great value. Sirich was holding Aaron's horse and was weeping and wiping his eyes on his sleeve.

'I thought we were followed as we rode from York to Fountains but my men dropped back a little way and could see no one. Perhaps they saw what we did and hid themselves.' Benedict looked at the two men and saw that they were armed with swords. They were not Jewish servants. 'Yes,' Aaron said, noticing his glance at the two men-at-arms, 'I often collect monies for the King and I am allowed this protection.' He spoke scathingly.

'Peter,' Benedict called to the servant boy, 'go down to the village, and tell them to keep an eye open for strangers.' He was glad to have an excuse to send the boy away, for he didn't wish him to witness the meeting between brother and sister. Then he led Aaron and his clerk up the outside staircase and into the hall.

There Francisca sat in the Knight's high-backed chair with the baby on her lap and young Jocelyn standing at her knee, clutching her skirt tightly and frowning at the approaching guest. Francisca lifted the little one on to her arm and rose to meet Aaron calmly. It was Aaron who looked nonplussed and he hesitated as he approached her. Then, he stepped forward boldly and, taking both her and the child in his arms, he kissed her on the cheek.

'What handsome children you have, and dark as I am, like our father was,' said Aaron.

Benedict heaved a sigh of relief. 'Come to the table,' he said. 'Our fare is plain but good, and thank God, we have plenty of it.'

They settled themselves at the table.

'How long is it since you went down to Fountains?' Aaron asked.

'A month perhaps,' Benedict replied. 'The lambing was going well until the weather turned, but since then we have been so busy I have been nowhere. There have been poor folk from the hills going down towards Fountains all this week.'

'And not only from these hills,' said Aaron. 'The Abbot has set up a camp for them at the gates of Fountains, as big as a large village. The monks have put up some of their travelling tents, but there isn't shelter for all. I suppose the promise of food is enough to attract them and they are sleeping in the open, wrapped in their cloaks.

'It's cold weather for that!' said Isabelle. Aaron swung round at the sound of her voice and looked startled, perhaps at the clear evidence of her increasing age. Until that moment Benedict had not realised how much older she looked, and he felt remorse for having brought her to this hard living. Aaron went forward and embraced her and she burst into tears, sobbing on his shoulder and speaking incoherently.

The boy Peter entered and stared at the strangers from a stool by the hearth.

'Your property is in good order, Master Benedict,' said Aaron. 'I see you have benefited from the labour of my father's old servants.'

Benedict reddened and hoped the boy hadn't heard. 'Yes, we have made the whole place good again and Isabelle has made the house habitable.' He was suddenly aware of the stark difference between his house and Aaron's, and the reminder that the servants had been Josce's both startled and hurt him. He wondered if Aaron had always thought of him merely as a servant, for when he lived at Coney Street he had forgotten his real status and had always thought of himself as one of Josce's immediate family. He turned then to Peter on his stool by the hearth.

'Had they seen strangers in the village?' he asked.

'Nobody rode through the village, but one of the shepherds came down from the hill while I was there and he had seen the track of horses on a path above.'

Benedict looked anxiously at Aaron, but Aaron continued with the conversation as though nothing had been said which could cause anxiety.

'But you must have had a bad harvest for two years past. Even in the Vale of York the corn yielded little; up here in the hills it must have been very poor, hence this distress.'

'We have always been able to save some seed corn, but I pity the hill folk. Our own villagers will be fed, but our neighbours at the head of the valley are in difficulties,' Benedict replied. 'March and April are cruel months.'

As he spoke he recalled that Sir Jocelyn had promised to feed the village if the need arose, yet there was something about his promise of charity that made Benedict feel uncomfortable. He remembered what the Knight had once said, that when he had the opportunity of trading food he would do so in exchange for the villagers' freedom from customary labour. Had that chance come at last?

The meal was laid before them and Aaron glanced curiously at his sister from time to time, obviously unable to comprehend the fact that she never spoke. He tried several times to ask her a question and she looked at him pleasantly, as though she believed he could read her thoughts. Meanwhile, someone else would answer for her and eventually he gave up the attempt to make conversation.

Isabelle had taken the younger child on to her lap and fed titbits to young Jocelyn who stood beside her. It was this which demolished Aaron's composure and they saw that he was weeping too.

'I remember your feeding Miriam in just that way,' he said when he had recovered himself, and that set Isabelle weeping again, to the surprise of the child and of young Peter, stirring a pot on the fire.

'Tell us, Aaron,' said Benedict, 'of affairs in the great world outside. What of King Richard?'

'Well, the King vanished on the return from the crusade, you must have heard.'

'Yes, but it took time for the rumours to reach us here, for I had not been to Richmond for some time. How was it that no one knew where he was?'

'First Duke Leopold of Austria had him. Richard had insulted him at Acre and he intercepted him, crossing his territory on the way home. Then the Duke sold our King to the Emperor who did not wish anyone to know where Richard was, and so the King languished in Germany. All the time his brother, Prince John, was spreading rumours that he was already dead. How those brothers love each other!'

'So, all we heard was true,' said Benedict.

'But there were further ramifications, of which you were perhaps not informed,' said Aaron. 'Philip, the French King, wished to buy him from the Emperor and to release him only upon the promise that the Angevin possessions were divided and weakened. Luckily the Emperor knew his onions, as they say, and hung on to his prize, putting up the price at the same time.'

'And was it true,' said Benedict, 'that Prince John hurried to Paris and vowed to divorce his wife and marry the French King's sister?'

'What wickedness,' said Isabelle. 'You would think they would know better.'

'Morality is not their strong point,' said Aaron. 'Philip and John then tried to persuade the Emperor to keep Richard in captivity or to sell the King to them, which again forced up the price of the ransom. But the Emperor was too wise to trust those two and, as soon as Richard and the Emperor came to terms, it is said that Philip sent a message to John saying, "Look to yourself, for the Devil is loosed."'

'The Devil's brood indeed, and for all this we have to pay,' said Benedict. 'One hundred and fifty thousand marks, and only half of it raised as yet. This is a burden we should not have to shoulder at a time of poor harvests.'

'And you will easily be able to calculate what interest such a sum could be earned if I had the luck to have it,' said Aaron, smiling.

'You surprise me,' said Benedict, 'by your application to business affairs. I used to think . . .' here he hesitated, for he could not continue with the idea which had been in his mind – that Aaron would have made an ideal knight.

'What else is there for a Jew in a Christian land?' asked Aaron. 'An apostate Jew can become a soldier, it has been known, but that is not my way. I am faithful to my religion and therefore I must be either a scholar or a merchant. You, Benedict, should have been a scholar and I, desiring a more active life, can find it only in trade,' his voice dropped, deprecatingly. 'Then, what other course is there than to become rich? In riches there is some security in this alien world.'

Benedict remembered Josce's words, which he seemed to hear again, in the stillness of the room: 'Riches do not bring safety, Benedict, particularly not for Jews . . .' He forbore to repeat the words to Aaron, there was no point in doing so. Instead he said, 'I see you have achieved one of your ambitions. The black palfrey is as beautiful a horse as Belazzar.'

Just then the dogs rose up and rushed, barking, to the door. There came cries from below which startled them all. They listened and heard above the barking of the dogs, 'Help us, Master Benedict. Give us food and shelter for the night. Pray, master, help us feed our children.'

Benedict rose hastily from the table and went out and down the steps. Those inside could hear him speaking and then he called for Thurstan. Next they heard one of the great doors to the undercroft being dragged open, and Benedict reappeared and ordered Isabelle to take bread to the people below.

But before she could move, they heard the sound of a horse outside and Sir Jocelyn's voice shouting angrily at the people below. He entered the room, bustling as though to show his annoyance, drawing off his gauntlets and swinging his cloak from around his shoulders before ever looking at the assembled company. His eye fell upon Aaron and he stared coldly at him. Aaron stared back just as coldly. Sir Jocelyn turned a red and angry face upon Benedict.

'What is this rabble at my door?' Then, seeing Isabelle on her way to the stair-head with a basket of bread, he demanded angrily, 'You are now feeding these people! If we once start to feed them we shall have as many here as are gathered at the gates of Fountains. What are you thinking of do you want to ruin us?'

'These people must have food!' Benedict said, firmly. 'It would not be Christian to let them go hungry and it is still a long way to Fountains. They have come down from the high valleys where things are even worse than they are here. Think what a winter they have endured, and no food available at this time of year unless it was stored from last.'

'I will not have it!' The Knight roared, his face growing dark with fury. 'What food there is to spare shall go to the village, and in return they shall promise to give me the labour they used to give my father. He wasted this land, just as you would!' and he raised his fist as though to strike Benedict. 'My father was like you, full of what he called Christian charity, and where did that get him? He gave them their freedom for money, and you saw the state to which this manor had sunk. Now is my opportunity to set right the natural order between this place and the men of the village. You will not waste that food, I say!'

'Might I remind you, sir, that the money we have is my wife's marriage portion,' said Benedict in a level tone, but with increasing anger showing in his tense jaw and rigid back. 'With that we can purchase the help we need. You will not reduce these people to servitude again.'

'And who rescued you?' the Knight shouted.

'Josce of York rescued me,' Benedict replied.

'If I had not brought you here . . .' the Knight was in a passion, and as he spoke he was looking not at Benedict but at Francisca and then at Aaron, who returned a very level gaze. Sir Jocelyn fell silent, but his face was purple. He put out a hand and grasped the edge of the table. Then he turned and fell, and struck his head on the hearth.

# 30

It was the spring of 1199. Benedict and Francisca were happy in Birkdale. He had grown accustomed to her silence, recognising that it was a refuge for her from the pressures of life. Only occasionally, when he longed to discuss something and hear her views expressed, did he become annoyed. Then he might speak irritably to her, and regret it later.

He paid for a free-lance to do his knight service to the Honour of Richmond and devoted his time to the management of his farmland, for now that Sir Jocelyn was dead Benedict was free to farm as he pleased. But that was not his only business. He knew as much of trading as he did of farming, and had bought a share in a ship. Henry of Fishergate, who leased the King's mill in York and with whom they had sheltered on the night of the massacre, was his partner in a ship which traded from York through the waterways as far as Lynn, and had once taken a load of wool round the coast to London for Aaron. It was not customary for knights to engage in trade, although he knew that some in the Derbyshire Peak had leased the rights to mine some of the lead which was abundant there.

Benedict sold some grain to merchants in York, but wool and grain were the only commodities which left the manor of Birkhau. The timber was used for building and repairs. The small coppice-wood was made into hurdles and strong baskets or burned for charcoal and traded with the local smith for horseshoes and other ironwork.

Aaron he rarely saw, for he was now the King's own moneylender and spent most of his time in London where he had been appointed by the Crown to be Arch Presbyter of the Jews. One of the consequences of the York massacre had been the organisation by the Crown of the Jewish moneylenders. In every large centre there was established an Archae of the Jews, where every debt was registered and the copies of each starr were kept. Both Jewish and Christian clerks were appointed to oversee all the transactions, but Aaron had been set over all. Benedict was secretly proud of this, though he spoke about it to nobody but Francisca and the servants.

News came that King Richard had died in France, and young Jocelyn said, 'Will there be a coronation? Can we go to see it and King John?'

'No,' said Benedict. 'It will be at Westminster and I do not like to be among crowds. No, it is too far.' The boy looked at his father's face, curious that he should suddenly have become so serious and stern.

Benedict was thinking of the future. Life under King John would not be easy. Despite having provided Alyce with a small portion, and having lent money to Sir Philip, which he was sure he would never see again, Benedict felt that his sons would be secure. With Francisca's money and the profits from his trading venture, which he kept in Sir Jocelyn's old wooden chest, they were richer by far than their neighbours. However, Benedict took care that people should not see just how rich he was. Many a knight only ever had a handful of coins in his house and a show of wealth was quickly noticed. He even allowed the neighbourhood to think that Sir Jocelyn had spent everything, and that what he had, he earned by his own efforts.

He often rode down to York to confer with Henry about the boat, and they were thinking of purchasing a second vessel. What Benedict didn't know was that on these visits he was often noticed, and that reports of his movements were relaid to Malebisse. After his last journey John the goldsmith's son, ever eager to earn easy money, had visited the house near the Lendal Ferry and on that occasion he had been lucky, for Sir Richard was in residence.

'He must have the Jew's gold. The townspeople said that it had all been thrown into the moat before the Jews killed themselves, but how could anyone throw that far? A man could not scatter coins so far from the tower as to clear the mound and fall in the water. If they had thrown their money down we would have found it in the grass the next morning. We looked hard and long but never discovered a single silver penny.'

'You say he is rich?' Malebisse asked. 'He makes money from trading. Perhaps that is what he lives on, for those manors in the hill country do not make a fat living.'

'I wouldn't mind having one. I have always fancied myself a knight with a grand house like my father had and an elegant wife,' said John.

The knight looked at him with disdain. 'How did he come to be living there? I have asked certain people, but they either do not know or will not tell and I suspect it is the latter.'

'Some say he is the bastard of a knight who held of the Honour of Richmond, but I have never been able to get to the truth of it,' said John.

'Try Henry the miller. You may get something out of him,' Malebisse replied, turning into the house and closing the door behind him.

It was the year 1200. Some had said that the world would come to an end, but the spring had passed peacefully and those who had been disappointed to find that the world still flourished now cast dire warnings about what might yet happen at the year's end.

Benedict was sitting with Thurstan and Sirich on a bench by the wall of the manor. The afternoon was warm and the two children were playing on the short grass with some pebbles which they had carried from the stream. Jocelyn was now nine years old, and Simon seven.

Each boy was engrossed with his play and neither looked up, but they talked as they made patterns with the different colours of the pebbles. Simon sat back, gazing with satisfaction at the three white pebbles he had arranged in a row.

'. . . And if you are bad,' he said, 'when the world comes to an end, the Devil will take you to Hell.'

'Then I will not believe in the Devil,' Jocelyn replied.

'You must believe in the Devil, because it is so,' said Simon.

'Because you say so,' Jocelyn replied. 'And you are only seven years and not old enough to know anything.'

Thurstan interrupted, 'Because the priest and the Church tell us so.'

'But how do they know?' asked Jocelyn.

'Mercy on us!' said Isabelle, coming down the steps behind them. 'The child asks how the Church knows. The Church knows everything. If the Church says you must believe in God and the Devil then you must believe.'

'But how do they know?' Jocelyn asked again.

'It is written in the Bible,' said Isabelle with finality.

'But who wrote the Bible?' asked the boy.

'God wrote it, so it must be right,' said Simon. 'Look, the Holy Trinity! My pebbles represent the Trinity.' He sounded very pleased with himself and Isabelle rushed across the grass and disturbed the short row.

'That is blasphemous. You cannot represent the Trinity with pebbles,' and she crossed herself as she turned back to the house.

'The Trinity is represented in glass in the church window,' the child objected.

Jocelyn was not interested in Simon's pebbles, his mind still dwelt on the original problem. He left his play and came to stand by his father, looking down at the ground and scuffing the sand with his foot.

'Father, how can you believe in something just because somebody else does?'

'Bless us, what does the child mean?' asked Isabelle, now half way up the steps again on her way to the house.

'Well, if somebody said he believed that swans were black and I can see for myself that swans are white, should I believe that they are black although I can see by looking that they are white?' Benedict felt a great bond of sympathy with his elder son, for he had often pondered on such questions himself. He remembered how, in Josce's house, these problems of belief and perception were freely discussed. It was dangerous, however, to question the teachings of the Church and he decided he had better intervene.

'In the matter of swans you must believe your eyes, for God gave you eyes to see, but in questions about God you should follow the teachings of the Church.'

The boy looked at his father and, to Benedict's dismay, there was a look of doubt on his face.

Simon had replaced his row of three white pebbles and he stood up now, dusting the sand from his hands by rubbing the palms across the front of his jerkin. 'I believe what the Church says in everything. If the Church said that swans were black and not white, I would believe them,' he said.

'That's a good boy,' said Isabelle as she disappeared through the door above.

Francisca was seated by the fire, darning a pair of Simon's hose.

'Don't you bother yourself with that, my dear,' Isabelle said. 'Go out in the sun and keep an eye on those two boys. They are discussing matters of the Church like grown men. I do not like to hear it. It is not natural in children.'

Francisca ran her finger over the darn once or twice, regarding it with satisfaction before she looked up at Isabelle.

What a pity it is, she thought, that the children cannot be allowed to question, but I suppose it is right to protect them by insisting that they accept whatever they are taught. It is safe for me only because I appear to be a Christian. The habits have become so fixed in me that I no longer notice what it is that I am doing in church.

Her thoughts were interrupted by Isabelle. 'I think Simon will go into the Church. He has always been a serious child. What a thing it would be if he became a great man in the Church.' She was sweeping the ashes towards the centre of the fire, and she looked up to see Francisca going out into the sunshine.

'I have decided to take Jocelyn with me to York tomorrow,' said Benedict, as Francisca joined them on the grass. 'I must talk to Henry about the ship and arrange for a time when he will be able to store my wool clip, and I have heard that King William of Scotland may be coming to York.'

'I want to go too,' said Simon, and from the tone of his voice Benedict expected a tantrum to follow.

'You must stay with your mother, you are not old enough to ride to York.'

'Jocelyn could ride on Blackie, and I could ride in front of you on the saddle as I do when we go up to church at Middlestead,' the child protested.

'I have business to conduct and, while Jocelyn can amuse himself, you have to be watched. You fell into the mill leat last time, do you not remember? I do not wish to be encumbered with children.'

'You always take Jocelyn! I am older now, I will not fall into the leat!'

The discussion ended with the usual tears and stamps and threats, and on this occasion the child grasped a handful of grass, and flung it at Jocelyn. Before Benedict could do anything about it, Isabelle had hastened down the steps and, grasping the furious Simon by the wrist, had dragged him into the hall, away from retribution.

Benedict and Jocelyn rode down from the hills the following day. The weather was fair and the boy enjoyed the journey. He felt relief that his younger brother was not with them, for Simon was always arguing, which distracted him from his own thoughts.

While the two were riding towards York, John the goldsmith's son was sidling in through the great doors of the King's mill, and had been standing in the shadows just inside for some time before Henry noticed him.

'These sacks,' Henry had been saying, 'are to go to Catte Street in London for Master Aaron.' His man nodded. 'And those over there, marked with a piece of red wool on the corners, are for Selby. You will not forget?'

'No, I will load them this very afternoon,' the man replied, and then he turned and saw John.

'What do you want?' he asked.

'Do you have any work?' asked John.

'You couldn't work if you tried,' the man replied, grinning at Henry, and turning to go. 'You don't know the meaning of an honest day's work.'

As soon as the man had left, John sidled over to where Henry was standing, counting the sacks with wagging finger. 'Do you know a man called Benedict, master?' asked John.

'I know several Benedicts,' Henry replied, still preoccupied with his stores.

'You know this one. He has business with you. Fair hair, about my age.'

'Why do you wish to know about anyone who has business with me?'

'I think I knew him when we were boys. We played together. I would like to speak to him and ask how he is.'

'If you know him, then speak to him when you see him in the street. Why come bothering me when I am busy?'

'I thought you might know for certain if it was the right man. Did he live in York when he was a boy? Is he married to a lady with copper-coloured hair?'

'If you know,' said the miller emphatically, 'that this is the man you knew as a boy, I do not see why you have to ask me.'

'But you know the man I mean. Tell me, is he married?' wheedled John.

'I don't know men's wives. Men's wives do not conduct business with me!' Henry replied.

'Is he coming here again soon?'

'Get out of my way,' Henry replied, moving to get round behind a stack of sheepskins. 'I have work to do if you do not.'

'If he comes again, let me have word. You will do that won't you, Master Henry?' and John moved, crablike, towards the door, waiting for an answer which was not forthcoming. He returned to the house near the Lendal Ferry.

'I couldn't find out anything today, Sir Richard, but I'll make it in my way to watch for him coming again. I won't fail you. Do you have a coin or two about your person, for I . . .' here his voice trailed away as the door was shut in his face.

It was late in the afternoon before Benedict rode into York on a good bay horse, with Jocelyn trotting beside him on a young black pony which had to be ridden with care, for it was full of tricks. They rode straight to the King's mill and John missed them, for he was down in a ditch, sheltered from the wind, gaming with some of his riverside cronies.

Henry sent young Jocelyn into the mill where his wife made much of the child and gave him a bread cake sprinkled with poppy seeds. In the granary Henry was saying, 'That idle loafer, the son of Peter the goldsmith, has been here this morning. He pretended at first that he was looking for work, but he gave that up after a while and started asking questions about you.'

Benedict frowned. 'What questions?'

'First of all he said he knew you and that you played together as boys, but then he asked about your wife. I told him I did not know the wives of every man in Yorkshire!'

'I do not wish everyone to know my business, and I think this John spies for Sir Richard Malebisse. If anyone ever asks about the lady we had with us on the night of the riot, you should tell him that we left her with her kin at Chester and have not seen or heard of her since. I would be obliged to you, Master Henry, if you would not only keep fat John at bay, but have someone keep an eye on him, if you have a man you can trust sufficiently.'

'Indeed I will. I fear I know what he wishes to learn and he shall not learn it here,' Henry replied.

# 31

Benedict had watched his sons with wonder as they grew. How was it that two children from the same parents could be so different from each other?

Young Jocelyn at fourteen years seemed to his father to be an amalgam of himself at that age and of Aaron. The boy took everything in his stride. He found no difficulty in mastering Latin and French and had inherited some of his father's talent with numbers. Yet he was also a fine horseman and skilled with bow and sword. Benedict had had a strip of land cleared and sanded so that the boy could ride at the ring with his lightweight lance. He would watch as, over and over again, the boy would canter briskly toward the hanging ring and never miss his aim.

He loved the boy so much that sometimes he was frightened by the intensity of his feeling. He watched with anxiety, fearful that some harm might befall the youth, yet he gave the boy freedom, for he was anxious also that young Jocelyn should have the liberty to develop his talents.

The younger boy, Simon, was quite different. He had never seemed at ease with the world. He did not like to play with other boys but preferred to read whenever the light was good enough. He seemed to be suspicious of everybody he met, weighing their words and judging them severely.

Benedict entered the hall on a glorious morning in the summer of 1205 and saw that Simon was sitting, as usual, in the patch of sunlight under the window. The father stopped there, frowning, and regarded the boy's bowed head for a few moments. He had wished his boys to be scholars, as their grandfather had been, and he wished for the thousandth time that he were free to tell them the truth about their ancestors. The children had been well taught, he had seen to that. He had begun their lessons in reading, and when they were able to read aloud with little hesitation Francisca had listened to them, the book on her lap, her finger pointing the way across the lines while they mastered first Latin, then French, but Benedict was not happy today to see Simon thus engaged.

'Why are you not out with your brother on the hills? It is fine weather.'

The boy started, and raised his head with what Benedict took to be reluctance. There was a moment of irritation and disappointment, but then he remembered the boy's grandmother, Hannah, keeping her finger on the place in the book if she were disturbed, and he smiled sadly at the recollection.

'You should be out and taking exercise. Your brother is just coming down the hill, do you see through the window? Why not go to him?'

'It is better that I should attend to matters of religion, Father. My brother Jocelyn should do likewise.'

Benedict turned to watch young Jocelyn as he came down the hill with Thurstan, a bow in his hand, and he sighed with regret and turned again to see Simon's head bowed over his book. Jocelyn took a healthy interest in everything which was going on around him and was on friendly terms with all the people of the valley. Simon, on the other hand, was determined to enter the Church. Nothing which Benedict said would make him change his mind, though the boy was too young yet, and Benedict puzzled again about what to do with the him.

There was to be a fair on the following day at Otley, and Benedict determined then that he would take both the boys with him. Simon should see more of the world, and Jocelyn would be delighted, he knew, to see all the activity, the goods for sale, and the traders who brought tidings from far and near.

Isabelle had fallen on the stone stair one night during the previous winter and had broken her leg. Benedict would think of her whenever he stood at the top of that outer stair, and of her prediction that someone would meet his death on them one winter when it was icy. He remembered with a shudder the weeks when she had lain on a pallet by the fire, groaning first with the pain of the injury, then with the fever. At last her leg turned black and everyone said she would soon die. He had sat beside her until she had died in the early hours of a cold morning. Every so often he would think he heard her voice and turn quickly. How he missed her! She had been more than a mother to him and to Francisca, and he was glad that she had nursed his sons. Did Jews and Gentiles go to the same Heaven he wondered? Had she found them there? Did she nurse Miriam on her lap?

Since Isabelle's death, Sir Philip's oldest daughter, Judith, had come from Hopestones to live with them and to serve Francisca as her lady. She was a brown-faced, rosy-cheeked young woman who liked to be outside whenever the weather was good. She knew how to lamb a ewe and calve a cow and was almost as useful as any man, but her mother despaired of her and had sent her to Birkhau to learn finer manners.

She was learning how to keep house, for the manor of Birkhau was famous for its orderly housekeeping and for its dairy produce; Isabelle had set a high standard and Francisca passed it on. Judith learned by example and they communicated by signs.

The manor had seen certain improvements since the death of old Sir Jocelyn. There was now a proper staircase to the sleeping loft and the bed was hung with fine red cloth and laid with linen sheets. Benedict had, at last, had a dairy built on the north side of the manor house, and it was a great pleasure to the women to work there in the heat of the summer, separating the cream from the milk, wrapping the butter and cheese in cabbage leaves on the cold stone table.

Peter, who had helped Isabelle in the house, was now a shepherd, and Toc, the boy who had replaced Peter, swept the house, turned the spit, milked the cows, and took the cattle to the woodlands to graze when the time was right. But there was still plenty of work for the two women to do. They tended the poultry, made ointments and syrups for the winter, and strewed the floors with sweet-smelling herbs, as Isabelle had done. While the light was good they sewed and in the evenings they plaited straw for baskets and skeps, and sewed pairs of hose while the men spoke of the adventures and tribulations of the day.

It was a good spring, with apple blossom in plenty and the promise of a fine hay harvest. The lambs were strong and healthy, and there were none of those cold, wet mornings which kill lambs more quickly than the snow. The three cows which had been overwintered had calved, and one of them had given birth to strong twins. Twins of any kind were not welcome, but these, having survived, were regarded by the villagers, who looked everywhere in the spring for signs, as a good omen.

# 32

On the day of the sheep fair in Wharfedale, Francisca and Judith were gathering watercress downstream from the manor. Barefoot and with their skirts lifted knee high, they waded about in the water like two children at play. Suddenly, the sound of a horse's hoofbeats made them stop and watch the place where the path emerged from the woodland. From the trees rode a man on a bay gelding who, to Judith, seemed to be a stranger; Francisca, after staring intently at him for a few minutes, grasped Judith by the elbow. The girl looked up enquiringly and Francisca frowned, looked towards the man, shook her head very slightly and gave the girl a little push forward to indicate that she was the one to answer questions. She turned and waded to the other side of the stream, setting the golden king-cups swaying on their stems. Then she pushed her way into the bushes and disappeared from Judith's sight.

Judith waited anxiously for the horseman to arrive. If only Francisca could speak! The rider had the appearance of a groom or man-at-arms, though he rode unarmed. His age, she judged, was about forty years. She was acutely aware that Benedict was not at home and that her own father was out on the hills with his men.

'Is the manor of Birkhau far ahead?' he called while he was yet at a distance.

'Not far, you will see it from the top of this hill,' Judith replied, pointing up the valley.

'Does Sir Jocelyn still live?' the man asked.

'Whose messenger are you?' she asked in return.

'You're a saucy maid,' he replied.

'I am the daughter of . . . ' she began haughtily, so as to put him at a distance, but then she stopped – perhaps it was wisest to tell him nothing.

'I beg your pardon, my lady,' the man answered, but with mockery rather than respect. Judith was confirmed in her suspicion that there was something wrong here, and that Francisca had recognised the man as one who would be unwelcome at the manor. With another saucy remark, the man rode on and Judith turned and waded as quickly as she could through the water.

'Who was that?' she asked, and Francisca turned, looking strained, even frightened. Then Francisca put down her basket of cress on the bank beside her and took tight hold of Judith's wrist. She drew the girl up beside her and, picking up her basket, led the way upstream, quickly but cautiously, at a distance from the manor so that they could see but not be seen. Entering a clump of hazels, they stooped to peer through the branches. Across the stream and a distance of grassland they could see the front of the house, and there was the bay horse, tethered to the wall at the foot of the stair. The man was alone and was staring about him. Francisca waited no longer, but took to the edge of the wood and, with Judith following closely, avoided the road all the way to Hopestones.

As soon as Lady Beatrice saw them she hurried forward. 'Whatever has happened?' she asked, leading Francisca to the settle by the fire. Francisca was very pale. Sweat stood on her forehead and she pressed her hand to her chest, leaning forward and breathing with difficulty.

'A man rode up out of the wood while we were gathering cress and Mistress Francisca must have recognised him, for she hid, and when he had gone on his way to Birkhau, she drew me after her and was careful to hide all the time we were passing the manor house, and even coming up the hill on the way here.'

'Thomas! Go down to Birkhau at once,' Beatrice commanded. 'Take the pony, but don't gallop up to the door or you'll call attention to yourself.' Even as she spoke his mother took from the boy's hands the harness he was lovingly polishing. 'Don't speak so the stranger can hear, but find out who he is and let them know secretly where Mistress Francisca and Judith are.' Turning to Judith she asked, 'Did you say that Sir Benedict is away?' The girl nodded, and her mother turned again to her young son. 'Now take care, child, this man might be an enemy. Tie the pony up behind the house so that the man can't see it.' Then she remembered something else. 'In fact, you must ride on the grass, not on the track so that he won't hear you. Now have you heard me, Thomas?'

'Yes, madame, I'll go if you'll only let go of my arm, and I'll do as you say, I'm not a fool you know.'

His mother cuffed him across the head, but very gently, as he dodged away and ran out to get his black pony.

'That boy is a little rogue, but he will go carefully and bring back news within the hour, mark my word.'

'That man called me little,' said Judith indignantly.

'He did, did he? Then he is a rogue indeed to speak so to a lady, but I suppose you were both wading about in the water like cottagers.'

'How else can we gather cress, mother?'

'Now, never mind about cress, or your dignity, or anything else for the moment but Mistress Francisca's health. Take her to lie on my bed. She needs to rest and if this man should appear at our door, she will be out of sight.'

Francisca lay on Beatrice's bed, but she never closed her eyes, starting at every sound and clutching at the bed sheets if footsteps approached. She had the strange, almost blue colour around her lips that Beatrice had noticed before. Judith hoped that her little brother would do as he was told for a change, and be quick to bring back news and possibly instructions about what they should do. He was all too fond of thinking of some embroidery to any errand he was given. She tried to imagine what was happening down at Birkhau, and why Francisca had been so alarmed by the man on the bay horse. Who could he be? Were there others behind him? Was he riding on ahead to spy for enemies who might threaten Birkhau or even Hopestones? Sirich and the boy could hardly defend the house. What was it about Birkhau? There was some mystery concerning its people.

Mistress Beatrice fidgeted about, offering food to Francisca who shook her head wearily in refusal. Then Beatrice went restlessly to and from the window which gave only a restricted view of the road. The window space was filled by a wooden frame, covered with the stretched caul of a newborn calf, and this she removed so that she could put her head out and see further down the track. She locked the door against she knew not what, but her own husband was away and she knew it might be evening before any of the men returned to Hopestones.

'I wish I had sent Thomas for the men before I sent him down to Birkhau,' she said, wringing her hands.

'Shall I go down through the woods, mother?' asked Judith. 'I need not approach too near. I shall be able to see the house from a distance.'

'No, don't you go as well, my love. Wait. Let us see if Thomas returns within the hour. If he does he can go then and fetch the men.'

Thomas did return within the hour, and surprised his watching mother by approaching from the head of the valley.

'You didn't see me, did you? I was very clever and went right on past Hopestones and round by Grindstone cliff and down beside the stream . . .'

'What a waste of time. Tell us what the man is about and what happened at Birkhau.'

'Well, I did as you said, madame. I rode fast for most of the way and then I made Blackie walk and passed around the back of the house and put him into that little place beyond the pigsties.'

'What about the man!'

'I could see his horse and I had to jump off and grab Blackie round the muzzle, for you know how he always whinnies when he sees another horse. Well, I got him into the yard, as I said, without him making any noise, and I shut the door to put him in the dark and gave him some hay to quieten him. He's used to that stable, because that is where Jocelyn kept him when he was his.'

'Will you stop talking about that wretched pony and tell about the man!'

'The man was sitting on the steps – I crept round the bottom side of the house you see – the man was sitting there, and Sirich was standing above him on the steps and the door tight shut. I couldn't see the boy just then. Sirich was asking something . . . yes, I heard, "What happened to the horse?" and I thought to myself, well, there is the horse, tied at the side of the archway, but they must have been talking about some other horse, for the man said, "Sir Richard ordered me to take him with them."

'Then Sirich said, "You didn't have to obey," and the man said "What would you have done?" Then Sirich said, "But you stayed with Mala . . . Mala-something," I can't remember.'

'Malebisse!' said his mother, and she did not sound pleased.

'What then?'

'Well, then I jumped out of my skin. The boy, Toc, had come up behind me and he reached out and pulled at my jerkin. I dodged back behind the wall with him and I whispered "Who is this man?" and he beckoned me and we went to the back yard. Then Toc said, "He is groom of the horse to Sir Richard Mal-e-bisse."' Thomas looked at his mother again for confirmation. She nodded and he continued, '"Malebisse is an enemy of my master. This man has come to spy." So I said, "Is he followed by others, do you think?" and Toc said he didn't know, so I said, "Stay here and keep out of sight, but listen to what is said. I'll ride down through the woods on my pony and see if there are others coming up the valley." So I did that. I took Blackie out and . . . '

'No more about the pony. What did you find?'

'I rode down as far as the village, and the people there said the man had ridden alone and they had seen no companions. So I told them to send a lookout further down the valley and have a boy ready to run all the way to Hopestones if any strangers came.'

'That was a good boy.'

'Then I rode back and came at the manor from the rear again, and I was just leading Blackie into the yard when this man came round the house, leading his horse. He looked surprised to see me and he said, "Are you one of the sons of Sir Benedict?" I said, "No, I have ridden down from Hopestones to see if they are at home." You see I knew they were away at the fair with their father. Then the man asked me where Sir Benedict's wife was, and I said she was away from home. He asked me where, but I said I didn't know. He asked me sharply then, if she was at the manor of Hopestones and I said, "No, I told you I have just come from there." Then he asked me how she looked. I couldn't think why he should wish to know, so I gave him a wrong description because I didn't like him and it seemed the best thing to do.'

'How did you describe her?'

'I said she was fair and bonny, with light hair.'

At this, Beatrice laughed aloud, 'You told no lie, but that description would never serve to know her by!' and they all relaxed a little. Thomas looked very pleased with himself.

'You haven't heard how I came home,' he said eagerly.

'We need to know more about this man first,' said his mother. 'Now, what else did the man say, and what did Sirich do?'

'Oh yes, Sirich came into the yard and saw us there. He frowned at me because I suppose he thought I might say the wrong thing, so I said, "This man wishes to know where the mistress is" – you see I was careful not to call her by name – "I have told him she is away, but I don't know where she is." Then Sirich looked much better in the face, I thought, and he said, "Yes, she is at Malton." Well, then I knew for certain that things were amiss, nobody from Birkhau ever goes to Malton, and then Sirich said to me, "This man wishes to stay the night, but I have told him there is sickness in the house and everyone is away except myself to nurse the young man." Now, don't you think that was good for old Sirich. He is very old but his wits are sharp.'

'It was very good for such an old man,' said his mother, nodding. 'But what did the man do then and where is he going to stay?'

'Sirich told him to return by the way he had come and to stay at Fountains.'

'And did he go?'

'Aye, he went, and I followed him, but I didn't take that bad Blackie because he would have whinnied. I went on foot, very quietly in the woods, almost alongside the man and he stopped at the village and I hid behind a hut and listened. The man asked the village people how my lady of Birkhau looked and they stared at him as though they were deaf and dumb!'

'You are sure none of them spoke to him?'

'Only the blind shepherd who sits by the oak tree in the sun, but he asked him who he was and questioned him sharply and told him nothing.'

'That was good,' said his mother. 'But why, then, did you have to ride all the way past here and come down again to the house?'

'You never know, there may have been somebody following me,' the child replied, with a great air of self-importance.

'Here is a bit of bread with honey for a good boy,' said Judith, handing her brother the treat and patting his head. He grasped the bread like one starving and dodged away from the caressing hand.

'This is all very well,' said Mistress Beatrice, 'but what if he meets someone at Fountains who tells him how my lady Francisca looks? That she is slim and tall with reddish golden hair, he will know for sure that Sirich was telling him lies. Then, if he tells them about the sickness at Birkhau, they might contradict him.'

'But sickness can strike so quickly, mother. It could be the case,' Judith replied.

'God forbid,' said Beatrice, crossing herself.

'Amen,' said Judith,

'I think you fret too much,' said young Thomas, his mouth full of bread. 'The man has a look about him which will keep men's mouths shut, and people hereabouts don't like strangers.'

'The boy speaks the truth,' said his mother.

In the late afternoon, when the men of Hopestones had come in from the fields, Thomas was sent again on his pony to see how the land lay at Birkhau, and to discover whether it was safe for Francisca to return home. She had turned on her side in the bed and was staring at the fire, breathing more easily, and with a little colour in her face.

It was some time before Thomas returned. All was well, however. Sir Benedict had returned with his two sons and had been told in the village all that the people could remember about the man on the bay horse. They had sent two of their young men to follow the horseman, and the two had instructions to trail him all the way to Fountains. One of them had already returned; whilst the other had stayed at the monastery guest house so that he could watch and listen to what the stranger said, and might follow him in the morning when he left.

Benedict and his sons had arrived home to find the door barred and Sirich in a state of unaccustomed agitation. He had begun, even while he was opening the door, to tell them of Aldred's visit.

'Who sent him?' Benedict exclaimed. 'He did not come here of his own volition; Malebisse must be behind this!'

'He is still a member of that devil's household,' said Sirich, and it was then that Thomas arrived, bubbling over with his story and eager to tell it to his idol, Jocelyn.

'So, tomorrow young John the smith's son may return from Fountains and we shall know more,' said Benedict. 'In the meantime, the men of the village will warn us if any more spies appear.'

Thomas was sent home and they waited for Francisca and Judith to return.

'While we were travelling to Harrogate we saw Jews, Sirich,' said Simon. 'I never saw Jews before. I will tell my mother when she returns.'

Sirich looked quickly at Benedict.

'They looked pretty much like everyone else,' said Jocelyn. 'I wouldn't have known them if those people had not been calling out after them down the street. Are they very wicked, father?'

'No, people cry out against them because they are not Christians, but Christ himself was a Jew,' said Benedict, and Simon looked curiously from Sirich to his father, puzzled by the frown which passed between the two men. Then he exclaimed excitedly, 'I do not understand why they cannot acknowledge Christ. They have been shown by many miracles that Christ is our True Saviour, it must be the Devil who teaches them. They must be converted!'

'Simon wishes to enter the Church, father,' said Jocelyn.

'I know he does,' Benedict replied, looking hard at the younger boy as he spoke.

'You should be glad that my life will further the work of God,' Simon exclaimed, looking almost defiantly from one to another. Nobody spoke, and he turned to his father, saying accusingly, 'When I was a baby, a man came here. I know, because Peter, the boy we had in the house when I was younger, told me so. He said the man greeted my mother with a kiss. Was he the Jew known as Aaron of York?'

'He was,' Benedict replied, looking across at Sirich again, unhappiness in every line of his face.

'Do you have dealings with this man?' Simon asked, his voice rising imperiously.

'What dealings I have are not your concern!' Benedict was angry now. 'When your mother returns, I want no more talk of Jews!'

Young Jocelyn, always anxious to smooth relations between his father and his brother asked, 'Who was the man who came today?'

Benedict sighed, and answered, 'A servant of Malebisse who is no friend to this house.'

'Is the money we have a loan from the Jews?' asked Simon, who seemed insensitive to the atmosphere he had created in the room.

'No! Our money has been made from the manor and from my share of the ship. You will have money to take with you into the monastery, never fear.' With that, Benedict got up and strode to the window.

'You are bitter against me, father, and against Holy Church. You have always favoured Jocelyn. I shall pray for you.' And with that, Simon flew to the door and down the outer stair.

Benedict turned and looked at Jocelyn. 'What shall I do with your brother?'

'Why not send him into the household of the Archbishop of York?' the boy answered with a smile. 'Let him go there and he will see how the great of the world live. If he finds favour he may become steward in some great household, or even enter the service of the King. When he knows more of the world he may not wish any longer to enter the cloistered life.'

Benedict smiled. How like Josce the boy was, and he remembered the words of Josce, one warm summer's day, when they had rested from their work in the cool of the hall at Coney Street, '. . . and to enjoy life, eh Benedict?' How he wished he could tell the boy of his ancestry.

'So,' he said, 'you have seen how the great of the world live have you, my Jocelyn?'

The boy reddened and looked at the floor.

'You are learning wisdom, my son. The great of the world indeed. The great of the world . . . ' The boy raised his head and looked curiously at his father.

'Come, let us walk to meet your mother,' Benedict said.

They walked uphill, but not on the track towards Hopestones. Benedict strode towards the outcrop of rocks where Francisca liked to sit in the sun. Benedict stopped at the top of the rise and looked about him. There was no sign of Simon.

'Gone up to the church at Middlestead,' said Jocelyn, following his father's thoughts.

'He is determined on this course, but what of you?' Benedict asked.

'I would like to enter the service of my Lord de Lacy, if that would not give offence to the Constable of Richmond. My lord might take me abroad with him. I would like to see the world. Would you ask about this?'

'He would take you, that I know, for he has told me how he would like to have you in his company. But is this your best course? These young knights who swarm in the great houses are not of good repute. There are too many young men who cannot afford to marry and have no settled life. Would you not like to be enfeoffed in this manor, or some other?'

'In good time, father, but now I long for travel and adventure and to make my fortune.'

'It is time I told you more about the money,' said Benedict. 'I shall be able to give a good sum both to you and to Simon. However, you must be cautious in everything you do and say. I cannot tell you my whole history, but I will tell you this: the marriage portion which your mother brought was greater than you could ever imagine. It consists of coins, which will not buy as much as they did at the time but, even so, you will never starve, and there are some gold chains and other ornaments there. When we married I had old Sirich bury some of it, and when my father died we hid another sum separately. Now, if your brother persists in his ambition to take holy orders, you must have the first and greater sum and he shall have the second. Unless I am robbed in the meantime, you shall also have what is in the chest, that is the money which the ship has earned for us.'

'And how must I account for the possession of this fortune?' Jocelyn asked.

'If you were to serve Lord de Lacy for a time and then return to this manor, you could represent it as the spoils of the tournament.'

'Like William Marshall!' said the boy, his face lighting up.

'He is the greatest of knights,' his father agreed. 'If you were to copy him in all things, I would be proud.'

'He made his fortune himself, did he not?'

'Aye he did, but riches are less important than honour, never forget that. William Marshall is an honourable man.'

'I do not wish to leave you, and I will return as soon as I have seen something of the world and had some adventures. Do you think the Constable of Richmond would grant this manor to me if I proved myself as a knight?'

'That would depend on the situation at the time. There has always been doubt about this little piece of land. The Constable may be told to sell it, or to exchange it for something nearer to Richmond itself. King John is a changeable man, and never forget that Fountains has its eyes on all the small properties which border its own. This one lies almost surrounded by monastic land. If the King should need money, he might part with outlying manors. There was a time when I wished to have it made an hereditament, but then the old Constable died. Now let me tell you about the money. Here, behind the rocks, is the greater hoard, and up there,' he pointed to the top of a little knoll, 'is the rest, and even that is more than any knight hereabouts has. It is buried under the boulder which lies between the three pine trees. Sirich and I rolled the rock over it when we had finished. That is your brother's fortune. Now do not forget, and say nothing!'

Benedict felt deeply depressed at the thought of losing Jocelyn, but he did not allow the boy to see it. They walked on then to meet the women, and found that Judith and her mother were supporting Francisca on either side. She smiled, however, when she saw Benedict approaching.

# 33

Jocelyn had been away for six months and Benedict had taken to walking the hills alone. He hardly missed Simon, who had recently joined the household of the Archbishop of York to serve and to learn and, perhaps, to sow the seeds of a fortune in the service of great men. But for Jocelyn he had such a deep and abiding love that he was almost distraught when the boy had left. Young Jocelyn was everything he could have desired. He was adventurous without being wild. He was brave but not rash. He was ambitious, yet he loved the farms and the farming folk who had surrounded him in childhood.

Benedict's grief had increased with time. Thurstan and Sirich watched him with dismay. Each day they expected him to return to his former spirits, but he avoided their company, striding over the hills all day long and often staying away all night. He sometimes sat silently beside Francisca, holding her hand and gazing into the flames, but things only grew worse. Soon Francisca was left to the company of Judith and the servants whilst Benedict would disappear for days at a time.

He returned on a cold evening in April to find Judith awaiting him in some agitation.

'Thank God you have come. My mistress is ill, she lies in bed!'

'What is it? Have you sent for your mother?' he asked, throwing off his cloak and making for the stairs to the sleeping chamber.

'I sent Thurstan to fetch her, but they seem to be a long time . . . ' Benedict left her twisting her hands together in the middle of the room and staring at the door as though willing her mother to appear. She turned to continue but he had already disappeared into the sleeping loft. She followed him, still glancing over her shoulder at the door, and climbed three of the steps, and there she stood, listening. She glanced again at the door as though uncertain whether to wait for her mother, then she continued up the new staircase.

Judith heard Benedict's voice asking rapid questions, but then he faltered and she heard a voice; a woman's voice, so low that she could not distinguish the words. It was a second or so before she realised that Francisca was speaking! She stopped where she was, but the floorboard had creaked under the pressure of her halting foot and Benedict turned slightly. He looked at her without seeing her, and immediately turned again to where Francisca lay, unseen by Judith in the darkness of the bed hangings. The girl stepped forward again, and heard Benedict say, 'Oh, why did you never speak?' and then, 'There, my love, be still, I know, yes, I know.'

Judith could tell that he was weeping, and then she heard the unfamiliar voice of the mistress whom she had known since childhood, and the voice which she did not know said, quite clearly, 'I always loved you.'

He was holding her hand, which felt pathetically fragile. There was silence for a while and then Benedict cried softly,

'Oh no! Do not go now. Please do not leave me now!'

'Where are my boys?' Francisca asked.

'They are gone away,' Benedict replied.

'But you are here,' she said.

'I will send for them. Simon could be here quite soon. Do not leave us. Oh Francisca, do not leave us,' Benedict pleaded.

'I love you,' she said.

Judith sank to her knees and began to pray. Benedict had put his head down on the edge of the bed, his arm across Francisca's body, and there he remained, sobbing.

Judith heard the door below open and her mother's voice ask where Francisca was. The boy at the fireside answered that she was above, but although he must have heard Judith's prayers and Benedict's cries, he ventured to say no more.

Judith rose and crept down the stairs, and as she came into the circle of light around the fireplace, she tried to speak, but was choked by tears. Thurstan cast himself down on a stool and wept with his head in his hands.

'Dear God, what is it?' Dame Beatrice cried, crossing herself and putting down the basket she was still holding.

'She has gone, mother,' Judith sobbed. Then they all fell to their knees in prayer. Dame Beatrice rose at last and went over to the fire, saying to the servant as she sat down, 'Fetch the priest as quickly as you can. Judith, you should have sent for him earlier!'

'I had no idea she was so ill, mother. I thought only of sending for you; how was I to know she would die, she was well this morning. It was only the pain in her chest again, and she went to lie down. Then I heard her moaning and went to look . . . '

'We never know when our hour is come,' her mother replied. 'We must wait now for the priest, and then you must help me to prepare her body.'

Judith fell to sobbing again, and then they heard Benedict move across the floor above and watched as he descended the stair, oblivious of the upturned faces.

'She spoke, at last,' he said as he approached them, a dazed expression on his face, his eyes never meeting theirs.

Beatrice crossed herself twice. 'That must have been the answer to my prayers. Every day I prayed to the Virgin to restore her speech,' and she fell again to her knees to give thanks.

'Did you hear, Judith, what she said?' Benedict asked, turning to the girl but seeming to look through her.

'Yes, I heard,' the girl replied, wiping her eyes on her sleeve.

'The priest is coming,' her mother said to Benedict, in a tone which was meant to comfort him, but he replied, 'Yes, I suppose he must. He is a good man. I do not think she would have minded . . . '

Beatrice looked puzzled, then thinking that she understood, she exclaimed, 'I know he calls her his housekeeper, but he is married. I do not like a married priest. Still he is nearest, it would take too long to send to Fountains . . . ' Then she suddenly remembered Simon. 'We should send for Simon!'

'Simon?' said Benedict, a look of complete bewilderment on his face. 'No, send for Jocelyn!'

Benedict spent the next few days like one in a trance. The neighbours tried to talk to him, but he did not reply. On the day of the funeral, all of which was arranged by Dame Beatrice and the priest, he remained silent. It was as though he had changed places with his dead wife. Now, however, he did not walk abroad, but sat beside the bed where Francisca lay. They could hear him talking to her softly. Sometimes they were able to coax him down for food and to warm himself by the fire, but he would return to the bedside almost immediately.

Simon returned from York just in time for the funeral and, seeing himself as destined for high position in the Church, he was disdainful of the humble parish priest. None of this seemed to impinge on Benedict's conscious mind. Before they set off for the church he did speak, but what he said had no meaning for any of the villagers.

'Now she will be here, without them. I wish I could bury her with them, but they were never buried, were they? They should have been buried with honour.'

'Everyone is buried, Master Benedict, unless they are drowned in the sea.'

'Who were these who were never buried?'

'What did he say?'

297

'Where did they live, Master Benedict?'
'Who were they, did he say? When did they die?'
'Who? Who is he talking about?'

Benedict heard none of these questions, and when the neighbours asked Sirich and Thurstan what their master was saying, they shook their heads and said her death must have turned his mind.

Privately, Thurstan said to Benedict, 'She may be with them now. Who knows? Perhaps the Jews do go to heaven,' but he received no reply.

Jocelyn could not be informed in time of his mother's death, for he had achieved his ambition and had gone to France with some of de Lacy's men as page to de Lacy's brother Richard, so he did not know of his mother's funeral.

Francisca was buried in the ground near the church at Middlestead, which stood on a high point, further up the valley. The priest tolled the bell. The earth was scattered. The women sobbed. Benedict seemed unconscious of what was happening.

A meal was laid out on a tressle in the nave of the church for all who cared to stay. During the meal, Simon spoke to his father again about his attitude to the Church, and bid him have a care for the state of his soul. Before the young man left for York – and he showed no sign of wanting to stay – he had again introduced the subject of the Jews and asked his father whether he still had dealings with them.

'You shall have your inheritance,' his father replied wearily. 'You may join the Church with my blessing when you are old enough. That is enough. What my dealings are with any man are my own affair.'

At Birkhau, Benedict sat by the fire, and would climb the stair to sit beside the bed as though she were still there. This continued for a month, and, when his wits returned, he longed to see Jocelyn and sent a message to Pontefract by one who travelled in that direction. It would be passed on, from mouth to mouth, until it reached Jocelyn in France.

As he gradually became aware of the world around him, his thoughts turned frequently to Aaron. He wished to see him again. No word had been sent to Aaron. He would not have been able to attend the funeral, and Benedict had been in no state to make the secret arrangements necessary to convey a message to York. But Aaron was all that was left of the old life and, eventually, Benedict sent Thurstan down to York to discover whether Aaron was there and, if not, when he would return.

Thurstan was told that Aaron was in London and might return at the end of the following month, but none in his house could be sure, for his affairs were diverse and he was now in one place, now in another. They promised to send word of his return.

During the intervening weeks Benedict was in a frenzy of impatience, for he had conceived an idea which would not let him rest. He would go down to York and have Aaron write his history so that his sons should know from whom they were descended, and what they owed to the Jews. Simon's patronising air infuriated his father, and the fact that the young man knew nothing of what had gone before made his father all the more angry.

He walked the hills alone, day after day, deciding what would be written on the parchment and envisaging the effect it would have when he showed it to his sons. The activity distracted his mind from his need for Jocelyn.

'When Simon sees, written down, who his grandfather was and learns that Aaron of York is his uncle, then let him talk!' he would repeat to himself as he trudged through the tussocky grass and waded across the peat hags, unseeing. He dismissed the idea of telling his sons himself, only of having them see it written in a parchment. Why he could not tell them face to face, was a question he did not ask himself.

He tramped the hills, while the house below him became dirty and ill-kept. Thurstan and Sirich and a young boy were all his household now. He remembered, as he walked, all the things which had pleased Francisca. She had loved the little birds particularly and would sit for hours watching them feeding and listening to their song. He also recalled the times when her silence had annoyed him, and now he felt remorse for those few occasions when he had been impatient with her. And, most of all, he regretted his neglect of her.

'I should have stayed with her,' he told Dame Beatrice. 'I must have been mad not to notice that she was ill. If I had been there, I might have done something.'

Dame Beatrice could only deny that his presence could have prevented Francisca's death. Of that she felt sure, but she regarded Benedict's obsession with Jocelyn as great foolishness, even as a sin. When she returned home, she protested to Sir Philip: 'No man should love his children so, it is wrong to love those around us better than we love Christ,' but her husband made no reply.

299

# 34

In the autumn of 1206 the time came for Benedict to journey to York in search of Aaron. He rode alone, passing people on the road without seeing them.

Aaron had heard from his servants of his sister's death. He began by telling Benedict that he had said the prayers for the dead, according to Jewish rites. Benedict nodded gravely, and the two sat down to a private meal in the solar.

'I feel there is something else you wish to tell me,' said Aaron when they had finished and were sitting on either side of the fireplace. He was concerned at the feverish brightness of Benedict's eyes, and his inability to rest.

'Yes. My sons know nothing of their grandfather,' Benedict clasped and unclasped his hands. 'Simon, who wishes to enter the Church, has been taught by the churchmen to hate the Jews. It hurts me to hear him, but I cannot tell him the truth . . . '

There was silence between them for a while and Aaron waited patiently.

'I wish them to know about Josce and what he did . . . all the good that he did. I wish them to know how charitable were the Jews to me. My sons must be told how the Jews died and who it was who was responsible. It is right that they should know.'

'Then why do you not tell them?' asked Aaron, smiling slightly.

'I . . . I shall leave them the parchment after I am dead. Then they can read it, not before.'

'The parchment?'

'Yes, I wish you to write it out on a parchment for me.'

'You, Benedict, are perfectly capable of writing out this parchment for yourself. Why do you need me?'

'It may be that I shall live for many years, or that I shall die suddenly. The parchment must be kept until my death. It would be better that it were written in Hebrew so that none shall spy out its content. When I die, Jocelyn will have to be sent for, perhaps out of France, perhaps from the Holy Land. During that time others might see it. Also, if I were to die suddenly, with the story unwritten, they would never know.' Benedict leaned back in his chair.

'What good will it do them to know that they are part of the Jewish . . .?' Aaron hesitated. He had been on the point of using the word 'faith' when he realised that this did not apply to his sister's sons.

'They should know,' said Benedict. 'They should know of the nobility of their grandfather and of the sacrifice he made in order to save me. Without Josce, they would not have had life. They are part of Josce and Hannah.'

'And will they wish to know that I am their uncle and that they have cousins? For I have three children of my own,' said Aaron.

Benedict did not seem to have heard.

Aaron smiled. 'Very well, it will please me to write this story, but shall I compose it myself?'

'No, no, there is no need,' Benedict said, starting as though awaking from a dream. 'I have wrestled with the matter for several months. I can dictate it to you. The Hebrew characters are quickly written, you can put it down as I tell it to you.'

'You are quite sure about this matter?' asked Aaron.

'I have never been more sure of anything,' Benedict replied.

Aaron called for his clerk to prepare a parchment and pens, and while they waited Benedict got up and paced to and fro across the room.

'Have you told your sons where to find their inheritance?' Aaron asked.

'I have shown Jocelyn where it is hidden. He can reclaim it at any time.'

'Suppose you die? Simon would be at the house first, as like as not. He might take the money he finds in the house, and think it all there is. Then, Jocelyn coming back from his wandering, might find another man at the manor, and would never be able to dig up the treasure unobserved; he would have nothing.'

'I must leave it to chance; Jocelyn could not have taken his share when he left. He has ridden off to serve de Lacy. How can a squire keep such a sum in safety, travelling around, living in other men's houses?'

'You do not trust Simon?'

Benedict did not answer.

'Then why not entrust it to me and I can give it to your sons when you die? Do you not trust me?'

Benedict was too concerned with his problems to notice the humour in Aaron's voice, and replied in a tone full of anxiety.

'You might die before me and the King would seize everything you have. I have thought on all these matters. I could not explain our relationship under those circumstances. The King would take everything; Francisca's money should have been forfeit to the King when your father died. No, no, I cannot cover every contingency,' and at that moment the clerk arrived with the parchment, asking if his services would be required.

'No, I shall write this myself,' Aaron replied, and as the clerk left the room he added, smiling, 'I see that my clerk thinks I am lending money.'

Benedict however, did not smile. The matter was to him of the utmost gravity. He took a seat opposite Aaron and began to dictate.

'I, Benedict de Birkhau, born in the eighteenth year of King Henry the Second, was the bastard son of a monk of Meaux and raised by his brother, Sir Jocelyn de Birkhau, son of Enguerrand de Birkhau who held the manor by knight service in the days of Earl Conan . . .'

# 35

It was a year later, and John the goldsmith's son was sitting just inside the door of an alehouse in Goodramgate when he saw Aldred, one of Malebisse's men, passing by on the other side of the street. He went to the door and called the man over.

'Your master hasn't sent me any money by you, has he?' John asked.

'What makes you think he would have done so?' asked Aldred.

'Because I sent him information. He promised me money if I would find out.'

'Betsy!' Aldred shouted, in the direction of the back kitchen. 'Bring me some cider so that I can wash a bad taste out of my mouth.'

'But how can I get my money?' asked John.

'I wish you and your money at the bottom of the river,' Aldred replied.

'Malebisse has been waiting for this news for some years now. I sent a message by that little boy he has waiting on him, but I never had a reply. It was a week ago if not more.'

'That little boy. Oh, that little boy. Isn't he the apple of my master's eye? I wish he were at the bottom of the river as well.'

'But how can I get the message to Malebisse and get my money?' John persisted. At that moment the alewife banged down a pot of cider on the table and demanded her money.

'No come on, Betsy, you know he doesn't pay regularly. I'll get some wages next week and then I'll pay you, my dear one.'

'Don't give me any of your dear ones,' she replied.

'I'll tell you what we can do,' said Aldred to Betsy, who had now taken a seat at the end of the table. 'If John here will give his news to me, I will convey it to my honoured master, Sir Richard Malebisse of Wheldrake and Acaster, then he will pay me and I will pay John and John will pay for this pot of cider.'

'I won't trust you with my message,' said John.

'Oh, he won't trust me with his message. Is your message any good?

That's what I'd like to know. Is your message worth passing on to my revered master?'

'It is good news. He will welcome it. It proves that Benedict had to wife the . . . ' but there he stopped. 'I will not give the message to you, for you will sell it to Malebisse and then where shall I be?'

'Betsy, will you be witness?' said Aldred. 'Will you stand as witness that this man John, son of Peter the goldsmith, an ancient lineage if ever there was one, has given to me a most valuable piece of information and that I have undertaken to pass it on to Sir Richard?'

'I can't get near the door. He has a man ready to drive me away. It may be the only way of sending him the message,' said John, almost to himself.

'Then come on, man, if you want to see your money. Tell us the message.'

'He asked me to find out,' said John, but then he hesitated. 'You will give him the message?'

'Yes, man, spit it out.'

'Well, I discovered that Benedict de Birkhau, who was once my father's shop boy – there is no justice in this world! – is rich now and rides upon a fine horse and was knighted,'

'Get to the point,' said Aldred.

'Well, he must surely have the Jew's gold because he ran off with the Jew's daughter!'

'That's not much of a message, is it Betsy?' asked Aldred.

'He has been waiting for this news for years, I tell you,' John said, slapping the table with his hand to emphasise the point.

'Well, I don't call it much of a message. I don't think I will bother to tell Sir Richard. He might kick me out and it wouldn't be the first time he has done that.'

'I tell you this is the news he has been waiting for,' said John.

'I must be off,' said Aldred. 'I was on the way to the castle when you stopped me with all this folly.' He left the alehouse and set off in the direction of the castle, but as soon as he could, glancing round to see that he was not followed, he ducked down an alleyway. Then he made his way back to the house near the Lendal Ferry.

'So, you discovered this, did you?' asked Malebisse. 'It is of interest to me.' He called to his page and asked the boy to bring a purse of money. Aldred's eyes lit up and Malebisse smiled to himself. When the purse was brought, he opened it and took out two coins which he gave to Aldred.

'I don't think you obtained the information. You went to Birkdale for me before and came back empty-handed. I think the information came from that fat fool, and if he is such a fool as to trust you with his information then he deserves nothing and you deserve only a little. Now, away with you and see if my mail coat has been repaired.'

# 36

It was a summer evening in the following year when Sir Philip came down from Hopestones to see Benedict. He wore a serious expression on his face.

'Do you have more news of this interdict? Does the Pope mean to cut us off from all the offices of the Church?'

'I care not what he does. It seems to me that King John is right in this. Why should he have Archbishop Langton thrust upon him? Langton is but a tool of the Pope. The barons and knights I encounter at Richmond are not disturbed by the interdict. We have suffered worse than this!'

Sir Philip fidgeted in his chair and Benedict looked at him curiously.

'You are not old, Benedict,' said Sir Philip. 'Have you thought of marrying again?'

Benedict was surprised. He had not thought of it.

Sir Philip spoke again. 'If Simon joins the Church he will have no children. Then, God forbid, but these things do happen, if young Jocelyn were killed in some battle or tournament, you would have no grandchildren. Furthermore, I need a good husband for my Judith, and she is not so young now, more than twenty years, I think, and there are younger daughters still to be married, I must consider them.'

Benedict smiled. Judith, he knew, was twenty-one. He had recovered some of his old spirits. 'Does she wish to marry me?'

'The girl has plenty of sense. She recognises a good match when she sees one. She knows the house and knows your ways and can keep the place as it used to be.' He looked around as he spoke, for the house was not as it had been. The floors were not swept so often, the hearth was untidy, there was dust on the top of the cupboard and on the food hutches.

'You do well to look around you, Sir Philip, and you are right, Judith could put it to rights,' Then Benedict thought he might tease his neighbour. 'But what had you in mind for a marriage portion?' he asked.

'I am not rich, as you are,' Sir Philip replied, looking a little uncomfortable. 'But you are not in need of money, you could perhaps make her a suitable dowry and her brother may be able to provide a little for her in the years to come.' Sir Philip did not sound, thought Benedict, as though he were convinced of this himself, and he smiled again, but took care that Sir Philip should not see it.

'What of any children we may have? If Jocelyn returns, hale and hearty, and finds a brood of young children here, he will be surprised to say the least. He will have to share what he . . .' here Benedict stopped, for the fact that he would leave money to Jocelyn was not to be broadcast.

'He is making his own fortune I hear,' said Sir Philip and he will not need for anything. A young William Marshall, or so people say. Did he not hold a rich French knight for ransom recently?'

The two men smiled at each other across the hearth. Sir Philip took as great an interest in young Jocelyn as he did in the fortunes of his own son, the harum-scarum Thomas.

'Then if he is to follow William Marshall in everything, he must next find himself a rich wife!' Benedict laughed.

'That is the first time you have laughed in many a long day,' said Sir Philip with satisfaction.

'Tell Judith I will gladly marry her,' said Benedict, 'and I will find a dowry for her, never fear.'

Benedict sent for ale, and the two men drank until late. It was dark when Sir Philip stumbled up the hill to Hopestones with his good news.

A year and a half had passed. News came from Jocelyn now and then, brought by knights who returned from France and who were destined for the castles of Richmond or Pontefract. It was never long after that before the news reached Benedict, for anyone who travelled in Birkdale liked to call at the manor of Birkhau. He thought of this favourite son with every passing day, and though he was always still anxious for his safety, he was calmer now.

Judith had indeed made the house pleasant and comfortable again, and Benedict had been delighted when a daughter was born to them in the April of 1208. They called the child Isabelle, after the old servant, which pleased the brothers, now growing old and infirm. The naming had caused some disquiet at Hopestones, for it had been thought that the child would have been called Beatrice, after her maternal grandmother. Judith was surprised, but Benedict could not tell them just what a special place the old servants held in the family's history.

Little Isabelle had the fair hair and blue eyes of her parents and was the pet of the households at both Birkhau and Hopestones, though they tried not to love her too much in case she died young. She was an inquisitive child, direct in her address, and her self-confidence pleased Benedict. The child brought him more joy than he could have imagined and helped fill the place in his heart which Miriam had once held. As she grew, he often found himself looking for the resemblance in little Isabelle to his dear Miriam, but then he would check himself, remembering that there was no blood relationship between the two children.

The whole family was sitting outside on the short, sheep-nibbled turf before the manor in the evening sunlight. Benedict's great chair had been brought down. The women of the household were spinning and singing quietly as they sat on the steps, letting their spindles drop over the edge. The kitchen boy had gone down to the stream to fish. They watched him moving along the water, and he was within calling distance should he be needed.

Thurstan was old now. Benedict looked at him, and dreaded the day when he and Sirich should become as feeble as the old man who had kept the fireside when they had first arrived at Birkhau. The two old servants sat on a long bench, their backs to the wall, their legs stretched before them, and Benedict thought of the long hot days of his childhood when they had sat thus in the garden behind the house in Coney Street, or with Henry the miller beside the mill leat. Then he had played beside the stream, as the boy was doing now.

Little Isabelle was sitting on the grass near the feet of the two old men and winding a piece of rag about a stick she had found. The stick had a nob at one end and a little offshoot on one side which she fancied was an arm. She talked to it as she dressed it.

'That's a queer-looking baby you've got there,' said Thurstan.

'It's a good baby,' she replied, closing her mouth very firmly and continuing to wind the rag about the stick with great determination.

'What do you call it then?' asked Thurstan.

'Francisca, she's called Francisca.'

'Who gave her that name?' he asked.

'I did. It was a lady who lived here and she was very sad, but she's gone to Heaven now.'

Several of them glanced across at Benedict, and saw that he wiped his eye and looked away to the stream where the boy was fishing.

# 37

As the years passed, the good relations which Benedict enjoyed with both the Constable of Richmond and Lord de Lacy made him the natural choice as go-between. In any matter of delicacy he was used as envoy, so that he spent many weeks away from home, travelling not only between the three castles of Richmond, Pontefract and Chester, but about the widespread domains of these two great Honours. He became well-known, for he had to appear at manorial courts and deliver closed letters from one Honour to another. In this way he heard all the news and the tales of King John which were circulating everywhere.

Returning in the August of 1211 from a journey to Hereford, where he had represented de Lacy at the Bishop's court, he was getting down from his horse in the courtyard at Pontefract Castle when the Butler's servant hurried across to him and bid him come to the Butler's own room. Benedict entered the apartment to find Sir William de Lonsdale, the ancient uncle of his friend, already seated there.

'There is no need to hurry with your messages, Sir Benedict,' the Butler said. 'Come, sit by the fire with us. Sir William has been asking me for news of the wife of Briouze. Have you heard what happened?'

'We all know that Briouze owed a debt to King John who demanded that Briouze give his two sons as hostages for his debt,' replied Benedict, 'and that Briouze offered forty thousand marks for the King's goodwill, but the King refused, for it was the lady Matilda he wished to capture. So the King then took an army to attack Briouze's lands on the Welsh borders. That is well known.'

'But I met a knight who had been present when Matilda, the wife of Briouze, declared that she would not give her sons to one who had killed his own nephew,' said Sir William. 'It was those words, they say, which sealed their fate.'

'This is true,' said the Butler. 'Briouze took his wife and sons to his kin in Ireland, men of great power who were prepared to defy the King.'

'That is so,' Benedict replied, 'and you will have heard that the King followed them to Ireland with an army. But did you hear that Matilda fled with her sons to Scotland?'

'Is it true that a Scots lord sold them to the King?' asked the Butler.

'I was told that story,' said Benedict. 'But whoever it was who betrayed them John captured them, of that we can be sure. On the way here, I heard that she and the children had starved to death in the castle of Windsor.'

'May God preserve their souls,' said Sir William. 'Could the King behave in that manner to a woman and her children?'

'The King conceives great hatreds for those who stand in his way,' said the Butler. 'Like his father and his brother, King Richard, his temper is beyond all comprehension. The Devil's brood indeed.'

'But this was not done in a fit of temper. The persecution of Briouze has lasted for four years now,' said Benedict. 'I have seen the King's temper, but this is different.'

'Does that confirm what men have said? Is it true do you think that the King murdered Prince Arthur?' asked Sir William.

'Nobody ever saw Arthur after he went to stay with his uncle,' Benedict replied. 'Hubert de Burgh, who had charge of the Prince, declared he had saved the boy when John sent men to blind and castrate him.'

'But it was de Burgh who first put it about that the Prince was dead and then denied it. What are we to make of that?' asked the Butler. 'And if the lady and her sons entered Windsor and have not been seen since that time then I fear they must have perished. It will do no good for anyone to demand that the King produce them, for he did not produce Prince Arthur when the Pope demanded it.'

'The King's demands for fines and amercements are truly terrible,' said Sir William.

'But let us not forget those which his brother, Richard Coeur de Lion, imposed when he wished to go crusading, and men forget also that Richard's ransom was a crippling imposition.'

'The debts incurred to raise the ransom money drove many lesser knights to borrow more than they could ever repay. Some have lost their manors and become mere husbandmen,' said Benedict, remembering how he had saved Sir Philip from such a fate by giving him money from his hoard.

'Once Richard was dead he became a hero, and John is no worse than his brother,' said the Butler. 'But it is time now for us to go into the hall, for my lord will be ready to dine. I see Sir Richard Malebisse has arrived. Now there's a man who always falls right side up. Despite his part in that riot during the first year of King Richard, he has been in good repute, first with Richard, then with John.'

'Yes, it was as I thought. A part of his land was confiscated and returned to him for a paltry fine,' said Benedict.

On these journeys, Benedict had often sat in the same hall with Malebisse, but he had managed to avoid any close contact with that surly and dangerous knight. Since the day on which Aldred the groom had come prying to Birkhau, Benedict had felt that eventually there would be a confrontation. Now as he entered the hall, they were almost face to face. There was no means by which he could avoid meeting the eye of Malebisse, who stood near the central hearth of the great hall, warming himself at the fire, with two of his squires close at hand. As Benedict entered, he caught sight of Aldred, who came from among a crowd of servants and approached his master. Benedict skirted the people standing about the fire and passed at a distance, but still he saw that Aldred looked in his direction and whispered to Malebisse, who turned and looked across to where he was. It was immediately obvious that Malebisse did not wish him well. Malebisse seemed to him to be bigger and more powerful than any man in the room, and to bode nothing but evil. It seemed to Benedict that there were only the two of them in the hall.

Benedict knew himself to be a man of importance and under the protection of two great overlords, yet before this broad, surly, dangerous man, he felt again like a boy of ten years. He glanced at the high table where sat Lord de Lacy, he looked around the room where men were seated in irregular groups at the long tables, talking and drinking. He glanced again at Malebisse and his men and found that Malebisse was regarding him with a long and level look, without warmth and with an interest that was intense and single-minded. Malebisse then took a man by the arm, saying something to him, and the man turned and he also looked at Benedict.

Benedict dragged his eyes from that broad and sullen face and marched up to the high table, but still he felt Malebisse's eyes boring into his back as he walked. His close friendship with the Lord of the Honour of Pontefract gave him confidence. He knew he could also rely on the Constable of Richmond, yet the look which he had received from Malebisse bode no good. There was many a long mile between one castle and the other, where he might be waylaid. Malebisse did not need to show his hand; he had others who would do his bidding. Who, Benedict wondered, was the man whose arm he had taken?

The letters he carried were handed over and de Lacy bade him sit beside him. Benedict was surprised to find that he needed this close proximity. He was like a child who hurries to its parents in times of danger. Many of de Lacy's tenants were present, old friends and acquaintances who came to him warmly, putting an arm around his shoulders, laughing with him and passing the wine jug. He found that he not only needed this show of affection but required that Malebisse should see it too, and should know that he was not friendless. But that safety might last only as long as these men surrounded him.

Benedict stayed the night at Pontefract and the next morning helped the clerks to write and seal more letters for him to take to Richmond. He had verbal messages, too, for the Constable and for sub-tenants in the vicinity of Richmond. Some he would deliver himself, the rest would be passed on to those who would travel north towards Durham, or up the long valleys towards Westmorland.

He left at noon. There were certain horses in the stables at Pontefract which were kept specially for the use of messengers and Benedict never rode far on his own horse, but always left it at Fountains or at a Richmond manor, to await his return and the last leg of the journey. The horse he had today was familiar to him, a plain, brown animal, capable of some speed, and such was his anxiety about Malebisse and the possibility that he was being followed that he used his knowledge of the terrain to go out of sight from time to time, and watch from concealment anyone who rode the same way. Malebisse had stayed at Pontefract and it was said that he rode southward, but Benedict was afraid that he might be followed by some of Malebisse's agents.

# 38

Benedict changed horses at Aldborough, where he had a message to leave, and as it grew dark he found himself safe in Richmond. The Constable was feasting and again Benedict felt the security of friendship, for every man in that hall was enfeoffed to Richmond and they would protect each other. He spoke to one of his neighbours about Malebisse. The other had no good word to say of that knight and offered to escort Benedict part of the way home. Then Benedict felt ashamed of his fear, and the next morning he rose with new confidence and did not speak to the Constable of the encounter but took the horse offered him and set off over the hills towards Birkdale.

Now his thoughts were all of home. He looked forward to sitting by his own hearth. If the child were asleep he would have them wake her and show her the present he had bought for her. Then she would sit on his knee and fall asleep there and he would carry her to her bed. The child was three years old now, and slept with one of the female servants, but whenever she awoke she would come to look for him and whenever he arrived home she was glad to see him.

In his saddle-bags he carried all kinds of luxuries. He had been down at Woebley, one of de Lacy's manors in Herefordshire, and carried dried apricots which had been grown in the Bishop's garden. From the fair at Richmond he brought cloth for a new dress for his little darling and a root of ginger and some almonds for Judith.

He stopped at Jervaux for food and to change to his own horse for the last leg of the journey. Just as he was leaving he hesitated and asked the gatekeepers if any strangers had been seen. They told him no, but as he was turning his horse to ride from the gates, he asked again, 'Have you seen Sir Richard Malebisse, or any of his men?'

Again they answered no, and with relief he rode away. Now that his anxiety had abated, he could enjoy the sights of his own country. He had come to love the rough hills, the rushing streams, and the wind-warped rowans which grew in perilous clefts of the rocky cliffs.

He came to the brow of Dallowhead and made then for Hollins Gill, where the little stream dived in among trees to plunge down the steep side of the valley. Before he entered the trees he could see, against the pale sky above Burn Edge, a wisp of smoke from the chimney of Hopestones below him. Far up the valley he heard the bell of the church at Middlestead, calling the villagers to evening prayer.

He looked up the valley and, as on that other occasion in his youth, he noticed that there were fields where the hay had not been cut and he glanced at the sky. Would it rain during the night? Would his neighbours be able to cut that late crop during the next few days? On the opposite hillside he saw the men dragging hay into the stackyard on a sled, and he remembered having seen the same activity when he had been to Richmond so long ago, on the occasion on which he had first met de Lacy.

On that other evening he had ridden home thinking of Francisca, and a great sorrow came over him now. Judith was a good wife but she was not and never could be what Francisca had been to him. He felt a pang then at the thought that he had neglected her in those last days for love of the son who had left them, and he sighed. He should have stayed with her.

He set his horse down the wooded cleft which would lead to the track he needed, and the horse sank to the hocks in the deep loam. The trees closed over him and it was dark. Then, on his left, he heard something moving – not the sudden startled movement of a wild animal, but a regular shuffle and pad of feet which kept pace with him as he rode down. No wild animal kept pace with a human. In sudden fear he began to turn his horse, to ride up on to the open hill again, but before he could turn in the narrow path, there came, not from the left, but from the right, a rush of feet in leaves, of snapped twigs, of broken boughs and before he could even look round to see who or what it was, rough hands were dragging him down.

'We have him, boys!'

He felt a fierce blow to his head and another fell on his shoulder. He writhed to get away, but strong hands held him and soon he could move not a muscle.

'Now, where have you hidden the Jew's gold?'

'What do you mean?' he asked, groaning then with the pain.

'Come on. Where is it? Is it in the house?'

'There is no gold,' he gasped.

A strong blow on the side of his head made him dizzy.

'How many men do you have at the manor, answer now!' and another blow struck him in the small of his back, making him cry out in pain.

'How many men?'

The house. They must not get into the house. The child must be safe, no one must get near that child. What could he do?

'There are armed men,' he gasped.

313

'How many?'

'Four,' he managed to whisper, before more blows jerked him this way and that, and his arm was twisted up his back.

'How many?'

'Four,' he gasped again.

'And we are six,' the voice said, triumphantly.

They dragged him to his feet and began to march him downhill. He could hear a horse following, his own, he supposed, led by one of the ruffians. Who were they? Were they merely outlaws, discharged men-at-arms with no master and nothing but robbery to sustain them? How near were they going to pass to Hopestones, or had these men already robbed that house?

'He has it all right. Sir Richard is sure of it and we daren't go home without it,' one of the men said. So, they had been sent by Malebisse!

He tried to think of some means of drawing attention to his plight. If they came near enough to Hopestones, he might be able to shout, but they must not open the door, they would become vulnerable themselves. He must let someone know, but how?

He stumbled and allowed his legs to sag so as to slow the progress of the party, but they jabbed at him with some unseen weapon so that to avoid further pain and injury he was forced to his feet again and made to stumble reluctantly on. He could feel the blood trickling down the backs of his legs.

Now they were on a level patch of ground and he managed to raise his head and judge the distance to his neighbour's house. Two hundred yards perhaps. He must not shout too soon, but what was that? From ahead came the sound of a horse, cantering fast on the stony track, but it wasn't coming towards them, it was going on, down the hill towards Birkhau and the village. What could it mean? Had they been seen? He prayed that it was so, but he knew that the hillside down which he had come was in deep shadow. How could anyone have seen the attack? Yet why was someone riding fast away from Hopestones? He allowed himself a faint gleam of hope.

They passed Hopestones, but apart from the sounds of his captors' feet there was no sound. No light shone out and no welcome voice demanded to know who was abroad so late. Now there was only a short distance of deserted track with no chance of finding help, and Birkhau lay just ahead with no men-at-arms, no strong son to save him, and no one to protect the child. Jocelyn, Jocelyn, why could he not have been at home? Benedict made a last desperate effort to escape. He twisted himself about and flung himself this way and that, but they knocked him to the ground, and kicked him severely in the ribs and about the head until he was almost unconscious.

He thought he lay on a wooden floor, and that a man and a boy were kicking him, and then there was sudden shouting and a scream and feet running away. Hands were exploring his battered body and he shouted out with pain. He wondered if the scream he had heard had been his own. Then, gently, he was lifted and carried on something hard and flat. This must be one of the new hurdles, he thought, and became anxious that they had removed it from a pen and that the sheep would escape. He tried to tell them about the sheep, but they did not seem to hear.

# 39

Benedict lay in bed, but he knew not for how long he had been there. Judith came and went with milk and ale for him to drink and that morning he had swallowed some chicken meat which had been cut up very small.

Sometimes he knew he was in his own bed at Birkhau, but at others he found himself in York or London, or at Richmond or Pontefract. He talked with many people, with Geoffrey de Padley, with Sir William Bagshawe and with Philip de Lonsdale. Sometimes he would see his sister Alyce, dancing, with bells and cymbals ringing, and then he would find himself again in his bed with the light coming in through the open shutters and the comforting sound of sheep on the hill.

When he had become conscious his first thought had been for the child Isabelle, and he had not settled until they brought her to him and he saw that she was safe and sound. The child was weeping, but he could not raise his voice to comfort her, nor move his hand to stroke her hair. He could not remember what danger had threatened the child, but he was a little easier in his mind and slept for a while. Then he dreamed again and began to call the name of Malebisse and cried out for Jocelyn to save him.

Today was better, however. The chicken had made him a little stronger and he lay now staring at the small piece of moorland which he could see through the open window. Now and then the white sheep would cross the heather and a small bird came and perched on the window frame. But there was something he must do, something he must tell them.

Below in the hall he could hear voices, and soon one of them distinguished itself from the general conversation. It was young Thomas from Hopestones, telling the tale in his usual excitable way, dramatising some event for the amusement of the company.

'I was riding up to Middlestead and I saw them hiding in the wood above, and knew they meant some ill, so I tied my horse up and crept up on the southern side of the beck, quietly, among the trees. There were six men, I reckoned – and I was right, there were six were there not? – and

316

I got so close that I could hear them. They were asking when he would come and complaining of the cramp. Then they said that if he didn't come that night they would attack the house. Well, I didn't know which house they meant, but my father was at home, so they couldn't be waiting for him. Then I realised that Sir Benedict might return from Richmond by that way and that he would be home sometime soon.'

Benedict heard Judith's voice from the hall below and pictured her, a broad, stout, comfortable woman now, as her mother had been, but not, thought Benedict, ever as strong a character as Dame Beatrice.

'You are lucky they did not hear you, creeping about in the woods. It is impossible to be absolutely silent. I shall be short of a brother if you will go adventuring always.'

'But you don't know that beck side like I do,' Thomas replied. 'There is a little spring which seeps into the ground and it's all peat there. You can walk silently for a long way, and there was enough light for me to see where the peat ran out and the dried leaves and twigs began. I knew what I was doing all right.'

'Yes, you always say that, but one day you might not be so lucky,' Judith replied.

'Don't be so dismal, sister. I saved you all, didn't I? I am wasted here, I really am. Why am I not abroad with Jocelyn, saving castles and raising sieges? Why do I have to stay here, kicking my heels in this Godforsaken place?'

'There you go again, taking the name of God in vain. You'll come to no good end, brother.'

'I'll come to no good end hanging about here, that is certain. Now let me get on with my story.'

'You've told it before,' his sister said.

'But Matthew here hasn't heard it,' Thomas replied, and proceeded with his tale. 'Once I knew who they might be waiting for, I wondered whether to work my way up on to the top of the hill, for if it was indeed Sir Benedict he would be coming down the valley side, not up it. I returned to my horse and mounted him. I had decided to go down to Hopestones to tell them what had happened and then to work my way up Ellerbeck and on to the tops, but as I rode away down the track I heard the skirmish in the woods above me and knew it was too late to stop him. So I set heels to the horse and as I passed Hopestones and then Birkhau I shouted up to them to beware. There was no point in stopping at either house, for we haven't enough fighting men between the two to keep an angry ram at bay.'

'So you made for the village?' said the voice of Matthew de Middleham, who must, Benedict thought, have come down to ask after him. Then he remembered that Matthew was paying court to Judith's sister at Hopestones. The young man had other things on his mind.

'It seemed the best expedient,' Thomas replied.

'Well, it was successful,' agreed Matthew.

Then it was that Benedict's wits cleared sufficiently for him to remember what it was he must tell them, and he cried feebly for Thomas.

'What was that?' asked Matthew.

'It was my father,' Isabelle's childish voice answered, and he heard her rush to the foot of the stair and begin to climb.

'There's my darling,' he whispered as she came to the bed and put her hand on his forehead. 'Will you fetch your mother and Thomas?'

The child stooped at the top of the stairs and called down, 'Thomas, fetch my mother and both of you come up here, my father wants to speak to you.' The child returned then, and stroked his face with her small, soft hand.

After a while Judith's voice sounded below and he heard feet on the steps. Judith hurried to the bedside and Thomas stood awkwardly nearby, blotting out the light from the window.

'Tell Thomas,' Benedict said in a weak voice, 'to get out of the light.'

'You must be feeling better,' said Judith, and she held a beaker to his lips so that he could drink. He rested then a while, and they waited patiently until he had regained his strength.

'Send for Jocelyn,' he said.

'We sent for him almost a week ago. Thomas rode to Richmond and asked that messages should be sent immediately. It will take some time for the message to reach him. He is still in France. The Constable was concerned about you and has sent men out to search for the men who attacked you.'

'He will not find them,' said Thomas. 'They were Malebisse's men, of that I am certain, and he will protect his own. I have good news, however. Philip de Lonsdale was here yesterday to ask after your health, and he told me that Malebisse rode home from Pontefract and he is ill abed with something which is like to carry him off.'

Benedict was too weak to respond. There was something more important even than the imminent demise of his old enemy. He had still not given them the message. They stirred, as though to leave him, and he roused himself.

'Wait. Tell Jocelyn that he must go to Aaron of York.'

'To Aaron!' repeated Judith. 'Why ever would you want him to do that? Are you in debt, husband?'

Benedict lay still, recovering his strength for the next effort.

'He must go to see Aaron, who has something for him, something of importance.'

This time there was no comment on his request. It seemed that they were all so surprised that they had nothing to say.

'Promise me. Promise you will tell him. If he doesn't return, tell Simon to go. Will you promise?'

'Aye, we will promise, Thomas and I,' Judith replied.

'Thurstan, send Thurstan,' said Benedict feebly.

'He's always asking for Thurstan,' said Judith to her brother. 'I keep telling him that Thurstan is dead, but he doesn't seem to hear me.' She turned to the bed. 'He died, Benedict, Thurstan died two years back. Do you wish to speak with Sirich? He can't get up the stairs, but I'll take him a message.'

This time Benedict understood, and he was appalled to think that Thurstan had died. Why, he had seen him only yesterday. He had spoken with him about . . . But he forgot what it was.

'Tell Jocelyn to see Aaron, and then to speak to Sirich. To Sirich,' he repeated, and then he fell back on his pillow.

Judith went to him with the beaker, but she drew back and looked up at her brother with frightened eyes. 'He's dead,' she said.

# 40

Jocelyn rode across the Vale of York, looking about him at the familiar landscape, but his thoughts were elsewhere. He could not savour this return. It was to his father that he had rehearsed the telling of all his adventures and he had no wish to tell them to anyone else. His father, dying so tragically, had never known adventures such as he had had. What a quiet life they lived in Birkdale. Yet he had been told at Pontefract that Malebisse was behind his father's death. Malebisse was himself dead, had died only a week after Benedict. What lay behind it all? What was the old quarrel between his father and Malebisse?

The message from home had been a terrible blow and Jocelyn regretted that he had not been able to come home for so many years. He recognised now that the words so often spoken by old men were true. Life does not go on for ever. Why had he not come home before this? He had put off his return many times. It had been too late to attend his mother's funeral when he received the message that she had died. He had thought his father would live to a great age and that a year or two more wouldn't matter, and time had passed without his noticing it, so busy had he been. Now he remembered the happy times, when he had played with his brother Simon on the grass before the manor, and how his parents had sat in the sun to watch them.

It was seven years since Château Gaillard, so heroically defended by Roger de Lacy, had fallen to the French King and, ever since, Jocelyn had been hoping for a new crusade. He longed for adventure and the stories he had heard of the Holy Land had fired his enthusiasm. He had been as disappointed as any English knight at the reversal of English fortunes in France, the more so because he had not arrived in time to take part in the great events. However, he nursed a small flame of hope. The Pope had long been exerting his influence to stop the war between France and England so that he could send their armies to the Holy Land. That would be Jocelyn's opportunity.

He had not wished to leave France at a time when there seemed every opportunity for adventure. Adventure was to be found out in the great world, not here in the north of England. These were stirring times and here he was, riding towards a remote valley in the Yorkshire dales, where nothing ever happened.

Yet it would be good to see his friends again, and at the thought of them his spirits lifted. Was Thomas as reckless as ever? Was old Sirich still living? Jocelyn knew he had been with the family even before he himself had been born and might be able to unravel some of the mysteries which seemed to hang over the manor of Birkhau. Yes, he would speak to Sirich.

Jocelyn wondered if there were beautiful girls to be found here, for it was time he had a wife. To spend a month or so in Birkdale might not be so tedious after all.

The village people came out to greet him and he remembered how his father had loved the people of the dale. He rode up through the wood and saw, as he emerged, the pool where his mother and Judith used to gather watercress. Then he remembered with a start that he had a small sister now.

There was the house, smaller than he remembered it, but no Benedict, no Benedict . . .

Sirich appeared at the door above him, but it was a strange servant who took his horse. Then Judith appeared, stout, and so much older than he remembered her. He had kept an image of her in his mind as she was when he had been a child and she had been about fifteen years old.

He climbed the stone steps and entered the hall. Everything was as it had always been. The fire, the long table, the carved hutch under the sleeping loft, the pile of pallets, and the great carved chair. His father's chair. Judith took his arm and he turned to her and wept.

After he had been sitting on the settle by the fire for some time and had recovered himself, the child appeared. She was between three and four years of age. Jocelyn was intrigued by her. He knew that she knew he was sitting there, but she pretended that she did not know. She had a little basket over her arm in which lay a wooden baby. The child crept under the big table and took her baby out of the basket.

Sirich was sitting opposite, across the hearth, and Judith brought some warmed ale and gave a flagon of it to each of the men.

'Your father gave us a message for you when he was dying. I couldn't ask anybody to write it for me and you know I cannot write,' she said.

'What was it?' asked Jocelyn.

'Well, it was very strange, and I hope it doesn't bring us trouble,' she said, twisting her apron about in her hands. 'He said you were to go to York to see Aaron the Jew, and then he said you were to speak to Sirich.

Now why would he say that? Why should you not speak to Sirich first?' She turned her head to look at the old servant as she spoke, but he did not look up at her and made no reply.

'Did my father owe money?' asked Jocelyn.

'Well, if he did, the sooner you get down to York and find out, the better!' said Judith. 'If we owe a large sum, I shall have to take the child and go back to Hopestones.' She sniffed and wiped her eye on the corner of her apron.

'No, it is not that,' said Sirich, but when they pressed him for more information he refused to reply.

'There has always been a mystery about this house,' said Jocelyn. 'I wonder why I must go to see this Jew of York?'

# AUTHOR'S NOTE

The massacre of the Jews of York haunted me in my childhood, but forty years went by before the event occurred to me as the basis for a novel. The paper *The Jews of York and the Massacre of 1190* by Professor Barrie Dobson (then of York, now of Cambridge University) provided me with the scholarly information I sought, and in reading it I became determined that the novel should not only tell the story of the York Jews, but should be the vehicle for my thoughts on the temporal power of the Church and the origins of landownership in England.

My plot is based largely on historical events, and I have tried to depict the real characters in these pages as they were described by their contemporaries. Josce and his partner Benedict did go to London to take the presents of the York Jews to the King – whether the presents were delivered or not we may never know – and I have stayed as close as possible to the records in describing the coronation procession and the subsequent riot. Josce's wife was called Hannah, Old Benedict died of his injuries at his house in Northampton, Rabbi Yomtob came to York from Joigny, Henry of Fishergate was the lessee of the King's mill, Sir Richard Malebisse and his followers – again historical figures – were scarcely penalised at all, whilst the leading citizens, who had taken little or no part in the York riot, bore the brunt of the King's displeasure, being imprisoned until they paid fines according to their wealth.

The title of the novel is taken from a commentary of the time, but in this story I have put the words into the mouth of a preaching monk, who was indeed killed during the riot by a boulder, flung by the militia.

Josce's children, the servants and young Benedict are inventions, but many of the lesser characters – William de Lovetot, Roger de Lacy, Isaac de Skeffling, Briouze, Alan the Constable – were living at the time. Only in the case of Sir William Bagshawe, Godfrey de Hethersedge and the family at Padley have I had to invent members of families who lived in the manors of those names two hundred years later, and I hope that we shall meet their descendants in subsequent episodes.

The city of York and its walls are so familiar to us that we tend to think that the city has always appeared thus, but York in the twelfth century was surrounded by an earthen bank. The castle in which Josce's family perished was a wooden construction. The newly built minster was more squat and sturdy than the splendid cathedral which towers over the modern city.

As regards the twelfth-century Jews, they were indistinguishable from members of the French and English upper classes in their dress and manner. This is borne out by the fact that in subsequent centuries laws were made which forced them to wear distinctive marks on their clothing so that it was possible for the first time to tell them apart from Christians. At the time of which I am writing, the hitherto easy relationship of the Jewish and Christian merchant classes was beginning to crumble under the combined onslaught of the Church, the crusading movement and the hatred of those who had borrowed money.

Some of the places – York, Peveril, Richmond, Padley, Langthorpe and Camp Green at Hathersage – I have described accurately; others I have deliberately disguised, and readers will have to cudgel their brains over Birkdale and Clungford Lacy. I have taken great care over the houses, food and general way of life of the people of the time. I will not enumerate my own reading list, as it would occupy many pages, but those who wish to read further in the history of the twelfth century might like to look at Doris Mary Stenton's *English Society in the Early Middle Ages*, W.L. Warren on King John, Michael Adler's *Jews of Medieval England*, and S.O. Addy's (now sadly out of print) *Evolution of the English House*.

You may be wondering about the Great House in Coney Street. It is fairly certain that it stood where the shop premises of Leak & Thorpe is now situated. I visited the spot in 1987 to refresh my memory, and wandered down the alley beside the premises. There, I found to my dismay that someone had chalked a swastika on the door of an outhouse.

Janet Ball

# ACKNOWLEDGEMENTS

If Dr Alan Burgess of Wolfson College, Cambridge, had not devoted so many hours to unscrambling my errors on the word-processor, this novel would not have appeared for another year: to him I owe profound thanks. To Professor Barrie Dobson of Cambridge University, I am greatly indebted for his splendid paper *The Jews of York and the Massacre of 1190*. Dr Peter Addyman of the York Archaeological Trust was most helpful in the early stages in describing the general aspect of the City of York during the twelfth century. Any mistakes, however, are entirely my own, and here I must confess to having moved the date on which Roger de Lacy changed his name, so as to avoid problems of identification for the general reader.

To Dr Alison Binns, of King's College, Cambridge, and to the long-suffering members of Hartington Grove Quaker Meeting and of the Department of Applied Mathematics and Theoretical Physics I am grateful, for they patiently read the work for me whilst it was in progress, and endured my moans and groans when the going got tough. Mrs Caroline Powell of Lucy Cavendish College searched the lists of vanished medieval villages and discovered Birkhau for me. Dr Oliver Rackham of Corpus Christi College gave advice on medieval woodlands, Mrs Tom Bagshawe of Wormhill advised me on medieval gardening, and Mr Tom Tomlinson of Hathersage discussed local history with me. Lastly, to many librarians I owe a debt of thanks for their prompt response to my requests for help and advice.